CLAWS & EFFECT

The Otherworldly Pets of Project Enterprise

Project Enterprise

PAULINE BAIRD JONES

ISBN: 978-1-962125-55-0

Foreword

Some years back, Veronica Scott and I embarked on a publishing adventure called *Pets in Space*®. For five years, we published one anthology a year and were thrilled with the response from readers.

While I am no longer officially involved with Pets in Space®, I wanted to collect the stories I wrote over that five years into one volume for my readers. I did revisit Pets in Space® in 2025 with *Echoes Beneath*, which I have included in this collection so that all the pets will be together.

The first five stories occur in my Project Enterprise universe, and I have added "The Real Dragon," as a bonus read, which stands alone. (Sort of. I did bring one of the characters from the story into my series.)

I hope you enjoy reading these collected stories as much as I enjoyed writing them!

Perilously yours,
Pauline

About Claws & Effect

The Otherworldly Pets of Project Enterprise

What do you get when you cross intergalactic danger, swoony heroes, fearless heroines, and pets that are anything but ordinary? You get *Claws & Effect*—a quirky, heartfelt collection of sci-fi romance adventures from USA Today bestselling author Pauline Baird Jones! 🐾

These aren't your average companion animals—they sass, slither, squawk, and occasionally save the galaxy. Buckle up for five fun-filled stories of love, laughter, and a little chaos, starring the galaxy's most unexpected MVPs: a caticorn, a chatty parrot, a prophetic python, a snarky frog, and one highly opinionated dragon.

🚀 **Time Trap** – Sergeant Briggs just wanted to recover and get back to work—not open a mystery package from Area 51 and accidentally unleash a woman claiming to be from the future and her sarcastic talking parrot. Now he's dodging threats from the Time Service Interdiction Force, helping save a base full of genius nerds, and maybe, just maybe, falling for a time-tossed troublemaker.

🔍 **Operation Ark** – Caro never expected to share a mission—or a spaceship—with a smoldering space pirate and a mischievous caticorn. Together, they must return alien refugees to their home planets while dodging a grudge-holding villain and their growing attraction.

⛊ **Cyborg's Revenge** – She's tired of heartbreak. He's tired of circuits. Can this bashful cyborg and his determined lady overcome betrayal, battle a terrifying enemy, and trust a snake who thinks he's the hero of the story?

⛊ **General's Holiday** – All General **Halliwell** wanted was some peace, quiet, and a chance to channel his inner Picard. What he got was a woman with a wild tale, a frog with attitude, and a crisis that might end in either planetary doom—or a first kiss worth the risk.

⛊ **Echoes Beneath** — Echoes Beneath is a science fiction romance adventure set in the Project Enterprise universe, with alien mysteries, planetary peril, found family, and love tested under pressure.

⛊ **The Real Dragon** (Bonus Short Story) – When Emma's pet bearded dragon starts typing (yes, typing), her dad's bossy bride-to-be may get more than she bargained for. One girl, one dragon, and a Texas-sized mess...what could possibly go wrong?

⛊ Full of romance, snark, interstellar shenanigans, and (very) unexpected heroes, *Claws & Effect* is your perfect escape into the paws-itively wild world of **Project Enterprise**. If you like heart, humor, and hot guys with laser blasters—and pets with plans—this collection is for you!

(The Pets are back! Pets in Space 10 releases Oct 7, 2025 for a LIMITED time! Preorder your copy now to meet my newest pet!)

Time Trap

"Of all the stories in *Embrace the Romance: Pets in Space 2*, Time Trap was the most fun!"

Hiding in time is not as easy as you'd think…

. . .

USAF Engineer Master Sergeant Briggs—only his mother called him by his first name—is not enjoying his birthday. A year older and ordered to recuperate on a quiet bay away from the Garradian outpost, he's ready to mutiny and go back to his beloved engines. When his friends send him a gift from Area 51, he figures it will relieve his boredom for an hour or so.

Until he turns it on and he gets his second present of the day.

Madison, and her parrot partner, Sir Rupert, are on the track of a traitor to the Rebellion when they time travel into a trap. Their only way out is via an old transport pad, but instead of sending them somewhere, it sends them back in time. Straight into the arms of the one man who could kick her tires and light her fires.

She would like to get to know the handsome engineer, but the trouble following her can get people erased from existence. The fact he's a hero, like her lost brother, just makes her want to protect him more.

Briggs doesn't trust time travelers—with good reason—but now he has to work with the unlikely pair because trouble is coming. Trouble that puts an outpost filled with geeks and ancient technology at risk. It's not the first time he's worked with a woman to save the universe, but it's the first time he's wanted to keep her for himself.

If only she were a little older...

With a Time Service Interdiction Force on their heels, can the three craft a plan that will save a base full of geniuses and technology and get them the happy ending they deserve?

This short story originally appeared in *Embrace the Romance: Pets in Space 2, Library Journal* Best Book of 2017 (eOriginal) and *USA Today* bestseller.

Chapter 1

MASTER SERGEANT BRIGGS—YES, he had a first name, but only his mother had ever used it—stared somewhat balefully at the crate delivered to him by the lowliest Airman currently stationed on the so-secret-they-weren't-even-supposed-to-think-about-it Garradian outpost. No one had wanted to be the one to bring it to him. Rumor was, there was a no-fly zone over his "recuperation sector." What a bunch of wimps. So he was kinda grouchy about being side-lined for his *health*. And turning a year older.

Who wouldn't be? Jeez, he'd been banished to a freaking hut. So he'd gotten shot. It was a graze. That maybe got an alien infection, but he'd kicked that to the curb. And what do they do? They park him on a bay overlooking a freaking ocean. It was hot, but it wasn't the heat bugging him. It was all this freaking fresh air. Like he was some kind of beach bum or suffering a mid-life crisis, instead of a guy who lived and died for planes and spaceships and the motors that made them move. His lungs needed engine fumes, not tropical breezes. He needed work, not a birthday present.

He glared at the crate. It didn't flee. Just sat there. Only two people he knew would be brassy enough to send him a birthday present, especially right now.

Sara Donovan and Doc Clementyne.

He could hear them laughing all the way from the Milky Way. They wouldn't be laughing when they turned forty five. Five years to fifty. How the hotel did that happen? He wasn't supposed to get older if he took a trip to a galaxy far, far away. He was pretty sure someone had promised him he'd get younger if he signed on the dotted line. Or if not younger, then that he wouldn't get older. Some kind of paradox or something.

About to stomp away from the crate, he hesitated. Donovan and the Doc did know him pretty well. Were they busting his chops? Or sending him a lifeline?

If they didn't want to drop and give him twenty when he got back to Earth, there'd better be something interesting in there. He pulled out his army knife—one on steroids—and selected a chunky blade. He applied this—with force—to the nails holding the lid down. Yanked the lid back and tossed it aside. There was a note on top of the straw. At least they'd been smart enough not to send him an actual birthday card.

WE FOUND *this in the Area 51 garage sale and immediately thought of you.*
Cha-cha-cha,
Donovan and Doc (and their significant others)
P.S. According to the files, this was collected on 2789645. Ring any bells?

AREA 51 GARAGE SALE. He chuckled. He should have known. Those two did know the way to make his engineer's heart happy. He dug through the straw, tossing it aside. The late afternoon wind would clear it away. The wind was like the tide. It came. It went. Every freaking day. Weren't even any damn birds chirping on this blasted place. What kind of island didn't have birds?

His hand struck metal, he felt around for the edges, and lifted it clear. Heavy little sucker. It pulled at his wound, but he ignored that and carried it over to the rough table he'd built on his second day of exile, using some of the driftwood washed in by the foxtrot tide. The local doc could tell him to take it easy, but she couldn't make him do it. If he'd had the parts, he'd have given the table an engine. And driven it back to the base.

He set the big disc down on top of the table and stepped back to study it. Not exactly promising. Looked like a manhole cover. Maybe those two were jerking his chain. Only his knowledge of Donovan and the Doc kept him from heaving it into the surf.

And the fact that Area 51 did not save manhole covers, not even for garage sales.

2789645? Actually that did ring a few bells.

He pulled up the stool he'd also made, and considered the item, rubbing his chin thoughtfully. If memory served—which it might not now that he was so foxtrot old—that was the first planet they'd dropped a team on back in the early days of Project Enterprise, when they weren't sure any of it was going to work.

The planet had had a barely habitable atmosphere, some algae that only excited the botanists and this. The geeks had studied it for a while, but had lost interest when it didn't do anything. No one had asked him to look at it then, and he'd had other priorities, so he didn't care.

Now? He might care a little.

He'd gotten that desperate.

Why had they sent him this thing? Something about it must have interested them. He leaned back wondering how they got their hands on it, and then how they got it to him for his birthday—all without getting him or themselves flagged and hauled in to explain. Until he remembered who they were. Alone, those two were danger-ous. Together? Lethal. He liked that about them. And they could dance. He'd always hoped to find a permanent dance partner—but he didn't hang out in the right places for that kind of woman.

He sighed. Reached out a finger and flicked the edge of the metal. He wasn't worried about touching it. If there'd been any danger in touching it, someone would already be dead. Or turned into an alien.

It was thicker than a manhole cover. No sign of a seam on the sides. He ran his hands across the top. It was rough, mostly from mild corrosion, he decided. His fingers found indentations that could be an alien version of screws or bolts. He lifted it up and studied the rim, rolling it left, then right. Lines were cut in the rim, not unlike a coin, but then his fingers found two depressions, side by side. He pushed them both. They gave, but nothing happened. Not a surprise. The geeks had probably done that much. He pulled out his cheaters—one of those gifts that keep on giving for crossing into over-forty range—and studied the rim. Was there a seam?

He turned it over. The bottom was dotted with multiple ovals that formed a circular grid across the surface. He touched one of the holes. It indented about an inch. He felt around. Was that wiring he felt in there?

"What do you do?" he muttered. The wind and the tide didn't know.

Time to see if he could open this bad boy up. Be nice to put one over on the geeks of Area 51.

Chapter 2

THEY DROPPED through the time tunnel in a dark rush, the landing a jolt that shook Madison all the way from her toes to the top of her head. Good thing she knew how to stick a landing. She didn't move and thought she wasn't breathing until her nostrils filled with the pungent scent of cleaning supplies and the dust their arrival had stirred up. With her knees still bent from the landing, she wiggled her nose, trying to head off an errant sneeze.

The fear of getting shot helped. This was their most vulnerable moment. It took a few seconds for all the molecules to settle, during which they were an easy target.

When no one shot them, she eased her weapon free and flicked it to stun. She wasn't supposed to kill people for fear of messing up the timeline. But they could kill her. So not fair.

After another moment of assessing silence, she pulled out her handy little scans-for-almost-everything device with her other hand, and flicked it on. The scanner had a fancier name but even its initials were too long to remember. With her weapon extended, she lifted the scanner up next to it and studied the faintly glowing screen, looking for something she might have to shoot, well, stun.

No other life signs, at least in the immediate vicinity. She adjusted the settings with her thumb, scanning wider. No one but them so far.

Of course, the opposition could be wearing a fancy heat-blocking suit, too. But for now the intel that had sent them here looked to be decent. She didn't let herself get optimistic. There was still a lot that could go wrong.

Sir Rupert's claws dug into her shoulder, as he poked his beak up out of his specially designed-for-him backpack. He wasn't good at whispering, so he used his claws to ask for an update. She felt the soft brush of feathers against her neck and lifted her index finger, her signal for "just a minute."

She changed the settings again, this time scanning for threats inside this room. Found nothing, which would be one of the reasons she'd chosen to arrive here.

Even the tightest security types didn't think about teching up the janitor's closet. Not that they really needed to double down in this room when this outpost was thick with beyond-the-latest in protection and detection technology—if their intel was right.

There should be—yup, there they were. The master security feed wires ran into, and out of, a box in the corner of this room. This would be the other reason she'd chosen to arrive here. One really didn't want to land in a motion-sensor-rich zone to take out, say, the motion sensors.

She navigated around a bucket, then a mop. Man, you'd think people would come up with a better way to clean in the future.

She scanned the junction box for alarms, then felt along the sides with her fingers—she liked to use high and low tech—and when she was satisfied there were no trip wires, she shone her light on what looked like a keyhole. She looked closer. Amazing. It was a keyhole.

She shook her head, pulled out a lock pick, and popped it open. The guts were high tech again, so she used her handy dandy line-tapping thingy, and soon she was looking at the station's video feeds on a small screen. She shifted between the various views, looking for signs of trouble. This station was, according to the intel, a kind of safe house and time travel research center.

As she studied the feeds, she also noted the arrangement of hall-ways, sleeping areas, offices, a couple of labs, the arrival and depar-tures room, and the inevitable time command center. It pretty much matched the map she'd been given prior to her briefing, and according to her time chronometer, she had nailed her time landing.

She gave herself a mental thumbs-up because her hands were full.

Once she was sure of her route, she fired up the recording program, just in case anyone was monitoring this particular time. While that was doing its thing, she went into the guts of the programming, studying their scanning and blocking tech.

She wasn't a geek, but thanks to good briefings, she played one during time ops. She frowned. It wasn't at the level she'd been told to expect. A niggle of unease created a nagging, unreachable itch between her shoulder blades.

If she could have, she'd have flashed out right then, but how did she explain the niggle to the very tough new guy, who probably had something to prove since he'd just been promoted?

Still uneasy, she turned off anything she couldn't false feed, then started her recordings looping. It was kind of old school, but Madison was really old school. And she liked to throw in curveballs so the opposition couldn't get a good file on her. Being predictable was the kiss of death in the time travel biz.

She went super high tech on the motion sensors. Motion sensors were evil. And sneaky. The motion sensors were easier to mess over than she'd expected, too. Her niggle went up a notch.

Sir Rupert must have felt her stiffen. He emerged from his pack and perched on her shoulder so he could ruffle his wings. "Well?"

"Too easy," she told him. Of course, there was no way to know if anything she'd done had worked until they opened that door. At that point they'd either get shot or not.

Their geeks could jump forward in time and get the latest devices, but so could the Time Service. It was a quiet battle of wits fought across the whole canvas of time, though neither side culled much tech from early in time.

Wasn't much call for catapults in a time outpost, or anywhere else she'd been. Though she remained hopeful. In her opinion there was something kinda majestic about hurling large objects long distances.

"One or two niggles?" Sir Rupert asked.

They might have done a few too many ops together. "I'm up to two."

"Tell me when you hit three," he said.

"Roger that."

For a parrot, he had some big, brass ones. And like her, he knew that so much access to so much tech meant these outposts were getting harder and harder to crack, even with good intel from their spies in the Service.

They both knew that the quality of the intel had been declining. Hard to pinpoint exactly when with time travel in the mix. All that bouncing around in time, sometimes she forgot what she knew and when.

It was the new guy, a former security chief on a space station, who had figured out they had a mole. Which could mean their spies had been erased or reprogrammed.

She closed the panel and turned toward the door but wasn't quite ready to cross the space between. She reminded herself this intel was supposed to be solid as a rock—one traveling through space and time. Which meant it was solid until it wasn't.

She still had doubts about a mole, or so Madison had heard, but *She* must have approved the mission. Madison also knew that the details had been tightly controlled. Only Madison, Sir Rupert, the new guy, and *She* knew about it. Even the geek who'd talked her through the tech didn't know when or where they were headed.

And Madison was the only one who had picked the exact time and place. Knowing that didn't help the niggle, in fact, it made it worse, but not quite to a level three yet.

Had Madison somehow given them away? She trusted everyone but *She*, but not because Madison thought *She* was a mole. It was *She's* utter ruthlessness that made Madison uneasy around her.

It was probably a good quality for a Rebellion leader, but it did make a lowly minion uneasy. Madison could admit that this prejudice could also have something to do with when she'd been born, at a time when heroes beat the bad guys by being heroic instead of ruthless.

She hesitated, trying to pinpoint where her uneasy originated from. Madison had been told it was almost impossible to jump back in time and change the outcome of an op—there was even an equation for it.

But "almost" wasn't for sure, and that didn't mean the opposition hadn't learned how—or that *She* would tell her minions if the opposition had closed that loophole. Frankly, the way both sides had agents bouncing around in time, it was miracle they didn't collide in transit.

So Madison had two rules. She never believed everything she was told, and she always expected the worst—without going full on pessimist about it. More in the vein of "it was what it was," with a little of "what will be will be" thrown in there.

She'd escaped the Time Service agents more than once because of her rules.

And because she believed the niggles in the middle of her back.

According to their intel source, the mole had been, or was here on this outpost right now, only in another time. Dwelling on him being here, but not *here*, made her head hurt. She worked better without a headache.

The science said that because all of time was aligned somehow —blah, blah, complicated equation—there were echoes, that these echoes could bleed through both time and space. There were certain species that could perceive these echoes. Wasn't it a nice coincidence that Sir Rupert was one of those species?

All they had to do was get in, let him look around, and leave without getting captured or wiped out of existence by the Time Service.

Easy peasy.

In other words, just another day—or millennium—in the Rebellion.

She realized Sir Rupert had left her shoulder. He was standing in front of a large disc that had been propped up against the wall, partly concealed by some cleaning paraphernalia.

"I haven't seen one of these for, well, for a very long time."

Madison directed her pinpoint beam at it. "What is it?"

"It's a transport pad. This is the precursor to the time travel launch pads."

"Seriously?" She shouldn't take the time, but they were in what the geeks would call a minor time flux. Which meant they had lots of time until they didn't. She joined the bird, running her light over what looked like a manhole cover. "You've gotta be kidding. Who had the nerve to use that thing?"

Sir Rupert regarded her with some amusement in his dark eyes. "I did."

"Oh. Well." She grinned. "No one ever said you lacked nerve."

He ruffled his wings, like he might be pleased.

"Let's get going," he said. He fluttered back up onto her shoulder, and worked his way back into the pack, his moment of nostalgia for the good old days over.

"You're the boss," she said, then added. "Keep your beak down."

Maybe if he dug his claws into her niggle, it would go away. Or at least give it a nice scratch.

She activated the door and when it slid back, she peered out. The silence—and lack of shots fired at them—were somewhat reassuring. She stepped out and turned left, padding silently down the hall toward the command center.

Chapter 3

BRIGGS FITTED the outside cover back in place. It had been an interesting exercise getting it open. A mix of WD-40 and a magnet did the trick. Sometimes you had to go low tech on high tech crap.

The interior had been interesting. Not as interesting as an interstellar engine, but better than an inanimate table.

He was pretty sure he'd found the break in the wiring—some duct tape fixed that—and then he'd traced said wiring back to what had to be the on/off switch on the outer rim.

The power source had been the most interesting thing about the disc. Even almost depleted, it looked like it packed a lot in a small space. He'd almost taken it out—that would interest the geeks more than anything about the disc—but he wanted to see if he could turn the sucker on first.

If he could get one over on the geeks at Area 51, well, that would be his second birthday present.

He tightened everything down, then turned it over so the dots were facing up. He had his cellphone—he couldn't phone home, but they'd launched a small satellite because the geeks missed being able to text—set up to record some video. Geeks always wanted proof.

He adjusted it using the selfie stick he'd gotten as a joke gift at the Doc's bachelor party. This he'd rigged into a crude tripod. Now he carefully zoomed it in on the disc and turned on recording. He circled back to the device, careful not to block the video.

He looked at the camera, he should probably say something, but he was better with tools than words. Didn't they say pictures were worth more anyway? He depressed the switch on the side and stepped back.

This time something happened.

There was a low hum that slowly built to just shy of annoying. He heard the moveable parts inside start to move.

First one of the dots turned faintly red, then red flowed across the top of the disc. More humming and moving parts sounds, and the circles turned from red to green all at the same time, sending beams of green light toward the sky at least six feet in the air.

Interesting. Still not sure what it did.

He was tempted to stick a finger into one of the beams, but he knew better. Funny how knowing didn't stop the wanting.

Oh, the human condition.

He looked around, found a stick, and carried it back to the beams. He poked it into one of the green lights. The stick glowed green, but nothing happened for a count of three, maybe four, then the end of the stick vanished.

Okay. Birthday present number three. Got to keep all his fingers.

And he now knew this thing did something. Wasn't sure what, but something. He went and shut off the video, then turned back to do the same to the disc, but right then the hum increased in intensity and the green lights began to pulse.

Chapter 4

THANKS to a sudden increase in her niggle—and a minor change in airflow—Madison ducked before the first shot sizzled past where she'd been standing.

Crouched behind a control panel, she fired back and was already changing position before that shot reached the other side of the room. She might have heard a muffled thump, as if someone had dropped to the floor. Hopefully it was not of their own freewill. Fire was returned where she'd been, then tracked to each side.

That would be why she kept moving.

Sir Rupert, who had poked his beak out of the pack so he could use his super power, now ducked back down, so far it felt like his claws were digging into her rear. The pack had some deflective qualities, which she hoped they wouldn't need.

Memo to self: if it niggled like a trap, it was probably a trap. It could be a fluke, she reminded herself. Maybe someone dropped in and found everything off.

Bad luck happened, too. It wasn't always a trap. Only time would tell which it was, an irony she wished she had time to appreciate.

She got a dig in the back, which meant Sir Rupert thought it was time to go.

Good idea, might be hard to make happen. She didn't have time to check, but she had a feeling all the station's stuff was back on.

Supposedly this suit would mask their location and they could do an emergency flash out even with blocking tech deployed, but a failed flash out would mark her position for them like a big arrow in the sky.

Not even she could tumble and dance herself out of the kind of fire that would attract. And—there was that thing about not believing everything she was told.

A stench was growing around this op that was making her question everything. But Sir Rupert would have told her immediately if the mole was in the op information chain.

They might still be able to jump out from the closet, if they could get there. Unless that gap had been left open on purpose, a gap in coverage designed to lure them in. All roads led to this being a trap, but that should have been impossible.

As if she hadn't learned that the impossible was only impossible until it wasn't.

She kept her body between Sir Rupert and the incoming—he was more important than she was—as she began to retreat along the shortest route back to the closet.

And—this is why she got picked for these missions—as a former gymnast, she knew how to move in ways even highly trained Time Service agents didn't expect.

She initiated an intricate and random series of tumbles, leaps, and rolls—careful to keep her pack from coming close to touching the ground, or any other objects, or being exposed to enemy fire. Music in her head helped, though she missed hearing the real thing.

As opportunities presented, she fired back and even went high at one point. No one ever expected that. She fired down on them from some kind of file cabinet, and then dropped down, using it for cover while she got her bearings.

Lots of shots incoming. And they were blue, which meant they were trying to stun her. For now. But the color of the shots told her something else.

This was a Time Service Interdiction Squad. Their best and brightest. Could it be Boris out there—she shut that thought off at the root. *Don't go there.*

If they caught sight of Sir Rupert, they wouldn't settle for knocking her out. They would not risk him getting off this outpost with what could be in his head.

Would their scanning be able to separate his profile from hers? The pack was supposed to prevent that, too. But...oddly enough, sometimes the super tech got too sophisticated for its own good and missed the small stuff. Like a parrot.

She would have liked to figure out what gave them away— apparently still hoping this wasn't a trap—but she was too busy dealing with what was.

She had a slight edge, or so she hoped. Unlike many of the other rebels, she'd never been a Time Service agent, so their intel on her should be limited to those scans taken during past ops, which varied based on the sophistication of the tech used at the time.

With time travel in the mix, she never said never. But at least they'd never had a chance to dig around inside her head. People could try to be unpredictable, but they tended to be unpredictable in ways that sophisticated tech could predict. Yeah, another equation.

She reached the hallway opening and flattened against the wall in a low crouch, angled so that Sir Rupert was protected as much as possible. She felt the vibration as more station systems came online. Didn't have time to see if they'd found her video loops. She was pretty sure they'd be able to track her soon, if they weren't already.

Just in case they weren't, she dug in her pocket for one of the pebbles she invariably kept there for moments like this, and tossed it well away from where she wanted to go. It clinked against the metal floor and a flurry of shots crisscrossed the spot. Still blue.

The volume of shots confirmed her suspicion she was up against a squad. Kind of flattering. In a not wonderful way.

None of the shots had come from the door she wanted to go through. Apparently she was supposed to just dive through. Because the best and brightest the Time Service could muster would leave one door unguarded.

She did a crouching roll across the opening—she did have a bird on her back—and fired multiple rounds through the opening, laying down a wide spread to clear her path ahead, then she was up, following her fire down the hall.

It was a nice narrow hallway with no alcoves to hide in. Hopefully the hostiles on her heels would be just far enough behind to give her time to get to the closet.

The doors lining the hall were all metal, so any that were partly open she lit up as she ran past. Amazing how hot a metal door got from even one energy blast. Her weapon wasn't set to stun. Not anymore.

She heard cursing, and at least one body hitting the ground.

Shots came from behind now, tracking after her like angry bees. She was still doing her gymnast thing, but the hallway was narrow.

She needed to get out of it and fast. She returned fire from a low position, her flip taking her into the shallow protection of the closet door.

Her shoulder was out just far enough to catch a blast that almost spun her away from the door. That wasn't a stun. But not a kill shot either. She staggered from the hit and pain, but managed to stick it. Sir Rupert gave a soft squawk.

"You hit?" She pressed in closer, angling to protect him, fired off some shots and hit the control to open the door, ignoring the pain spreading out from her shoulder and trying to cloud her thinking.

"No."

She fired another spread, then the door opened at her back, and they were inside the closet. The door closed and she fired on it, aiming at the handle and hinges until they glowed bright red. Only then did she reach up and try to flash out.

Not a huge shock when they didn't.

Might be damage from the hit, but most likely the opposition closed the hole they used to get in. Also meant their intel on the suit was wrong. Or they'd upgraded for it already, but—

"Blocked?" Sir Rupert asked, making his way back to her shoulder.

"Yeah." She should have tried to jump sooner—

"They locked this place down before they started firing," Sir Rupert said, as if he knew what she was thinking. Which he probably did. He was that smart. He didn't waste time bemoaning the failure of the suit to perform as advertised.

Multiple shots made the metal door rattle in its frame. They had maybe thirty seconds. Probably less.

"The transport pad," Sir Rupert said.

"Why did I know you were going to say that?" Had she had the same thought? Was that why she'd retreated here? Sometimes if felt like even she didn't know what she was thinking. She crossed to it and started to lower it.

"Not that side."

"Heavy bugger." She flipped it over, wincing as pain flared brighter in her shoulder. She blinked spots away, kicked the bucket and mop to the side so there'd be room for it to lay flat. She glanced back. Red spots were appearing on the metal door. Spots that glowed and expanded as the metal began to melt.

"Turn it on here." Sir Isaac's beak touched the spot, then he hopped on the device.

She depressed the spot. There was a hum, but it felt like a long time before the circles turned red.

She glanced back again, maybe ten seconds, and they'd be through. She pointed her weapon at the door, preparing to take a stand if she had to.

Sir Rupert was the one who had to escape. She took a quick look back, but he was gone. Just a pattern of green beams shooting up from the disc and piercing the ceiling.

"Man, I hope you know where we're going."

A pinhole opened in the door, growing rapidly as they concentrated fire on that spot.

The shots were red now. One red beam skimmed by her other shoulder as she scrambled onto the device.

The door burst open, weapons firing at, and sparking off, the green beams—then the room vanished in a tunnel that was both familiar and not familiar.

Just a transport pad, she reminded herself, but the ride felt like more than that. It was beyond rough. She tumbled and bounced around in the tunnel. Saw the white light coming and tried to slow down. Couldn't. Tried to aim for the center. Didn't think she'd nailed it.

She might be about to find out about catapults, though…

The transit sped up. Wasn't going to stick this landing. Be lucky she didn't break something. With a spin she flew head first through the center of the circle of light…

Chapter 5

SOMETHING CATAPULTED out of the green beams of light like it had been hurled, something that squawked loudly as it tumbled beak over claws, just missing Briggs' head.

The spinning tumble continued unchecked toward a stand of palm-like trees. Somehow it recovered, made a narrow pass between two tree trunks, then circled back to a landing on the peak of the cottage.

It ruffled its feathers as if annoyed, then began to preen itself.

A parrot? He blinked. The green body, with a band of red just above the beak looked parrot-like.

"That's not something you see every day." Particularly in this birdless place. Too bad he'd already turned off the video. No one would believe he really saw a parrot shooting out of that thing.

The bird looked up and Briggs had the odd feeling it had understood him. He'd heard parrots were pretty smart. He glanced back at the disc. At least now he was pretty sure it was some kind of a transport pad. Definitely needed to get the power supply out—

He heard the hum build again and turned fully around, just in time to catch what flew out next. Instinctively his arms wrapped around the very humanoid—very female—form it ejected.

He staggered a few steps and then went down. The sand was harder than he'd have thought. His breath rushed out as they slid toward the water, his arms still wrapped around the woman.

When they hit wet sand, they slowed, and finally stopped. He felt water soaking into his shirt and heard the waves hitting close to his head. Took him a couple of tries before he could grab some shallow breaths. Each one was filled with the smell of salt, woman, and singed something.

He could feel the female struggling to catch her breath, too. Yeah, she was definitely female. Almost every inch of her was pressed against a lot of him, creating a different problem in catching his breath.

In the sudden silence, the bird squawked once.

Over on the table, the disc's beams flickered, there was a popping sound from inside, and it went dark, smoke puffing out the holes on the top. Great. Now he didn't even have a depleted power supply to show the geeks.

"Ow."

Her voice was pained, but, well, nice. She took a couple of deep breaths that increased Briggs' male holding a female problem. He wasn't as old as he'd thought.

He would have shifted her off, didn't want it to get embarrassing, and he would like to catch his breath, but the thing digging into his ribs felt a lot like some kind of gun. If she twitched wrong...

She muttered something that could have been a cuss word.

"...that hurt."

It was something of a relief she spoke very American sounding English, but also a worry. What was she doing on this top-secret outpost? He'd bet real money this was not what Donovan and Doc had had in mind when they sent him the disc to play with.

The weapon retreated as she rolled off him and onto the sand. She didn't get up, just lay there staring at the sky, her chest rising and falling quickly.

He yanked his gaze off her chest and sat up. Only, the changed angle made her harder to see. Was that some kind of high-tech camo?

If it was, it was damaged. One second she was part of the horizon, next he could see her very nicely put together figure encased in a black suit.

She muttered again but all he heard was, "...buggers shoot better than I thought they could..."

She lifted the hand holding the weapon, then looked at it as if surprised to find it in her hand. It was impressive she'd kept hold of it during that landing.

She stared at it then looked at him. She seemed about to say something, but instead she rolled over and got up, the movement of her body smooth and graceful.

Oh yeah, she was a girl. If he'd had any doubts after the close proximity check. Almost idly, he thought, bet she could dance a great cha-cha. And he wished he could get a better look at that weapon. It wasn't like anything he'd ever seen, even around this outpost.

"You're flickering."

That sounded like it came from the peak of the hut. Briggs got up, not nearly as smoothly as the woman.

Because he was a guy, and he had his pride, he kept the wincing to a minimum. His wound had not liked the slam against woman or ground, though other parts of him hadn't minded the woman-slamming part.

He thought he saw her touch something near her shoulder, and the camo faded, leaving just the black suit. Now he could see it had lines of silver running through the tight fitting black.

He gave a half tug at the neck of his tee shirt. Very, very tight fitting. He'd have spent more time matching brief memory with reality, but, as if she just realized he might be dangerous, she lifted the gun and pointed it at him.

His gaze narrowed. He was not in the mood to get shot again. He made a half move toward her.

"Don't." She flicked something on the weapon.

He assessed his chances. He could take it from her. Did he want to? She looked like kind of cute standing there and the look in her eyes said she really didn't want to shoot him. There was definitely a glint of humor in her chocolate-brown eyes.

Her lips twitched. "Stun hurts almost as bad as getting shot." She rotated one shoulder. "And getting shot is the pits."

He couldn't argue with that, his hand lifting to cover his own protesting injury. He should have just taken it from her while they were on the ground.

His gut said she was dangerous, but something else told him she wasn't dangerous to him—at least—he backed away from finishing that thought. Took a tug at his tee shirt neck again. Damn the heat in this place.

"You okay?"

He started to answer, but realized she wasn't talking to him.

"I am fine." The bird squawked once, then flew down, making a neat landing on her shoulder.

All she needed was an eyepatch to look like a pirate, standing there with her shoulders back, her chin up, and her feet planted. Her grin was sassy.

"Thanks for breaking my, um, fall," she said.

More heat bloomed where it shouldn't. He opened his mouth to answer, but she holstered the weapon like a pirate. Then she reached up toward a now visible line of buttons situated just below her shoulder blade and pressed one of them.

There was a distinct pop and smoke jetted out of her suit from the back.

The bird glanced back. "Well, that's embarrassing."

Chapter 6

EMBARRASSING DIDN'T QUITE COVER it. At least the big guy, the very nice looking big guy—she flicked her gaze up and down—seemed pretty unfazed by their abrupt arrival—and failure to depart. He might even be kind of amused.

Madison might be impressed.

And, by the way, she'd totally lost her fascination with catapults.

She was lucky he'd been there to catch her. Of course, he was big enough to catch two of her.

She studied him. He had looked annoyed when she first pointed her ray gun at him, but now? Hard to say. Was that a twinkle buried deep in his eyes?

She liked the eyes, with or without a twinkle. Even drawn in a line, his mouth was—she ran a fingertip along hers and sighed. Made her gaze move on. Military haircut and bearing. The tee shirt was stretched across a chest she had good reason to know was well-muscled and unyielding. And yet, the landing had managed to be pleasant for all that.

His denim shorts exposed tree-trunk legs planted in a way that should have made her nervous. Okay, he did make her a little nervous.

He could probably take her down with his pinkie finger. She felt a little color steal into her cheeks as she recalled how it felt to be held against him. All of him. The iron bars of his arms around her. His afternoon beard had been nicely rough against her cheek, his mouth temptingly close.

Did he date older women? Who pointed ray guns at him?

Sir Rupert's wings brushed the side of her head, as he lifted off, circling the clearing, then landing on a rough-hewn table parked in front of a rustic cottage. Had she landed in *Robinson Crusoe* land? The guy sure looked the part.

Sir Rupert gave a small squawk, his version of a snort, perhaps, his claws lifting briefly. So what if the big guy was the only non-time traveling male she'd met in, well, she didn't know how long. It wasn't that relationships were discouraged in the Rebellion.

The new guy had a wife. But it was tough to get involved with someone who could be years younger than you, or crazy ancient, when you finally had that date.

At least it was easy to shake off the bad ones. Don't call me, I'll call you took on a whole new meaning in time travel.

As if he sensed her random and inappropriate thought processes, Sir Rupert ruffled his fathers and walked around the manhole cover.

Still troubled by the rustic setting, she considered the big guy, then decided he could have already taken her down if he were so inclined. She let her hand drop away from her weapon—oh yeah, that hurt—and walked over next to the boss.

"Won't that just take us back," she stopped, slanting a glance at the guy, "where we came from?"

The big guy appeared to hesitate, too, then walked to the other side of the table from her. "If I was asked, I'd say you depleted the power source and that thing won't take you anywhere."

He was a pretty cool customer. Despite the, um, rustic surroundings, he'd clearly had contact with tech. Fixing tech was not her skill set. Breaking it? Yeah, she had that down pat.

"No," Sir Rupert said, continuing to circle the disc as if that would somehow make it work again. He angled his head to look at her. "They knew right where to shoot."

Now that he'd mentioned it, she felt air from what must be a hole in the shoulder of her suit. And possibly some sluggish bleeding. And just like that the pain rose in a wave.

This made the horizon waver for several seconds and her stomach gave a nauseous bump. She firmly pushed it all to the back of her brain. Because the niggle was back between her shoulder blades.

The squad couldn't use the manhole cover to follow them here, so that might be a relief, but could they track them some other way?

She looked around again. Where was here? She turned back to the big guy, tried out a smile. It felt like it hit a deflector shield and fell into the sand at her feet with a painful plop. He crossed his arms over his chest—man, that was a great chest if his tee shirt wasn't lying—and she knew it wasn't.

"We don't care for Time Service agents around here."

Madison looked quickly at Sir Rupert. He was the boss.

"Neither do we," he said.

The big guys brows arched skeptically. If he'd had dealings with the Service, which he clearly had, she did not blame him.

"You're not Time Service…agents…" The sardonic tone faltered a bit as his gaze fell on Sir Rupert.

Okay, so he'd run into agents, but not Sir Rupert's *Militarian* species. That was interesting. What would he think when he found out the bird was in charge of the op? Sir Rupert gave her a tiny nod, though his glance also advised caution. Like she didn't know that.

"We're, well, I guess you'd call us the opposition." Tip-toeing through minefields was her thing, assuming it was an actual minefield. But emotional mine fields? Not so much. Her ears were starting to buzz as the pain indicated it did not like being ignored. "Do you mind if I sit down? I don't feel that great."

She got a hard stare from the big guy and a very brief nod. She gripped the table as she sank onto the stool. She leaned an elbow on the table and tried to slow her breathing. Cause each breath hurt like a son of a gun. Been a while since she'd taken a hit this bad. If it had hit her somewhere else—but Sir Rupert was right, whoever fired it had known right where to point and shoot.

Must be frustrating when he or she saw Madison vanish via the manhole cover. She would have chuckled, but that would hurt, too. Through a growing haze she met the big guy's hard, distrustful gaze. So why did she sense something else from him? Why wasn't she that worried?

"I'd let you point my ray gun at me, but it only works for me." She lifted it clear of the holster and set it on the table top, then shoved it toward the big guy. Sir Rupert let out a muted squawk that she took to be a protest. Or agreement. Sometimes it was hard for her to tell.

"DNA or handprint?" The big guy asked, managing to keep one eye on them, as he snagged her ray gun and studied it with what she'd call professional interest.

"DNA," she told him, her voice oddly distant from the rest of her.

He quirked a brow. "Ray gun?"

"It has a fancy name that I can't ever remember," she admitted. And that's what they'd called them in the books and movies from her time, a time where a girl like her wouldn't have got to look at one, let alone get to point and shoot one at bad guys.

She could tell by the way he handled it, he was comfortable with weapons. If her head would clear, she'd figure out what that meant for them. Beads of sweat began to track down the sides of her face and the wavering horizon began to blur. She needed to stay awake, to stay focused. There was her niggle...

Sir Rupert fluttered over to the edge of the table with a worried squawk. "You are injured. I should have realized..."

His words kind of faded so she missed the end. The horizon steadied for a second, long enough for her to see two moons, dim in the late afternoon sky, but definitely two moons hanging there over the big guy's shoulder.

She rubbed her mouth, her hand coming away damp with cold sweat. "This isn't Earth."

The big guy lowered her weapon, his gaze sharpening.

Sir Rupert looked up, his feathers ruffling.

"What year is this?" She tried to look around, but that was a very bad idea. Spikes of pain shot up from her shoulder, stabbing into her brain and everything spun fast enough to ramp up the nausea.

From a long way away she heard her voice say, "Usually I can make a good guess, but this place doesn't give much away." She tried to grin, but it felt like it wavered more than the horizon. She was talking too much, but couldn't stop herself.

"Who are you?" He had his Sphinx on, though he did glance at the bird this time.

"I am Sir Rupert." He ruffled his feathers importantly.

It might actually be his real name. Birds didn't have the same risks with sharing their real names. It was hard to track down a flock and pick out the one bird who could erase you from existence.

Time was not only fluid, but apparently had a sense of humor. Let's make sure, it said, probably snickering somewhere out there, that you remember people you can never see again, because they didn't exist anymore. And then let's put you in position to fix all kinds of time paradoxes. But not that one.

Never that one, thank you so much, Boris.

The big guy was looking at her now, she realized, though it seemed his expression had softened. Or her gaze was getting blurrier. Probably that one. He wanted a name, she realized fuzzily.

"Scarlet Doe." It embarrassed her to say it out loud. Even about to pass out from pain, she blushed. She met his ironic gaze. "I told them it was the worst fake—"

"Code name," Sir Rupert interposed.

"*Code* name, worst code name ever." The big guy's brows rose and his look said, give me something better than that if you want my help. She couldn't give him her real name, so she gave him the one she'd used in her head for so long it felt like her real name. "Madison. You can call me Madison."

Her insides tensed, despite the pain that caused, as the name dropped into the gentle sea breeze and rose through the air toward the warm, high sun.

The horizon didn't tremble or reverberate, at least not in a time-ish way. That's how she would have known that somewhere that name had registered with someone.

Real names in time travel were dangerous, existence threatening, but so was time travel. Besides, all they could do now was kill her.

For her, well, she didn't exist, though it had been a near thing, a fluke in time. But even she needed something to anchor her to her past, even if it was gone. It was so easy to lose yourself in time. And for someone who had been doing it as long as she had? That anchor was as critical to her survival as staying hidden.

They all knew it, so they were careful about using those anchors outside their own minds. Until now, not even Sir Rupert had heard the name Madison. Which begged the question, why had she told the big guy? And the answer came back in two parts.

He would know a lie if he heard it.

And for some reason she was too foggy to figure out, it was important he believed her. She wanted him to trust her.

"And you are?" she asked, then was sorry because he probably only had a real name.

"Briggs."

It felt like her chin sank deeper into the palm she rested it on.

"Briggs." She smiled at him, felt the cloudiness of her gaze, even as she worried at how much their arrival would put him at risk. "Nice to meet you, Briggs."

He frowned and stepped closer. "You are hurt."

"Yes." She felt the clouds going dark, felt herself listing to the side—felt those strong arms lock around her for the second time. "Thanks again," she murmured, her head dropping to rest against his truly wonderful chest as her lights went out.

Chapter 7

Briggs carried Madison inside the hut and settled her on his bed. Her waist was ringed with a belt loaded with neatly slotted equipment. The only one missing was her ray gun.

He removed the gear, then the belt, and tossed it aside. Only then did he lower her—feeling something stirring inside himself, a something not appropriate to the situation, as he did so. But doing it felt oddly familiar, as if they'd done this before.

Which was not possible.

So—maybe it just felt right, the kind of right that he hadn't felt for a long time. It hadn't been so long that he hadn't recognized the look in her eyes, an interest she hadn't tried to hide. Was it a tactical move? Hadn't felt like it, and the interest had stayed in there as the fog closed in, and took her down.

Before he could stop himself, he smoothed the hair back from her face, noticing how her lashes fanned across the upper curve of her cheeks.

Her skin was pale beneath her tan, revealing a sprinkling of freckles across a nose that tipped up on the end.

His gaze lingered on parted pink lips, noted the rapid rise and fall of her chest. He pulled his hand back, though his fingers wanted to linger on the soft skin and trace the lines and curves of her face. And then move lower…

She'd never make it onto a magazine cover. She was short, her body more compact than thin. Very fit, with signs of strength in her limbs and body. That was okay. He'd never been interested in half-starved waifs with big, sad eyes. What he'd seen of her eyes, they for sure they hadn't been sad. Serious, sassy, amused, and interested, but not sad.

She did interest him. He faced it because he needed to take care. If this was some kind of move on the base here, well, he had to make sure that didn't happen.

Madison. Even as he considered how this might be a play, his hands moved down her arms, then flexed her legs, trying to assess her injuries. He checked her ribs, but was defeated by the suit. She seemed to have been sealed inside it.

"Put your fingers here," the bird said, tapping its beak between her breasts.

He gave the bird a wary look.

"To open the seal on her uniform," it added.

Briggs decided he didn't want to know what the bird was thinking when he hesitated.

He touched the suit, careful to keep his fingers in the center. But his knuckles brushed curves as he tried to find a seam. Felt like a creepy guy, even when his thumb finally found something. He pushed and a gap appeared. He pushed a little harder and his fingers brushed against soft, firm skin.

He didn't yank back. That would be obvious, even to a bird. She didn't stir. Breathing a bit easier—okay, nothing was easy about this, but he doggedly worked to open it wider.

The vulnerability of her situation called to his sense of honor, the reason he'd joined the Air Force. To serve. To protect. But then there was that other call. It wasn't just a guy and a gal call, though it had started that way when she slammed into him.

There was something about her that had made a stealthy pass through his defenses, not just the base's. She was wrong for him in every way—including too young. He could be her father.

Maybe if he repeated that enough, if would finally sink in. But that wasn't going to happen while he was sitting here opening her suit while the warm, clean scent of her filled his nostrils.

Here he'd thought it would be better to smell anything but fresh, sea breezes. It was a reminder to be careful what you thought you wanted because the universe was listening and happy to show you where you were wrong.

He tried taking a deep breath, but that just made it worse, so he held his breath and finished exposing her from waist to neck. Underneath she wore a light weight tank top that hugged her skin and revealed the fact that the suit had seriously compressed her... chest.

Briggs massaged his temple, but stopped when he caught the bird looking at him in a way that was kinda unnerving. Like it knew exactly he was thinking. The skin he could see was smooth and also lightly tanned. No sign of tan lines—not that he was looking. Much.

He averted his gaze from the danger zones and eased the suit off her shoulders—sweat beading on his skin and hers—dang tropics— until the suit was folded down around her waist. Normally he'd have been interested in that suit.

Of course, he'd left normal when the parrot bounced out of the disc. His gaze accidentally tracked across her tee shirt and he found one reason to be glad it wasn't cold. Just the one, though. Because the heat outside was not helping him at all with the heat stirring inside.

"Where did she get hit?" His voice came out husky, but maybe the bird didn't notice.

"Back left shoulder."

He shifted her onto her uninjured side and all heat fled in the face of a cold rage that wasn't any more appropriate than the—his mind rejected lust. Oh, he wanted her, he admitted reluctantly, but well, he needed to move on. She needed his help. He studied her injury.

It was an ugly, sluggishly bleeding gash high on her back, partly inside, and partly above the rounded edge of her tee shirt. The force of something had driven bits of wires, small pieces of metal, and cloth into her skin, but—he studied it carefully—he didn't think it was deep, despite the debris.

He could probably patch it up, but—his thoughts strayed to the alien infection that had put him in the infirmary for several days….

"She should see a doc." And what would that involve? Their presence was a security breach that was going to be hard to explain. He glanced at the bird, who was perched on the bed examining her injury with a bird-like, but oddly professional, interest.

"It could have been worse," the bird said, relieved. "Can you apply first aid?"

The bird said. Had he just thought that? It wasn't a shock that a parrot, or parrot-looking bird, could talk. It even had the croaking overtones of a parrot. But this was *talking*, not just talking.

He shouldn't be surprised. They'd been looking for non-human, sentient alien life from the first flight of Project Enterprise. It was even possible this wasn't the first contact with a non-humanoid, since there were other ships out there nosing around. It was his first, however. Until now their people had had contact with only humanoid aliens.

Briggs nodded, dug his first aid kit out of his duffle. and opened it. He found the supplies he needed and started cleaning and disinfecting the wound. He didn't hesitate, even when she stirred and muttered in pain.

He'd tended battle wounds before. And this was a battle wound, no question.

He might have cussed under his breath, but he kept going. It had to be done. When he was sure it was cleaned, he studied the injury carefully. There were signs of scorching around the edges. His lips tightened. Someone had used an energy—a ray gun—on her. And she'd fired back, he reminded himself. Still pissed him off someone had hurt her.

He doused the area with antiseptic, waited for it to dry, then carefully applied Super Glue to close the torn skin. He sprayed on some pain killer, then covered it with a light bandage and eased her onto her back again. Only then did he look at the bird, trying to decide what to ask.

The bird hopped up on the headboard and looked around. "Are you marooned in this place?"

Briggs sat back, shifting to ease his wound, which was complaining about the workout, now that he wasn't busy focusing on Madison's injury.

Madison. That probably wasn't her real name either, but it meant something to her. He'd felt it, felt truth in it somewhere.

"I'm recuperating." His annoyance with this broke into his tone. "The base…"

He stopped that sentence unfinished. For all he knew, these two were attempting to infiltrate the base. Just because they looked like time travelers and she'd asked what year it was, and they'd appeared out of a disc, didn't mean they'd traveled through time.

It could be a simple transport pad. A decoy? Donovan's handwriting had looked genuine, but it wasn't like he could give her a call and ask.

And it might have been an unintended consequence. He had been the one to fix it and turn it on—something no one at the base or Area 51 would have approved. In his boredom, he'd been careless. He could face the uncomfortable truth now that he was forty-five and probably more mature.

"You are wise to take care. The people hunting us are ruthless and highly trained. If they find you useful, they will take you, and reprogram you to serve their needs." The bird moved one way along the headboard, then moved back.

"And if they don't find me useful?" Briggs asked, his gut tightening at the thought of the "useful" people at the base, including Doc Clementyne's brother, Robert. Robert, who had finally found happiness and purpose in his life.

"They will erase you from time. It will be as if you never lived."

He frowned. "But wouldn't that…"

"Do you think they care about fallout to others?"

"The time service—"

"…has changed," the bird said. "Absolute power corrupts absolutely. They began trying to fix and repair time breaches, but at some point their focus changed. And now it ripples back through all time in an unchecked rotten flow."

"But—" he started to protest, but how would he know that big events hadn't changed? Or if this bird spoke the truth. They were the 'opposition,' but that didn't make them allies. Even if he had a built-in prejudice against the time service thanks to Doc. The bird could be talking to earn his sympathy and turn him into a weapon against its enemy.

"The only place they take care is around large events, because these anchor time and time will push back."

If the bird could have smiled grimly, Briggs sensed it would have.

"They learned that lesson the hard way, but they did not learn enough."

Briggs studied the bird, but it was not like he had experience reading a bird's face for truth or lies. Odd that his gut felt it spoke the truth—the truth as the bird knew it, he decided.

"Why are they after you two?"

"We are hunting a traitor and they seek to stop us before we can return to our base with that information." The bird ruffled its wings and stepped lightly along the headboard again. "They did not factor in the transport pad or they would not have left it for us to find."

Was the bird sure about that? That thing didn't seem like the kind of thing you left lying around in an unsecured area.

"We found it in a storage closet, shoved into a corner," the bird said, as if it heard Briggs' thought.

Had it had the same thought?

"I can not be sure it was not part of the trap," the bird conceded. It looked around. "I do not think it meant us to come here, however."

Yeah, a trap that depended on him turning that thing on at the right time wasn't a very good trap. More like a lucky chance if these people were as bad as the bird thought they were.

The bird looked around now. "I did not expect to arrive here."

Briggs let himself grin. "Where did you think you were going?"

The bird regarded him solemnly. "Anywhere that wasn't where we were." It paused, then added, "But more useful than here."

Briggs' grin widened. He was kind of starting to like the bird. He grinned. "Yeah, I'm not thrilled to be here either," he admitted.

The bird regarded him in a way that might be thoughtful. "You should leave."

Briggs' gaze narrowed. There'd been a warning in there. Did it expect trouble to follow them here? He looked at the bird. "How do I know your trouble won't follow me?"

"It is our job to contain it," the bird said.

Briggs didn't try to hide his skepticism. Then his brows lowered in a scowl.

"They can't get here on that," Briggs pointed out, already sure that wasn't how trouble was gonna arrive.

"No," the bird's head bobbed as if it was aware of the irony, "but nevertheless, they will come."

Chapter 8

"I'm afraid I have to agree with Sir Rupert." Madison's voice was husky, but calm.

Briggs twisted around to look at her. The fog was clearing from her eyes, revealing worry. He saw something else in there though, something he recognized because he'd seen it many times during his years in the USAF.

The look of a warrior preparing to meet the enemy.

"And thank you for the third time." She shifted her shoulders. "It feels much better."

Better wasn't fighting fit, but he also knew when someone couldn't be talked out of a fight. Not someone with that stubborn jaw line.

"You're welcome." He kept his tone even with an effort. He wanted to argue with her. He wanted to grab her and change her mind the old-fashioned way. Not that he wanted to get caught with his pants down when the enemy arrived.

If they arrived.

And when had her enemies become his? A smile tugged at the edges of her mouth, and regret filtered into her expression. She could be his daughter, he reminded himself. It didn't help as much as he'd hoped it would because she didn't look at him like he was her dad.

Was it because he wanted her to be older that it seemed like she was older than she looked?

"You never said what year this is?" she prompted softly.

He hesitated, but couldn't think of a good reason not to tell her. "2017."

Her eyes widened. "Really?" She glanced up at the bird. It ruffled its wings, which could be its version of surprised. "But I thought—" She stopped, then asked, "Where…"

"That's classified." His non-disclosure agreement didn't say he couldn't mention the base to time travelers, but there were all kinds of clauses about not talking to anyone—including yourself—and getting shot if you did.

So it added up to not disclosing to time travelers in his opinion. And the kind of shooting in the agreement? It wasn't the kind that required recuperating in a hut or anywhere else.

"I need to get up." She reached out and he did, too, maybe to stop her, but her fingers slid between his, her palm brushing against his and he forgot about stopping her. Might have made him think about pushing her back down.

Warmth surged from where their hands touched and it felt like they'd always held hands and always would. There was the heat of desire in the mix, but also the warmth of a wood fire, the kind that invited you to settle in, to stay, and make something that lasted—

His fingers tightened involuntarily on hers. There was no fool like an old fool…

For several seconds, it felt like she returned his grip, probably just so she could swing her legs over the edge of the bed and rest them on the floor. Side by side, her head barely reached the top of his shoulder.

He waited for her to free her hand, but she didn't. If anything her grip tightened. Her breath came in quick bursts for several seconds and she bit her lower lip. He had to stop himself from reaching for her as she lost color, but after a moment or two, her breathing slowed and some of her color came back. Her lips formed into a thin, stubborn line.

She looked at him, her smile wavering a bit, and finally there was some sad in her eyes. He didn't mind because there were other things in there, too. If he died right now…well, he wouldn't be happy, but it would be better than seeing her walk away…

The bird flew over to the top of the rustic dresser, breaking into whatever was happening between them. It walked one way along the top, then back, almost as if it were pacing.

She hesitated, her shoulders stiffening as resolve pushed out every other emotion in her eyes.

"How big is our possible risk zone?" she asked.

It stopped, a wing came up, as if rubbing the lower part of its beak. "They'll come in on a tight beam because they won't know what they're jumping into."

"They won't like that," she said with a grin. "Couple of hundred yards? More? Less?"

The bird appeared to nod. "Less, I think."

Madison shifted a bit, so that she half faced Briggs, their hands still linked.

"Is that enough to keep your people safe?"

"If it wasn't, could you do anything about it?" he asked, though without heat. He figured she was trying to find out what she needed to know, without actually finding it out. He appreciated the effort, even if he wasn't sure it would work. She had no idea what this island contained.

She nodded. "There are some things we could do." She glanced around. "Defensively, this isn't the best location. Or the worst."

"The structure will give them something to focus on," the bird pointed out, his tone in the range of 'it was what it was."

Wary and trust contended for the upper hand inside his head. Last time he'd felt like this, he'd been trying to decide if he could trust Doc Clementyne—but he hadn't felt like this around Doc.

Then he had needed to only believe his head, not his heart. Could he trust either when all he wanted to do was sit here and hold her hand? Okay, not all he wanted to do. His lips twisted wryly.

"That should be enough," he admitted. If he'd put Robert Clementyne at risk, there was nowhere in time or space he could hide from Doc Clementyne.

She squeezed his hand one last time and then released it so she could stand up. This time she didn't face him when she said, "You need to go."

She didn't know he couldn't, even if he wanted to, which he didn't. He'd never walked away from an important fight in his life.

But there was more to it than this girl and his uneasy feelings for her. More that was both complicated and simple. It was his fault the base and its people were at risk. He'd opened the door these two came through. And he had to close it.

He couldn't die trying. He had to live and do it.

That was the simple part. The complicated part? He stared at her profile. He sure as hotel wasn't leaving her—these two to face the incoming alone. That wasn't in his DNA—though it was the first time he'd felt the need to protect a bird.

"No," he said, his tone mild, but firm.

She spun to face him, her head tipped to one side as, he guessed, she assessed his resolve. Finally she glanced at the bird. It almost seemed like it shrugged.

"We could use the help."

"The risk—" she said, but her protest lacked force.

"I'm guessing we don't have a lot of time to argue. Is the ray gun your only weapon?"

Her posture changed. Kind of reminded him of Donovan when she was preparing to toss someone on their ass. He rose, towering over her with his brows arched. Not that Donovan had ever managed to toss him. After a pause, she nodded.

"How many hostiles incoming?"

She wasn't the one who answered him.

"At least six. Highly trained and outfitted with dangerous and deadly technology they've stolen from the future."

Briggs mouth straightened into a line, and he shot a look at Madison. She seemed startled, but not annoyed. Was she surprised by what the bird had told him? Who was in charge? Who got to decide what? He could take orders, but—as if she sensed the question, she spoke.

"Sir Rupert is my," she hesitated, "...boss. I'm his bodyguard. It's my job to get him safely back to our base." He knew his gaze narrowed sharply because she added, "But it is always in my brief to protect innocents from hostile actions of the Time Service squads. You do not have to believe me, but I am as committed to protecting your people as you are."

"We are committed to that," the bird amended. "It is why we do what we do. To protect all living things from the damage done by the Time Service."

Because he couldn't do it to the bird, he directed a drilling gaze on Madison, using all the technique he'd learned during his years in the military. She didn't flinch or look away. Her lips might have twitched once.

"So," he said, finally, "six hostiles incoming?" That didn't seem too bad, even with fancy dancy technology.

"There might have been more than six who attacked us," she cautioned with a frown. "There was a lot of incoming fire, but they could have upgraded their weapons from our last, um, encounter." She rubbed her forehead. "I didn't get a look at any of them. Just heard one or two go down."

"So what's your highest estimate?" Briggs pressed.

Her lips twisted wryly. "They might wait to reconstitute their squad before they come after us. Or they might call in backup. Twelve is the most I've ever seen them risk on a single op." She frowned. "It depends on what they think they'll jump into."

"If they believe you are alone, injured, and cut off from assistance," the bird said, "they will not wait for backup."

"But..." she started to protest, then stopped. "They would have brought a full force if they thought we jumped back to our base. But they know the manhole cover wouldn't take us there." She looked more hopeful.

Briggs grinned at the "manhole cover."

"But..." she murmured, the look she exchanged with the bird was interesting.

"What?" he asked, adding impatiently, "I need to know."

"He is correct. He does need to know."

Madison shifted her shoulder as if it pained her, but she met his gaze with sober determination. "If they saw Sir Rupert during the op, they will come in at full strength and loaded to kill. They can not afford to let him return to our base alive."

Did he need to know why?

"I told you we were seeking to identify a traitor, a mole in our organization," the bird said.

He frowned as a thought occurred to him. "How will they track you?" From where he sat, the disc looked dead out there on the table.

Once more it seemed that Madison looked at the bird for permission.

"He needs to know," the bird said again.

"I do," Briggs said grimly.

Madison patted her waist, then looked around, found the things from her belt he'd tossed onto the bed, and went over to them. She sorted through the small pile until she found the one she wanted. She activated it and directed it at the suit, watching a small screen. She finally made a face, speaking to the parrot, not him.

"Yeah, it's got an active tracking beacon."

"What...the suit?"

She nodded.

"Can you turn it off?"

In normal circumstances no one could find this outpost, since it had cloaking technology, but these two had made it in, so that probably wouldn't keep out their incoming squad. He could summon help, lots of it, but he had a feeling that conventional defenses wouldn't work in this situation.

"Maybe," she said, but once again she looked at the bird. "They might already have a fix on it."

"You want to use it to draw them in," he said, because it is what he would have done.

"We could try to leave, but if they already have this location..." She shrugged and did it very well.

He'd meant he had to be a grownup and not look—more than once. Apparently he was not as mature as he'd hoped. He glanced up, found her watching, humor and something else in her eyes. If she weren't younger than him…She met his gaze steadily.

"It's the best way for us and for your…for anyone here. They don't know the terrain, won't know what they are jumping into, but if they follow the beam in, they'll be less likely to look around, at least until they've got what they want."

He frowned. "A couple of hundred yards isn't that narrow." Had she seriously thought she could cover that much ground?

"I assess they will come in at considerably less than one hundred yards," the parrot said. "Their scanning will see the trees as obstacles to avoid, so the clear space on the beach is where they will most likely land."

Madison nodded. "And they'll know, if I'm conscious, they won't have that much time. I will have sensed them incoming."

Briggs blinked, not sure what to say. She could sense that?

"She's a very good time jumper," the bird said. It began to pace once more. "I do not believe they saw me. I transported before the door was breached. They'll know you were injured and that your suit was damaged and that the pad was the only way out."

"You think they'll be overconfident," Briggs suggested.

"Not a good reason for us to be overconfident," Madison said. "Their tech will be formidable, even if they think I'm down or almost down."

Her worried gaze met his. He should care they were up against some scary dudes with scary stuff, but words lost their power when she looked at him like that. He was treading in deep water, no question, but if it came down to a choice, he had to choose the base, its people over her.

She gave a slight nod, as if she knew it and agreed. "So we fight."

"Was there ever any doubt?" the bird asked.

"How long do you think we have?" Briggs asked now, his brain kicking into strategy mode.

Madison frowned. "That thing wasn't supposed to send us through time, just space."

Briggs blinked.

"What happened before your transit?" the bird asked.

"There might have been some shooting," she admitted. "More shooting, I mean," she added, with a sidelong glance at Briggs. "While I was in the beams."

"The concentrated weapons fire must have boosted the power and the signal, enabling that pad to connect to this one," the bird said. It fluttered over to the back of the chair, and moved back and forth on this now. "It is only thing that explains it."

"I'm not going to ask what would have happened if there'd been no pad to connect to," Madison said.

Since she hadn't asked, the bird didn't appear inclined to answer.

It was nice to know he'd been right about what the disc did. He might be forty-five but he still had it.

"The other pad must have had a better power source," he mused, then gave himself a shake. It didn't matter now. "How long do we have to plan?" It was need-to-know.

Madison hesitated. "Oddly enough, the trip through time will give us more time. We might get three hours, but safe number is more like one hour."

One hour? Briggs tensed. "Then I need to make a call."

"I need to walk around, get a feel for the location," Madison said. She started to turn.

"Wait." She stopped, one brown lifted. "This is my turf. I know the terrain," Boy, did he know it. "I'm in charge."

She hesitated, glanced at the bird and nodded. "But Sir Rupert leaves the area. He can't be seen."

"During your call, could get me access to a computer," the bird asked. "I could endeavor to send out an SOS."

"You think help will come in time?" Briggs asked, not thrilled at more time travelers arriving.

The bird moved its beak from side to side. "There is not enough time, I know, ironic, but these are the limitations we live—or die—with."

"He could get the word out about our traitor," Madison said.

"I don't like it," Briggs said.

"Then I will go find some birds to, um, hang with."

Briggs blinked, not sure whether to laugh or grind his teeth. "There aren't any birds on this...in this place."

"No birds?" Madison looked shocked, then shook her head. "We're running out of time."

Briggs hesitated, then went with his gut and prayed it wasn't letting him down. "I'll arrange a safe place and a way to send your message." But he'd also make sure Robert was warned.

"Your plan," the bird said, "you must disable, not kill them."

"That's not—"

"Not all of them are willing," Madison said, clear reluctance in her voice. "And we don't know what impact their deaths would have on the timeline."

"You're in one batcrap crazy business," he said. "Okay, I know how to disable."

"Thank you," the bird said.

He shook his head. "I'll go make my call."

He stalked out the door toward the water. His chest heaved twice, then he lifted his radio.

MADISON STARED AT BRIGGS' back for several seconds, then turned back to Sir Rupert, but she didn't know what to say or even ask.

"Trust him," the bird said.

"I do." She glanced out the door again. "He doesn't trust me, us."

"No." His wings fluttered and he lifted off, coming to where he could look out the door, too. "You should collect your things and get out of that suit."

"If they don't see a heat signature connected to the suit—" she protested.

"Trust him to work something out."

She looked down at the bird, but he wasn't looking at her. He hadn't done this once already, had he? Not that he'd tell her if he had.

He would try to steer them away from where it went wrong— she rubbed her temple. It always ached when she tried to think her way through the paradoxes of time travel.

She was tired of it, she realized. Tired of doing the same operations, tired of looking for Boris—the one who had changed her life for all time. She chose to be happy, as happy as possible, because why give up more of her life to a faceless nosebleed waste of space. But she felt out of juice.

This place, that man, had made her realize how very fast she'd been running, trying to stay ahead of how alone she was. And how very much she wanted to not be alone anymore.

I don't know how many more fights I have in me. Even thinking the words made her realize she did know. She had one left, because she couldn't let that man down. She couldn't let him die because she'd made a mistake. She hadn't trusted her niggle.

That couldn't, it wouldn't ever happen again.

Chapter 9

BRIGGS HAD TOLD Robert not to get out of the chopper, but he was too much like his sister. The impossible not only didn't scare him, he thought it could be beat.

He grinned at Briggs, his curious gaze tracking past him to Madison and the bird. His eyes widened in delight and he passed Briggs, his hand held out.

"Robert," he flicked a glance back at Briggs, "and I'm not supposed to ask your name."

"Madison," she said. "And this is Sir Rupert."

Her smile was so natural for Robert, Briggs felt a stab of something that couldn't be what it felt like because Robert had a wife. But then he processed the fact she'd told him their names. Trust. She trusted them.

"How do you do?" the bird said, waving a claw in greeting, Briggs supposed.

Briggs lips compressed when Madison shot him a questioning look. He trusted her, he realized, but Doc—this was the brother that had been lost to her. Nothing could happen to Robert.

"We were wondering if you could take Sir Rupert with you. He kind of needs to send up an SOS to our base."

If anything Robert looked even more curious. "How do you do that?"

"Facebook," the bird said.

Both he and Robert did a double take.

"Facebook?" Robert slanted a look at Briggs.

"We all have an emergency account," Madison explained. "We use Facebook memes all the time to send messages. And those quizzes. Sometimes we use the quizzes."

"I don't," Briggs admitted, a bit dazed, "have an account. But—"

"It won't be instantaneous," Robert said, "but we should be able to get you connected. Emily loves Facebook."

Madison half opened her mouth, then closed it.

"His wife," Briggs said. She needed to know what was at stake here. And to know he trusted her.

She met his gaze, gratitude in the worried depths.

Robert half turned toward the chopper. "Let's get your stuff unloaded." He hesitated. "Sure you won't need more help?"

"We'll be fine. Just help," Briggs had to swallow, "the bird with his meme thing."

Robert laughed as the bird flew a small circle then landed on his shoulder. "I always wanted to be a pirate," he said, stroking the bird.

Briggs could be wrong, but he thought the bird rolled its eyes.

BRIGGS STARED out over water reflecting light from the waning sun. Night was incoming, probably at the same time as the bad guys —the guys he hoped were bad guys. It had been a busy almost hour, one far too short, since Robert had left with the bird.

Madison had traded her suit for some camo, though not without a protest.

"If you're in there, we won't have enough fire power." She was not going to be bait on any op with him.

So they'd filled the suit with bags of hot water and arranged it on the bed. He'd hesitated, then looked at her. "We may not have a choice. If we can't stop them—"

She nodded.

She wanted to kill them, he realized. There was more than getting shot in the shoulder that drove her, but he didn't have time to find out. He snorted silently. Time. What a mess time travel made of things that should be simple, straightforward. "Can you do this?"

He kept his tone neutral, but with a layer of hard he used when he sensed an Airman on the point of wavering.

She looked at him then. "I can do what has to be done."

She might as well have said, *I can do what must be done one more time.* She was at her limit. Maxed out. But she'd do it. He wanted to—but they both needed to get under cover.

"Will you do one thing for me?" she asked, her voice so quiet, he almost missed her words.

"If I can."

Her lips trembled into a small smile. "I promise it won't hurt."

She turned until she fully faced him and reached out with one hand, settling it lightly on his chest close to his heart. Her chin lifted. "There's not much time…"

She lifted onto her toes, her lips parted, but she was too short. His lips quirked, Briggs bent his head, and met her halfway. She didn't seem to know what she was doing, but it didn't matter.

He hadn't forgotten how to kiss a girl. His arms found their way around to her back and he pulled her close and maybe off her feet entirely. Desire tried to surge out of control, but he didn't turn it loose.

There was no time. No time…

He felt her stiffen and lifted his head.

"They're coming."

For half a second, he couldn't let go. Then his arms slackened. She stepped back. He couldn't, not until she created the distance. His hand shook slightly as he touched her hair one last time. He dropped his arm to his side, his fingers clenched.

"Right," he said. "Let's do this."

~

BRIGGS HAD HELPED Madison slide into the sniper's blind they'd built, one on either side of the target zone, then he piled foliage across the opening.

She dug deeper into the dead leaves and other debris as she heard his crunching footsteps taking him to his position. Plants gave off a heat signature, too, so the dense foliage should muddy hers, particularly when they had a nice clean one inside the cottage to focus on.

Their positions would also provide a good crossfire situation. She had two weapons—a tranquilizer rifle and one with real bullets, already positioned for sniping. She only had to shift her hand to grab a stun grenade.

She considered her instructions again, making sure they were clear in her mind before things went hot.

The plan was good. He knew strategy, was just the kind of person the Time Service liked to acquire. She had to make sure that didn't happen.

As the clock ticked down to zero, she felt calm settle over her mind, her body alert, but not tense. If this was her last performance, she intended to make it a good one.

They wore headset radios, tuned to a frequency his people were unlikely to stumble across, but they were only useful until the shooting started. Her headset crackled.

"Romeo Tango Golf," she heard Briggs say.

Ready to go.

"Mike Tango," she answered.

Me too. She felt the change as the time bubble formed.

"Hotel India," she said. *Hostiles incoming.* She lifted the tranquilizer rifle, tucked it into her shoulder, and prepared for her first target.

~

THE HORIZON SHIMMERED A BIT, and then Briggs saw six dark figures appear along the beach line. Almost immediately they were gone. They'd activated their camo, he realized but they'd be moving in toward the hut.

In the moonlight falling across the beach, he saw footsteps appear in the sand and grinned. No one had come up with a way to hide footprints.

They reached the table and stopped, probably looking at the dead transport disc. He activated the drone. It rose slowly, until it was about chest height, hovering in the shadowy doorway of the hut.

"What's that sound?" one of them asked. The footprints turned, first one, then all of them angled toward the hut. They began to track forward.

Keep coming, he thought, *just a little further.* When they were close enough, he sent the drone out of the doorway and activated the EMP device the drone carried. There was a flash of bright light.

Hello, electromagnetic pulse.

The drone went dead.

But so did their fancy tech.

They went from blending into the horizon to dark shadows backlit by the rising moons.

Madison fired her first shot, then a second. Nice. Two shadows down. The other turned toward the shots, giving Briggs a chance to lob a stun grenade into the middle of them. Another bright, blinding flash. Followed by the sound of muffled thumps into soft sand.

Don't move, he wanted to tell Madison. But their radios had been taken out by the EMP, too.

He waited for his night vision to return. There were dark lumps around the hut's doorway. But were they all down? He lowered his night sight and their heat signatures popped them out. No sign of movement. With his weapon ready, he kicked out of his blind and approached them.

Madison appeared out of the dark on the other side. He lifted a hand to stop her before she stepped into the light.

"Cover me," he ordered. He pulled out the plastic zip ties and secured the first guy, feet and hands, then moved to the second. One figure shifted a bit and a shot hissed out, hitting its target. The moving stopped. Even as Briggs secured each one, his mind was repeating over and over, "Too easy…"

A sharp cry, cut off before it was complete came from Madison's position. Briggs dropped down between two of the prone figures as something blue sizzled past, close enough for him to feel the heat.

A bright cage of lights dropped over him and the figures. He heard the crackle of it, felt its heat maybe two inches above his head. And from Madison's direction, he saw another one appear, trapping her inside.

MADISON FELT the niggle too late to escape the energy trap. The heat of it traveled along her weapon, forcing her to drop it. Then two figures emerged from either side of the hut, both with their camo already down. One circled the cage that held Briggs trapped.

"Sometimes it pays to be late to the party," the one closest to her said. His voice was icy cold, crisply devoid of anything that might give away his origins. He stopped and looked at his downed team. "We need to know what happened."

Briggs wasn't down in the sense this agent meant, but he was not moving. She did not see how it would help, but she clung to the faint hope as the man's attention shifted to her. She was the only one who appeared to be standing.

He walked over until they stood a few feet apart. His gaze traveled up, down, and then back up to her face. His gaze narrowed. His hand lifted and it took all her resolve not to flinch, but it was just a light. With her night vision lost, she couldn't see his reaction, but she heard his sharp intake of breath.

"Not possible," he said. "You're…not possible."

Her vision clearing, she studied him now.

"Boris," she said. "You're Boris. You're the one who erased my family." It was the only way he could have recognized her. Because of him, they didn't exist. She didn't exist.

"Boris?" The man seemed puzzled, though it was hard to be sure in the moonlight.

"Boris Karloff. The always bad guy."

Now he chuckled. "That depends on your perspective, I suppose. I did what had to be done."

"You erased my family, my brother, and the people he was meant to save died. You had no right to do any of it."

He shrugged. "Apparently I missed my target."

"I was away," preparing for the Olympics that had never happened for her, she thought painfully, "they came for me first. But they were not in time to save…" She couldn't continue. Didn't need to. He knew what he'd done.

His quiet laugh chilled her to the bone as he came closer. Stopping only when he was just shy of the shimmering cage that held her back from killing him with her bare hands.

She'd tried not to think about meeting him, because it would have eaten her up inside, but now that he was there? She wanted him dead.

"You really believe that? You believe they were too late?" He laughed again.

Madison felt cold go deeper into her bones as she stared into his cold blue eyes. Funny how fear changed the cold. Cold should just be cold.

He shook his head, his gaze mocking. "You were young, but surely in time you must have realized you were the one they wanted. It was never about your family. It was always about you."

The one true thing she'd learned during her time with the rebellion was how to hide her feelings. It served her well now.

She stared at him from blank eyes, while her brain raced, trying to feel her way to truth. His words would hurt later, if she lived, if she found out he was right.

This moment, the talking, it wouldn't last. He couldn't erase someone who didn't exist, but he could kill her. She was human.

And if she died, so did Briggs. And when he died, they'd search this place and find his people. She didn't know what was here, but she could tell Briggs believed there were people here the Time Service would want. Somehow she had to keep him talking. Time, almost she laughed, they needed time.

"And why was a thirteen-year-old gymnast such a threat to the Time Service?" She was impressed with the bored scorn that infused the question.

Girl gymnasts weren't that big of a deal when she was training. But she'd lost that dream, too. And why had she mattered to the Rebellion? No, now was not the time for those questions. If she wanted answers, she had to live.

"You don't know, do you?" His laugh held surprise. "You are one of the most gifted time sensitives in, well, history."

She didn't even blink. "And you didn't want that?" She didn't try to hide her disbelief. *Never trust a Time Service agent.* It was the first rule in the Rebellion.

"Oh, we would have, but your other gift was a deal breaker. They didn't tell you that you have a complete, built-in resistance to the mind wipe, did they? I'm sure it was just an oversight. There you have it. You couldn't be turned. No use to us, but very useful to the Rebellion. We couldn't risk you or any future heirs being out there, so you had to be erased." He paused. "How every clever *She* was to hide you from us. We never even had a whiff of you in all this time."

"Are you so sure you weren't mind wiped?" Madison asked, as hope faded. She could see death in his eyes. He was going to kill her. She couldn't think her way out of this cage. If Sir Rupert had called in help—it was possible they'd get here in time to clean up the scene. But she wouldn't make it. Briggs would die—or worse, be taken to use.

He shrugged. "I never needed to be persuaded to join. I like my job." He walked around her cage, looking her over like an animal being assessed for slaughter.

He was drawing out the moment so she'd suffer, she realized. He did like his job. "It's a pity," he said.

"What's a pity?" she asked, knowing he wasn't capable of feeling pity.

"That you won't live long enough to ask her if I've lied to you." He lifted his gun, letting her see as he flicked it to the kill setting. His other hand held the cage control.

He'd have to drop it to shoot her.

She might be able to move fast enough.

He stepped so that the tip of his ray gun almost touched the cage and was pointed at her heart.

Her breaking heart.

I'm so sorry, Briggs.

Chapter 10

BRIGGS FROZE, keeping his head down, his body slack. As he went down, he'd felt something hard pressing into his thigh. If it was the drone…inch by careful inch, he eased his hand down.

His fingers brushed against it, then curled around it. He traced it. Yeah, that was the drone, the EMP device still attached. He'd left the trigger back in the blind, but that would be dead anyway.

There was a chance, a slight chance, that the device had enough charge left. He'd not set it to full charge, just in case. Didn't want to cause any problems on the base.

His guard moved closer and Briggs lowered his lashes, feeling the dull thud of his heart as Boris spoke to Madison. It was clear he meant to kill her.

Don't think about it. Deal with it later if we make it. His fingers traced the shape, found the device. He was running out of time. There. His finger found the manual trigger.

"It's a pity you won't live long enough to ask her if I've lied to you."

Briggs pressed the button, praying at the same time.

The flash was smaller this time, but the cage disappeared. His guard was close and slow to react. Briggs took him down and out and was already headed toward the two figures silhouetted against the rising moons.

They disappeared into the shadows of the trees. He could heard the scuffle, the panting breaths of a desperate struggle. A grunt of pain and then silence.

Afraid to hope, Briggs darted toward where he'd last seen them—

Madison stepped out of the shadows, her face white, her eyes haunted.

He grabbed her and pulled her close, his hands running down her back, then up, as if to assure himself it was her, that she was alive.

"Is he dead?" He spoke matter-of-factly into her ear. A contrast to the frantic beat of his heart and hers.

She shook her head. "I...no." She inhaled shakily. "I wanted to but..."

She stopped. His grip tightened.

"Wait here. Don't move." He headed into the shadows, found the guy she'd called Boris, and dragged him out into the moonlight. He had a nasty swelling bruise on his chin and was bleeding sluggishly from a wound in his side.

Briggs used more zip ties on him and his sidekick. He angled his head and studied Boris's partner. She did look a bit like a Natasha...

Once he was sure they were all well secured, he went back to Madison.

She hadn't moved though now her body shuddered with shock. Now the words she'd exchanged with Boris came back with echoing force.

He didn't know what to say or do, other than to hold her again. He wanted to tell her it would be all right, but the words stuck in his throat.

How could anything be all right for her? She'd lost so much. Questions formed and were discarded before they were uttered. Nothing sounded right.

"I'm sorry," he finally said. "I'm sorry."

She looked up at him then. "I am, too."

MADISON SHUDDERED with the adrenalin that had carried her through the fight with Boris. He was a good fighter, but a lousy gymnast. The super power he hadn't seen coming. And the knife strapped to her leg.

She was still surprised she hadn't killed him. He'd been worse than she'd imagined. A cold, killing machine.

Maybe that was why she couldn't do it. It took her too close to the edge of becoming like him, becoming him.

"You," she was close enough to feel Briggs swallow, "could stay here, you know. We're a motley crew, so you'd fit right in."

She was surprised to hear, to feel herself chuckle. Knew she'd find him grinning, felt her own lips stretching into something like a grin.

It was a relief to feel the drama ratchet down. She'd never wanted to be one of the drama girls, not with the team or without. It was even a relief to feel the pain in her shoulder and the slow creep of blood from the wound she'd reopened—

She started to answer him, but stiffened instead, spinning to face the rippling horizon once more.

As *She* and the new guy's cells settled into this time, she stepped protectively in front of Briggs. *She* noted the movement and her lips twisted wryly. The new guy moved forward to examine their catch.

"Nice work," he said, his wary gaze moving between Madison and their boss.

"That's Boris," she said, adding, "the one who erased my family."

"He's dead?" *She* asked.

"No." Madison lifted her shoulders in a sigh. "I'm not like him. I'm not a killer."

The new guy straightened, eyeing Madison carefully. "What do you want me to do with him?"

"I want you to keep him away from me," she said. Briggs stepped up next to her, his hand on her shoulder.

"You had help, I see," *She* said. Her gaze returned to Madison. "You can't trust them, you know, him least of all."

"Even a Time Service agent will tell the truth when he knows it will cause more damage than a lie," Madison said evenly.

She's gaze flicked toward Briggs. "We can talk about this later—"

Madison felt Briggs grip on her shoulder tighten, then loosen, as if he'd forced himself to do it. She shook her head.

"I'm not going back. I can't do it anymore."

"You could still be a target—"

"I don't exist, remember?" Her lips twisted wryly. "And according to him, you can't rearrange my brain. So you're going to have to trust me. And leave me alone to get on with my life."

She didn't like it, but the new guy was watching.

"We're supposed to be the good guys, remember?" Madison said.

She thinned her lips, but she gave a half nod. "Sir Rupert..."

There was a raucous caw-caw from the trees, then he sailed into view, landing lightly on Madison's shoulder.

"I think this island needs birds," he said. "Not to mention someone who can make sure you don't interfere with...anyone's future."

Madison reached up and stroked under his chin. "Thank you," she said softly.

The slightest slump in *She's* shoulders was the only sign he'd tipped the balance. Her blank gaze tracked between Madison and Briggs. "I don't suppose you're going to introduce us."

"Not a chance." Madison met and held her gaze. "I've done more than enough time. You know that's true."

The new guy spoke again. "We are the good guys, are we not, ma'am?"

"Of course." *She* gave a shrug that was not quite casual. "You did good work. We'll all miss you."

"You'd better," she let iron filter into her tone, "miss me, I mean."

She glanced at the new guy and finally did sigh. "You have my word." She nudged one of the men with a toe. "You have no idea how good she is...was," she said. "You will miss her."

The new guy grinned. "At least we got our mole."

Madison's smile was real this time. She glanced at Sir Rupert. "Good job."

Now that it was decided, *She* turned brisk. "Tag them for transport," she ordered. With a half salute for them, she vanished in a shimmer of horizon.

"I'll keep an eye on her," the new guy promised, before he and the catch of the day vanished.

Madison tensed, reaching out with her senses, but there was nothing but the night breeze and the light from the two moons. And a man and a bird.

She gave a small chuckle, then laughed with sudden joy. It had been a long time...she sobered thinking about how long.

She faced the man. "I hope you meant it, because I can't go anywhere now."

Sir Rupert, as if he realized he was a bit in the way, lifted off, circling the clearing before landing on the table. Madison would have liked more space than that, but it was what it was.

The man rested his hands on her waist and she saw joy in his eyes, too, manly joy of course. But also hesitation.

"What's wrong?" she asked, lifting her hand so it rested against a cheek roughened by the beard he hadn't had time to shave.

"Today was my birthday," he admitted, with a rueful scowl. "That thing was a present sent by a couple of friends."

"Happy...birthday?" She couldn't remember the last time she'd been in real time to celebrate a birthday, or been with anyone who would have cared.

"I'm forty-five," he muttered.

Madison looked at him, trying to understand his problem.

"I'm a lot older than you," he muttered, even lower than before.

Her eyes widened and she couldn't help the half chuckle, half snort. "Sorry, but," she bit her lip. "You said this was 2017, right?" He nodded warily. "Briggs," was this the first time she'd said his name out loud? "I was born in, um, 1946."

She could see him doing the math.

"1946?"

She nodded. His hands slid further around her, moving up her back, then down her shoulders while heat built swiftly inside her. Heat and longing and an aching restlessness. His mouth turned up slowly, the smile sexy with lots of hot in his eyes.

"You're in really good shape."

"I try to work out and…and…eat right," she said, breathlessly, her lips aching for his. Had she only known this man a few hours?

"Do you know what my friend, do you know what Robert said, before he took the bird away?"

Madison almost lost her breath at this sign of trust and at the way his hand trembled as he smoothed the hair back off her face.

"What…did Robert say?" she asked.

"He said, you should keep her."

"Did…he?"

He bent his head toward her mouth. She pushed up on her toes, but his mouth was just a bit out of reach.

"Can I keep you, Madison?"

"Please," she said and finally his mouth covered hers. His arms banded around her, so that all of her was pressed against a lot of him.

He was a big guy. But now there was time to get to know all of him. Lots and lots of lovely time.

~

History of Women
in Gymnastics

While the most famous women gymnasts competed on the Olympic stage in 1972, women began to compete on the same apparatus as men as early as 1928. The floor exercise was added in 1932, and in 1952, the bar, beam, floor and vault events for women were added, making it entirely possible that thirteen-year-old Madison could have been training for the Olympics when the nasty Time Service messed with her life in or around 1958.

Operation Ark

She's a USMC Sergeant deployed to the Garradian Galaxy.

He was raised by the robots who freed him from slavery.

It's a match made nowhere anyone can figure out.

They clashed as enemies but joined forces to defeat a common foe. Now they're tasked with returning some freed prisoners to their home worlds. In the next galaxy. With an alien, a robot, and a caticorn. It was a bar joke without a punch line, though Carolina City has a feeling it is out there—like the truth.

Kraye isn't eager to return to his galaxy where the dark secret of his past lays in wait, but he's willing to risk it in hopes that Caro can teach him what the robots couldn't: how to be human.

Together they must face a dangerous journey, a lethal enemy with a score to settle, their unexpected desire, and an uncertain future if they make it out alive.

Can Caro and Kraye navigate the minefields—both emotional

and space based—to land a happy homecoming for the sentient animals in their care? Can the man raised by robots learn how to kiss the girl while the starchy Marine decides if she is willing to bend the rules for a happy ever after? Don't miss Pauline Baird Jones' newest Project Enterprise story!

This book was previously published in anthology *Embrace the Passion: Pets in Space® 3,* which is no longer on sale.

Chapter 1

THEY FILED in two by two, the click and scrape of claws and paws against the stone floor adding a discordant note to the music filtering quietly through Central Outpost's intercom system. Some of them paused for a last look around before starting up the lowered ramp of the spaceship *Emissary*.

At the head of the unusual column were the *Erinaceines*, a pair of hedgehog-like creatures whose waddle was almost on the beat. They had the pointed noses of an Earth hedgehog, but their coloring was brighter, more in the yellow and orange range.

Behind them came the *Pinyians*, most closely resembling pandas, but they had black and red coloring. They ambled in, following a wandering path, and pausing often to return the curious looks of the humanoids.

After the pandas were the two *Sulian Nebos*. According to the Kikk Outpost's biologist, these two were a green-footed version of the blue-footed booby. Their comically wide eyes explained the "booby" appellation, at least in their version, but it didn't help that they waddled like cartoons characters into the room and up the ramp.

The two pure gray *Cygninains* made an interesting contrast with the boobys. Their swan-like grace was somewhat blunted by having to herd their small brood of cygnets onto the ship.

The *Testudinians* should have appeared next, but even by another name—and in another galaxy—they looked like turtles and were as slow as turtles. They'd started first and would arrive last.

The lone *Harparian* must have wearied of following them, because she appeared next, the tuft of feathers on the top of her head weaving with the snap of her clawed feet against stone.

According to their biologist, her species was similar to an Earth Harpy Eagle, though much, much larger. With feathers that were a mix of gray, royal blue, white, and pink, she was as tall or taller than the humanoids in the hanger, giving her a wing span that was four times longer than she was high. Each of her individual claws were the size of a big man's hand, and they were so sharp, they glistened when they caught the light. Her black and gold gaze was fixed on the ship and nothing else. Her passage seemed to leave behind the scent of woods and high mountain cliff breezes.

And then they waited for the *Testudinians*. And waited some more. Finally, the turtle-like creatures appeared. They were about half the size of a Volkswagen Beetle—and would have looked at home with any of the painted psychedelic versions from the 60's. Their coloring was a strident mix of yellow, orange, and green, outlined in black. Before they reached the top of the ramp, the music had trailed off so that the slow scrape of their steps seemed loud in the quiet bay.

Only after they were out of sight did the scent of the sea drift past.

~

SERGEANT CAROLINA CITY, USMC, paused just inside the *Emissary's* bridge. She'd have drooled over the sassy alien tech, but she'd been there and done that while bringing the *Emissary* to Central Outpost.

Her copilot, Kraye, a super serious version of Jack Sparrow, was already seated in the copilot's position. Normally she wasn't interested in scalawags, but the guy could stack and shoot. She could admit to being intrigued, possibly even a little bothered by the sight of him. After a rocky start—technically her fault since it was one of her Marines who knocked him out—she'd sensed some reciprocal interest, but then he'd gone chill on her. She sighed. As the only human crew member on a ship of sentient robots, she could see why he might not have had a chance to develop people skills, and it was probably better if they both kept their hormones parked somewhere out of sight for the duration of the mission.

And speaking of robots…her attention shifted to the robot at the navigation station.

OxeroidR was big, square, and scary. The dull glow of his red opticals was the only "bright" element in his menacing facade. Though no weapons were visible, she knew he bristled with hidden ones because she'd seen them in action. While she'd never seen a live moose, this robot had reminded her of one from the first time she'd seen him.

Which made his later bonding with the flying squirrel incongruous, ironic, and hilarious. Not that she'd ever laugh at the robot or his purple-faced squirrel where they could see her. She wasn't stupid. Officially, the squirrel was a *Patagious,* and it had been one of the prisoners they'd freed during their recent military action. She wasn't sure if it had landed on the robot, or the robot had put it on his shoulder. But she hadn't seen them apart since.

Moose and squirrel. Her lips twitched. In her mind, she called them Bull and Rocky. Okay, she called the squirrel Rocky to his purple face.

Not that she was in any position to judge. During the same action, one of the prisoners had attached itself to her. The expedition's biologist had been unable to classify Tiger, other than to verify he was male.

His face was that of a tabby cat, with the requisite whiskers, pink triangle nose, soulful gaze—and a single horn protruding from his cat forehead. Behind the cute ears, the neck was long, sloping down to a horse body, hooves, mane, and tail.

The geeks on the outpost opined that Tiger—so named because

of his tabby stripes—might be the result of genetic tampering. Unlike the other animals on the *Emissary*, Tiger didn't speak Standard, a form of their Earth English that had been their unsteady communication bridge since the Expedition arrived in system. In an interesting twist, the Garradian language translator couldn't understand him either. Despite these signs he was not as sentient as the others, City still had doubts. Of course, she knew that cats could look like they knew-it-all and it was possible they did. It wasn't as if you could argue with a cat.

And, like a cat, Tiger knew how to get what he wanted. He'd not been approved to go on this mission, but she'd seen his tail whisk out of sight around a corner as she came aboard.

The last member of her bridge crew didn't need a seat. Rita, the ship's AI, had chosen her name. Apparently, she was a fan of Rita Wilson. Her favorite song? *You Were on My Mind.*

And then there was City's mission.

Operation Ark.

She wasn't Noah and had never wanted to be Noah, but it was hard to escape the parallels. Animal-like aliens. Safe passage from one place to another. The chance of stormy passage.

When she'd opted to boldly go to the Garradian Universe as part of the Project Enterprise expedition, she had anticipated action, adventure, and alien encounters.

And she'd experienced all three.

And now she was about to boldly go further than this galaxy.

With an alien, a robot, and a caticorn as her sidekick. It was like a bar joke without a punch line though she had a feeling it was out there—like the truth.

She took a calming breath and, trying to do it like Picard, sat down. She glanced at Kraye. "Let's do a final systems check with Ms. Rita's assistance, Mr. Kraye."

Was that an actual glint of humor in his eyes?

"Aye, aye, Sergeant."

Aye, aye, Sergeant.

"Bull, I mean OxeroidR—"

Oops.

"Bull is acceptable."

There was no way his flat delivery could convey humor, but City sensed some. Or perhaps she hoped for some. If the big guy hoped to reach full sentience, he needed to lighten up.

"Bull, inform our passengers to prepare for launch."

"Aye, aye, Sergeant."

Were they pulling her chain with all the aye ayes? Did they even know how?

"Ms. Rita, are we go or no for launch?"

We are go, Sergeant.

For some reason, this exchange brought back the memory of her high school boyfriend.

"Marines? Girls can't be Marines and even if they can, where's that gonna take you?"

She smiled as felt the *Emissary* come to life around her. *To the stars, sweetie. To the stars.*

Chapter 2

THANKS to the recently discovered Garradian comet drive, the *Emissary* should be able to make the trip to the various theres, and back again, in around a month, or possibly less. Of course, this estimate assumed that nothing would go wrong. City tended to be optimistic, but it was hard to be sanguine when there was so much that could go wrong.

It was unusual for a Marine Sergeant to be rated as a pilot without the NFO (Naval Flight Officer) and an officer's rank. City had considered that route, because she loved to fly, but she wanted to be a Marine, not their bus driver. Her pilot creds had helped her join the expedition. With space at a premium, even on a freaking big spaceship, it helped to be able to multi-task.

She might be surprised there hadn't been more push back about using the *Emissary* for this mission. Those in charge had speculated that it had been a diplomatic, possibly VIP transport for the lost Garradians. As with all things Garradian, the past was still something of a mystery.

In any case, it was better than cages in the hold of a crap pirate ship. And—this was almost City's favorite part—there was separation from the three diplomats that had been detailed to transit with them.

It wasn't that she disliked Joseph Faxton, the head of the team. He was nice looking in a mild-mannered way, kind of Clark Kent without the glasses and—she hoped—the "S" on his underwear. There were already plenty of unstable elements on this ship. City hadn't met Brittani St. Danniels or Dr. Lowe Dauwn, the other two human passengers. She hoped that by the time she did, the impulse to giggle would be under better control.

Even better than the quarters, this ship had the goods in both stealth technology and weapons to give them decent odds for a good outcome.

City liked decent odds, though she had worked—and survived— worse.

The *Emissary's* capabilities had tipped the scales on the mission from bat crap crazy to this might work. City had volunteered without hesitation. She'd worked with Kraye and Bull. Kraye was good in a fire fight, and Bull, well, he was a robot who had been designed as a super warrior—a super warrior with a flying squirrel for a pet, but still a robot with fighting creds.

She heard a plaintive half whinny, half meow.

"There you are." She made the mistake of meeting his big, 'I feel so neglected' gaze. With a resigned sigh, she knelt down and ran a hand down his back. It arched like a cat and he purred when she scratched around his ears and horn. "You know you're not supposed to be here."

The purring increased, and she sighed again. A Marine was not supposed to be owned by a cat, even if it was a caticorn.

"Good thing I got your dietary needs programmed into the system."

Tiger angled his head, his gaze meeting hers. The look was odd enough to make her wonder—but the Puss'n'Boots look came back. She felt its power, but let Tiger see her skepticism. At least she didn't have to worry about his claws in her back. It didn't seem like it should be possible for Tiger to increase the soulful, but he managed it. She chuckled, moving her fingers around so she could scratch his chin. "You win." She said the words, not sure what he'd won, and she'd lost. It all felt a bit paranoid. Though a little paranoia never hurt anyone in a galaxy far, far away.

A slight sound jerked her gaze up. Kraye stood in the doorway to his quarters, a look of actual amusement in his eyes. She rose, flushing a bit.

"He snuck on board."

"He is resourceful."

For the second time in about a minute, she found herself making eye contact that she probably shouldn't have. Though the heat that swirled into her mid-section was nothing like the warm fuzzy from petting a caticorn.

His gaze altered to curious, perhaps also puzzled. It was just her luck to be almost alone on a ship for a month with a guy who didn't know how to flirt, let alone make a pass.

She broke eye contact, her lips twisting a bit wryly.

"Your quarters all right?"

"They are optimal," he said. He glanced back into his room, his gaze well into the neutral zone.

City knew what he saw. They were comfortable, but practical. Not home. As nice as this was, the *Doolittle* and her cramped personal space felt more like home. Was the *Najer* his home? This was not the first time she'd wondered about his story, his history. How did someone end up being the only human on a ship of robots? How did that even work? But she didn't know how to bridge the gap without looking nosey, without being nosey, she amended wryly. He interested her. There, she'd admitted it, but he either didn't notice her interest or didn't recognize the signals. She'd even twirled her hair on a finger, something she vowed she'd never do while she wore the uniform.

Nothing. Not even a small flicker of "oh."

A small body bumped against her calf. She was glad for a reason to look down at Tiger.

"You hungry?"

He bumped her leg again, his meow-neigh pointed.

"Excuse me," she said, not sure if she felt awkward or disappointed.

"Of course."

She palmed the door control for her quarters and her caticorn trotted inside. She paused, trying to think of something to say, but he'd already gone back into his.

It was going to be a long month.

"I BELIEVE SHE LIKES YOU," OxeroidR said.

Kraye jerked around. He'd forgotten the robot was there. "How —" he stopped, his face heating. The question should have been who, not how.

"She played with her hair." A robot finger lifted, moving as if he had hair. Because he did not have hair, the action was unsettling.

"So?" He shrugged, as if he did not care.

"I have observed female humans doing this," the metal finger moved once again. "They also tip their heads to the side and angle their bodies toward the object of their interest."

His big square body adjusted into a disturbing configuration that might be somewhat familiar. But once again, it was more troubling than informative.

The robot resumed his normal configuration, rubbing his metal chin with two of his fingers. His head lifted. "Kraye, when we were in space dock, did you observe females there?"

Of course he had, at every opportunity. He could not say he'd learned much from these relatively brief observations. He'd also—more discreetly—observed the females who had filtered into Central Outpost after the successful military action. Much observing, not much learning. He half shrugged. "I am not interested—" He stopped, but it was too late.

"One can learn from observation of any female. The signals they use to create intimacy can be similar."

Was he really getting romantic advice from a robot? He wanted to protest. Those women on the space docks, well, he had considered accepting what they offered. He was a male with urges that were not unusual, according to the information he'd read on the subject. He had not because the risks to the ship, to his crew mates were too high for such casual experimentation. He was, as he well knew, the weak link on the *Najer*. As a human, he could be co-opted to betray them without even realizing it. He could be taken hostage in the belief that the robots would rescue him. He did not believe they would, but his belief was not relevant. If someone believed he was a way to pressure him, they would not hesitate. The knowledge of what would happen to him if he were captured had done much to tamp down his sexual curiosity.

And now, looking back at the casual curiosity he'd felt, and yes, interest in those dock-side women bothered him. It almost felt as if he'd betrayed…someone.

"She said I was her friend," he muttered. He'd looked up the word in their databank. It was not what he wished for from her.

"Friends do not play with their hair or—"

"I see," Kraye said hastily, fearful he would alter his configuration again.

"Females who desire friendship do not look directly at a male, then away, then look at them from the corner of their eyes," OxeroidR went on, as if he'd not spoken.

Had Caro done any of these things? She had glanced at him at times, but mostly they had been involved in battle, in shooting others, and protecting each other.

"When initial intimacy has been established, a female will touch a male on the arm, or, as intimacy increases, on the chest."

He touched Kraye's arm with his metal finger, then withdrew it. Then his hand rested briefly on Kraye's chest.

None of it felt particularly romantic.

"Look for small actions. Observe closely because some of their actions are barely perceptible. When a female is not interested, she will withdraw, shift away."

Observe closely. He could do that. He had been doing that since he met her. For the first time since this uncomfortable conversation had began, Kraye looked at his friend. He was a friend. A strange, tactless, mostly emotionless friend, but still a friend. But in the flat delivery, he almost sensed…old pain. He did not know how long the robot had been sentient. Had their sentience developed into a longing for intimacy? There were signs their robot Captain had feelings for a human female they'd rescued in the previous action. He did not know if those feelings were romantic in nature, or if any of the robots could act on romantic feelings.

"Human women will sometimes purse their lips in what is called a pout," OxeroidR added, much like one going down a list.

Thankfully he was unable to demonstrate this pout since he did not have a mouth.

Rocky lifted his head from OxeroidR's shoulder, stretching his small legs and extending his webbed arms. "My kind are more direct. We dance for our females and present our—"

Kraye winced as the Rocky showed him what he showed females. Pain formed behind Kraye's eyes. Had he thought it uncomfortable getting advice from a robot?

"Humans wait until later in their courtship for—" OxeroidR said.

Kraye hastily cut him off by waving his hand. "I, please…"

"Humans waste a lot of time," Rocky said, though his tone was more matter-of-fact than judgmental. "Perhaps you should talk to the *Testudinians*. They take a long time for everything."

If they talked as slowly as they moved, Kraye would be an old man before he learned anything from them.

He heard a discreet buzz and turned toward the opening with relief, giving it permission to open. The door slid back. It was Caro. He hoped she had not heard any of their conversation.

Her gaze moved between them and he could not stop the color that stole into his face.

"Sorry to bother you. I forgot to tell you that Mr. Faxton asked if we'd dine with them this evening." She grimaced. "I have to, but you don't. It's sort of a meet and greet thing."

"I would—yes, of course." He studied her as he spoke, but could see no sign of the romantic cues they had been discussing. She did not lean or angle. In fact, her back was most straight, her hands clasped behind her back and in no position to touch him. Her lips were a line, one that was possibly a bit rueful, and not a pout, though he was fuzzy on what was and was not a pout. Despite the lack of encouraging signs, he was pleased with what he saw. She was not a tall woman, but she was sturdy, capable and confident. Her light blue eyes met his with directness. He had a feeling she would know what a pout was, but lacked the courage to ask her.

He glanced at OxeroidR, who gave his version of a shrug. Rocky turned in a circle before curling up on the robot's shoulder.

Her gaze shifted past him to OxeroidR.

"You're welcome to come, too, Bull."

"Would it be useful?"

She considered this and then nodded, her lips curving in a wry smile. "The *Harparian* is...unsettling. Have you ever had dealings with one?"

OxeroidR turned his head in a negative. "We have only had dealings with space capable species."

Her brows drew together. "That's interesting. I think."

"My kind are not space capable either," Rocky told her, his head lifting from his folded front paws.

"But you've had contact?" she asked, her head tilting a bit.

"When I was abducted," Rocky said.

"That...could be a problem when we attempt to repatriate our passengers." She half grinned and shook her head.

"What?" Kraye asked.

"It's just—I've never been the little green man before." Her gaze met his puzzled one, and she added, "Sorry. It's an Earth joke. About first contact." She followed this with a smile that apologized and asked for a smile in return. "If you're interested, I'll explain later."

Kraye nodded. He was most interested, and he liked the sound of later. She left and he looked at OxeroidR.

With his opposable thumb, he gave him a digit up of encouragement.

CITY HAD EATEN MREs in a foxhole while under fire. That, she decided, was more comfortable than this. Rita was in there pitching. She had provided some soft, elevator music so the lack of dinner conversation wasn't painfully obvious. Everyone had their game face on—or in the case of the robot, he had his usual face on. On the surface, it was smooth and civilized as long as she didn't look at the *Harparian,* at the head of the small table, ripping her dinner to pieces with beak and claw.

The food dispenser had manufactured everyone's food, based on nutritional needs and personal preference, but it was still unsettling to watch. For City, this was the closest she'd been to the over-sized bird since freeing her from a cage in the hold of a space pirate ship. The tuft of feathers over her eyes acted as a hood to a gaze that was deep and old, like a mysterious pool in a fantasy tale. If emotions stirred in the black and gold depths, City was not equipped to read them, though that gaze did make the hair lift on the back of her neck.

A claw big enough to rip City's face off lifted a chunk of food to a curved beak—one bigger than City's hand with the fingers extended. She decided that watching the bird eat was bad for her appetite and shifted her attention to Joseph Faxton's discreetly sympathetic presence. He was seated directly across from her and Kraye was on City's left, with Bull at the other end of the table. Since Bull didn't need to eat, Rocky was doing that for him. Both of Faxton's team members were on his side of the table, though Dr. Dauwn didn't look as thrilled as a biologist should, in her opinion. City hadn't quite decided what to call Brittani St. Danniels, sitting not exactly demurely between Dauwn and Faxton. It felt a bit us versus them, but she didn't mind.

One of her Marine's who had volunteered to act as steward for the meal, bent over Faxton's shoulder and refilled his glass, then stepped back, coming to attention. City glanced around, noted that everyone who needed service had received it.

"Thanks, Private Spencer. You can go," *and I wish I could go with you,* she added to herself. The slight flicker of his lips told her he knew it. His last look was sympathetic. He'd have a tale to tell on the crew deck. She wasn't sure if it would get easier or harder to get volunteers if they had more of these formal dinners. Not that she could blame Faxton. When he'd signed up to smooth the paths for the expedition, she'd bet real money he hadn't planned on dinner with two of the scariest species in a couple of galaxies.

Dr. Lowe Dauwn—bet he'd gotten teased a lot as a kid—was not the stereotypical scientist. He wasn't even wearing glasses. His brown gaze was thoughtful and intelligent—which he'd have to be to make it onto the expedition. She did wonder about his light red shirt.

Brittani—Ms. St. Danniels—was flaunting her red dress. Not wanting to be judgy, City assumed the blonde hair was natural and gave her credit for not wearing foxtrot heels on a spaceship. She had to be smart, too, to be here. Faxton would have to be extra careful, so she'd have earned her passage with her brains. City told herself that the way she was trying to chat with Kraye was a diplomat thing and not a girl thing.

Facing the *Harparian* was OxeroidR—Bull—and Rocky. City thought she was used to the robot's contained stillness. Maybe it was the setting that made it creepy again. His hands rested on the tabletop on either side of the munching squirrel. His eyes, she realized, feeling her own warning hackles rising, they weren't moving side to side like they usually did. They were fixed on the *Harparian*.

It did make her wonder about how the *Harparian* had been captured and why. What was out there that could take the raptor down? That was a scary thought, one that put some more fade on her appetite. And on the heels of that thought…had she been captured? She sure didn't act or look like the others they'd freed. Menace and mystery wrapped around her like an invisible mist. All the others had been various levels of stressed and shell-shocked.

She might be glad that Bull was keeping both opticals on the big bird.

Faxton was also pushing his food around his plate, his fork not making that many trips to his mouth. He might be nervous, or maybe diplomats had to keep their mouths free for talking. Had he learned anything from his time with the *Harparian?* No surprise the

Expedition hoped to learn more about all the freed prisoners and their worlds, and possibly open diplomatic relations with some of them, but City wasn't on the need-to-know list, unless it affected mission security. Would Faxton tell her or recognize a risk if he saw it?

He faced her across the table, giving her the opportunity to study him without looking like she was studying him. He was a nice looking man, with an aura of calm confidence that made an interesting contrast to the bird's—and his assistant. If he was quaking inside, it didn't show on his smoothly polite face or in his gray eyes.

Faxton gave up on pretending to eat by setting aside his fork. He glanced at the bird, then smiled at City. "I don't think I heard where you hail from, Sergeant?"

His tone was diplomatic glass. His question earned her a prolonged look from Brittani. City had no doubt the lady was smart but was she wise to take this mission? There wasn't even a whiff of anything between her and Faxton, but they were trained to find out things, not give them away.

City set her fork down. She didn't mind giving up on her dinner. "Wyoming, sir."

"Call me Joe, please." Before she could respond, he added, "I drove across Wyoming once. It was a long, bleak drive."

Caro chuckled. "I'm from the north, the pretty part," though after her time in space, she'd be happy to see any part of it.

"The pretty part?" Kraye joined the conversation, though his tone sounded rough after Faxton's smooth delivery.

City gave him a slight smile. "Southern Wyoming is part of the plains, low rolling hills and desert, or inclined that way."

Britanni's smile at Kraye did not reach her eyes. "What's your home like?" Her lashes did a sweep, but her gaze, though curious, had some targeting to it.

"I live on the *Najer*."

City, sensing something in the briefness of the answer, cut in before Britanni could ask anything else. "Where are you from, Ms. St. Danniels?" Why did that extra "n" make her name more annoying?

"California, Sergeant."

"It's a beautiful state, too. You have beaches and mountains." She turned her gaze to Faxton. "I love mountains."

The *Harparian's* gaze turned toward her. "There are mountains on your world?"

Faxton's hand curved around his cup. "I used to be able to name all the major mountain ranges, but alas…"

"Do they soar? Are they high?" The question was quietly intense.

"Very," City said.

"Some reach so high in our atmosphere humans can't climb them without carrying oxygen," Faxton told her.

City sensed an extra level of alert from Faxton, and followed his lead by watching the bird as they waited for her response. City sensed she wanted more…on the height? But how did she explain altitude when they didn't have a common measure of it?

Even the biologist was frowning.

With a slight grimace, City lifted her hands, so they were about a foot apart. "This is what we call one foot. If you added together five thousand two hundred and eighty of these that is one mile. Our highest mountain is almost thirty thousand of our miles." Would the largeness of the numbers give her a frame of reference?

The raptor lifted a claw, moving it between City's hands as if assessing that distance and possibly calculating.

"Your highest mountain would be one of the lower peaks on my world." Her beak lifted, her gaze seemed to be seeing past all of them, past this ship to those mountains.

"You miss them," City said without thinking. "You miss home."

The beak, the gaze turned toward her again. She nodded. "How long?"

"Until we get to your planet?" City asked.

"Until we reach Teuhhopse, yes."

It hadn't been hard to show the raptor a small unit of measurement, but a unit of time? Without realizing it, she looked toward the robot and Kraye for help.

"You speak Standard," Bull said. "Do you use any Standard measurements for counting the passing of time?"

Her head shook. "We count time and distance by flight." Her wings lifted, sweeping so wide their tips brushed the opposite walls and a breeze ruffled City's hair.

"Are your people space capable?" Kraye asked.

"We fly toward the stars but we do not reach for them."

Somewhat cryptic. City pulled out the tablet that was her link with Rita when City was not close to ship controls. "Rita, can you give us a holo of where we are and our various destinations?"

Of course, Sergeant. Her voice through the intercom was less brisk than on the bridge.

The holo appeared in the middle of the table, turning slowly.

"That's *Emissary,*" she said. "We're just passing through the void between the two galaxies, between your region of space, and the Garradian space. We should reach the edge of your galaxy by ship morning." She stopped. This still wasn't helping them show her how long it would take. Maybe Rita could rig a time holo for the raptor's quarters and she could observe time's passage. Who wouldn't like clock-watching a flight through space? She didn't rub the place between her eyes where a headache was trying to dig in. "Our flight plan takes us to the *Testudinians'* world first. They are the closest to the boundary and we're hoping to get some up-to-date intel from them and from scanning as widely as possible." Could she, was she getting a feel for the distance by looking at the holo? "The *Sulian Nebos* and *Cygninains* are from sister planets."

"Actually," Dr. Dauwn piped up, "one appears to be the moon of the other."

"We will be able to accomplish both repatriations in one to two ship days," Bull said.

"You can't be more specific?" Britanni asked.

"It is not possible to predict dirt side time," Bull said, his tone not changing at all.

Faxton smiled. "I suspect we're the problem with your calculation." He turned toward the *Harparian.* "We are hoping to find out more about each species' home world."

"Why would you care?" Her tone was not more menacing than it had been, but City was close enough to sense her suspicion.

"We are a curious people," Faxton said, his friendly tone not altering either.

"I see."

It did not sound like she did, but City figured it was a good time to move on. She indicated the holo. "The *Pinyains* and the *Erinaceines* are from the same planet, so that shouldn't take more than a ship day for repatriation. How fast we can move between locations depends on local conditions." She didn't mention this was about the comet drive. There were certain phenomena in space where the comet drive was not safe. "Your planet is the deepest into this region, so…" her voice trailed off.

"We should make good time. This is a fine ship," Faxton said, smoothly. "A fast ship."

The *Harparian* looked at City, as if for confirmation. She nodded. "Depending on conditions, it can make good progress."

Would the raptor be content to be last to get home? She had the claws to make them do what she wanted though Bull would likely try to stop her. Maybe. All roads led back to one question. Who could she trust? This trip had happened because the robots had insisted it must. None of them wanted to get in a slug-fest with the killer robots, so here they were.

"There is much danger in the stars. The ship on which I was held, engaged in battles."

Had it? Well, that wasn't exactly a surprise. They had been pirates, bad guys.

"She is correct," Bull said. "This region of space is not well controlled by a central authority."

"We have a technology that should let us hide when necessary." Would it be effective, though? The pirate ship had gotten its claws on some Garradian tech that had caused their side problems during the last action. But this ship was supposed to be better, possibly the best the Garradians had ever had. Which begged the question why had they left it behind? If you were fleeing a galaxy, wouldn't you take your best ship or ships?

"We're going in as low profile as possible." That was one reason they weren't using the comet drive's top speed for their initial insertion. They were trying to balance energy use with stealth, and they didn't know what kind of a signature the comet drive left in its wake. Rita had believed their current speed was optimal for both speed and stealth. They hoped both, combined with their weaponry, would give them the edge they needed. Their mission would take them deep into the mostly unknown and what they did know, well, as Bull had told them, it wasn't optimal.

"I will try to explain our concept of time to you," Faxton offered. "Perhaps we can exchange information about both our peoples during this journey?"

It was a question carefully couched in diplomatic cotton. There was a long pause.

"Perhaps," she said.

Faxton's gaze met hers across the table. His shrug was almost imperceptible. No surprise the scary bird had trust issues. What would be a surprise? That none of them had them.

Chapter 3

THEY'D CROSSED into Kraye's region of space as the *Emissary* signaled ship's morning and Rita deployed the day's playlist. They did not count time in morning or night on the *Najer*. They belonged to no planet, so planet time held no meaning for them. For Kraye, his time was divided by work, food and rest, unless they were in a space port. Only then did they adopt dirt side time.

He assumed ship time was related to some military protocol required by Caro's leaders.

He had always had the choice to clean up aboard the *Najer*. As the ship's only human, he was also the only one who needed the water supply. He'd attended to his hygiene needs, learning from study and by observation when they were in space docks. His interest in Caro, and noting how the people around her conducted themselves, had added to his knowledge on many levels.

Water requirements aboard the *Emissary* were tighter, but he used his ration to freshen up before heading to the bridge for his scheduled shift. Despite being early, he found Caro already there. He knew what Caro knew. Rita, the AI, could have flown them there and back without anyone ever being on the bridge. He was used to being superfluous. This did not change his sense of obligation to do as Caro did, and monitor the ship's functions. His Captain had told him once that human eyes and human instincts had their place. This had proved to be true on a number of occasions.

Though Caro smiled and greeted him, he sensed the difference, concluding that being on shift was not the same as being on duty. This he could understand. The bridge was a place of business. But if they spent their off-duty meal times with the *Harparian* and the diplomat's team, his chances of observing Caro's possible female responses would not be optimal. It was not as if he could stare at her without others noticing. It was challenging enough that OxeroidR had noticed his interest and felt he needed help. The squirrel, well, he did not wish to think about his advice. He may have been raised by robots, but he knew better than to indicate romantic interest by dropping his pants.

Call me Joe, the diplomat had said. His mien was smooth, polished. Kraye had encountered many like him during his dockside interactions. He was less oily than most. Kraye might have sought opportunities to speak with him. He was the first human male non-business contact that Kraye had had since he'd been delivered from slavery by the captain of the *Najer*.

This rescue had occurred many years ago, but it was only recently he'd found himself thinking about that day and wondering why the Captain had done what he did. Kraye could have asked, but he was not certain he would like the answer.

He had hoped that this journey would be an opportunity to spend time with Caro, to get to know her. Prior to launch, it had seemed like more than enough time to discover if they could be more than friends. After last night, he was not sure several seasons of travel would be enough.

Watching Caro interact with other humans had only increased his confusion. Caro had appeared to respond to Faxton, but then she'd smiled at the doctor. And the woman, she'd displayed many of the signs he'd been told to look for, but was she interested in the doctor or Faxton? He supposed, he thought glumly, there would be more advice coming from OxeroidR and Rocky.

Clearly, connections could be built by talking about where they had come from, but he suspected his past would kill conversation, not build connections.

Nothing worth having, the Captain had told him more than once, is acquired without risk and effort. What was it that he risked by trying to get closer to Caro? His mind said there was no risk, but the pain in his chest disagreed. Without being obvious, he could see her hands out of the side of his eyes, could see them, small and competent as they worked the controls.

"We dropped out of comet drive about an hour before the wake up call," she said. "We're a few hours out from the *Testudinians* planet. This should be a quick drop but—"

The side long look, the grin she added, caught the breath in his chest. "They are not...swift creatures."

She chuckled at this sending heat punching through his mid-section like a plasma fire. Smiling at her in return was not life threatening, so why did it feel as if it was?

"You, my friend," she said, turning back to the controls, "are the master of the understatement."

My friend? Master? These seemed positive signs though he was not sure why. The fire settled into a smolder, but in his chest, the feeling was...warm. Pleasant.

Silence returned, then built. He studied his screens while his mind tried to find something, anything but the scary words. *I like you. I would like to hold you and touch your mouth with mine.*

It was too soon. He did not need a squirrel to tell him that. Last night the words had moved easily from one person to the next, except when they reached him, but he'd watched and listened. And failed to learn.

You are dazzling her, are you not. The squirrel could do better. At least it could dance. He shifted, so that his body angled more her direction and latched onto words that drifted past.

"Your world," he had to clear his throat, "it sounds pleasing."

Her lips turned up again. "I like our third rock from the sun." She leaned back, her gaze going distant. "I'm sure you're used to seeing planets from space but for me, when it was a big blue ball hanging there—" She gave a shake. "I wondered what I was thinking to leave."

"What did you leave?" The question popped out and for a moment he tensed because the question had almost been "who did you leave?"

She hesitated, and he wondered if he'd crossed a line. But she sighed and said, "My family. That was hardest because I couldn't tell them how far away I'd be. We keep in touch, but they have no idea where I am."

This seemed very strange, but what did he know of family?

"You miss them." He did not ask this. He felt it, saw it in her eyes.

"I do. I got an email from my mom in the data dump before we set out." She did something and an image containing several people popped up as a holo. Her gaze softened more. "That's my dad and my mom..."

He felt her longing, but something deeper and darker welled up from a place he did not know was there.

Another image appeared. "That's me with my brother and sister. Mom found it in a box of stuff and thought I'd like a copy. We're standing in front of Old Faithful, it's a geyser."

He did not know geyser.

"I think I was maybe ten there." She leaned back again, bringing the picture of her parents up once more, so that the pictures were side by side above the control console.

My parents. My sister. My brother.

Kraye stared at them as the darkness swirled closer and closer to the surface. It was a roar in his mind, but in the roar, he thought he heard crying—

"Are you all right?" Her hand covering his yanked him from the storm.

His throat was dry, his skin damp.

"I am fine," he said, surprised his voice sounded fine. The breath he was able to draw in hurt but not as much as the one before it.

"You sure?"

I had no parents. But that was not possible, was it?

"I—" the lie died at the look in her eyes. "I do not...remember parents." A memory stirred again with the words, but so did pain. The darkness. He pushed back, and the memories subsided.

"But—" She stopped. "Were you...adopted?"

"I..." He did not want to say the words, but—she needed to know. Then he'd know. But he could not watch her face as he said it. He stared out the view screen. "I was a slave."

Her hand on his tightened almost to the point of pain. He had to look then. Her face with tight, her eyes stormy. She was disgusted—

"Bastards. But you're free? The robots—"

"I am free." The words helped. "I am free," he repeated, his voice stronger. "I ran away. But they—the Captain rescued me." He tried to think of more he could add, but what?

His life could be summed up in those three sentences. *I was a slave. I ran away. The Captain rescued me.*

She was quiet for a few moments, then she said, "Families form in lots of ways."

Were the robots his family? He did not know a lot about family. He did know they were his crew mates, his friends. He nodded. He did not want her pity, but at least he had her attention. The edges of her mouth turned up.

"I'm trying to imagine what it was like to grow up with...them."

He glanced at the picture. "It was not like that. But..." The smiling faces of her family caused pain to echo from some deep place in his mind, but her touch anchored him in the now. "It was good." It was safe, which was ironic since the robots had many enemies, and yet it had, and still felt...safe.

"I'm glad." She hesitated. "My dad used to say where you start isn't as important as who you become." She tipped her head to the side. "He'd like you."

The pain retreated further. Would he? He opened his mouth to say—he was not sure. He did not get the chance.

Alarms blared.

We have a contact.

~

"HAVE THEY SEEN US?" City asked, snapping to attention and pushing to the side what she'd learned about Kraye. She'd think about that later. The hologram of her family vanished, replaced by tracking information on their unknown contact.

That is not known.

Did Rita sound a little incredulous that City had asked? She didn't—yet—have the attitude that the AI at Central Outpost had, but give her time...

They weren't cloaked but the *Emissary's* skin had stealth capabilities. What no one knew was how well this worked in real space.

"I'm going to try a course change and see how they react," City said. Out of the corner of her eye, she saw Kraye nod. It would take time for both the course change and for the bogey to see it and react. So she had time to note that this super alert Kraye was, well, sexy. His thin intense face and the combo of his relaxed but alert body conveyed confidence. His dark skin made his hands pop against the controls. Those hands might have prompted not-on-the-bridge thoughts if she hadn't been on the bridge. She admitted to herself that she'd liked having him on her team when they went toe-to-toe with the bad guys in their last action.

He'd already pulled up all available data and brought their weapons systems online. This might not be his ship's bridge, but it didn't matter. He was as home here as she was.

She wished she could read his thoughts because even his body language was close-lipped—unlike Faxton. The question she had about the diplomat, was he interested? Or was he interested in appearing interested? He and his assistant had been so not interested in each other, she figured they must be a little interested. She didn't care if they were heating up the alien sheets together. She did care if they wanted to use her as cover.

She could wish that Kraye showed a little interest and not just to get Faxton to back off. She half frowned. Could he? Would the guy raised by robots know how to flirt?

I was a slave. I am free.

Guy had to be left with some issues. Usually, she tried to avoid guys who were major fixer uppers. She looked at dating like buying a car. You could love the lines, but a smooth finish was not an indicator of what was under the hood. She didn't expect perfect, but no one wanted a break down.

"They are reacting to your course change," Bull said, from behind her, making her jump a little. She hadn't heard him come onto the bridge.

"So they can see us," she muttered. Did that mean stealth only worked in atmosphere? Or was something else giving them away?

"Let's cloak and see how they react," she said. "We do not want to bump heads with anyone unless we have to." Not this early in the mission. She hit the intercom. "We have an unknown contact. Get to a secure position and strap in if you can." Even the turtles had a sort of docking station. "Rita, please activate the stasis shields around the habitat when you can." The shields would hold the water—and anyone in it—in place if they had to execute maneuvers that would negatively impact loose objects.

Aye, aye, Sergeant.

She bit her lip on a grin. Rita seemed to love the military stuff. "Let's hope we won't need it."

The bridge was quiet while they waited for the physics of space to work out. City almost asked Rita to give them some music to fill the silence, but resisted the urge. She liked to feel and hear the ship around her. More than once she'd felt a change before the instruments registered it. Even the small throb of music could come between her and the ship.

Contact has slowed and is scanning intensely.

"So they did see us. Now they can't. Or they are pretending they can't." She glanced at Kraye. "You and Bull operate in this region. Can you look at the scanning and see if you can identify our bogey?"

"Of course, I mean aye—"

"Of course is fine." She shot him a quick grin before turning back to her controls, her gaze scanning the data much like their scanners were giving space a going over.

The hatch opened behind them. She started to turn and look, but stopped when she heard a soft whinny-meow.

"Not a good time, Tiger."

The tiny clip-clops didn't retreat. There was a jump seat—she took a quick look back and sure enough, Bull had dropped the jump seat for him and secured the harness. City gave a resigned shake of her head.

She input evasive maneuvers programming, a series of small, but random course changes that should be hard to predict. She didn't want to light them up with a lot of power usage either. "Do we have any more data on the bogey?"

"They are continuing on a course to our original position, but at reduced speed," Bull said. "They know we are here, but I do not believe they can see us."

I concur.

Was it her imagination that AI's tone got warmer when she talked to Bull?

"Sergeant?" Bull's tone was the same as it always was, so it was weird she had the feeling he was puzzled. "There is...I am uncertain how to describe..."

"Describe what?"

"We received the coordinates for the *Testudinians* world from them, did we not?"

"That is my understanding," City said, half turning to look at him.

"It is not there."

City blinked. "A trap?"

"It was there when we entered the system, but now it is not."

She was pretty sure the Death Star hadn't got to it. So that left
— "They, what, cloaked their whole planet?"

"It would appear so."

She opened her mouth, but closed it again, tension in her jawline. In her last briefing with General Halliwell aboard the *Boyington*, he'd mentioned a lost expedition ship and a sanctuary. He had a report by some geeks who had found data that the Garradians were working on a planet-wide cloaking tech. So it wasn't totally impossible, she supposed.

They are transmitting a message.

"Can we receive—and understand it?"

I am attempting a translation.

The pause was impressively short. Rita might be crushing on Bull, but she wasn't letting it distract her.

I believe the language is Testudinian.

"It's a turtle ship?"

I believe so.

"Can you confirm, Bull? And let's see if we can get a feed to our *Testudinians*. We might need them to smooth things over." While she waited, she leaned toward Kraye. "Did we know they were space capable?"

"I did not know," he said, a sudden grin softening his face.

The smile, even at half strength, suited him. He needed to smile more. She thought about what he'd told her. Not a surprise he didn't smile much. Her return smile might have been warmer than she considered suitable for the bridge. She turned back to her controls. Maybe she'd pick Bull's, um, processors, see if she could get some intel on what Kraye liked. So she could see him smile again.

"Mr. Faxton, can you get on the comms with us? We might need your expertise if this is who we think it is." Should she ask about their missing planet? It wasn't on her mission brief, she decided reluctantly. And she wasn't a geek. Did she even know the right questions to ask without revealing something she shouldn't?

"Aye, aye, Sergeant."

She glanced at Kraye and thought he looked surprised. "It's why he's here."

～

"THAT WENT a lot faster than I thought it would," City said, relaxing back into her seat. For the first time since they'd been lit up by the turtle ship, she realized how tense she'd been. And that she was hungry.

"It is optimal that this ship can remotely transport objects," Kraye agreed.

If he was tired, it didn't show. For a face with the potential to be mobile and fascinating, he kept a tight lid on his muscles. Which was probably not that surprising for a guy raised by a bunch of robots who couldn't break out in expression if their lives depended on it.

"It would have taken longer to make the transfer," City agreed, rotating her shoulders to ease their stiffness.

"We also acquired intel that might prove useful," Bull said.

City released the lock so her seat could rotate her around to face him. "Can we trust it?"

The turtles had appeared glad—no, that wasn't quite right. They weren't terribly expressive either though they had more capacity than the robot. Their huge sad eyes might have reminded her of Eeyore. They hadn't invited any of them back to their missing planet and had said they'd require time to consider it when Faxton proposed further diplomatic contact. And since not even the *Emissary's* sassy sensors could "see" a cloaked planet, they had no idea what it was like. It was a disappointment. What was the fun of "boldly going" if you couldn't also 'boldly' see something?

Not that City blamed them. Some nasty humans had kidnapped two—or more—of their people, most likely intending to add them to soup. She couldn't imagine what else the slow-moving species could have done for the bad guys.

"Trust?" Bull didn't shrug, though that might not be something he could do. "No, not without verifying. The *Najer* could tap into the beacons and satellites situated around the system. I brought some of that programming with me, but it has limitations."

"Limitations? Like what?"

"The *Najer* has technologies that this ship does not. It would not be advisable to risk compromising this ship's systems, so we will not have the same level of access."

Even City knew he was talking about hacking. She nodded.

"One of the things I am seeing in what you sent me, they are advising against traveling directly from here to the *Sulian Nebos'* planet. Rita, I need you in on this, too. If this intel is good that's a lot of ship activity happening along our planned route. What are our options?"

A hologram appeared in the center of the bridge, giving all of them a view of where they were and the other intended destinations. Rita added labels to possible hazards. City studied the hazards, a mix of magnetospheres from astronomical objects and spatial instabilities. "It's kind of like a trail through a mountain pass, isn't it?" Lots of places for an ambush. "So what's a better option?"

"I am running our options," Bull said.

City might have sighed a little. Too bad they couldn't bust a move to the *Harparian's* planet. She knew she'd sleep easier when the bird was off the ship. Which gave her an idea—admittedly one cribbed from the robots.

"You guys fire probes so you can get a look ahead. Could we do that? I'm thinking of Teuhhopse, the *Harparian's* home. Get a heads up on any problems we might encounter there?"

A probe is possible.

Rita sounded intrigued. Or like City, she wanted more information on where they were going. "High mountains" wasn't cutting it for them.

Tiger wriggled out of his harness and approached the hologram, studying it as intently as they were. "Got any ideas?" she asked him. He turned and stared at her for a long moment, then lifted a hoof and batted at one of the planets, as if it were a ball she'd asked him to play with. His interaction with the hologram made it ripple like the surface of water.

"Thanks, Tiger—"

That is very interesting, Tiger.

Rita almost sounded excited.

Bull might have come to attention. "There are anomalous forces in that region. If we did a comet drive jump to the edge of the region, as we dropped out, momentum should carry us into the *Sulian Nebos* region from this direction." His metal digit traced a path. "It is a less obvious approach."

"Would we be able to slow down in time?" City asked, looking at

his equations. "And what about possible hostiles around that—"
What was it, anyway? "Unstable…nebula?"

I can provide braking at the optimum time.

"And our momentum will confuse any hostile forces lurking
there. We will…"

"…blow past them?"

"Something like that," Bull agreed.

"If something is lurking near the planet, our arrival should
provide enough confusion that will give us time to assess threats,"
Kraye said.

City nodded thoughtfully. "It's a plan. Do we need to deploy the
probes before we go into comet drive?"

Probes?

"Well, if we're going to look ahead, maybe we should look at all
of our ahead?" It didn't sound grammatical, but Rita seemed to
understand.

I will prepare them. We should launch just prior to initiating comet drive.

"Make it so," City said. Okay, she'd been waiting for a chance to
say that and she was the only one who'd get it—

Her caticorn made this sound that almost sounded like a
chuckle. She looked down, running into his Puss'n'Boots gaze.
There was more to him than met the eye. And that was saying quite
a bit.

"Rita, you okay if we take a break to eat? Meet you back here in
thirty?"

"I will remain here," Bull said, "Can Rocky go with you to
obtain sustenance?"

"Sure," City said. Was this how Noah had felt on the ark?

Rocky launched himself forward, landing neatly on Tiger's
back. As she followed them out the hatch, she wondered if Noah
was the right comparison. At this moment, she felt more like
Barnum or Bailey.

≈

LUNCH DIDN'T TAKE LONG, so City decided to drop down and see how her Mikes were doing and also check on the remaining passengers. The *Emissary* had lost its stale ship smell when they all came on board, but the aliens were winning against the humanoids. Even with scrubbers, there was an odd mix of river and stable that came in whiffs, or lingered in unexpected corners. The smell built as she left the Mikes and dropped down to the cargo deck. It wasn't unpleasant, but it was earthy and on the pungent side.

With the turtles gone, the swans had the run of the small waterway that had been jury-rigged for their aquatically inclined passengers. City noticed that as they drifted gracefully past a chunk of fake greenery, they almost appeared to disappear. Bird calls preceded the green-footed boobys—the *Sulian Nubians*—from a stand of fake bushes. They regarded her with comic solemnity from their huge eyes, but before they could speak—if speaking was their intention—the black and red pandas tumbled out of another huddle of fake greenery. They rolled over and over until they bumped against City's leg. Kraye grabbed to her arm to steady her, then staggered himself when one of the panda's wrapped all four legs around one of his legs.

The other panda hugged City's leg and asked, "Are we there yet?"

"*Are* we there yet?" This sounded like a small chorus. The hedgehog-like creatures rolled into view and tipped pointed noses and dark eyes up, blinking slowly as they waited for City's answer.

She bent down and eased the panda's paws off her legs, then sat down. Tiger settled under one armpit and the panda under the other.

"Rita, can you give me a flight plan holo for our guests?"

A less detailed holo appeared before City and the animals clustered around it, one of the swans leaving the water to draw closer and study it.

"We've had to modify our original flight plan," she admitted. "We're trying to avoid possibly hostile contacts." She pointed out the modified route, tracing it with her finger. It looked a bit crazy seen this way.

"We approve," the hedgehogs said, their squeaks perfectly synchronized. And when one shifted, she realized the other did so, too.

It must have been awful for them to be separated. She reached out her hand, not daring to pet the spiky things, but letting their noses nudge against her hand.

"I'm sorry," she said.

"For what?" they asked.

"About what happened to you."

Two pairs of eyes studied her for what seemed like a long time.

"We will heal when we are home," they finally said.

"I'll do my best to get you there."

"Are we there yet?" Kraye's panda asked.

She met his gaze over the panda's head and grinned ruefully.

Chapter 4

THEY DROPPED out of comet drive space, the pull of it still strange to Kraye. Granted this was only the third or fourth time he'd traveled this way, but perhaps it was not possible to get used to the sensation of being stretched one direction, then the other, then compacting forcefully before smoothing out.

He watched the controls, tracking their momentum as the scanners kicked on, searching for dangers in their path, particularly those close enough to be of concern. He almost smiled. As predicted, they'd—as Caro put it—blown past a small cluster of suspicious looking ships. They'd planned to arrive at the *Sulian Nebos'* planet first, but the course change had brought them to the *Cygni-nains* instead. Their scanners were updating in waves as Rita applied the "brakes" so that they didn't also blow past their destination.

Thanks to the probes they'd launched they knew a little more about this planet and it had not—yet—cloaked.

"It's an ocean world?" City asked, "or just this side?"

He did not let himself look at her profile as she studied the probe data. Doing this made him wish to trace the line from her hair to her chin—with a pause to trace the curve of her mouth. He wished—

"There are land masses, but they are scattered rather than concentrated," OxeroidR said, "Based on the life signs assessment, inhabitants are either amphibian or avine. We will not be able to transport the *Cygninains* and their offspring to the surface. The atmosphere is not compatible with transport energy."

"Mr. Faxton will be happy about that," City muttered. "Dr. Lowe Dauwn, too."

Kraye glanced at her, wondering why her lips twitched whenever she said the doctor's name. She caught him looking, so he arched his brows.

"It's his name. On Earth, we say 'give me the low down.' It's like a briefing."

Kraye found it easy to smile, forgot about the clues to how she saw him and enjoyed looking at her, basked in the warmth in her eyes.

"They have provided coordinates for our shuttle," OxeroidR said.

City held his gaze, then half shrugged and turned back to her controls. While Kraye had not had a lot of personal time alone with City, as in no time alone with her, Faxton had not been in the mix at all, so it was almost like being alone with her. Other than OxeroidR, Rocky, and Tiger. So almost alone. At least it had been semi-alone time without the necessity to be on high alert or in a fire fight. The fingers of the hand closest to his tapped on a section of her station that did not have control functions.

She spun around, her gaze moving between Kraye and OxeroidR. She straightened as if she'd come to a decision.

"One of my functions as a Marine is to protect US diplomatic personnel. Mr. Faxton and his team will want to be on that shuttle. Unless we can identify it as a high-risk situation, I have to let them. I'll be the pilot with three of my Mikes—my Marines." Her gaze still moved between them. "You're both good in a fight, but I can't have all our key people in that shuttle. I need one of you to stay here."

Kraye's gaze jerked to OxeroidR. "You should stay." He could stand in for many people whereas Kraye could only ever be one person. The fact that he did not wish Caro to travel on the shuttle with Faxton and without him was not relevant.

Caro looked at OxeroidR. "Do you agree?"

After a long pause, the robot slowly nodded. "I can complete the mission."

Kraye exchanged a rather wry look with Caro. They both knew he could have done the whole mission with just he and Rita.

"I'm going to go talk to the…swans. Rita, the bridge is yours."

She rose and Kraye found himself standing as well.

"May I accompany you?" he asked.

"Of course. Bull, you're second seat with Rita."

"Aye, aye, Sergeant." He rose smoothly and took her place.

When they were in the corridor, with the hatch closed between them and the bridge, she asked, "Is he being ironic when he aye, ayes me?"

Kraye hesitated. "I do not know if he is able to be ironic," he admitted. "They are sentient, but emotions are difficult for them."

They turned and started walking toward the lift.

"That is not to say they are incapable of intense loyalty." He hesitated, then said, "They are complicated."

"Life," said Caro, "is complicated."

The lift opened, and they entered. As it closed, he realized he was alone with her. No Rocky or Tiger. Just the two of them. It would not last, so he should do…something. He turned so that he fully faced her. Her chin lifted, her expression losing worry for curiosity.

"Seems like they'd be too much and too little at the same moment."

For a moment he did not understand what she meant. "Yes. That is what it is like." Living with sentient robots. Wanting her. He wanted to say more. The lift was dropping. It would open and the chance would be gone. "I do not know your words."

Her eyes widened, she seemed to hesitate, then the line of her mouth softened. "You're okay." She touched his elbow.

She touched him. If OxeroidR was correct, this was a positive sign.

"I like you." The words dropped into the space between them like asteroids. Her eyes widened and soft color stained her cheeks. The wait for her to speak felt longer than a light year of travel. Her lips began to tip up at the edges, the lips he wished to press with his began to part—

The lift door swept open.

"There you are, Sergeant," said Faxton, his clever, knowing gaze moving between them before he stepped into the lift, forcing them to separate. "I was hoping you could brief me on the plan for repatriating the *Cygninains.*"

THE ONLY SOUND that broke the silence as the shuttle lifted off were twitters from the cygnets, with an occasional admonition from their mama and papa. At least, City thought they were a gal and a guy. She hadn't looked under their tails and didn't plan to.

She glanced at Kraye. Even judging by his usual, he was devoid of expression. This was probably the first time he'd gone on a mission without at least one of his robot crew. While Bull hadn't broken out in expression either at their parting, Rocky had seemed anxious. At any rate, he needed an emergency lick of a body part she'd rather not see.

She might miss Bull, too. There was something reassuring about a huge robot with who knew how many built-in weapons he could deploy in a blink. And he was fast enough to cover point and six at the same time.

As to Faxton and his team, she'd given each of them the opportunity to use the comms for their diplomacy efforts. She might be a little impressed they all wanted to go head to, um, beak with the aliens.

"Amphibians and avines," Caro murmured. "Under water and over land. Dr. Dauwn finds that intriguing. I wish we had a better risk assessment. Intriguing could go either way." If they waited for one, this mission could be longer than the months Noah was stuck on his Ark. So she was going with her gut—and sometimes against it. Actually, her gut was neutral on this one. The hair on the back of her neck wasn't standing up, but her right eye kept trying to twitch.

Through the passenger cam she could see her rifle squad of Mikes sitting facing Faxton and his team. No one could look like they weren't looking at Brittani like a Marine could look like they weren't looking. And she'd given them a lot to look at back there. Ms. St. Danniels had donned her uniform, too, a gray suit that packed the impact of a red dress. Dr. Dauwn went against geek trend with his fairly well cut brown suit. His tie had been a little crooked but Britanni had fixed it. Mr. Faxton had had to straighten his own tie. She'd given Kraye a thorough once-over, but he wasn't wearing a tie and didn't notice the look over.

City was starting to like her, though she thought the foxtrot mike heels were a mistake. City was expecting a soggy landing.

One thing she'd done when she couldn't sleep was do simulations for both the *Emissary* and this shuttle. Sadly, the shuttle did not have the sassiness of the *Emissary*. At least it could cloak, it had shields, though these were limited by the shuttle's power capacity, and it could do some pointing and shooting. These were also limited by space and power.

City set a course for the LZ provided by the *Cygninains*. Advance scanning and the probe data had identified abundant life forms, both above and below the water line, but no radio or power signals, no sign any of them were space capable. Maybe it was this making her eye want to twitch. Why did the swans speak Standard albeit a bird accent? Had they learned it in captivity or on their planet? Even before her deployment to another galaxy she'd learned that ducks that looked like ducks weren't always ducks. And she had three people who really wanted to talk to the ducks. If she'd have had her way, they'd have dropped down, dropped off the birds, and lifted off again.

But this wasn't just a repatriation. It was an attempt to open diplomatic relations with a non-human species. Apparently, that was a lot more interesting than talking with alien humanoids. Faxton didn't admit it, but it was obvious the cool factor was part of what lured him into this "boldly going" further than they'd already "boldly" gone.

Her guys were packing regular projectile weapons and a nice selection of ray guns they'd picked up in Central Outpost. Lethal force was only authorized as a last resort. No one wanted to mess up future diplomacy by killing the wrong species. But she was also not about to let her Marines die on their ray guns. They were good guys. They'd do their best. They all would. She just hoped it would be enough.

"Approaching atmospheric insertion," Kraye said. He was acting as navigator and backup pilot for the mission. Bull was monitoring their comms from the *Emissary*, but no one knew how the atmosphere might affect communications. It was compatible with their lungs, which was weird, and the shuttle had its own decontamination protocol, and then the *Emissary* had another one. But the humidity was going to be a bitch.

"Adjusting course for atmosphere entry," City said. She felt the drag start as they nosed in, watched the heat build up on the shuttle's skin. It stayed within an acceptable range, even as the atmosphere thickened. As soon as the drag overcame momentum, she fired up in the in-atmosphere engines. Kraye gave her the course, and she made the adjustments, bringing the nose down until they broke through the cloud cover.

Spread out below them was a blue water world with tracings of green and brown, like a quilt design.

"It's beautiful," City murmured.

"I have initiated threat scanning," Kraye told her.

Her eyes moved constantly over the various controls, reading and processing the information. This was a different operation. Usually she was with her team, moving forward with all of them on the alert. At the controls like this, with all their lives resting on her reacting fast and in the right way, it felt off.

"We have a contact," Kraye said. "Biologic. Big."

"Shields," she ordered tersely, activating the forward view screen. "Hotel sierra."

Its wingspan was as wide as their *Harparian*, but this bird was pure gold with a white under belly. It turned, and she got a good look at its face.

"It looks like an…owl," she said as it played chicken with them. She decided to turn first. She'd never played chicken and didn't intend to start now. She banked the shuttle to the right and lost visual on it, though tracking showed it banking left, then coming around. "We can probably outrun it, but do we want to?"

"We could ask the *Cygninains?*"

City considered it, then nodded. The owl was banking, diving, and basically dogging them. She activated the intra-ship comm. "Mr. Faxton, I'm going to send some video back there. Could you ask our passengers about the intent of this species?"

"Aye, aye, Sergeant."

Kraye worked the controls, sending them the feed. After a few minutes of dancing with the owl, Faxton came on the comm.

"They wish to know if there is a function to broadcast sound."

City blinked. "They want to talk to the big owl."

"They want to talk to the big, er, owl, yes."

"Let me see what I can do."

"I am looking as well," Kraye said. Then, "I believe we can broadcast now."

She slanted him a grateful look. "Give it a shot, Mr. Faxton."

The sounds were also audible on the small bridge. Painfully audible. But it helped. The big owl swooped several more times and then dove into the boiling mist below.

"Resuming course for our LZ," City said. She glanced at Kraye. "Get the translation program running. See if we can find out what they said."

KRAYE DIDN'T TAKE his eyes off the sensor data as Caro set the shuttle down on a small island of solid ground in a large lake. The nose of the shuttle looked out on a shifting scene of blue-green water and thick mist.

Caro leaned over and did a last check of the atmospheric readings. "Darn, we can breathe, though gills would be helpful."

He did not know what this meant, but he nodded and returned her grin. Each time he did this, it got easier. The *Najer* did not make many planetfall landings. There was too much risk. Even contact with space station docks involved risk for a ship as wanted as theirs.

Caro pushed back and rose. "You're on the con, Mr. Kraye." She hesitated, her gaze meeting his, the expression one that puzzled him. "I'll keep the radio open. Yell if—well, you know when to yell."

"I do." He wished to go with her down the ramp, but he understood her need to have him here on the bridge. "Have care." He wished to reach out to her, but he did not. She'd called him Mr. Kraye. This was official, business. Her hand came to rest on her shoulder and her gaze once more puzzled him.

"I'm glad you're here," she said. Before he could respond to this, she'd turned and left.

I am glad you're here.

This seemed encouraging. A shuffling sound drew his attention as Tiger jumped onto her vacated seat.

"You should not," he said, even as he reached out t0 run a hand down its back. They had something in common. They both wished to be near Caro.

THE RAMP LOWERED on a world of blue, green and white, with swirls of gray and purple, too. The air damp rushed in, bringing with it the smell of water and plants. Not being a scientist, City didn't know what else to call all that green crap, even if they'd been on Earth. Which they weren't. So not on Earth. In truth, it felt like and looked a movie set, not a real place. City was stacked on one side, at the top of the ramp with Fox on her six. On the other side, Jenkins was stacked with Spencer. It was hard to feel outnumbered with Kraye reading her the stats on the approaching life signs. They were few, but they were Marines.

Oorah.

She gave the signal, and they started down the ramp. No one hesitated at the edge. They stepped down, mud oozing up to cover the top of their boots. She and Spencer cleared their point while the other two cleared the rear. Something was out there. Kraye could see them on the sensors, but they didn't have eyes on anything. Weapons ready, she eased up to the edge of their small patch of ground. She tested the edge with a foot. Spongy but there was something hard under the sponge.

"What's out there, Mr. Kraye," she asked through her head set.

"I see twenty heat signatures holding about twenty feet out from the point of the land mass."

Faxton's voice came over her head set. "The *Cygninains* say their, um, people won't appear until they see them."

Everyone had trust issues. "Send them out."

"I would like to go with—"

"Let's see if there is anyone for you to talk to first." She did not want his team in their way if things turned unfriendly.

Her other Marines were providing as much coverage as they could as the swans waddled down the ramp. They'd left the kids behind, she noted.

"Let's take a less aggressive posture," she ordered, lowering her weapon, so that it pointed at the ground.

The swans stopped about halfway between their forward and rear positions, clear of the ramp, but still within a zone where they could protect them. The air was cool, but sweat beaded on her upper lip and her hackles rose. It was too quiet. Even the water was still. When City considered how almost casually she'd signed on for this mission, it made her brain hurt now. She seriously needed to have her head examined.

"Anything on the sensors we should be concerned about, Mr. Kraye."

"The life signs are on the move."

The water almost at her feet confirmed this as it lapped softly against the small shoreline.

Life signs under and over. "Do we have a way to tell how deep the water is around our position?"

Kraye read off a number that was deep enough to make her take a half step back. The ripples grew, the angle suggesting something was moving across the surface, but she couldn't see a bean. She opened her mouth to ask why when suddenly she could see shapes. They slowly resolved into a cluster of swans very like theirs.

They drifted just off the bank, holding their position with, she guessed, only their webbed feet. They were incredibly beautiful though their silence might be creeping her out. With barely a ripple on the water surface, the swan delegation reformed, most of them falling back to form a "V." The lead swan emitted a sound that was a cross between a chirp and a bark. One of their swans answered. The conversation bounced back and forth for about a minute, then their swan turned to look at City.

She or he said a word that City couldn't begin to understand, and followed it with, "…will speak to Mr. Faxton."

A name? Or a designation?

She tapped her head set. "Come on down, Mr. Faxton."

The lead swan shot forward, then lifted from the water, passing near City's face—not a great smell—and landed near their swans. With or without parental consent, the cygnets followed Faxton and his team down the ramp. Oh yeah, Brittani's shoes were a mistake. She sank in the ooze up to her ankles. City gave her props for grabbing Dr. Dauwn's arm and removing both her muddy shoes. City was about to protest, but she was smart enough to climb back up on the ramp. Dr. Dauwn elected to stay with her, though he looked about him with more animation than she'd seen so far. He had a camera, but he didn't lift it up.

It wasn't until ten minutes into the diplomatic dialog that Kraye started sending her rough translations with a fifty percent accuracy rating. It sounded like they agreed in theory that being allies would be acceptable. They were not open to exploring that theory at the moment. It sounded a lot like "don't call us, we'll call you," only with what?

Something, maybe the sense of movement out of the corner of her eye, had City glancing down at the water barely a foot from where she stood. It moved, the ripples horizontal to the shore now.

She realized there was a shadow where there hadn't been one. A shadow that reached into the drifting mist in both directions. And then a line of fins broke the surface. A long line of fins.

"It will not eat you."

City tore her gaze away with difficulty—and kept her weapon pointed down with even greater difficulty as the shadow continued to flow past. At her feet stood one of the swans, with her cygnets circling her like many small planes.

She swallowed. "It won't?"

"It eats," a wing swept against a bush and it said a word City didn't recognize.

"It's an herbivore," Dr. Dauwn breathed out, his tone somewhere between awe and horror as the end of the thing finished its pass with a twitch of its tail fins.

"It was curious," the swan said.

"Okay, well," City swallowed dryly again. "We should probably wrap this up."

Dr. Dauwn lifted his camera. "May I take a picture, capture an image of you?"

City couldn't figure out why it felt like this amused the swan.

"You may." She lifted her beak toward the camera.

City resisted the urge to say, "Cheese."

Dr. Dauwn pointed his camera toward more than the swans and was the last, except for the Marines, to retreat back up the ramp. Before City's Mikes were up the ramp, the swans had faded into the mist.

AS SOON AS the ramp closed, City gave the order for Kraye to lift off. City joined him in the cockpit, giving her caticorn a look. When it didn't move, she picked it up, took the seat and let it settle in her lap. "If anything happens, you book it," she said, sternly. All this earned her was a limpid look from the caticorn.

She let Kraye keep the con while she activated their bottom cameras, but the mist, as if it had the ability to think, blocked their view of water. They reached the upper atmosphere without being buzzed by the owl and Kraye set a course for the *Emissary*.

She activated the comm. "Dr. Dauwn, when you download your images, I'd love to take a look at them."

There was a pause.

"I have downloaded them and there is nothing to see," came the despondent reply.

City looked at Kraye. "Nothing?"

"Not nothing but—I will send them to your control station," he said.

There was a ping as the images arrived. City pulled up the first one. He was right. They were not nothing, but they weren't anything either. They were pictures of the mist. No birds. No huge fish. No colors. Just gray mist.

'That is..." Kraye stopped.

"Not how it looked when I was out there." She sat back and rubbed her face. "Rita, you got anything spooky on your playlists?"

The Addams Family wasn't quite what she had in mind, but it would have to do. She petted Tiger with one hand, the other tapping along with the music on the arm of her seat. She was a Marine, so she couldn't say they were in over their heads. But there were no regs against thinking it.

Chapter 5

THE EMISSARY HAD ENTERED a high orbit over the planet of the *Sulian Nebos* and transported the green-footed creatures to coordinates provided when the probe and scans determined it was also a planet without the capability to talk to them. The densely covered planet also had no landing zone large enough for the shuttle.

Faxton and his team managed to hide their chagrin, but the three of them had been decidedly morose at dinner as they left orbit and set a course for the planet where they would drop off both the *Pinyains* and the *Erinaceines*.

There were signs that they'd been spotted by less than friendly sources. OxeroidR, who had been monitoring channels official and not official, was not certain the questions were about them, but he was concerned.

"Is there any way for them to predict where we are going based on where we have been?" Caro had asked.

"They would need passenger specific data to make such a determination based on our past movement."

"I hear a but in there," Caro said.

"Our energy signature is not typical and—" he stopped once again.

"—one of our former passengers could have talked." Caro bit her lip. "The only ones who seem to have 'rat us out' technology was the turtles." Her hand ran absently down Tiger's back. He arched and emitted a humming sound. "Are we sure we handed them off to their own kind?"

It was true that none of them had seen anyone on the *Testudinian* ship.

"The *Testudinian* passengers seemed certain they were speaking with their own kind," OxeroidR said.

"Doesn't mean they weren't fooled. Or they spilled what they knew for reasons of their own. That might explain the cool welcome at our other stops." Caro sighed. She spun around and faced OxeroidR and Rocky. "What do you think, Rocky? Are we being paranoid?" Rocky tipped his head to the side as if puzzled. "You spent more time with them than any of us."

Rocky scratched the side of his head and appeared to consider the question. "We occupied adjoining cages or cells," he agreed, "but we did not talk amongst each other. There were…rewards for sharing…" His voice trailed off.

"So, we should assume our last two stops are known." Caro's tone was flat.

"It is better to be prepared," OxeroidR agreed.

She muttered something.

"I did not hear—" Kraye began.

"We have a saying on my planet, one about good deeds not going unpunished." Her smile was wry.

Kraye echoed her wry. They had had no time together. Caro had asked him and OxeroidR to do practice simulations—and she'd asked OxeroidR to "up the level of difficulty to impossible." Her Marines were also doing sims, using probe data they'd collected so far.

When they'd left on this mission, there had been a business-like air about them all, but their sense of purpose had taken on a grim edge now. The signs of interest had turned into signs of pursuit, signs significant enough that they'd sped up their transit to the planet where the *Erinaceines* and the *Pinyains* were to be repatriated.

It had been a wise precaution. The probe data showed at least two ships known to them patrolling the system.

"We can go in cloaked," Caro had told them, "but we'll have to limit our ground time." Her gaze had been apologetic when she directed it at Faxton. "I'm sorry, but none of you can go down."

He'd started to protest.

"There won't be time for talking down there. You can talk to them before we disembark, but that's it. We have to do two drops and our passengers are picking the LZ's, not anyone down there. There won't be anyone to talk to because we're not telling them we're coming. We have probably already been betrayed at least once." When Faxton still showed in inclination to protest, she added, "We could lose more than a pair of shoes this time. I'm not risking your lives or the lives of this crew."

"What about Teuhhopse?"

She'd bit her lip then. "We don't have probe data back on it yet. If you can get more out of Lady Yodrirka, I'm willing to discuss one or all of you going down. But what we do will also depend on what we find when we get there. I'm not going to promise anything. I can't."

He'd finally nodded and left.

"I think he's finally realizing how bat crap crazy it was to sign up for this trip," she'd said, when the hatch had closed behind him.

"If you are not stopping," OxeroidR said, "I should fly the shuttle."

Kraye stopped an instinctive protest. He well knew that the robot was more than able to accomplish the mission and he—or Caro and her Marines—would only get in his way.

"I concur," he said. She was correct, the level of difficulty was rising. Someone had talked.

Caro had considered the request for what felt a long time. "I don't like sending anyone out without backup," she said finally, her tone reluctant enough to indicate she was considering the suggestion. She did not like it, but she was a wise mission commander. She needed to use her available assets in the most optimal manner.

"I," OxeroidR pointed out, with something that was almost amusement in his computer-generated voice, "am my own backup."

That had surprised a laugh out of Caro, one the softened the worry in her face.

I can act as his backup.

"Rita would be useful," OxeroidR admitted in his version of almost surprised.

"I hate to lose you up here, Rita," Caro said, frowning.

I can be two places at once.

"That's a skill I would not mind having," Caro said, her grin appearing. "Alright. I'll take it under advisement."

"SO YOU THINK they might be able to see the energy signature from our comet drive?" City asked. They were in her ready room. It was a total *Star Trek* moment, the room and the incoming risk— which took the edge off her squee moment.

Bull gave a solemn nod. "The data is not clear on whether it is safe to cloak while in comet drive. We will be visible when we drop into normal space."

"If we have to be visible, we might as well launch the shuttle then. We're programmed to drop out close to the planet. After a deeper dive into the probe data, there appears to be a humanoid presence, along with indications that someone down there is space capable." This would increase the level of difficulty for the shuttle landing. She looked at Bull and Kraye and knew what they wanted to ask. She appreciated their restraint. She hated to do it, but Bull was right. He was the best...team for the job. "I concur with your assessment on who should be in the shuttle, Bull. We need to prep the shuttle and finalize your LZs."

"I have been consulting with the *Pinyains* and the *Erinaceines*. They are willing to share their LZ and agree that any approach to either of their colonies will increase the risk to us and them."

Or they don't want us to know where those colonies are. Their motives didn't matter unless they were lying, too. She'd been considering deploying two shuttles, but she didn't think Rita, a fairly new sentient, was ready to go into battle.

"What else do you need for your part of the operation?" she asked. She would be a fool to discount any advice from him. He'd been designed and programmed for impossible operations—which she hoped this wasn't one.

If you could get Mr. Faxton to quit whining, that would be helpful.

City bit her lip, exchanging an amused look with Kraye. Rita was definitely developing a personality. "I'm a Marine, not a magician. Sorry about that."

She understood the diplomat's frustration. What he didn't understand was that up here or down there, neither would be a cake walk. Both ships were probably going to be dodging bogies and possibly under fire. She tapped her controls, pulling up a representation of the system they were about to drop into. The data was old, of course. Their probe data was a snap shot of how it had been. None of those ship positions were current, and it was possible they'd be facing more than two ships by now. She frowned at it.

"Rita, can you add our drop in point?" City was a decent strategist, but this was not her arena. It flashed onto the holo. They would have to drop at an angle, or they'd run into the planet before they could apply the speed brakes.

"What's our braking path?" Kraye asked. Rita added that, too.

"If you were setting a trap for us, Bull, what would you do?"

It looked small in the holo but it was a lot of real estate—or space estate—they'd be navigating when they got there. If he'd been human, he'd have taken a breath and time to think, but he was robot and could do thousands of simultaneous calculations in a nanosecond.

"Without the complicity of the planet authorities, they won't be able to set mines."

It was the qualifier that was troubling. "Could they get that kind of agreement?"

"The usual—" Kraye hesitated.

"Suspects?" City offered.

He smiled. "Yes, the usual suspects for this kind of interdiction would not be able to secure an agreement with a legitimate government."

Legitimate. Another troubling qualifier.

Actually, the fact that their passengers didn't want to arrive through official channels might indicate the government wasn't legit. Which brought her back to: what had she been thinking to do this? Usually, she was level-headed and matter-of-fact. She did her job, and she was good at it, but this was not her job. And yet here she was. Her gaze intersected with Kraye's and she felt a tremor of unease, an inkling of why she said aye, aye instead of "yeah, that will never happen."

She'd trained with guys, worked with guys all the time. There were women in the military but there were a lot more men. Tall ones. Short ones. Middle range ones. Jerks and heroes. She liked some, didn't like others. She'd dated some, kissed a few, but…

She shouldn't be thinking about kissing, not here and now. She'd let her thoughts go down the rabbit hole to something she had neither the time, nor the inclination to face. Of course, thinking about not facing it was a lot like facing it because she had to know what she wasn't facing to not face it.

Okay, so she liked Kraye. So she felt more comfortable with him than anyone she'd dated. She might even get tingly and warm around him and yes, she wondered what kissing him would be like. But that was it. Totally it. Nothing more to see here, so thoughts move along.

Luckily no one had been inside her head because the conversation had continued without her. She checked back in, and after a moment, realized they had decided they needed to assume that anything and everything could go wrong so they should plan for all of it. She nodded like she'd kept up.

Kraye sent a look toward Bull. "So sensor nets are probably their best option."

"I do not believe they wish to destroy this ship unless forced to."

She felt a twinge of unease, which did not surprise her. Who wanted to be captured by aliens? "There hasn't been time for news to filter back about what we did to, you know, the spider?"

Kraye looked at Bull. Bull looked at Kraye. Kraye shrugged, possibly because Bull couldn't.

"So, what's the plan? You know how to beat the net thing, right?"

～

KRAYE WENT with Caro to the cargo bay to bid the *Pinyains* and the *Erinaceines* farewell. The habitat was quieter with the stream of water turned off. Neither species required a water habitat. The small channel where the water had cycled had been moved to the side and secured with special restraints.

Faxton and his female were not in sight though the one called Dr. Dauwn was in the clutches of the *Pinyains* when they entered. He did not appear to mind. When the two bear-like creatures released him and rushed them, he rose and straightened his clothing.

One bear tumbled against Kraye, almost knocking him to the ground.

"Are we there yet?"

Caro's gaze met his over their heads and his heart gave a strange lurch, as if it had moved in his chest. He did not know if he could trust his sense that something had changed between them. It seemed as if her eyes probed his, asked him something. He must get it right or—he did not know what might happen, just that it mattered to get it right.

Caro's caticorn nudged the leg not being clutched. When he looked down, he nodded toward Caro, the look in his eyes very aware.

"Caro." The name escaped his closed throat. It was only the second time he'd used her name since she gave him permission to do so.

Her head tipped to one side, and he realized she knew this, that she had noticed.

"I am glad I am here." Releasing the words lightened the heaviness in his chest, eased his breathing, though his heart felt as if it pounded as hard as if he were in a battle. There were more words he wished to speak to her, but this was a start. A good start, he realized, as a smile bloomed on her face.

The movement of the creatures made her stagger as the other demanded, "Are we there yet?"

She glanced at Kraye once more before kneeling to face the creature.

"We're almost there."

He sensed the words meant more than a destination for their passengers, or perhaps it was that he hoped that her words meant more.

IT HAD BEEN EASIER than she expected to turn control of the *Emissary* over to Kraye for the drop into normal space. She was a pilot, but not a combat pilot, no matter how many practice sims she'd gone through. And she hadn't made sergeant by not using her resources to their best effect.

That didn't make it easy to be in the second seat when her people's lives were on the line.

She activated her comm. "Bull, are you a go for shuttle launch?"

"We are a go, Sergeant City."

He might have to always sound calm, but it was reassuring at the moment. If anyone could get the *Pinyains* and the *Erinaceines* safely home, he was the man, or the robot. She just hoped they had a ship to return to when he finished his part.

Their other passengers were strapped down. City had briefed the *Harparian*, who left no doubt she was not pleased. Boy, was there no doubt. City had offered to let her use one of the other shuttles as a hide while they worked things out. To her credit, she'd refused. Or she'd figured out that being stranded by herself in a shuttle wasn't optimum either.

It had started to sink into Faxton and his team that things were about to get hot. He'd probably had a very different picture of how this mission would play out. Reality bites sometimes. She'd thought it, but she didn't say it. Instead she offered them a shuttle hideout, too, with a bit of Rita at the controls. He'd hesitated longer than the bird before refusing. Maybe he'd been a diplomat so long, he couldn't do expression, but he nailed sober.

"Counting down to normal space reentry," she said, broadcasting ship wide. "Brace for bumpy."

She didn't tell Bull to do anything. He'd know what to do faster than she could think it, let alone say it.

The bridge was silent. No music. Rita's sentient presence was on the shuttle with Bull and Rocky. She couldn't hear her breathing because her heart was thumping too hard as adrenalin began to bleed into her system.

Her body registered the change as the ship dropped into normal space. The stretch in one direction, then the other. The snap back to normal until Kraye applied the speed brakes. Bumpy got super-sized as he tried to slow enough for the shuttle to launch.

Sensors flashed and blared all over her board.

"I'm guessing those are caused by the sensor net," she said, her hands moving on the controls as she nudged the system to give them an update on system threats.

"Very many sensor nets. Someone has invested much in capturing this ship," Kraye said, almost absently.

He had gone into what City called his robot mode. No expression, gaze hyper-alert. He was a dang good ship driver, too. They'd discussed pre-programmed evasive maneuvers, but Bull made the case for trusting Kraye's instincts, well, he'd suggested it and since he was the super soldier, that was the same as making the case.

The *Najer* had a special program for confusing sensor nets that this ship did not have. So Bull had rigged up something that would broadcast code that wouldn't stop it but would give it a headache—and hopefully enough time for them to get cloaked before anyone got a lock on them.

Her heads up display began to update. One, two, four, five bogeys. It could have been worse. She must have said this out loud.

"They split their forces in case we changed our plans and set course for Teuhhopse instead of coming here," Kraye said, his tone as flat as Bull's.

"We've got two close enough to shoot at us." And she couldn't put her shields up until the shuttle was launched and was far enough away. Somehow she managed to watch their forward speed drop, and the countdown clock for the shuttle launch. "They have launched something at us."

She tracked the incoming. "It's going to miss—did they fire a warning shot at us?"

"Bull theorized they wished to capture this ship."

Which was all well and good if they didn't accidentally hit the shuttle. It was going to be close, but Bull could see the same data she could. Time seemed to stretch and slow even though the tick of seconds did not change on her console. The warning round passed close enough to rock the ship, or that might be caused by the shuttle—

"Shuttle is away." This time the countdown was shorter, but it felt like they were all in slow motion as she waited for, then activated shields and cloak.

They'd bounced tactical ideas off each other, everything from a full stop, low systems to a balls-to-the-wall, move-and-shoot, keep them off guard strategy. Though City personally liked the more aggressive approach, she hadn't been sent here to start a war, even if that war might be with friends of the spider they'd stepped on.

The factor they couldn't predict was how well this unknown enemy could track them. They'd counted on the cloak before and found out the spider had had Garradian sensors. This ship was the last and best—but that didn't mean every system was shiny. If even one of the bogey's could "see" through their cloak, they were hosed.

So they'd decided on a fox and the hounds strategy, designed to determine how much the enemy could see. The system had a few smaller planetary bodies and anomalies they hoped to use to mix things up. All they needed was to know how good the enemy could sniff and to not get shot.

In addition to the comet drive, the ship was equipped with a regular jump drive, similar to the ones the Project Enterprise ships used. These drives could make smaller jumps—which also left a trackable energy signature—but some of the smaller bodies and rocks had magnetospheres they could use to confuse their sensors.

"Initiating the first jump," Kraye said.

"I'll keep an eye on the hounds," City murmured.

THE WARNING SHOT made the shuttle rock as it passed them, nudging them off course. The deliberate miss confirmed OxeroidR's assessment that the goal was capture. What was not clear was who or what was the priority target? How much information had been passed on? The *Testudinians* had known the ships passengers, but would not have known much about the *Emissary's* capabilities. Had they known he was on board?

It was often the case that they became the priority target once it was known he or his other ship mates were around.

He made the course adjustment even as his internal systems continued analyzing the external threat profile. He was capable of flying this ship, asking questions, and feeling concern for the *Emissary* without impacting his effectiveness. He was also unable to escape his internal assessment of their chances. His programming gave them below even odds. Oddly enough, he was more optimistic than his programming. Kraye was a good pilot for a human and the sergeant had a pleasingly devious mind. And he was, as the sergeant would say it, pretty badass.

"How are we doing?" Rocky asked. He was strapped in the co-pilot's seat for the flight, though OxeroidR was not certain how well the harness would secure his small body.

OxeroidR missed having him on his shoulder even though his robot body could not feel him there.

"We are not being targeted by any of the hostile ships as yet."

Then we will prepare for ground interdiction.

Rita did not sound overly concerned. Her words were for Rocky. Their processors had already exchanged data on a possible problem before they'd boarded the shuttle.

"But they can't see us," Rocky protested.

"As we pass through atmosphere, it is possible we will become partially visible to some tracking systems."

And we don't know what systems they have.

Systems that could track them could have been provided by the hostile forces as payment for letting them attempt to intercept the *Emissary* in their system.

OxeroidR activated the shuttle's communication systems. "We will be entering the planet's atmosphere. The ride may become uncomfortable."

The *Pinyains* and the *Erinaceines* had been carefully secured for the ride, but he wished to keep them informed. It was, as he knew, challenging to be cut off from the information stream. Their former masters had done this, not aware that it was torture for the beings they considered mere machines.

When do you anticipate a problem?

"When we are entering the atmosphere or soon after. It will be harder for us to adjust course at entry acceleration."

I am detecting surface weapons coming online.

KRAYE MIGHT HAVE FELT a measure of relief when they reached the magnetosphere without taking any hits. It had taken time for the enemy to register—track?—their movement and react. And it had taken more time for him to see their reaction. While a battle was never a good option, if it could be avoided, navigating was more optimal in atmosphere than out where thrust and counter thrust had to be calculated. It also took longer for a change in momentum once thrust had been deployed.

They'd had a plan, but the movement of the enemy had already forced them to change tactics.

Caro, who became even more strategic under attack, had been proposing—and sometimes—discarding ideas, even as she kept him informed about enemy movement. Some he'd had to disprove, but others showed promise. He particularly liked the one where they activated the phase cloak and slipped inside one of the smaller planetary bodies orbiting the larger planet and watched the hunt.

The only problem with this plan was that it did not have an option for retrieving the shuttle. If their enemies were clever—and he had already seen signs they were both clever and dangerous—they could fall back, forming a screen between them and the planet, forcing them into a confrontation if they wanted to rendezvous with the shuttle. They'd seen the shuttle. They would know its purpose. If the ground forces did not take it down, then it represented their last, best chance to capture them all.

What he wanted to do was draw the enemy away from the planet—an enemy who would not wish to be drawn away. *Emissary* would have to present a tempting enough target to get all of them to abandon their picket line.

"They are barking around us," Caro said, sounding satisfied. "Just like hounds on the scent."

Out of the corner of his eye, he saw her tapping a finger on her lips. If they survived this, he would be brave. He would find a way to taste those lips.

"Of course, they also know where we are, which was not the plan."

Kraye gave a philosophical shrug. "It is what it is."

"Yeah, but I want it to be the is that I want it to be." She shot him a quick grin. "They won't be easy to shift. We need them to think that what they see is real without getting real if you know what I mean."

He blinked. She'd said the same thing in a variety of ways, but this might be the one that made his mind hurt the most.

"What about that nebula? Can we do anything with that?"

"It will not provide as much cover as a magnetosphere."

She stiffened. "What about a probe? Could we send one toward the nebula when we know the shuttle is heading back our way?" She zoomed in on the nebula. "It's not as far out as I'd like, but nothing really is. Don't you hate when all the spatial things hang together?"

He blinked again. "Yes." He was not certain what he agreed to, but he believed it would improve his chances for kissing if he agreed with her when he could.

"I wish we had Rita for this. Well, we'll see what I can do, won't we?"

～

THE GROUND DEFENSES launched on the edge of too late. It was all OxeroidR needed. The missiles passed over them as he dropped the shuttle down to the tree line. He knew he could pilot the shuttle in extreme conditions. He was not certain the shuttle could handle that level of extreme.

"A positive outcome is not certain," he told Rocky.

The small creature seemed to relax in the seat. "It is what it is."

If he had had a mouth, he would have smiled.

As his processors made minute course changes to avoid sudden obstacles, his sentient self wondered —not for the first time—what Rocky saw, why he had become his friend. He was more than a pet. Unlike the sergeant's caticorn, Rocky was a sentient being who could have gone home, had he desired it. While he—or his other crew mates—could not articulate the compulsion they felt to return these species to their homes, Rocky alone seemed to understand.

"Are you prepared, Rita?" he asked, as they closed on the coordinates their passengers had given them. He did not have to ask this, or discover if she were scanning for additional threats. She would be doing all she could, just as he was. The actual drop off should not be difficult. Even his processors could not produce a reason for their passengers to betray them, but he could not discount the possibility.

I am ready. There was a pause, then just ahead of the sensor alarms, she added, *a weapon has locked onto us.*

His processors located a series of canyons that might serve him if they could reach them in time. And if the shuttle could handle the braking and then bank it would require to enter it. He kicked up the speed, edging even closer to the ground.

"I thank you for being my friends," he said, the countdown to impact and the turn perilously close together.

~

"THE SHUTTLE IS BEING TRACKED by a heat seeker," City said. If they lost Bull, their chances of finishing the mission and getting back to Garradian space dropped pretty close to zero. If might also cause the scary eagle to lose confidence. It was hard not to ponder those claws. If she decided to take over and try to make a better deal for herself, none of them would be able to stop her.

The hounds sniffing around their patch of magnetosphere had launched various non-lethal weapons at them, creating some insta-bility that could, as Kraye had pointed out, result in a negative outcome for them. The turbulence was also making their human passengers airsick. Space sick? If there'd been time, City might have barfed up something.

"There is some kind of energy building in that bigger ship," she told Kraye.

Kraye, whose expression of robotic calm had not altered, shot her readings a quick look.

"That is concerning," he said. "They are trying to disrupt the magnetic field. This could also disrupt our engines. We will have to leave whether the shuttle is ready to rendezvous or not."

And when they did, the bogeys would know what to do to flush them out if they tried to use one of the other magnetospheres.

"I think my probe is ready to fire." Lucky for her the program-ming was already in the system and Rita had left enough of herself behind to help introduce a glitch in the programming so that the cloak would appear to be failing. The harder part was getting the glitch-glimpses to look like a ship and not a probe. If she were inclined to panic, all she had to do was remind herself that even if it worked, they were probably hosed.

~

THE SHUTTLE HELD TOGETHER, though it put out many warnings indicating it was not happy. The narrow canyons required the attention of many of OxeroidR's processors and the heat seeker had climbed, found them and was trying to reacquire.

I am deploying our counter measures. Our LZ is in thirty clicks.

His processors automatically translated this into a distance he could understand. He activated the comm. "Prepare to disembark. We won't have long on the ground."

It was as well the *Testudinians* were already gone. Had they been betrayed or the betrayers? It troubled him that they might have delivered them back into captivity.

He began to slow the shuttle, braking slowly at first, but as the numbers ran down, he upped the reverse thrust.

There is no sign of other pursuit. No life signs in the LZ.

The shuttle whined in protest, but stopped and dropped down. He activated the back hatch and the comms at the same time.

"We are there."

AT FIRST ONLY THE bigger ship started after the probe, but after a tense wait, the other ships broke their line, too. It was the first encouraging sign since they'd dropped out of comet space.

"They all want a piece of us," City said. "Shuttle is heading our way."

Ground fire followed them up.

Kraye had already started the *Emissary* in that direction.

"If we slow down to pick them up—" Caro began, her gaze on the numbers.

"We will not make it. OxeroidR knows this, too. I have set an intercept course. I will attempt to match their speed and angle for boarding."

City opened her mouth to protest, but he was right. The shuttle would have one shot at it, but once inside…

"What if I activate the field we used to protect our passengers? It might cushion the impact."

Kraye gave a sharp nod.

City said "make it so" to herself and activated the field. And then she activated the comm.

"Brace for impact."

OXEROIDR TRACKED their flight path and that of the *Emissary*, making necessary adjustments to avoid ground fire and make their intercept. The enemy ships had turned back from their pursuit of the decoy probe. One of the smaller, faster ships would get there before them if he slowed too much. He considered the hanger bay. They would need at least one shuttle at their next destination. Could he bring this shuttle in without critically damaging the *Emissary*, the other shuttles, or themselves?

The comm crackled.

"I've activated the energy net we used for our passengers. Can you point your nose toward the cargo bay as you come on board?" Sergeant City asked.

"I can," he informed her.

Rocky gave him a skeptical look. "You can?"

"I can try." For a nanosecond he considered breaking off the approach and ramming the incoming ship. It would allow the *Emissary* to escape, but what happened when they reached Teuhhopse?

As if he followed OxeroidR's thoughts, Rocky said, "They'll never make it without you."

This was true.

They broke free of the upper atmosphere. On his systems, he tracked the shuttle and the *Emissary* as they closed on each other. The *Emissary* dropped its cloak and fired something at the forward enemy ship.

For the first time in a long time, he felt time move both fast and slow.

The *Emissary* grew larger on his view screen and his tracking screen.

The bay doors retracted, some small debris was sucked out as it decompressed.

He reversed thrust.

The shuttle slowed but not enough.

They were inside the bay.

Heading toward the parked shuttles and the back wall.

He activated a brief side thrust.

There were sounds of metal screeching as they changed direction.

The cargo bay doors came briefly into view.

They slammed into the energy net with a lurch.

He saw Rocky launch toward the view screen.

Caught him just prior to impact.

His body slammed into the restraints as he and the ship jerked forward and then back.

Lights flashed on the comms and alarms sounded.

He tried the comms. "Shuttle is on board."

Chapter 6

Everyone looked hammered but the *Harparian* and Bull. Rocky looked like he was taking a nap on the robot's shoulder, so she wasn't sure which camp to put him in.

If there'd been a safe place to be dropped off? Faxton and his team would have begged for it. This was not the adventure they'd signed up for.

"In the past, I could have identified several places they could wait in relative safety," OxeroidR told them during yet another meeting in City's ready room. "But I do not believe there is a safe place in this system for any of us."

And that, City knew, included their destination: Teuhhopse. City sighed silently as she studied each one of Faxton's team.

Brittani had acquired a black eye during their rendezvous with the shuttle, and she packed up her dresses, her foxtrot mike shoes, and her smooth facade. She looked like someone who had figured out that wearing red on this ship was a bad idea.

Dr. Dauwn, on the other hand, looked like the absent-minded college professor who was late for class. He was someone City hadn't figured out. She looked at him and saw him, but...he was also out of focus, the edges soft rather than sharp like Britanni.

Faxton. City considered him as she waited for his response to OxeroidR's risk assessment, he might have her a bit puzzled, too. Bland had mostly given way to grim, but he wasn't whining anymore. He'd finally realized that none of his people should be here. If he'd lobbied for this, well, he should have remembered that curse.

Be careful what you wish for.

His gaze moved briefly from Brittani to Dauwn and then he said, "We'll stick with you."

City nodded. Her eyes felt like grit and she didn't know if she'd get any bunk time before the next round of FUBAR started. Standard operating procedure, in fact. "All right then. Rita, what's our damage assessment?"

She and the robot had been checking things out, both through the system and visually. The cameras had sustained impact damage, so Bull had broadcast a view of the damage and Rocky had scouted around with a camera on his little noggin. They'd taken out the port lift to the cargo bay. Luckily, the starboard lift still worked. They'd need it to get to the two shuttles that were left. She offered a silent prayer of gratitude that Bull had only clipped one and completely missed the other.

"There would be more damage if you had not used the energy net," Bull told her.

Did the robot read minds now?

There is some collateral structural damage to the hull in that section. I would not advise using the comet drive at fullest speed until it can be assessed at a repair facility.

Yeah, they could stop by one of those space stations, oh wait, everyone wanted to shoot them or capture them. No wonder Faxton looked discouraged. He'd come here to make friends. It was not his fault they'd picked a bad neighborhood. At least General Halliwell should understand if—when they made it back. He'd run into trouble his first hop out of their galaxy. At least she hadn't started a war, at least not yet.

"So we can't get to Teuhhopse fast." She'd been hoping to bust a move and surprise the opposition, put them on the hop this time around.

I believe that we can travel at two-thirds speed.

So faster than they'd been going. That was something. She waited for someone to ask why Rita hadn't used the word "safely" but no one did. They'd all figured out that nothing about this operation was "safety approved."

"Do we have a plan for when we get there?" Faxton asked.

"We have only begun receiving data from the probe," Kraye said.

"Have you had a chance to look at it?" City asked. He shook his head. "Well, let's see it." They might as well know the worst.

The hologram formed in the center of the table, spinning slowly as it gave them their first look at the region around the planet of Teuhhopse. City inhaled sharply. This was out of date, thanks to the laws of physics, but— "Is that right? No bogeys? Nothing?"

"I also expected to see enemy ships," Bull said.

She could tell by the movement of his red eyes that he was processing the incoming data. She bit her lip, considering the whys and wherefores of this change in tactics. She did not assume they weren't going to make a last try at the ship. Or their passenger? She was a scary looking bird, but what else might she be?

"Isn't it good that there are no ships waiting for us?" Faxton asked.

Poor guy actually looked more cheerful. *Dude.*

"It's a different kind of trap," she said, finally.

"I concur," Bull said.

Faxton's face fell. "But…"

"They realized that we were ready for them the last time," Kraye said. "Most likely they have deployed signal buoys that will alert them when we arrive."

"Well, we can't plan for their plan until we see what's involved in getting Lady Yodrirka home." She used the word deliberately. Home had emotional resonance. It was why they were here and not for a diplomatic score. "Let's zoom in on the planet surface, Rita."

The hologram began a slow zoom in on Teuhhopse.

There is a humanoid presence.

Her tone was a bit tour guide, which almost made City grin, except she was too tired to waste her energy on a grin.

Only one of the concentrations of humanoids has indications of technology and possible space capability.

"May we see that concentration?" Bull asked.

Rita brought that region in close. At first City saw mountains, then trees came into view. It took her several seconds to realize the trees and possibly some of the mountains were buildings. It was a sense that they looked wrong, more than a certainty about them. Lights twinkled in a murk that looked like a scene from a *Star Wars* movie, but these humanoids didn't live in treehouses. There weren't bridges and hanging vines. The trees weren't trees. The mountains nestled near the fake trees looked constructed, too. Too much precision along the edges. The colors were right, forest and mountain, the scene washed with greens, browns, grays, and blues. It was the same color palette as the swans' world, but these were richer, more vibrant and yet the end result was somewhat the same.

Camouflage. All of it designed to merge with the larger environment. If this was reality? It was possible it was a hologram.

"Can you add heat signatures to the current view?" she asked.

Rita obliged. The dispersion of the signatures looked right. How did the "hiding" work for them? Surely they weren't the only space capable types with heat signature detection technology? "What do you think, B—OxeroidR?"

"There is deception intended."

But without a closer look…bang went Faxton's last hope. She looked at the scary bird.

"Do you know what they are trying to hide?"

Her feathers ruffled as if she shivered. Could birds shiver?

"I have not been inside the tree city."

City considered pushing back against this non-answer, but she also didn't want to give Faxton hope. They had no reason to check out the tree city.

"How many heat signatures?" Kraye asked.

Around ten thousand. Not all are humanoid.

Rita tightened the view. The smaller signatures could be pets, or non-human citizens, she mentally amended. She glanced down at Tiger, sitting alertly on her lap. He appeared to be studying the holo as closely as everyone else. Not for the first time, she wished she knew what he was thinking about things, if for no other reason than that he'd been all over the ship, listening and perhaps hearing conversations. He was her version of "if only the walls could talk."

And there was also the fact that Tiger seemed to be the only species on board that Lady Yodrirka didn't appear to mind. When City had freed the bird from captivity, Tiger was the only other freed prisoner that had sat with her. It was a puzzle among many puzzles she didn't have time to be troubled about. A puzzle she hoped didn't come back to bite her on the butt.

"What about the other humanoid locations?" City asked. She ran a hand absently down the caticorn's back. His fur was more cat-like than a horse, which she did not mind—though the tail was all horse tail.

The view zoomed out and then closed in on one of the other locations.

This one made no effort to hide, either the people or the rustic nature of it. This was more than structures and heat signatures. They could be seen. Crude huts, smoke fires, and a population that looked like it was straight out of a dystopian movie.

Something in the way they moved bothered her.

"Why the difference?" she murmured, glancing at Kraye.

He stared at the hologram, his body oddly rigid, the color gone from his face. His hands rested on the table looking unnaturally relaxed. As he felt her gaze, his head turned her direction and the look in his eyes killed any questions she might have asked.

Her caticorn jumped from her lap to his and leaned in. Kraye's hands lifted from the table to rest lightly on the caticorn's back and one of them trembled briefly before going still once more. Her caticorn purred-neighed and nuzzled against Kraye.

No one else appeared to have noticed the byplay, so she turned her attention back to the hologram. As she watched, some kind of airborne craft buzzed past the crude village. Heads lifted, the people freezing in place until it passed them.

I was a slave. Now I am free.

Resignation. That was what she saw in the way the people moved. This felt important, but she couldn't figure out why. These people were not why they were here. If not for the previous attacks, they would have tried to make contact with the humanoids in the other city. There was no point in trying to open negotiations with people who weren't 'out there.' But now she wanted to drop off the *Harparian* and get the heck back to their own region of space.

She looked at Lady Yodrirka as she asked the question. "What about the *Harparians*? Can we take a look at the mountains?"

The Lady didn't move, but her stare bored into City.

There are many high peaks, but there is some metal or element in them that resists the probe's scanners. It did not pick up any heat signatures comparable to the Lady's from the high peaks. Or the low peaks. Or anywhere.

She changed the image to the mountain peaks, but it was like looking at a smudged photograph. Were they seeing what was there? It felt wrong. All of this felt wrong.

There is one other area of possible concern.

"Let's see it," City said, after another quick look at the still rigid Kraye.

The holo zoomed in once more, the dive into an area of old, not quite dead forest made her stomach bump like she was on a roller coaster. The view steadied. Her hands curled into fists.

"What is that?" Faxton asked.

"Webs," City said, surprised at how calm she sounded. "Spider webs." She paused. "I hate spiders."

KRAYE STARED at the simulated view of outside this spaceship while he fought through waves of—he did not know. It was worse than any storm he'd experienced on any planet. But this was a storm inside. He did not recognize these feelings or the memories trying to break out of some dark place in his memory.

Memory. How could he remember, with such fear, something he'd never seen before?

Why did the sight of that village fill him with panic? His hand covered his chest. Pain, it...hurt. Grief? Was that what he felt? He lifted a hand, surprised to find his face dry. Inside it felt as if he cried like a child—

The word triggered flashing images, many too fast in their appearance and disappearance to register. But faces. Crying. A child crying, begging...

He would not, he could not—

His door buzzed, and he swung around, relieved at the distraction, but fearing what might be seen on his face. He fought back to a place of calm, but it was not a secure perch. More like a high place in a stormy flood.

"Open," he said.

The hatch slid back and Caro stood there, her expression concerned.

"Are you all right?"

I am not. I never will be again.

"I am well." The lie came out stiffly.

She hesitated. "Can I come in?"

He wanted her to come in, to hold him, to pull him out of the storm. He wanted her to leave before she saw into its dark heart—

He nodded.

She entered, and the hatch slid shut.

The silence weighed on him. He wished to turn away from her eyes, but the concern in them held him in place, offered faint hope that his fear and panic did not disgust her. She moved closer and then closer still.

The warmth of her pushed at the storm and he twitched.

Her hand lifted. He watched it, strangely detached, as it approached.

She is going to hit me.

The thought startled him out of his detachment. Caro would not hit him—her hand, her palm settled against his cheek and sent

136

warmth, healing warmth out against the flood, the storm. He shuddered.

Her other hand settled on the other cheek, her gaze holding his.

"Did you come from Teuhhopse, Kraye?"

"I do not know," he almost gasped the words, his head drooping until it rested on her shoulder. Her arms circled him now, held him close.

"Do you want to know?" she asked.

Did he? No! His soul cried out. Inside he shrank from it, huddling like a child. *A child.* He'd still been small when he'd been brought on board the *Najer.* Then he had believed he'd exchanged one master for another. As time passed, he'd realized he was not a slave on the *Najer.* It was a refuge. It took longer for it to become home, or for him to become a member of the crew. What he'd been before his two lives? He hadn't known there was a gap.

"No." His voice was quieter. She anchored him here. He turned his face into her neck and inhaled her scent. His hands came up, landing lightly at her waist. She did not pull away. He'd never been this close to a female—but was that true? A distant memory taunted him from behind the storm Caro had pushed back. A soft embrace carrying the scent of the rain and wood. The memories threatened to drive them apart. His hands clenched, then slid around her. He held on. It seemed as if his life depended on it.

He'd felt desire when he looked at her, but right now he huddled into her warmth, clung to the peace she promised if he could just get close enough. He sensed, he did not know how, that if he turned aside now, he would lose more than Caro. She deserved a man who was whole, one brave enough to face the storm.

"But I must know."

She eased back, her hands resting at his waist, their warmth a lifeline, her gaze steady and kind. She looked weary, and he felt guilt stab through his need for her. He smoothed her hair back, surprised his hand was steady.

"You are weary."

"It won't kill me." Her lips quirked at the edges.

"What?" he asked, not surprised his voice was rough edged.

She shook her head. "I just...am I the only one who wonders what we were thinking to do this in the first place?"

"No," he found he could almost smile. He hesitated. "Everyone should be able to go...home." He said the word with the realization that its meaning for him was blurred, out of focus.

"We have a similar saying about not leaving our people behind."

"And do you always secure them?"

She shook her head. "Sometimes we fail, but we try, because we'd want that for ourselves, we'd want to be brought home."

His heart chilled. She was speaking of their dead now. She feared she would fail to bring her people home. Now he touched her cheek. The skin was soft, his touch releasing her scent. He inhaled it greedily. Her home was far from his, in more than light years. If she went home, he would lose her. He was starting to realize how much he feared that, feared it more than what he might find on Teuhhopse.

"Then we will try," he said.

CITY WAS NOT THRILLED to be alone with Lady Yodrirka, well, almost alone. Tiger was curled up on one of the ready room chairs, his cat's ears up, his expression alert and interested. In fact, he kind of reminded her of a referee, the way his head turned to her, to the Lady, then back to her.

City had never felt so Picard. Ready room for starters. Her hands were clasped behind her back, her chin was up, the table was between her and the bird. The uniform was different and there was no Earl Grey tea, but she channeled him because she needed to be the Captain at this moment.

She needed the bird to talk.

The bird was still, not even her eyes moved as she watched City. Those eyes. It took channeling Picard and all the other *Star Trek* captains to hold it.

"You wished to speak with me, Sergeant City?"

Her voice was as deep and old as her eyes, with the timbre of a mountain storm.

Yeah, it was that cold.

Was the "Sergeant" a push back against the captain channeling?

"Yes, I did. You've seen what's happened at our other…stops. I don't know if they are after you, your ally, OxeroidR, or both of you—"

"You don't believe this ship is an attractive acquisition?"

"I'm sure that this ship interests someone. Now. But no one knew about it before. We think the *Testudinians* either talked or were coerced into talking."

"The robot knew. And his human."

"We both know that if OxeroidR wanted to take this ship, it would already be his."

The bird's head moved in what could be a nod. For the first time, she moved, turning to pace slowly over to a painting that had come with the ship, her claws clicking ominously against the uncarpeted flooring. City didn't know where or when the painting had been created. It was a place she wouldn't mind seeing. A place of blue mountains and a purple lake. Both familiar and alien at the same time.

"True." She turned to face City once more.

"Bull and I have been looking at the probe data. We've identified an area where we can drop you off. This time we'll take the *Emissary* down, use the scan dampening effect of your mountains to confuse them. You fly your way and we fly ours."

The Lady continued to stare at her. Not a feather ruffled, so why did City feel distrust emanating from her? What was her deal?

"We are concerned about ground defenses. Can you give us any insights to what we might encounter during atmosphere entry?"

"Such as?"

"Ground to air or ground to space weapons? Be a pity to be shot out of the sky this close to your home."

The Lady walked the other direction, then turned to face City. "You are not going to open communications with the humanoids? That is what your Mr. Faxton desires, is it not?"

Faxton had started to set his sights on getting home. City cocked her head. "Should we?"

"Is that not what you do? Make treaties with other humanoids?"

"That knowledge is above my pay grade, but from what I've observed, we've only recently encountered non-human species. Mr. Faxton's brief for this mission, with the help of Dr. Dauwn, who specializes in non-human species, was to explore our options there." Jeez, she sounded like a diplomat. But had she been careful enough? She let her gaze do some boring into the bird's. "But my interests are about the security of this ship and everyone on it." She paused. "You fly high. Surely you have a good handle on the risks on your own planet."

"I would avoid the treehouse city," she finally said. "The hut dwellers are…acceptable, but what use will they be to you?" It was her turn to pause. "Unless you also see them as a…resource?"

"Resource." City felt the chill all the way to her toes. "You mean slaves."

"The others let them exist, provide some assistance, protection from the *S'Kassidaens*, and in return they pay tribute."

The *S'Kassidaens* were the spiders. "Tribute. What kind of tribute?"

"Ask the robot's human."

City clenched her hands behind her back. "I'm asking you."

The hooded gaze slid away. "I think you know."

"What is your relationship with the humans and the *S'Kassidaens*?" City was shocked at how calm she sounded.

"We stay as far away as we can from them."

City considered this. "Except you didn't."

"I…surrendered to them." Her wings extending and beat the air angrily. The force of it almost rocked City back on her heels. "They found my nest. My mate was killed. My fledglings were taken. I had no choice."

City dropped into a seat and rubbed her face. "Do you know what happened to them after—are they still alive?"

Perhaps it was something in her voice or her face that caused the bird to tuck her wings back in.

"I have seen them twice since. On a video link."

This was bad. "Do you know where they are?"

"In the *S'Kassidaen's* den, of course. If—"

City bit her lip. "What's to stop them from using them to make you surrender yourself again?" Even if she tried to free them, they knew they were coming. Or they would know by the time the *Emissary* was in Teuhhopse space.

The wings beat again. "I cannot leave my young in their hands. I will do what I must."

City eyed the talons flexing against the metal floor—leaving long gouges in it. So just turning around and heading home wasn't an option. And if they released the Lady, not only would she surrender again if she couldn't free the kids, she'd be a captive with a lot of information about them, about the expedition, and about the Garradian Universe.

Spiders. Were these the kin of the one they'd stepped on? Spiders had lots of babies, didn't they? She rubbed her temple. Okay, they had spiders. *We have a robot.* With a flying squirrel. And her Marines—Marines she couldn't order to do this. It was so far outside her brief.

She sighed. "Could we tune our sensors to find the—your young?"

"Why would you help me?"

City met her gaze without flinching. "You know we now have a mutual security issue. If they get their hands on you, they'll ask you about us, about this ship, where we came from. And you'll tell them to protect your young."

Her head nodded.

"But beyond that, we embarked on this mission to get you home. All the way home. Even if I am not…thrilled that the scope of the mission has expanded, we both know Bull won't stop until you and your young are safe." And he was the only one who could stop her taking over the ship to make them keep going. It was ironic knowing that he'd probably help her do it. "We could drop him in close, he frees the kids, they fly—"

"They cannot fly. They would not allow me to teach them to fly."

Birds that couldn't fly. City wanted to bang her head against the desk. Or a wall. "How big are they now?"

"Near my size."

It almost seemed as if the bird was amused about the piling on.

"Do…they have the same trust issues you have? Will you be able to convince them we're the good guys?"

She looked away, then back. "I do not know."

City would like to think this would make a difference with Bull. But it wouldn't. He was the only one not afraid of the bird. She glanced down at the grudges in the metal. Maybe he should be.

"Rita, can you work with the Lady to find her young?"

If they are there, I will find them.

City was not sure—no, it was better if they turned out to be on Teuhhopse, because Bull would insist on flying all over the place looking for them. For a robot with millions or possibly billions of processors, the dude could sure be single minded.

THEY'D DROPPED out of comet drive one jump away from Teuhhopse so they could get an updated look at the space around the planet. Bull believed they should launch another probe.

And they needed to share the plan with the team.

City was pleased that Kraye looked more like himself. What he'd learned had rocked him. It had rocked her. But she had a feeling he was used to quick recoveries. It had only been a few hours since they'd held each other. It felt longer.

She'd offered him one of the shuttles to see if he could find his past, but he'd refused. His lips had twisted wryly. "My past is—I prefer the present. I look to the future."

Had his gaze held hers with special significance? She'd hoped so as they'd entered the ready room together.

Okay, she liked thinking that too much.

Today the ready room looked bigger because there were fewer

participants in this council, with one new addition: her second in command, Corporal Jenkins. He was a good Marine and would take over if something happened to her. And her men needed to know. Boy, did they need to know.

Bull was there with Rocky. Tiger had settled near Lady Yodrirka. Rita was always with them. It didn't take long to brief them on what she'd learned and then Rita showed them where the not-so-young were being held.

She and Bull had seen the data and had had time to process it. Okay, Bull had had time to process it. He was calling the shots because he was their only hope.

At least the hostages weren't being held in the spider den as the Lady and City had feared. She had a feeling it was a much harder target. She'd seen *Lord of the Rings* and *Harry Potter*.

But she and Bull agreed that the appearance of it being a softer target was part of the trap being set for the Lady. On the plus side, the enemy might not be expecting them to help the Lady. It depended on how good they were at planning for the unexpected. Bull believed they needed to expect them to plan for everything or they weren't planning for the unexpected. This, while mind bending, also red lined the plus side.

So far all they'd observed in the probe scans were humanoids moving around the encampment. But that did not mean that the spiders wouldn't be there.

City didn't need Bull or the Lady to connect the dots for her. The tree people "protected" the hut people from the spiders by working with the spiders. It was on a spider's ship where they'd found the captured bird. Those spiders got around which was a strong incentive not to give them access to intel on where this ship came from. This brought her back to, yeah, exceeding the mission brief, but not a lot of other options here.

"At our last look, the space around the planet is still free of bogeys. We think they have deployed buoys around the planet and are planning to hop in once we set one off." City figured they'd bring as many ships as they could get there but the bad guys lived with the same laws of physics that they did.

"How do you plan to deal with incoming bogeys?" Jenkins asked.

"We can't stop them from seeing us when we drop into normal space," Bull explained. "We will switch to cloak. They might also be able to track us by the turbulence the *Emissary* will cause when it enters the atmosphere."

"You're taking this ship down to the surface?" Jenkins might be having trouble with his stone face. "With all due respect, ma'am, this ship will be a sitting duck on the ground."

City's smile felt a bit evil. "Not necessarily. The mountains where the Lady's people live have some interesting sensor dampening properties. If we can locate an LZ there—"

He grinned. "They won't be able to see us."

"Exactly. And, as we're doing our atmospheric insertion, we'll grab what intel we can and adjust our plan if necessary." City gave Bull the nod to continue.

"We'll go into the mountains well away from where we plan to land, drop down and launch the shuttles, heading straight for our secondary LZ."

This time Jenkins blinked. "Straight for?"

"This ship has a phase cloak," City said. "It will spend energy, so we can't do it all the way to the encampment, but if they pick up anything, we'll be far enough from the *Emissary* when we switch to regular cloak. Even if they can track our movement somehow, they won't be able to track anything back to this ship."

His grin was wider this time though his eyes might also be a little wide at the thought of flying straight through a mountain. *Don't think about it* was the best she could offer if he asked. He didn't.

City turned to Bull. "Would you brief them on what happens next?"

He nodded and extended his body upright. A hologram activated in the center of the table.

"The young are located in an encampment that is centrally located between these three hut dweller settlements. It is possible that these settlements provide labor for the encampment."

The view moved in.

"There is humanoid activity during daylight that diminishes significantly after night fall."

The view changed to night.

"We've noted when the activity is at the lowest. That is when Bull and the Lady will go in," City said.

"Just Bull?" Jenkins did not look pleased.

"Once they have located and freed the hostages, we'll drop in and pick them up," City said evenly. She didn't mention persuasion might be necessary. It already looked enough like a Charlie Foxtrot. "There is a landing pad in the center that is large enough to accommodate one or both of our shuttles."

"Are you certain they won't see your shuttles approach?" Lady Yodrirka asked.

"It depends on the skill of their scanning tech," City admitted. They had to assume it was top notch.

"We can also make it harder by flying the shuttles in low, like just above the trees," Jenkins said.

City slanted Bull a look. "I know someone who can do that."

"You have two shuttles," the bird pointed out.

"We can tie the flight controls together," Bull said. "I will fly both shuttles during our approach, landing as close as possible. I will send a signal when we are ready for pickup."

City angled to look at the bird. "Can you be our eyes in the sky until we neutralize any opposition, at least until Bull needs you?"

"You do not wish me to be on the ground."

"You can hike to the encampment with Bull if you want to," City said, holding her scary gaze.

The bird gave a sound that almost sounded like a laugh.

"We can fit you with a head set so you can stay in touch, warn us if you see anything we need to know." Once she was on the ground, that edge went away but Rita would have the shuttles sensors cranked up, too. A lot of finger-crossing on this op.

"Questions? Concerns?" She surveyed her team.

"You gonna make some of us stay behind and guard the diplomatic team?" Jenkins asked.

"I'm going to let you volunteer to remain, but if no one wants to stay, Rita will watch out for them, won't you, Rita?"

A part of me will.

"She can be in two or three places at once," City told Jenkins.

He blinked. *"Oorah."*

"Indeed."

CITY FACED Faxton in the small communal space on the VIP deck. He looked ragged around the edges, but he managed one of his smooth smiles.

"No one shooting at us?"

"We're parked in a fairly remote sector in this system while we ready for the last hop," City said. "So far that's working for us."

He might have winced. "This is not the journey I expected."

"No." She'd known they wouldn't get what they expected, but it was obvious she hadn't set her expectations low enough either.

"You all have a role, tasks to perform." His wry smile was almost real. His expression rueful when he met hers. "I had hoped that we, that all of us would have more time to become acquainted."

City blinked tired eyes. Was that personal interest in there? Had he expected the love spaceship?

"I could have used more downtime," she admitted, especially more sack time. She shot him a look as if he'd heard her thoughts. Alone, thank you. Maybe if she hadn't met Kraye—

"I've been running sims—simulations." She'd been trying to get better at everything she might face out there. Bull had cranked them up so high she died during most of them. She didn't continue the confession. It would not build his confidence to find out she'd been practicing her combat flight and fighting skills and done a lot of dying while doing it.

"Will the *Emissary* be dodging around while you drop off the Lady?"

City considered him, then shook her head. "No, they'll be expecting that. We're going to land. You saw the data, or rather you didn't see the data about the Lady's mountains. We think we can hide there."

"Hide?" A frown spread slowly across his face. "Why would we need to hide? Aren't we going to land and release the Lady?"

City took a deep breath. The command structure was a little iffy here. He might think he was in charge. "We're going to launch a rescue mission."

He blinked. "Rescue?"

"The Lady wasn't captured like the other prisoners we found. She was forced to surrender because her offspring were being held hostage. This whole exercise is for nothing if we don't rescue the kids because they'll just force her to surrender again."

He stared at her. "And since they know she returned on this ship, they will require her to tell them all she knows about us and where we came from."

His shoulders rose and fell in a sigh. He turned away, paced several steps and turned to face her again.

"We have their location. We're going to try to get in and out as quietly as possible, using the remaining shuttles."

"You're going to leave the *Emissary*—" He stopped, turning to run a hand over his hair, then turning back to her. "And us. My team."

"Yes."

"And if they find the *Emissary* or you do not return?"

"Rita will lift off and initiate comet drive. She'll get you home." City might have crossed her fingers behind her back. Rita would have to get clear without getting destroyed. But if she could get the ship into comet drive, they would make it home.

"Possibly leaving you all in enemy hands?"

"Rita knows she can't rescue us if we get captured." Nor could she retrieve their bodies. She was a great AI, but she was not a magician.

"It could be a trap," he pointed out.

"It is a trap." It was City's turn to sigh. "I don't think they can plan well enough to deal with Bull—OxeroidR."

"He is a formidable opponent," Faxton agreed. He looked

down, then up, holding her gaze. "I'm not staying here. I took the training before joining the expedition. I…want to go with you."

His tone did not inspire confidence. He was scared. Smart man. And that was not the request she'd expected.

"With all due respect, sir, that training—"

"I realize it is not up to your level, but I passed. We all passed," he repeated. He gave her a wry grin. "I can shoot straight."

Why did the term "friendly fire" come into her head?

"You don't think the others—"

"Dr. Dauwn, perhaps not. I won't speak for Brittani, of course, but I expect her to make the same choice."

"Why?" While they were in the Teuhhopse system, there was no truly safe place, but they'd be better off with the ship, with Rita.

"I…we came to make a difference. If this is the only way, then I will go. In battle, numbers help, do they not?"

If the guns were pointed the right direction, but she did not say this. She nodded. "All right, but I'm asking everyone to verbally confirm their voluntary participation." If only Rita made it back, she wanted the truth known.

"Of course.

"Once I have that, I'll get Jenkins to set you up with gear." She hesitated. "The plan is to move as soon as we set down on Teuh-hopse. All personnel will need to be on board the shuttles before we make our last hop."

And it was unlikely that Faxton would have the opportunity to point, let alone shoot at anything. They were going in quiet and fast and getting out quiet and even faster. She ignored the chill dancing down her back as she left him.

THE BRIDGE of the *Emissary* was quiet. Even Rocky had left to eat. City entered and sank down into the co-pilot's station next to Bull. She might still be shocked that Faxton and Brittani had opted to join the assault force. Or she was too tired to feel anything.

No surprise Dr. Dauwn wanted to stay with the ship. He was a scientist and older than everyone else. Did he mind being left with a sentient AI? His absent-minded persona was too deep and wide for her to know.

She tapped the console, bringing up the list of people who had given their verbal agreement to join the rescue mission.

"Which shuttle should the Lady go in?" Perhaps what she really wanted to know was could they trust the bird not to betray them? There was no question that this was risky. She and her offspring could die. They could all die. What kind of premium did the bird put on freedom? Or would she rather live, let her young live in captivity?

Bull angled his body so that she could see the red slits of his eyes. "The *Harparian* should go with Rocky and me. The rest should deploy with you. The *Harparian* and her young will return in our shuttle."

"Once she's lifted off, I'll put a rifle team and Kraye on your shuttle?"

"Yes." It is possible he hesitated. "Your diplomatic team is going with us?"

"Not the scientist." He might look like he was inventing flubber, but he knew better than go into a possible hot zone. She hoped the other two would leave their red shirts on the *Emissary*. Or change their minds. "Do you trust her?"

Bull did not ask her who she meant. "I do not."

"But you'll try to help her."

"If we do not, then I will be required to kill her. We cannot risk her surrendering to the *S'Kassidaen's*."

"She knows too much." They'd already talked about this. "If it was me, I would want us to try," she admitted.

"You are honorable," Rocky popped his head up to say.

She eyed the squirrel. "You could stay here, you know."

The squirrel circled his patch of robot three times and then curled up once more.

"He can help," Bull said. He turned back to his controls. "Tiger will come with us, too."

149

Tiger? City blinked. She opened her mouth to protest, but closed it. Was she going to argue with the robot? Or a caticorn?

"You need to assign an operation name," Bull reminded her.

"Let's call it Operation…Motley Crew," she said.

CITY PAUSED with just the lower part of her battle armor in place. In an odd display of caticorn tact, Tiger had turned his back on her while she changed. Under the armor she wore her lightest weight uniform. Now that she was decent, she sank down by him and ran a hand down his back. He ramped up his purr, the one with a bit of neigh in it. And some whinny. It was strange, but comforting. Reminded her of sitting on the porch with her Grandma's cat on a warm summer day.

Wow, did that feel far away.

"I won't say there is a safe place to wait, Tiger, but if you stayed with the *Emissary* and Rita, or the part of Rita, you'd have a better chance." She'd seen close up scans of the area around the encampment. Trees as tall as redwoods, with massive trunks and huge patches of alien ferns—with leaf edges that looked like sharp spikes. A ground mist clung to all of it, hiding what could be lurking under there. He had the horn, but it only pointed one direction.

Best case, only she and her Marines would deploy around the shuttle while the hostages and the rescuers boarded. It was likely that the time of greatest danger would be after lift-off.

He looked up at her, his cat eyes so soulful she felt guilty for trying to save his life. He carefully angled his horn away from her and nuzzled against her hand, his purr-neigh increasing.

"What's your story?" she murmured, scratching under his raised chin.

He blinked. With a sigh, she gave him a final pat, rose and reached for the rest of her body armor. She slid one arm in, catching sight of the caticorn watching her with a look that was not cat-like—a look that disappeared when her gaze met his.

What *was* his story?

"WE'RE KEEPING the operational names from our last operation," Caro said, pacing in front of those involved in Operation Motley Crew. Kraye had blinked when he heard the name, but lacking a frame of reference for the term, he did not waste time pondering it.

She pulled up a hologram showing the ships and personnel.

"Golf Sierra Alpha, or GS Alpha, will include Bull as Alpha1, Rocky as Alpha2, Tiger as Alpha3, and the Lady Yodrirka as Alpha4. Once on the ground, the Lady, Alpha4, will fly cover."

Had she winced when she gave Rocky a code name? Kraye was not sure. He had seen her wince when she gave Tiger a code name. He noted some of those in the room looking at the caticorn on a chair next to the Lady, then exchanging looks.

"Golf Sierra Zulu, or GS Zulu, will carry everyone else. The order of command for our team is me as Zulu1, Kraye as Zulu2, Jenkins, you're next in command as Mike1 and Reid is Mike2. Spencer, you're Mike3, Fox is Mike4, Burns is Mike5, Knight is Mike6. Mr. Faxton, you're Delta1 and Dr. St. Danniels you are Delta2. I realize the code names might present some difficulty to our diplomatic team. Please practice them and do not, I repeat, do not use real names or real locations over the radios."

She said this, he was sure, for the benefit of the two Deltas. She pulled up another visual, a map this time.

"This is our area of interest. We've divided the encampment into zones. Zone one is where we'll land the shuttle or shuttles after Alpha1 gives us the pick up signal. Our first LZ, our strike zone, is here. Only myself, Zulu2, and the Mikes will disembark here. Mikes will deploy first and clear the area. At that point, the Alpha team will deploy."

She nodded to Kraye, and he took up the narrative.

"Our task will be to keep the shuttles secure so that we can pick up the Alpha team when they call for us. Once we receive the pickup code, the Mikes and Zulu1 will board Golf Sierra Alpha. I will board Golf Sierra Zulu. We'll lift off and fly low and cloaked for Zone 1. Unless directed by Alpha1, only GS Alpha will land for the pickup with GS Zulu providing aerial cover fire."

His insides clenched as he thought of Caro in battle without him, but she and OxeroidR were correct. He had more flying battle experience than Caro.

"What about us?" Faxton asked.

"If GS Zulu has to land, it will be your job to protect the shuttle, keep it from being boarded by hostiles," Caro said. "I believe you've both been doing sims for that scenario?"

Faxton nodded. St. Danniels appeared surprised, then also nodded.

"You've all received a map that shows how we've divided the encampment into zones. Memorize those locations. Alpha1 will use them when he calls us in." Her gaze centered on the two Deltas. "Knowing where other members of the team are, and staying where you're assigned, should keep anyone from taking friendly fire. *Anyone*," she emphasized.

She paced in front of them, her hands clasped behind her back, then faced them with a tense smile.

"We're planning for worst case. We do not expect a fire fight. Bull is, well, this is his thing. Our main task is to get the hostages safely on board the shuttles and get the crap out of there."

Kraye knew why. Once they were in the air, they faced a different kind of challenge. And if they made it back here—he closed off his thoughts. *Focus on the task in front of you.* Wise advice from his captain.

"Questions?" City asked.

"It sounds complicated," St. Danniels complained.

She was dressed quite functionally, Kraye noted, and showed no signs of discomfort, except around her mouth and eyes which were pinched with tension, he supposed.

"It is complicated. You did live fire exercises during your training, didn't you?" Delta2 nodded. "It's like that only worse. And we can't afford you or Delta1 to shoot one of us. Those of us with more experience will have heads up displays in our headgear that will give us the location of everyone on the ground. We won't shoot you, so don't shoot us. Please."

"But how will we know?" she asked. "Will I have a heads up thing?"

"Trust me, you don't want a heads up display. If you're not used to it—If we approach the shuttle, we'll inform you via radio. Using code identifiers. You have my permission to shoot anything or anyone who doesn't warn you they are incoming to the shuttle." The female did not seem reassured, so Caro added, "Your weapons will be set to high stun. It will hurt, but it won't kill anyone."

She looked relieved. "I'm basically a pacifist. But I'm also totally opposed to taking hostages and things like that. Separating kids from their mom."

Caro lifted a hand, massaging her temple as if it pained her.

"Well, you picked the right time to help out," Caro said, her tone more polite than pleased. "Have I missed anything?" Her gaze moved from one person to the next.

Kraye saw no sign her Marines moved, but she appeared satisfied. He sensed the two diplomats did not know what else to ask.

Caro paced again, then stopped.

"If you get cut off or captured, activate your emergency beacon." She lifted her arm, showing them where it was located on the wrist. "This is the *last* option to use. And you need to realize, if this mission goes south, there may not be anyone to come. The armor also has a self-destruct here." She pointed it out and then paused, her gaze once more tracking around the room. "The hostages were probably moved to the compound as bait for the Lady. This is not a soft target. We are hoping to strike before it is fully hardened. We have to have a care for the hostages. They don't. That's why we'll start with non-lethal fire, only going lethal when we are sure the target is the enemy and you have no other option to neutralize a threat."

She paced once more, the scrape of her boots against the metal floor distinct in the silence. She stopped and faced them for the last time.

"This is your last chance to stay with the ship. There are risks in staying. I'm not going to lie to anyone, but your chances of getting home alive are better here. When we leave this room, we're heading down to the shuttle bay. If you don't make it, well, it means you're not crazy. We'll adjust force placement before boarding the shuttles if anyone drops out."

For the first time, the edges of her mouth moved in a half smile.

"Let's move out." She turned toward her headgear, but stopped before securing it. "Kraye? A quick word?"

He felt surprise, but nodded, waiting until the room had emptied before moving closer to her. She met him half way.

"We're going into battle and, well," she said. "I just wanted—" She arched up on her toes and pressed her mouth to his.

Heat flared. His arms slammed around her, dragging her close. She met him halfway again, pushing to be close to him. Their battle armor was the only reason he did not go up in flames. He kissed her, moving his head one direction, then the other. Each drag of her lips against his healing even as it burned with an inner fire.

Her radio buzzed, and they fell apart. Her face was flushed, and he assumed she dragged in air as desperately as he did because of the way her shoulders moved. She rubbed her face. Her smile lit the fire inside him again, but they were out of time. He touched her cheek with a hand that visibly shook.

"I—" he did not know the words, so he pulled his hand back, touching his heart.

She touched her heart, too, then activated her radio.

"We're on our way."

Chapter 7

THE *EMISSARY* DROPPED into normal space. This time they didn't have to wait to cloak. City didn't fool herself this meant they hadn't been spotted. The space around Teuhhopse was still clear of space traffic, but City didn't let that get her hopes up either.

Initiating an avoidance maneuver while awaiting next course to be plotted.

Rita, at least a piece of her, and Bull were driving from their shuttle. City and Kraye were on the scanners in theirs though neither fooled themselves into thinking they could find anything faster than Bull could.

Thanks to the laws of physics, they had a small window of opportunity before they could be seen and that information transmitted to wherever their enemies were hiding. Of course, while that information was traveling to their enemies, their scanners and Bull were scanning for a safe place to land before the enemy had time to react to their arrival light.

City checked on her passengers through the video feed. Looked like everyone was strapped down. Her Marines were wearing their usual stone faces. Her two Deltas had their diplomatic faces in place, but both of them gripped the arms of their chairs hard enough to turn their knuckles white.

"I have located an LZ for the *Emissary*. I have located an LZ for the shuttles. Sending you the data," Bull said, over the radio.

"He's fast." She glanced at Kraye, feeling no embarrassment over the heated kiss they'd exchanged. Mostly she hoped she'd get to do it again.

Kraye half smiled. "He is that." Even though he was as out of the flying loop as she was, his expression was intent, focused on what the data told them. He'd be studying their flight path after shuttle launch in case he had to take over the controls.

The course change for planet insertion was slight, only visible on tracking. They'd dropped in as close as they could to where they wanted to go in. This was also near the region of the scary bird mountain ranges. They hoped to shorten the time their entry track was visible. They'd arrive at dusk and reach the encampment when it was dark and movement was at a minimum.

It felt like the silence was ticking—slow ticking, the waiting kind of ticking. She missed Tiger's purr, she realized. Felt her stomach clench with worry for him.

"Let's pipe some music in, Rita," City suggested, once more eyeing her tense Deltas. She wasn't sure it helped them. At least it filled the silence with something. One of her Mikes started to tap his fingers on his knee in time to the music. The others looked like they were cat-napping.

She felt it when the *Emissary* entered the upper atmosphere, felt it as the ship encountered resistance and then was rocked by turbulence. It was, she knew, only going to get worse. Currently the mountain region was experiencing strong winds with potential rotors. Bull indicated confidence in the ship and his ability to fly it. She had asked everyone to take advantage of a Garradian air sickness reduction device prior to their strap down. So far it appeared to be working. No one was green. Or puking.

This was the hardest part. Once they were moving, acting, it got easier. Action was always better than being strapped in a seat wondering if you'd missed something.

The *Emissary* began braking maneuvers. Readings showed below zero outside air temperatures. Thank goodness they weren't going to be outside in that. Their final target zone was a temperate seventy degrees now that it was night, the mist on the ground thickening.

"Bull, can you confirm the shuttles can fly in current temps and wind speeds?" It had been her idea to park in the mountains though Bull had given her plan that interesting twist. They would still be exposed to the elements for a short period.

"I can confirm."

Tough little ships.

The ride was brutal. City had a new respect for hurricane hunter pilots. The buffeting was so bad, she saw, but didn't feel it, when the *Emissary* banked between two jagged mountain peaks. She felt their braking maneuver, however, because the buffeting amped up. For several tense minutes, she thought they were going to crash into the side of the mountain and then they were on the ground sliding up against the mountainside, then rebounding until they finally came to a stop. A small snow slide tumbled down, the snow sizzling against the hot hull.

"That was a seriously good landing, Bull," she said. He didn't respond. Perhaps he didn't know how. With the engines off, the howling of the wind and the ice hitting the sides of the ship were loud enough to be disconcerting. Their current position was somewhat sheltered, thank goodness. But Dr. Dauwn wasn't going to have a fun time here by himself—though it was probably still better than the time they were going to have.

"Switching to shuttle control." Bull's voice was flat over the radio, because he was a one note guy. "Prepare for lift-off."

With control of both ships, he activated the phase cloak. They would head in, and gradually angle down, through the heart of the mountain. Depending on power usage, he'd pick their exit point and they should emerge into the open at a lower altitude and in a location their enemies could not possibly predict. At that point, they would switch to regular cloak and fly at tree height to their LZ. Tree height was still pretty high because this planet had some seriously tall trees.

"Don't open any doors while we're gone, Dr. Dauwn," City said over the radio. Not that he could. Rita would keep it all locked down while they were gone. "We'll catch you on the flip side."

"Yes, Sergeant." His voice lacked his earlier vagueness. If he was regretting his choice to stay, she couldn't tell.

She checked her passengers once more. Her Mikes looked like they were all now catching some Z's. The Deltas had lost about half their diplomatic calm. Good thing they couldn't see what she was about to see. They might wet their battle armor.

The shuttles lifted off together. The hardest part was not being in control. Through the view screen vid, the other shuttle disappeared as the phase cloak activated, though it was still visible on her controls. She knew from the controls that Bull had activated the phase cloak on their shuttle, though she couldn't "see" it happen since she was inside the shuttle. She tensed when the side of the *Emissary* drew closer. They passed through the outer hull, but the view of the now approaching mountainside wasn't confidence building either. The wind hit them like a hammer once they were clear of the *Emissary*. She made herself breathe evenly as they approached the side of the mountain, Bull accelerating both shuttles. City tried to look away, but it was not possible.

They reached rock—and passed into it. They were moving fast enough now that the strata of the rocks appeared blurred. Even with the meds, she might get sick. She looked down, tracking power use and shield stress to distract herself. At least the wind wasn't in here.

"Heat against the hull is rising," she noted. Was it friction against the shields or were they close to a magma tube? "Do you copy the heat buildup, Bull?"

"It is within an acceptable range," he answered, "but I will adjust course."

This meant they'd emerge from inside the mountain sooner than planned. Was it better to burn to death inside a mountain or get shot outside one? She honestly didn't have an answer.

As the inside of the mountain continued to rush past, some strata were cut with red lines that could be magma. She didn't check. She didn't want to know. Bull had kicked their speed up the top edge of safe. A Bull out of hell? When she thought she couldn't bear it any longer, they burst free of the mountain and out into the winds. Her shuttle rocked, and she clenched her hands so they wouldn't try to correct course. She checked the readings as the cloak shifted from phase to regular. Power usage was higher than they'd hoped, but still in the safe range. No stress damage, though they'd pushed that line, too.

"Wind's not as bad down here." Still wasn't great.

They'd emerged at a higher altitude than planned, so Bull steered them into a course that felt a lot like a nose dive. He used reverse thrust to slow them down as the tree tops rushed toward them.

She felt the ship strain as the nose came back up, then slammed back in her chair when he kicked into high.

Bull had some big brass—she stopped the thought. From this day forward, she was substituting Bull out of hell for bat out of hell and eliminating big brass anything from her thoughts. She checked the timing to their LZ.

"Rita, stop the music." She activated her comm to the rear of the shuttle. "Prepare for first stop in fifteen."

KRAYE'S GAZE moved from the view in front of him to the controls counting down to the moment OxeroidR would give him control for the final approach to their landing place. It ticked down swiftly, even as OxeroidR braked for the landing.

"Dude can multi-task," Caro murmured next to him.

He did not look at her. He could not afford to take his eyes off his controls and she had the power to distract him. He could not multi-task as well as the robot, so he did not think about their inter-action before boarding the shuttle, well, he did not think about it much. It was also in the distraction column though it gave him considerable incentive to survive this mission so that he could do it again.

"I have control of the shuttle," he said. The shuttle quivered some as he took over control, applying what Caro liked to call the speed brakes. Another screen gave him a countdown to the LZ. The robots had perfected the stop and drop as it tended to confuse tracking, and taught him to do it, too.

On tracking, he saw the other shuttle stop and drop first. He followed it in, feathering the controls and braking hard. The shuttle made a tight turn over their landing spot so their sensors could take a quick look.

"Looks good," Caro said. "Put her on the ground."

This shuttle had vertical lift and descent functions. He switched to this even as the engines protested the fast stop. While the shuttle made a fast descent through the small break in the trees, he checked power usage, shield strength, and other systems integrity. The shuttle hit harder than he liked, but they were down.

He cut the engines. They needed to save power for the assault on the encampment and then, once they completed their mission, they would need to do all of this in reverse to get back to the *Emissary*.

"No sign yet that anyone knows we're here."

She did not sound relieved. Like him, she did not assume that the enemy would give them any preview of their intentions. They would pounce when they thought this ship, or those on it, were vulnerable.

"Rita, what's the atmosphere like out there?"

It is acceptable.

This was as expected. Its humanoid population was much like theirs. And the probe's readings had shown it was within the acceptable range for them. Their Garradian battle armor also filtered out harmful toxins and bacteria, as well as allergens, he'd heard Caro tell the female Delta.

Caro was already on her feet, palming the hatch open with one hand, while the other lowered her face mask. "Delta 1 and 2, you wait on the bridge."

Neither one protested, just moved quickly to obey. Caro shut the hatch behind them. Her teams were ready except for their Infrared —IR.

The lights in the cabin lowered until they were completely off.

"Turn on your IR," she ordered.

Ahead of them the hatch began to lower, revealing the dark outlines of a forest. The hatch hitting the forest floor caused the thick mist to retreat in slow rolling waves.

"Clear," she ordered.

The two rows of Mikes ran down the ramp, spreading efficiently out. Kraye and Caro followed them to the edge of the ramp and stopped, their weapons ready.

"Anything on the sensors, Rita?" Caro asked.

"Small life signs only."

"Roger that. Mike1 and 2?"

"Clear."

"Clear."

"Alpha team, deploy," she said.

"Roger that," came the flat reply.

IN STARK CONTRAST with the wind-blown, jagged peaks where the *Emissary* waited, this forest was on the edge of steamy. Thankfully, the alien battle armor they'd found on one of the Garradian outposts provided some temperature adjusting capability—though it had to work hard when the adrenalin kicked on.

The trees seemed to reach up and touch the stars sweeping across a carpet of deep, dark blue. Fern-like plants clustered around the wide bases of those trees. Some trees were straight and tall, others twisting and turning in curves that gave it a fairytale ambiance that City was sure would not last. Any small heat signatures had scampered away when the hatch had lowered.

Alpha4's heat signature had swept over them, bringing City's heart into her throat for long seconds, then she'd headed for the encampment. According to her heads-up display, Bull—Alpha1 still beat her there. The robot could move when he wanted to. If the heat signatures were reading right, he had Rocky on one shoulder and Tiger on the other.

It was strange to feel worried and puzzled.

They started getting video from inside the encampment.

"Okay, let's get ready for phase two."

She and her Mikes headed back inside their shuttle. Kraye climbed into the other shuttle.

She kicked Delta1 out of her seat and fired up the engines. The sims were great for practice, but there was nothing quite like the feel of an engine firing.

She hadn't removed her headgear, so she could monitor the video feed from Alpha1. He was good. He made sure to give them a 360° view as he penetrated the encampment. The video was IR, so it took her a few beats of her heart to realize what the perimeter fence was.

Web. Densely woven web.

He zoomed in briefly, then moved on. Would these spider creatures be as large as the one they'd stepped on during the last op? He'd been as big as Jabba the Hut, eight legs—the two front ones curving forward like crab claws, and eight eyes in two rows. Big, crap-brown and disgusting with human blood dripping from his fangs.

Alpha1 was inside the perimeter she realized. Bull could out ghost a ghost. He almost gave her robot envy. Just inside the perimeter were single size, evenly spaced huts. They started at the gate—the only way in or out it appeared—and continued all the way the around. Inside the circle of huts were three larger structures with barred windows.

"Has Alpha3 been able to give us a more precise location of the hostages?" Zulu2 asked over the radio.

He'd asked City's next question. She wished she could ask—and get—an answer to the questions that lingered about the big bird. Would she betray them? Would she know *her* kids? If others of her kind lived here, it was possible that other hatchlings had been captured. And the biggie: what had she been forced to do to keep the kids safe?

As she circled up there, what was she thinking? What was she planning?

"I see movement from one of the structures." This was Alpha2's whispered croak. "It appears to be a guard patrol."

City studied their positions on her HUD. The heat signatures were close to Alpha1. She wasn't worried about him being spotted. They could probably bump into him and not realize who he was. But if the bird wasn't really with them—

The video view changed abruptly. Who—it had to be Rocky. It moved forward in jerks and bumps. It might do to her stomach what their flight through the high winds had not.

"Where—" she started to ask. Then she realized where he was.

"He's inside one of the prisons," Kraye said.

She felt her skin chill inside her body armor, a chill it could not warm.

There were birds, birds like their bird, but also humans. Children and adults.

OXEROIDR WAITED until Rocky had run through all three prisons before processing his next action. Only the middle building housed *Harparians.*

Six of the bird species and about sixty humans were behind held in the three buildings, about five were children.

Rocky flew silently from the barred window and landed on his shoulder.

"They are not all prisoners," he whispered.

"How?"

"Too well fed."

Ah. He postulated that not all the cells would be locked, only those with true prisoners, and that the fake prisoners would be armed.

He ran through the video Rocky had broadcast, marking targets, at the same time formulating a plan. They'd packed the prison. Only five adults and the five children appeared to be actual prisoners. The human prisoners were separate from the *Harparians.* The children in one prison, the adults in the other. He could neutralize the fake prisoners in all three. Logic said he should focus on the birds. If he did not, the situation could become exponentially more complicated.

He lifted Rocky and Tiger from his shoulders, setting them down in a deep shadow next to the central prison.

"Wait," he said. As he moved toward the entrance to the first building, he sent a written message to Zulus 1 and 2.

Launch. Prepare to land both shuttles in ten minutes.

As a device emerged from his frame and melted the door lock, he spoke once, his voice barely loud enough for the radio.

"Alpha4 now."

He'd passed through the two outside prisons and was back with his two companions before the Lady dropped silently down next to them in the shadows by the middle prison structure.

He turned his attention to this lock.

The door swung silently open. He held up a metal hand, signaling her to wait, and entered. When he returned to the opening, the only sound from inside was the fluttering hum of sleeping birds. He looked down at Tiger.

"Now," he said. He looked up, meeting the *Harparian's* gaze. She appeared as if she wished to say something, but instead she followed the caticorn inside.

∾

BOTH SHUTTLES ON THE GROUND? City studied the video coming back, but none of it was from Bull.

"We're lifting off," she said into her rear intercom. "Strap in and get ready to deploy." She activated her private comm with her Mikes. "We're landing both shuttles. Prepare to defend both and assist in boarding passengers."

She watched Kraye lift off in Golf Sierra Alpha. She followed him and was on his six as he accelerated toward the encampment. They stayed low enough that the tops of some trees scraped the bottom of the hull.

They came in fast. She reversed thrust, engaged vertical lift and dropped down next to GS Alpha. She dropped cloak and lowered the rear hatch as she yanked off her restraints and grabbed her weapon. The hatch slid back. Her Mikes were already down the ramp.

She felt a twitch in her gut and said into her radio, "Kill your IR." She hadn't turned hers on and was grateful when the center of the compound lit up like a fairground.

OXEROIDR CAUGHT up with the *Harparian* and passed her as Tiger, with Rocky on his back now, approached the two cages that held the young.

The *Harparian* gave a soft call. The young stirred, ruffling their feathers.

One made a sharp sound, but Tiger's horn began to glow—a glow only visible because of the darkness in the prison. A low hum also came from Tiger.

OxeroidR quickly unlocked the cages, and the birds came out, casting uncertain glances at their mother, but falling willingly in behind Tiger.

"Take them to Golf Sierra Alpha, my friend," OxeroidR told him.

"That was the plan," the caticorn said, breaking his long silence. He trotted toward the door just as the outside lit up as if it were day.

THE DOOR to a structure to City's right burst open and Tiger galloped out, that was the correct word, Rocky clinging to his back and four *Harparians* running after him. City hoped that was a good thing.

Mom and Bull came out on their heels.

She didn't have to ask her Mikes to help out. She pivoted toward the other shuttle, running to help Kraye—Zulu2, who was taking fire from that direction. Her HUD gave her heat signatures, even without the IR, thanks to OxeroidR and Rita.

It was a lot like the sims, only the incoming fire blazing perilously close was real.

Energy pulses. Estimate in disable, not kill, range.

So they were looking to take prisoners. Good luck with that.

She fired a burst, using the blunt nose of the shuttle for protection, then pulled back as multiple bolts hissed past, one striking the shuttle with a prolonged sizzle.

On the HUD she saw Tiger, and the kids were almost to Golf Sierra Alpha. Zulu was closer, but whatever.

With her own eyes, she saw a blur that her HUD identified as Alpha1 head into the nearer prison structure. Were there more birds in there?

Cries and shouts blended together with the babble of battle chatter.

She saw something approaching on her HUD. Something big, something almost as fast as Alpha1.

Crap, a spider.

She leaned out, kicking her weapon to kill and stepped out, firing repeatedly. It staggered back, but kept coming. Kraye joined fire with her and the thing began to fall back.

City turned, her back to Kraye spraying that area with cover fire. Then they dodged back between the shuttles as they took a brutal round of incoming fire.

"We got passengers trying to board, Zulu1," she heard Mike1's voice. "Taking heavy fire."

"Rita, fire up the GS Alpha engines and prepare for lift off," she ordered.

She started toward the rear of the shuttles, checking her HUD. Alpha1 was in the furthest structure. What...

Humanoids. Children.

City bit back some curses she'd learned from her Sergeant. "Delta1 and 2, we could use some extra cover fire."

She moved forward, concentrating on an area delivering heavy fire down the passage between the prisons and the shuttles.

On her HUD she saw Alpha4 and several birds running toward her, then bodies low to the ground. Tiger was with them, she realized with a shock.

Some fire diverted toward him. She stepped out and caught their attention.

The birds and the caticorn ran up the ramp.

"Zulu2, get that shuttle in the air. Give us some cover fire."

"Roger that," Kraye said. He fired on a position, then ran up the ramp. It closed on his heels.

Bless you, Rita, City thought, as it began to lift off. She didn't know what made her look up past the rising shuttle. It took her a minute to realize what the dropping bundles were.

"Spiders. We've got spiders overhead."

KRAYE DROPPED behind the controls as he heard Caro's warning. Rita handed over to him. He took it up to ridge height of the structures and started it moving in a slow circle, firing forward and rear guns at the dropping strands and spiders on them.

One dropped on his forward screen, lifted a leg and stabbed it at the screen. A small star of damage grew larger when it struck again.

It took fire from the ground and dropped away, its legs curling in.

Suddenly the Lady was on the bridge with him.

"Can you open the hatch enough for me to get out?" she asked.

He hesitated, then nodded. "Don't let anything in."

"I won't."

Over the cries in his headgear, he had not picked up on the soft hum, but through the hatch he heard it now. Whatever it was, it seemed to be keeping the younger *Harparians* quiet.

The hatch slid closed, he lowered the rear hatch as much as he dared. He heard the Lady say, "I'm clear."

He closed it and saw a much larger spider making a run at Caro's position.

~

CITY SAW the dark shadow rushing her and fired. And fired again. It slowed, but still came at her. She was aware of figures running or being herded to Golf Sierra Zulu by Bull.

"All Mikes and Deltas, start retreating to GS Zulu and cover Alpha1."

Her back slammed into the side of the shuttle.

"Rita, fire it up!"

She raised her weapon as spiders continued to drop around them.

A figure ahead of her fired clumsily at a spider and it pounced. The figure screamed. A female.

Delta2.

City turned and fired, knocking the spider off her. Delta1 ran to her and helped her. City tried to cover their retreat to the shuttle, but a spider dropped onto Delta1, trying to pierce the battle armor with fangs and pinchers.

City fired.

"Your six, Zulu1!" a Mike warned her.

She whirled and fired. "Fall back to the shuttle!"

On the HUD Alpha1 had herded all his humans aboard and now he stood at the base of the shuttle doing his robot thing.

City didn't know how to describe it. The Mikes contracted their perimeter as the spiders, perhaps realizing Bull was their greatest threat began to target him.

It gave them a chance to get on board. She counted her Mikes. She was short one. Using the HUD and her eyes, she found him under attack from two spiders. He was on his back, trying to keep vicious pinchers from stabbing into his face plate.

She fired, running toward him. Bull must have helped out because the other spider tumbled off him. She grabbed his arm, helping him up. He slung an arm around her shoulder as they staggered toward the ramp.

"Go," she pushed him toward another Mike and then turned back. Checking her HUD for anyone she might have missed.

The smell of singed bug got through her face mask. Cries and shouts, incoming fire added to the chaos.

"Take out the lights," Alpha1 ordered.

Above her, Kraye turned the hovering shuttle and targeted the encampment lights.

At the base of the shuttle, Bull held off a circle of snarling spiders.

"Lift off," he ordered.

"But…"

"Leave the ramp down."

"Right." She loosed off some shots and then turned and ran toward the bridge. "Lift off, Rita, but leave the ramp down."

The Mikes clustered by the open ramp, firing on anything trying to board from above.

As City ran, she was aware of huddled figures holding crying children. As the shuttle rose, there was a thud as Bull landed on the hatch ramp.

City hit the close button. A last spider tried to crawl in, the screams of their passengers louder than the fire that decimated the creature.

The hatch finally closed. City sank down in her seat, possibly ready to breathe a sigh of relief.

We have bogeys approaching our position.

KRAYE TURNED the shuttle to face the incoming ships as Golf Sierra Zulu rose to take a position next to his.

"Cloak and shield," City's voice came calmly over the radio. "Prepare for incoming fire."

"Do we return fire?" he asked.

"Negative." This voice was OxeroidR's. "They will wish us to fire to reveal our position and course."

"What is our course?" he asked.

"Transmitting," City said. "This time we're going to put some distance between us."

He did not like this, but he adjusted his heading. "I will cover our six." He had a thought. "Did Alpha4 board your shuttle?"

There was a long pause.

"No." City's voice was flat. Then Kraye heard, "Alpha4, come in." There was no answer. "Can we find her with the scanners?"

"If she lives, she will make her way to the *Emissary*," OxeroidR said. "We must focus on getting her young there."

He had a point. They had enough trouble following them—warning signs posted. More ships had risen from the forest—ships positioned between them and the mountains.

"Looks like they have figured out where we've hidden the *Emissary*," Caro said. This time she sounded resigned.

"Can we use the phase cloak to pass through this line?" Kraye asked.

"We can," OxeroidR said, "but we might not have enough power to get through the mountain."

"So we fight our way through or take the long way back?" Caro said. "Any preference?"

"We take the long way," OxeroidR said.

He'd barely said the words when Rita delivered more bad news. *Multiple ships are arriving in Teuhhopse space.*

"THEY ARE ACTING like they can see us," City said, glancing at Bull. He'd not taken over the flying yet, which surprised her. He could fly both ships, plot their course and come up with a plan for getting out of this system. *Cause he's a robot, r-o-b—stop it, Caro,* she told herself sternly.

"The trees," Bull said suddenly. "If there are more spiders in the trees, their webs could sense movement, perhaps track us."

"So they probably tracked us from the point where we overflew the trees coming in." But they'd thought they could trap them on the ground in the encampment. She contacted Kraye and let him know they'd need to adjust course again and why. All the time, her brain was playing what if?

Rita could bring the *Emissary* to them, but then the *Harparian* wouldn't know where to find them.

Another, smaller line of ships popped up on tracking.

"They're building a box," City said.

"AND THERE IS the last side of the box," Kraye said. They had open comms now. Both shuttles were flying a parallel course, with Golf Sierra Zulu at a higher altitude than this ship. He had full shields and cloak engaged. Rita kept a wary eye on power usage for both shuttles. Once they were back on the *Emissary* their powers sources could be recharged, but they'd used considerable power both in their approach and during the battle.

"What are they up to?" Caro murmured the question as if asking it of herself. "Oh, crap."

It seemed to Kraye that he felt her stiffen over the comm.

"They must have those two doomsday weapons with the crazy names, too." One of them negatively interacted with shields, turning them into deadly weapons right next to the hull. The other was a super charged heat seeker. Both were illegal, but apparently readily available to bad guys.

"A Trozzerd Emitter 3DXZ and a Beugrimt Seeker 55THT." OxeroidR's voice did not change as he added, "That is unfortunate."

"Does it work against a phase cloak?" Caro asked.

"I doubt anyone can answer that question until—" OxeroidR stopped.

"Until we survive or die?" Caro put in.

"Yes."

"DID I actually volunteer for this mission?" City muttered. "Is there any way to determine which ship has those things on board?"

"When they begin charging it, the sensors on the *Najer* can detect a Trozzerd Emitter 3DXZ. I am not sure this ship was programmed to detect a weapon that wasn't available when it was built."

"I don't like disclaimers," City said.

"Excuse me?"

"Never mind. So what are we looking for when it powers up?" No way was she going to try to say either name. It would be like being in a campy sci-fi movie.

"Heat."

Bull almost sounded thoughtful. "Rita…"

I am on it.

Was Rita starting to pick up City's slang?

"Could we fire on it before it fired on us?"

"Once we fire, the other ships will know our general location. They can saturate the region with fire," Bull pointed out.

He was just full of good news today.

"Maybe we can narrow the choices," City suggested. "These ships aren't all created equal. They seem cobbled together if these scans are close to accurate."

My scans are never close to accurate. I cross my T's and dot my I's.

"Sorry, I just meant, these are unfamiliar ships to all of us."

"Not to me," Bull pointed out.

City glanced at him. He looked off balance without Rocky perched on his shoulder.

Both he and Rita went silent, which she took to mean they were communicating at a processor level. Since Rita was busy, City started a power usage assessment without her.

Basically, they could do one more, limited phase cloaking. Fifteen minutes tops. Longer than that and they wouldn't have enough power to make it back to the *Emissary*. She asked if it had accounted for wind speed they were likely to encounter. The number went down to ten minutes.

Something started to flash on her console.

"What's that?" she asked.

They are broadcasting a surrender or die message.

"COULD the ship broadcasting be the lead ship?" Kraye asked.

"I am tracking the signal back to the source," OxeroidR said. After a pause that had more to do with distance than the robot's processors, he said, "There are indications of a heat buildup inside the broadcasting ship."

"It's right in our way," Caro complained. "I've got ten minutes of phase cloak. Can we make a run at it and pass through it before it can fire that thing?"

"We cannot go full throttle. The power usage—" OxeroidR paused.

"Would be detrimental to our ability to reach the *Emissary.*" Caro's sigh was audible over the comm.

"We should accelerate to three fourths full power," the robot said. "There is a risk. If they fire before we reach them, it will lessen the time until the weapon impacts with our shields, but it is our best option."

"Might as well go down in a blaze of glory. I'm not excited about getting captured by the spiders," Caro said.

"I have started a countdown to optimum phase cloak deployment on both control consoles," OxeroidR said.

"They are sending a video broadcast," Kraye said, as he accelerated the shuttle to the recommended speed. The other shuttle accelerated, too.

"Can we see it without them getting a bead on us?" Caro asked.

Suddenly his front screen was filled with a loathsome sight. Eight eyes, a row of four above a row of four, peered out of a bristle of brown and black fur. Its front legs curved forward with shiny pinchers on the ends. Fangs marked where he assumed a mouth to be. Fangs that dripped with something red. Another leg appeared, holding…Kraye inhaled sharply and heard Caro do so as well.

It was a human leg.

"Let's fire on that ship," Caro said, her voice both shaken and grim.

"We should fire simultaneously," OxeroidR began.

Wait. Look.

On the tracking screen, something sleek and fast shot out of the cover of the trees, curving in an arc that took it close to the bottom hull of the spider ship. Starlight gleamed on something as it raked along that hull. It turned sharply and made another run.

On the video, the spider's mouth opened in a scream of rage. The ships with it tried to fire on it—on *her*. It was the *Harparian*. She moved in a complicated series of moves that led the fire back on the ships. One of the ships closest to the spider ship exploded, ripping a hole in its side. It exploded, taking out the ship next to it and down the line.

"Sympathetic detonation," Caro said, admiringly. "Gotta love it."

Chapter 8

BOTH SHUTTLES RENDEZVOUSED with the *Emissary* at the same time as the Lady. Caro climbed stiffly out of her chair and rubbed her face. She vaguely remembered what tired felt like. She missed it. Didn't know how good she'd had it before she slid into total exhaustion zone. She didn't have the energy for a deep breath, so she took a regular one—it almost wiped her out—and opened the hatch.

At first look, she thought everyone in the passenger section was dead. Then she realized they were asleep—or they had been. Her guys stirred first. They'd removed their headgear and looked as weary as she felt, though they started to come to attention. She waved that nonsense off. A couple of first aid boxes were open, the contents tumbled about the deck. St. Danniels was slumped in her seat, held there by the restraint straps.

Their other passengers were huddled into three small groups of adults strapped in with children because there weren't enough seats. The children appeared to be asleep as well, or in shock. The adults, well, they looked pretty shell-shocked. Faxton was seated near them, his eyes closed when she entered. One arm was in a sling, she noticed. His eyes opened, and he straightened. He looked like he wanted to ask her something, but couldn't remember what.

"We're back on the *Emissary*," she told him. She looked at her Mikes with apology. "Let's get these people to the infirmary or into quarters and then take turns getting some rest." Her gaze moved back to Faxton. "Have you been able to talk to them?" Were they real prisoners or kidnappers after all them was the question she wanted to ask?

Before he could answer her, a woman at the end of a short row stirred, her hand smoothing the hair of the child she held. The child shifted in her hold and straightened, knuckling his eyes.

His hands lowered, and she sucked in a shocked breath.

He was a mini Kraye.

THE MIKES RELOCATED the humans before she gave the order to lower the hatch on the shuttle Kraye had flown. The Lady had been pretty patient and stayed out of sight of the humans until the flight hanger was quiet.

City wasn't sure what she expected. Actually, she was trying not to expect anything. But still…

The birds weren't strapped in. Instead, they had used their talons to cling to the arms of the seats, their bodies in what she'd call the brood position. For some reason, this position made their eyes appear more hooded and ominous than upright. In the heart of this small flock was her caticorn. His horn pulsed with a light. She frowned and put a finger to her ear as if to clear it. Was that a hum?

"Tiger?" she asked.

"Actually, my name is Glurone, but I prefer Tiger."

She'd known that caticorn could talk. She cleared her throat of annoyance and asked, "So you're a *Harparian* whisperer?"

At her elbow, the Lady laughed.

City turned to face her. "So now what?"

The Lady hesitated.

"There aren't any of your kind left here, are there? You're the last?"

"Yes." She looked away, her feathers ruffling in what could be a raptor sigh. "Could your Rita find that planet in the picture?"

"The one in my ready room?" Man, that sounded so Picard. The Lady nodded. "Rita?"

I can find anything.

City arched her brows, then resolved not to waste energy on that until she'd had a nap.

"We would like to go there."

"All right." She was not going to argue with a bird that could take down a spider ship. All they had to do was get by the twenty or so ships that had arrived in system while they were dodging spiders. Easy.

Kraye appeared in the hatch to the bridge. Oh right. She needed to tell him about—

More ships have entered Teuhhopse space.

She was not sorry that disclosure would have to wait.

Chapter 9

CITY HAD HAD a drink of something that Bull claimed would help with the tired. It was not a shock it worked. And she did not ask what was in it. She, Bull, and Kraye were back on the bridge of the *Emissary* studying the bogeys arrayed against them. More ships kept arriving, allowing them to build a pretty decent net around the planet.

It was possible these enemies had learned from the mistakes of the last spider. Random ships were broadcasting surrender demands, bouncing the signal off the blockade ships and some satellites they'd popped out when the first ships arrived, so they couldn't get a fix on where the signals originated.

City nodded at the image of an even bigger, scarier spider that was going out with the surrender demand. Apparently it planned to eat them.

"I wish we knew what ship this bad boy was on."

Bull said nothing. No surprise there. A tired half grin appeared and disappeared on Kraye's face. She returned the grin, then looked away as guilt stabbed her.

"That's a tight net," she observed. She frowned. "Could they know something about our comet drive that we don't know? I mean,

I don't think I know how far out we have to get before we can turn it on."

This silence felt different. The HUD hologram flickered as if Rita were thinking. Or looking? It was not a surprise that her thinking or that Bull's thinking didn't take long. It did surprise her when Bull's cranium turned her direction.

"It would be inadvisable to activate the comet drive from inside a ship."

Did she know that?

"We're not inside a ship."

City was glad it was Kraye who pointed this out. Gave her a chance for a half second nap.

Activation requires some forward movement, but I can find nothing that prohibits an in atmosphere launch.

"It can create instabilities in the area," Bull added his cents.

Rita put up a simulation of in-atmosphere activation.

"And a hole in the mountain," City noted. "Should that bother us?" It's not like they'd received a warm welcome here and the area was *Harparian* free. The simulation continued through the launch out of the atmosphere. More instabilities. Looked like it would either blow a hole in the blockade or send them into tumbles in a variety of directions. Couldn't see the downside of that either. She frowned. "What's the downside for us? Risk assessment?"

It is possible we could blow up.

That always seemed to be on the table.

"The risk is higher than normal because our hull has been weakened," Bull said. "But it is still within the acceptable range."

She swiveled to face him. "What's the acceptable range?"

He pointed a metal finger at the blockade. "It is better than attempting to get through that."

"Good point. Let's get everyone secured. I'm guessing it's going to get bumpy while we're trying to catch our hurricane force headwind."

∽

IT TOOK about a half of one of Caro's hours for her men to report that all personnel were secured. She also took time for a status report on their passengers.

Dr. Danniels had a bad spider bite. She'd been put into stasis in the small infirmary for transport back to the Central Outpost in the Garradian Galaxy. Faxton had bruises and a sprained wrist. Their new passengers, both *Harparian* and humanoid, were dehydrated, hungry and tired. Quarters and food had been provided. Rita was on guard duty because Caro's Mikes were as tired as she was.

Kraye admired the way she commanded this ship and the people on it. When she needed to be the one to do something, she did it, but when it was optimal to let her best people act, she stood back, she trusted them and treated everyone with respect. And she kissed, well, he lacked experience with which to compare this to, but it been a more than optimal experience that he longed to repeat as soon as possible.

For this last, risky play, she'd turned over the flight controls to Rita and OxeroidR. Kraye was in the second position and she was behind them in navigation.

"Rita and I have made the comet drive calculations," OxeroidR said, the lack of emotion in his voice somewhat comforting to Kraye.

Almost, he could believe he was back on the *Najer*.

To minimize power drain, we will drop the cloak and use the vertical lift until we are in the full force of the wind.

"We believe that the mountains will continue to mask our movement," Bull added.

He glanced back at Caro, wondering how she felt about this belief that was not a certainty. She gave him a wry grin and a thumbs up.

"Once we have a sufficient tail wind, we will activate the drive at half power."

This should minimize the impact on our surroundings and lessen the stress to the ship's hull.

"What about the blockade? Does it soften the impact on them, too?"

No.

"Good." She activated the ship-wide comm. "All personnel, prepare for lift off. I repeat, lift off in two minutes. It's going to get bumpy but it won't last long." There was a pause, then she said, "Make it so, Bull and Rita. Make it so."

Kraye did not understand the hint of humor he heard in her voice but it helped as the engines began to fire up. Did he feel regret at leaving this place with his questions unanswered? Perhaps. Life, his captain had told him more than once, was not tidy.

"Making it so," OxeroidR said.

"Cloak down," Kraye said.

The engines came fully on. Kraye could sense nothing concerning in the hum where his feet rested on decking. The forward view screen showed the snow blowing in broken patterns as the ship began to rise. The slope of the huge mountain had sheltered them somewhat from the raging winds and it appeared they had collected snow on top of the ship, because it began to slide off, obscuring the view for a several seconds.

The ship jerked when the full force of the wind found them, but the engines held. The ship spun so the all that wind was on their six.

And then the ship quit fighting the wind, let it take them. The force of it slammed him against the back of his seat. Only the robot and AI could have steered them through the peaks at their current speed.

"I hope everyone believed us when we said strap in," City muttered from behind.

Several orbiting ships have launched weapons at us.

"So much for, they won't see us," City said. "How long to comet drive ignition?"

"Ten of your seconds," OxeroidR said.

Caro had long seconds, Kraye observed, as he tracked the incoming missiles and their launch clock.

"Initiating comet drive," OxeroidR said.

Space stretched around them, first wide, then long, and finally in both directions. Inside the stretched bubble, he thought he saw flashes of light, then the stretching stopped. His body returned to its regular configuration.

There was a long moment of silence on the bridge.

"How close?" City asked.

"Not close enough," OxeroidR said calmly.

Kraye saw the data and arched his brows, but the robot was right. If the incoming missiles been close enough, they'd be dead.

"Do we know what we did to them?" City asked.

Sensors don't work during comet drive initiation.

"Oh well, you can't have everything." She unstrapped and stood up. "I'm going to catch some z's, get some rest, if you don't mind taking the bridge, Bull?"

"I do not mind."

Kraye hesitated. He wished for sleep, too.

"You should rest, too," Caro said, looking directly at him. "And, I need a word with you, if you don't mind?"

"I do not mind." How could he mind? Each moment in her company was a gift. And possibly there would be kissing. He followed her into the passage way. She glanced around, bit her lip, then lead him back into the ready room. Though they'd kissed here, he sensed this meeting was not about kissing.

"We're less likely to get interrupted in here," she said. She walked away from him, coming to a stop in front of the image of a planet with high mountains and beautiful lakes.

He joined her. "Is this where the *Harparian* wishes to relocate to?"

She nodded, took a deep breath and turned to look at him. Her eyes were wide, worried, and lines of exhaustion had dug grooves around her eyes and her mouth.

"This can wait—" he lifted a hand and smoothed an errant strand of hair back. He felt a deep longing to hold her while she slept, to be there when her eyes opened fresh from her dreams.

She reached up and caught his hand, clasping it with both of hers.

"It can't." She stared at him. "I don't know if you saw, but Bull freed some humans in that camp, too."

He frowned, trying to recall this from the jumble of the action. "I...no, I was focused on the *Harparians*." Why had OxeroidR freed humans, too? Except he knew. None of his shipmates could see captives and not try to free them. "I know it was not the plan, but he, I do not know much of what they think, but I know they are most opposed to slavery and captivity." He breathed in and then out. "They freed me."

"I'm not angry, okay, I might have been annoyed. It did make it more interesting than I'd planned down there. But..." Her clasp on his hands tightened. "Kraye, there's a woman, a mother, at least, I think she's his mother, she acts like his mother to the little boy. He —" She paused, then released the words in a rush. "He's a mini you. Your short twin. Maybe your...brother?"

He heard her words, but it was as if the winds of Teuhhopse surged into this room. It roared through his mind, forming a vortex around his heart. The only thing that kept him from being swept away was Caro, her hands holding onto him.

"I've been thinking about it. If the turtles talked, maybe they realized you were on board and brought them to the encampment as hostages. We know they kept the Lady's kids to keep her in line." Perhaps something in his face alarmed her. "It didn't work. Bull, well, Bull was Bull. They are here. Free."

His lips moved. He swallowed, his other hand coming up to clutch hers. "I do not know what to do." Or what to feel, he admitted. He'd lived too long with robots who were emotionally challenged. He'd believed he had no family. That he'd come to being as a slave.

She gently freed one hand and turned them toward the door. "Why don't we start by saying hi?"

Her fingers curled into his and the buffeting calmed a little. "I could...that seems...possible."

Just shy of the door opening, she turned suddenly, her arms sliding around him and holding him tightly against her. He felt her heart pounding against his chest and his heart leaped in response. Her head tipped back. "You looked like you could use a hug."

The hand he lifted to her face shook. "I...yes."

She turned, leaving one arm around his waist. "Let's go meet your, well, let's go meet them."

~

CITY ENTERED the quarters where Kraye's possible mom had been taken. She'd hoped to smooth things, but she wasn't needed. The woman had looked up, the cry she gave bringing tears to City's eyes. She'd stepped back from Kraye, letting him take one step toward her. Then another. His shoulders heaved and she could still feel the way his heart had pounded when she hugged him.

One hand reached out toward the woman and she ran toward him, throwing her arms around him, and pulling his head down on her shoulder. City didn't understand the words she said, but the stroke of her hand on his head was universal, as were the tears that rained down her face.

Chapter 10

City emerged from her quarters feeling almost as human as their humanoids. It had taken her a while to fall asleep. The tosses and turns hadn't been about what she wanted. She was a Marine. Marines knew how to home in on a target.

No, the question that came between her and her sleep was: what did Kraye want?

The guy had been raised by robots. He'd probably been given a data file on the facts of life, but without the context, did he—could he know what he wanted?

Okay, she had a feeling he figured out want, but what about love?

City's target was the happy ever after. She wanted what her parents had and what too few people believed in anymore. She could give up the walk down the aisle, but not the "I dos." It was ironic that it felt like she'd be taking advantage of his inexperience with relationships if she told him she loved him. Oh, she wasn't worried about him managing the mechanics. Couples had been figuring that out since the beginning of time and he'd caught on quick during their kiss.

But…just because she could see a future with him didn't remove the fact that he'd probably never seen a healthy romantic anything. Could he *be* in love? Could he know love when he saw it?

He'd experienced loyalty. She could see that in him. She knew he was both brave and clever, that he fought like a Marine, and refused to give up. The thing was, inside her Marine exterior was a woman. She had emotions, and she hadn't seen a lot of that around Kraye or his crew mates.

Could the man who'd been raised by robots learn the tender emotions?

Exhaustion had finally won the battle. She'd wakened more rested but with her questions unanswered. Taken them with her through her one-minute shower and out into the mess area for breakfast. She fabricated something and sat down, activating the table's built-in systems unit.

The last thing General Halliwell had said to her when he handed over the symbolic keys to the *Emissary* was, "Don't break it, don't bend it."

Well, it wasn't broken, but it was bent. She'd landed one diplomat in stasis and it looked like Dr. Dauwn had a broken ankle. She should probably look into how that happened. Faxton had come out a bit like the ship, with some bruises and bangs. But for three people who'd shown up wearing red, well, they weren't dead.

Her Mikes had also taken some damage, but they were all going home.

This did not mean she wouldn't have a lot of explaining to do.

She pushed her food around on her tray, looking up when the lift swished open. She tried not to look disappointed when Faxton entered. She started to rise, but he waved her back and sank into a seat opposite her. He leaned back, adjusting his sling and then offered her a wan smile.

"Are we really on our way back? No more stops?"

"No more stops." They didn't have enough resources on board to do anything but get back.

"How long?"

"Are we there yet?" She countered with a grin that quickly faded. Had the *Testudinians* betrayed them or been captured? She'd never know, and that was going to haunt her. It wasn't going to be fun reporting to the General that the Expedition and outposts might have been exposed. None of their passengers had had access to the command deck, but they had ears. Had they taken care in what they said around them? And they'd know who was with them. Everyone they'd taken home would be a target of the spiders.

City looked up and caught the same shadows in Faxton's face.

"Did we do any good?" he asked.

City half shrugged, but with the memory of Kraye and his reunion with his mother in her mind, there was no way she could call it a wash. "What kind of outcome do you get in an Earth-based diplomatic effort?" she countered.

He acknowledged her hit with a wry look.

"My grandfather served in the Korean War," she said. "Not long before he died, he told me he thought they'd failed. That all they'd done was destroy Korea, left it devastated. Then my cousin came back from a trip to Seoul and told him about a visit with the man he'd met. My cousin told the man that his grandfather had been there and the man teared up. He told my cousin that my grandfather needed to return and see what he'd done, that he needed to see what they'd done with the freedom so many had fought and died for."

City pushed her plate away and leaned back, her gaze on Faxton. "Some things take time. You plant the seeds and wait."

He nodded slowly, rose awkwardly to his feet. "Thank you, Sergeant." He started toward the lift, then turned to ask, "You never told me how long?"

She chuckled. "Longer than it took us to get here. That's all I know." She waited until he'd entered the lift to gather up her tray and take it to the disposal and cleaning unit. She lifted the lid and set it inside, then started the cycle.

Maybe that's why she didn't hear anything until he spoke.

"Caro."

She tensed, then turned around. He'd rested, too, though like her, it would take more than one good night's sleep to recover. He had bruises, some she could see, some, well, those she could see in his eyes. She wanted to hug him again and maybe get a kiss. She waited, though, seeing him again for the first time.

The first time she'd seen him, she thought him a Jack Sparrow look-a-like. Now the idea seemed crazy. His features were a bit Sparrow, his skin—sporting a couple of bruises—as smoothly brown. His shoulder-length brown hair lacked the dread locks, but had added to the impression. He'd combed it, tied it back and shaved. Without the facial hair he looked younger. Not even twenty-four hours with a mom and even his posture seemed better. And the expedition-issue jump suit definitely toned down the pirate vibe. His brown eyes were wary, but some of his shadows retreated.

He met her gaze without flinching or looking away though it appeared to City that he struggled for words. Finally his lips twitched.

"I do not know what to say," he admitted.

"Words aren't streaming into my brain either."

He took a step her direction, so she did, too. It was a small room. At this rate it would only take a couple of days to get within touching distance.

"I learned many things from the crew of *Najer*," he said, turning as if to look into the distance, or perhaps the past, "but…"

"You didn't learn how to talk about your feelings," she finished when he seemed unable to go on. "Funny thing, where I come from, guys sometimes have trouble talking about their feelings."

His lips twisted. "Do they know the name of the feelings they cannot talk about?"

"You have a point there." Thanks to all the chick flicks, it was hard for her to talk about her feelings with a guy. Maybe coming at it sideways would help. "Are you happy about your…mother? Is she your mother?"

"We believe so."

"Did she say what happened to your…father?" City asked this carefully.

"He died. That is why she was allowed to keep Naric, my…little brother."

City leaned a hip against the side of the table. "That's...I'm sorry. Is all this freaking her out?"

He gave a confused head shake. "Freaking?"

City indicated their surroundings. "Is she finding it strange? Unsettling to be on this ship hurtling through space?"

"Yes, but she is free. Naric is free."

There was that.

"I have promised her that she is safe."

Was there a hint of question in there?

"She is as safe as we are," City told him. "When we get back, well, we'll figure out what she'd like to do, where she might like to live."

"Are there worlds with people, safe worlds?"

City hesitated, not sure she knew the answer to that. She took another step toward him. "You know that nowhere is completely safe, but we'll—I'll do my best. She'll be free." Her lips twisted. "You know your crew will make sure of that. It was Bull who got them out."

His lips widened in a smile. "They are most...empathetic... despite their lack of expression and emotion."

City felt her own face relax into a smile. "I keep having this feeling there is more to them than meets the eye—then I think, holy crap because there is so much that meets the eye."

He laughed and somehow managed to get two steps closer from the action. City had to meet his two steps. This wasn't poker, or diplomacy, but it seemed like the right thing to do. Now the small-ness of the room was working with them. She was close enough to see the lines fanning out from his eyes. There were gold and green specks in his eyes, too, though she'd need to get closer to be sure.

As her heart rate sped up a little, she wondered how old he was. Old enough she knew he was a man and not a boy. Old enough to know what he wanted?

"Caro, I do not know the words your people use for—" He thumped his heart with his fist. "There is a storm inside. It pushes me—"

Okay, that kicked up her heart some more. "Where does it push you?" It felt like all of her being leaned toward him, but she couldn't move. Not yet.

"To you." He took another step, a bigger one.

Now she was close enough to inhale the clean, male scent of him. If she stopped now they'd almost be chest to chest. She took half a step instead, not quite ready for chest to chest.

She licked her lips and saw fire flare in his eyes. "In my culture, we have something called the relationship talk. For the most part, women like it more than men."

"Relationship, that is how you relate to each other?"

She nodded.

"Why would they not like this? I would appreciate clarity on this."

Yeah, you're an alien, she didn't say.

"Sometimes men like to spend time with women, but not get serious." Before he could ask, "Serious is exclusive and could lead to what we call marriage. That's when you tell each other 'I love you' and decide to live together, have a family together. Commit to each other for always."

He shocked her by stepping up, one hand on her waist, the other settling over her belly. Low down where her womb was. Her knees may have wobbled.

"A child. With you? This would be—" His gaze lifted and met hers. "That would be a happiness I never thought to have. To live with a woman such as yourself always. There is heat around my heart and so much fear."

"Fear?" The word came out as a croak as his hands moved to her cheeks, then slid around to the back of her head, easing her gently against the length of his body.

"That I dream." He smoothed strands of hair back, his brown eyes full of wonder.

For her.

"Is this love?"

She couldn't nod because his strong brown hands held her gently but firmly. She licked her lips again. "Yes. I mean, I think so.

Because I feel the same way." She covered one of his hands with one of hers. The thumb of his free hand stroked across her lips.

"This marriage you speak of. How is this accomplished?"

She sighed. "We need someone with the legal authority to do the ceremony. General Halliwell could do it." If he would. He'd had to do a lot of Expedition-Alien weddings though. He should be used to it.

His arms slid around her, his hands running up, then down her back. "And with this ceremony, we would belong together?"

All she could do was nod.

"You should kiss her already," a voice broke in.

They glanced to the side and found they were being observed by Tiger, Rocky and Bull. Rita started playing a love song in the background.

City opened her mouth to object and shrugged instead. "It is tradition."

"I like this tradition," he growled, covering her mouth with his.

City's toes curled in her military issue boots as she kissed him back.

Cyborg's Revenge
THE CYBORG CHRONICLES BOOK 1

They say you can't go home again, but what if it is the only way to truly be free?

Rap solves problems large and small. He solved them when he was human, when he was a robot, and now that he's mostly human again, he's still solving problems—though eliminating the threat from his old Master is a biggie. He'll need his pet, Snake, and his new friend, Nelson, the AI inside his head. And then there's Ale. He thought he knew all there was to know about Ale.

He was wrong.

Her human form is making his head spin and his heart hurt. He'd like to get closer to her, but he was a geek who didn't know how to talk to women before he became a robot. He can't imagine facing the Master without her, but how can he risk her life on an impossible mission?

Now that Ale is a human again—mostly—her new beating heart is pounding for Rap. It's a pity that he's inscrutable, and she's got a huge secret—one that could be the key to ending the threat from their former Q'uy Master—or doom them all to captivity once more.

Can the shy guy and the lovesick gal defeat their greatest enemy and find a happy ending? Only the chatty Snake knows for sure.

The Plan

"A goal without a plan is just a wish." Antoine de Saint-Exupery

IT WAS READY.

Rap—formerly robotic unit RaptorZ—took a deep breath, trying to ease the tension in his shoulders and back. His chair creaked and he almost sighed. He used to be able to work around the clock without the aches or the creaks. He hadn't needed a chair at all while in his previous unit. But he wasn't a robot anymore. He reached out and used the datapad to flip through the plan again. Not that he needed to. It was burned into his brain. That hadn't changed with his transition back to mostly human.

The plan was as solid as he could make it. It was simple in concept—and complex because of how the enemy might respond—but he'd considered and planned for most variables. That he could foresee them was a skill he'd been born with. That it was also the reason he'd ended up a slave of the Master was unfortunate, but he wasn't a slave anymore. And this plan should ensure that he and his crewmates continued to be free…if it worked. The risks were great, the outcome in doubt.

That was the problem with plans. No matter how carefully he planned, stuff happened. As a robot he'd been able to react swiftly to rapidly changing dynamics. This body was much slower, but he couldn't have executed this plan in his previous unit. And the only reason this human body had a chance was because of its cyborg enhancements.

You are welcome.

The AI, Nelson had come with the enhancements. Or the enhancements came with the AI. There was no question Nelson was key to making them work properly. But having a voice inside his head was an acquired taste—one Rap was still acquiring. At least it didn't have the same attachment to playlists as the other AIs in the outpost. So far, here, aboard the *Najer* was the only place where music wasn't being piped almost continuously through the communication speakers.

Your plan is imperfect.

Nelson was correct—

I am always correct.

Rap didn't dispute this. It felt too much like arguing with himself, even though he knew Nelson was a separate entity operating inside Rap's head.

"It is all we have," Rap pointed out, startled by the sound of his voice in the otherwise empty room. If not stopped, the *Q'uy*, and V'ruwak in particular, would move against them again, harder than the last time, and they'd barely survived that.

With a slight frown, he closed out the file and sent a copy to the captain's console. Using his hands, instead of being directly connected to the computer, still felt clumsy and painfully slow.

I can create a connection for you. It won't be quite the same, but it will be faster.

Nothing quite like being called slow by an AI. "Maybe later," Rap said. He was unsure how he felt about using Nelson or giving up control. There was a sense of something from Nelson that could have been understanding. Rap was not sure.

I respect your ethical issues. It hesitated, then said, *Snake was wondering if you had time to address some concerns.*

Rap hid a sigh. He might miss the days when Snake's hissing was just that—hissing. Now that Nelson could translate, he realized how much Snake said on a daily basis. He could understand Snake's pent-up frustration and need to talk. She was the only one of the species that had been liberated from pirates, who had not had a chance to tell her story. *She. Her.* He'd thought Snake was a male for no reason he could explain.

"Didn't you look under her tail?" Dr. Rachel Grant had asked, her gaze openly amused.

He'd shaken his head, rendered mute by the presence of two females. Even before becoming human, he tended to lose most of his ability to speak. Or to think.

This is true.

Rap ignored the interjection, but that didn't make the truth go away. This left him at a considerable disadvantage with Snake. Before he could think of a response to her comments, she'd moved on to something else.

He gave a gesture of assent in Snake's direction and the flow of hissing—words by Nelson—began to flow.

Thank goodness for Ale—AlebatorR, his old friend. Not that Rap had any idea how old AlebatorR was, but Rap had done many missions with him. Ale was highly experienced in the mission critical skills Rap needed right now. Rap needed him to be at his side for the plan. There'd be no surprises from good old Ale.

"ARE YOU OKAY?"

Ale had been asked variations of this question since Dr. Rachel Grant had assisted in the process of transferring her human consciousness from her AlebatorR unit to her cloned body. By now she should have an answer. She should know what "okay" meant.

All right. Proceeding normally. Satisfactory or under control. Correct, permissible, or acceptable. Meeting standards. Well enough. Agreeable, all right, copacetic, ducky, fine, good, hunky-dory, jake, A-OK, palatable...

Ale repressed a sigh, hoping Jett did not notice. She was grateful for the accumulation of nanites that called itself Jett. It had assisted her greatly in this journey from machine to mostly human. Ale might be less grateful Jett loved rock and roll. It was a good thing the nanite could cure the headache it caused when it "rocked out."

Just tell them you are fine, sweetie.

Ale considered this suggestion and realized she'd heard the phrase exchanged many times between the humans occupying this outpost in the Garradian Galaxy.

Um, you're human, too, sweetie.

The other humans in this outpost, Ale mentally corrected, though the first felt closer to the truth. She did not yet feel like one of the humans.

"I am fine," Ale said, watching Rachel from beneath her lashes. She might miss her previous unit's ability to scan a target without looking at it.

Rachel's not a target.

This was true, but it felt as if Ale were Rachel's—problem. Jett had no comment for this, Ale noted.

I can neither agree nor disagree. Not enough data, sweetie.

Rachel had one hip propped against the counter that was part of the small kitchen in Ale's current quarters. Normally a medical person would live there, but the quarters had been empty when Ale needed to leave the hospital bed and was not quite ready for wider interaction. Even with Jett's help, Ale had struggled to control the cyborg enhancements that made her, actually, not completely human. Or a bit more human if she decided to look at it on the bright side.

Which you never do...

"It's a lot to deal with," Rachel had pointed out, when Ale exhibited frustration. "You're coping with returning to your cloned body and leaving your unit, and, well, everything."

It was true that returning to her body had been more difficult than she'd anticipated. But being watched by Rachel and her staff did not help. And being isolated from her crewmates like Rap...

She pushed that source of stress to the back of her mind. She was getting better at it.

When you have to do something that much, you're not actually getting better.

Ale ignored this and lifted her chin so that her gaze met Rachel's.

Rachel appeared to be relaxed, but her intent gaze belied that. Ale noted that Rachel's body was imperfectly aligned with one hip jutted out and one foot tucked behind the other. It was common for the humans to do this, she realized.

Ale felt her own near-perfect alignment, from her rigidly straight spinal column to the careful arrangement of her feet. Her hands rested on her almost-touching knees, the fingers lightly flexed.

You need to lighten up. Relax.

Was it more comfortable to be out of alignment? Ale moved one hand forward and eased one foot back. The urge to restore both to a more balanced position caused the tips of her fingers to tremble.

You can do it, sister.

Ale twitched, not where it could be seen, but inside.

No, really, you got this.

Almost imperceptibly, Ale moved hand and foot back into place.

Maybe next time, sweetie.

Jett's encouragement did not abate the spike of anxiety. This caused a flicker of metal to appear on the backs of her hands for a moment.

Rachel bit her lower lip, an indication Ale believed, of doubt.

"You are concerned that I am not yet stable and in control." Ale angled her head as she'd seen other humans do. "Are you not?"

Rachel hesitated, then nodded. "You're the only crew member, so far, who has returned to your own body."

Ale felt her brows rise—a strange sensation—and said, "This is not my 'own' body, Rachel. That body died when I left it for my AlebatorR unit."

"Returned to your cloned body," Rachel corrected. "How do you feel about that?"

"About becoming human once again?" Ale's brows drew together. Rachel's lack of precision was confusing.

If you think their words are confusing, you should see inside one of their heads.

Ale did not know how to respond to this interjection. She had been inside a human head before and currently was back inside...a human head. In contrast to her cybernetic unit, she could agree it was less orderly, bordering on chaotic.

Sorry.

Ale sensed Jett's embarrassment. Now that was confusing. How could an AI, no matter how sentient, project emotion?

Didn't you feel? You were an AI, too.

It was a fair question. She had felt, but she had not *felt* like this. And she had been a sentience inside her unit.

Um, so am I, girlfriend.

"Is my experience dissimilar from the others?" Ale asked.

"Yes...and no, I guess. They left bodies for their cybernetic units, but so far everyone else has chosen a new body, not a clone of who they used to be."

"This concerns you?" Ale asked the question to deflect—or postpone—the moment Rachel asked why she had done this.

"Well, CabeX seemed surprised," Rachel said.

The captain of the *Najer*, and the man who had saved her life, would be surprised by her choice. For that matter...

"I surprised myself," Ale admitted. This was a version of the truth. She'd never expected or hoped to return to her old body. And when the chance came, she would have chosen another body, too. She'd had nothing but sorrow in her old body and it would be insane of her to return to *Q'uy* territory as herself, no matter how long it had been since her death. Only Jett, and the cyborg enhancements that came with the AI, made a return possible. They were protective, but they also allowed her to hide who she was. Now she held up one hand and called the metal plating out of her hand. It flowed across the back of her hand and up her fingers, the tiny platelets shimmered silver and blue in the room's lighting. She stroked the metal composite with her human hand. It was not as strong as her robotic unit, but it was better than fragile human skin.

The Earth Expedition members had not encountered her kind —if there any of her kind left to encounter. It was possible she was the last of her species. She was not sure CabeX had known what she was when he offered her an escape, though in her experience CabeX always knew everything.

"Do you feel in control of the cybernetics now?" Rachel asked.

Ale looked up, held Rachel's gaze as she hid the metal once again. She turned her hand, released some on her palm, then hid those again.

"Yes," she said. The moments when anxiety brought them out were fewer, the breaches slight. She flexed the human fingers, feeling the movement of muscle under the skin. Jett had assisted her early on when Ale couldn't make the enhancements retract, but now Ale could control them on her own. Ale did not know—and feared to ask—if Jett intended to leave at some point. Ale might find its taste in music unfortunate, but she had grown used to having the AI... around.

I heart you, too, sweetie.

Ale felt warmth around her heart. It was somewhat like the warmth she felt around Rap, though the sensation was also different.

You don't have the hots for me.

There was no point having the, er, hots for Rap. He'd gained a human body but retained his inscrutability, and seemed mainly to care for his *BoaConscript.* As a human, she could admit she felt uneasy around the large Snake. Unlike the other rescued species, Snake did not communicate with them.

She talks plenty. You just can't understand her.

Snake's hissing was communicating?

She digs you.

Ale was not certain what this meant.

She likes you.

The Snake liked her. She supposed that was...optimal.

It is if you want to get close enough to jump Rap's bones.

She didn't—

Liar.

Ale turned her attention back to Rachel, wondering if she'd missed a question. Rachel did look puzzled, but her next comment somewhat alleviated Ale's concern.

"I've—we've—noticed—" Rachel looked away, bit her lower lip, then returned her gaze to Ale's, "—that you haven't looked at yourself. Don't you want to…see how you look?"

"I know how I look," Ale said. Her last view of her human face had been burned into the databanks of her unit, and journeyed with her consciousness into this cloned body. Though it also felt strange, there was something familiar about the height and weight of this body. She remembered the things she had done. She knew what she'd lost in giving up her robot unit. She'd liked being powerful. The cyborg enhancements helped her retain some of that power, but not all, yet she'd chosen to do this, to go all the way back. Why had she risked so much?

The heart wants what the heart wants, girlfriend.

Ale resisted the urge to rub at the tiny ache over where her human heart beat. The last time she'd seen Rap was just before they began her transfer. In a way she did not understand, his new body suited Rap, though she had not seen his previous human form. Of course, the body was not as tall as his unit had been, but it had a powerful frame, a sharply carved face that felt as if it had emerged from the metal of his old frame. The face had distinct brows over intense brown eyes. Facial hair stubbled the area around his mouth —Ale's mouth quivered before she could firm it—and a straight nose. His high forehead reached up to hair shaved short. He reminded her of the mercenaries—she cut the thought short when it caused her insides to heat up unexpectedly.

He's a bad-A dude for sure. Jett's tone was admiring. *But he's a marshmallow inside.*

Ale might have frowned. What was a marshmallow?

Soft and sweet. Nelson says he's way smarter than he looks.

Nelson was Rap's AI. How did smart look? Ale wondered. As

units, they'd all looked like, well, different kinds of robots. But she'd been the least smart of the crew.

Now don't go brain-shaming, girlfriend. You've got some serious IQ in your brainbox.

Of course, linking her mind with an AI had enabled her to learn, but she'd been the only one to come to the crew without a specific skill set, the lone human who had left her only value behind with her body. She'd worked hard to perfect her battle skills because that was all she had to offer. Always she'd wondered, if CabeX had known who he pulled out of this body, would he still have saved her? She did not wish to know the answer to that question. There was no doubt in her mind that if V'ruwak had known she still lived, he'd have thrown every resource he possessed, including every robot in his inventory, into getting her back. But he hadn't known.

She lifted a hand, tracing the curve of the now-human cheek. No, she did not need to see herself in a mirror to remember.

Ale eyed Rachel carefully, wondering how to phrase her next request, wondering if she really wanted it. But even if she didn't, Rap needed her. They'd both received the cybernetic enhancements for the upcoming mission. The mission that everything important to her, and to him, hinged on.

Smile, sweetie.

Smile?

Let me help you out with that.

The edges of her mouth moved, the edges tipping up. After a nudge from Jett, Ale said, "I feel ready to return to the *Najer* now."

RAP LISTENED to all of Snake's "concerns," which seemed numerous and not all equally essential at this time and then talked to his friend about the mission one last time before he went to meet the captain in the ship's ready room. This very human space had been an ignored room until the crew started to transition back into human form. Rap climbed two sets of ladders to get to the command deck, then turned a corner in the passage to the ready room and came face-to-face with a female.

They both stopped. She looked startled. His jaw dropped. His throat closed.

She was the kind of female that took processors offline. Her widened eyes were the green of a nebula, iridescent and mysterious. Vibrant titian hair was pulled up into a careless knot on top of her perfectly sculpted head. A straight nose sat above lips that—his brain quit working at even this minimal level, while his eyes cataloged a body well suited to the perfection of her face.

"Rap," she said. Her rounded lips compressed into a sultry line that dried his throat and caused heat to suffice his body.

He opened his mouth, but no sound emerged.

Your body's key signs are indicating a high level of stress.

The metal nanites flared on the skin of his arms and hands, catching the light in black and silver patterns. His lips pursed as they tried to ask "who?" This time a croak broke the silence.

The lips curved in a smile that felt like it stopped his heart.

"I guess you wouldn't recognize me," she said. "I hardly recognize myself." The chest—more heat flooded his extremities—rose and fell in a sigh. "I'm…Ale."

Ale. The name reverberated through his frame. "You're not…"

She shook her head, setting the titian curls dancing, light finding gold. "No, I'm not…male. I'm sorry. The captain thought it was better…" The words trailed off, and her gold-tipped lashes swept down over her eyes.

"Yes." Now, when he could have used a little help, Nelson had gone mute, too. His gaze swept her from top to bottom and a thought penetrated the shock. "You're…"

"Teimanein," she said, giving a slow nod. "Well, half. A mongrel."

Sadness marred the perfection of her eyes. Horror for her began to reduce the shock. The Teimaneins had been hunted almost, if not all the way, to extinction. Their beauty was legendary and their blood was said to hold the power of long life. Despite what his eyes told him, he could not make the connection between AlebatorR and this woman.

"You…"

Her smile was wry. "It was an excellent hiding place. And I would not have left it without…" She lifted her arms and the metal of the nanites emerged, covering her from top to toe. Only her eyes were visible now.

"Your eyes," he managed. Their color was also a giveaway.

The nanites emerged, turning them red. The nanites could not hide the blue and silver perfection of her form, but other species had well-formed bodies. He nodded, but his throat remained dry and tight. He felt like a troll standing before her. And why did that matter? he asked himself. Then he remembered his plan and the part he'd hoped he—*she*—would play in that plan.

"You can't go back—"

"I have to," she said. Her gaze held his for a long moment as the nanites retracted back into her skin. Turning, she gestured down the passage. "The captain is waiting for us."

Rap was not sure what was harder to see. Ale as a human or covered in blue and silver.

You do not need to decide now. But you should follow her.

Now heat flooded his face as he forced his legs to move.

SOMEONE NEEDS *to break out in expression, sweetie.*

It wasn't going to be Ale. She'd lived her whole life—human and robotic—hiding how she felt.

You could break the silence, then.

She licked dry lips and opened them so that words could emerge. "So, it is decided." It was not a question. That had been answered earlier with another. Did they wish to live their lives waiting for the *Q'uy* to strike or end the threat and secure their freedom? Even now they knew V'urwak would be preparing for another assault on them, and on this galaxy. He would have received data bursts from the ships he'd sent the last time, and that data would only heighten his lust for them and the technology here in the Garradian Galaxy.

This wasn't just about their continued freedom—though all the crew of the *Najer* wished to retain their freedom—but about the danger they'd brought with them. The humans here had given them aid and sanctuary. They had fought with them during the last attack and had assisted greatly in defeating that attack.

It must be acknowledged. They lived because of those who inhabited this outpost. This debt must be paid. It was their turn to risk everything. And she....

"I don't like it," CabeX said.

Of course not. It would be the first time he did not lead them into a fight.

"Rap and I are the only ones who can do this," Ale said, though it had been said before. They were the only ones with the cybernetic enhancements that could hide and protect their human bodies. And those enhancements would also be the bait to trap V'ruwak—that and the fact they'd be flying back with the two ships he'd sent to attack them. He would desire to know what happened and why those ships had not returned before now.

The thought of facing V'ruwak made her newly human blood chill in the veins. But she felt something else stirring in her memory. Something about her mother...a longing to know....

"The Earth Expedition leaders won't be happy about this," CabeX said, not as if this concerned him, but rather as an observation.

"They can't act without a committee," Rap observed. He kept his gaze turned away from Ale. He hadn't looked at her since his first protest about her part in this sortie. Her heart hurt. If he didn't care, at least she could be with him until...

She frowned. Until what? The restless stirring increasing, and she almost flinched back from the dark and cold she sensed down there....

~

SNAKE SLITHERED NEXT to Rap as they entered the outpost's ship bay and headed to where the captured robot ships were. The *Exarch* and the *Khanri* looked much like the *Najer* on the outside, but Rap was not deceived by exteriors. How could he be when he and his crew mates had perpetrated the deception they were robots who had become sentient? When their very human consciousnesses had hidden inside the robotic units for so long? Rap was not—or had not—been given to deep reflection once he'd left his human form behind. He'd been a scientist, a researcher in the same lab where most of the crew had been trapped, enslaved by V'ruwak. Together they'd been forced to work on the technology that had resulted in the robots forms that they used to escape from V'ruwak—the robots that V'ruwak used to compel others to do his will. It was CabeX, with Rap's help, who arranged for them all to escape. The risk factor had been high but they had been motivated by the desire to not just be free, but to live free.

If he'd just wanted his freedom from everything that was intolerable, he could have killed himself. In truth, he'd wanted freedom for something better. And he wanted to quit hiding from his past. He wanted to live so he could resume his real studies, not those forced upon him. He wanted to live—well, he wanted to live.

Most men would rather deny a hard truth than face it.

Rap did not acknowledge this interjection because he was not sure what Nelson thought he denied. He inhaled deeply into his new lungs. He lived. He was free—mostly. They were still hunted by V'ruwak. And now V'ruwak knew they and the *Najer* were somewhere in the Garradian Galaxy. It was a lot of space to search, but as long as he hunted for them, they would never be completely free. Their new human bodies gave them an edge, made them harder to find. But that assumed no one would sell this information to V'ruwak, that betrayal was a thing of the past, too.

Rap was not the only crew member who did not believe in this fantasy.

They all wished to be truly and completely free of this threat. Rap had no illusions that other threats might appear, but V'ruwak —made all else pale in comparison.

Rachel had told him he needed a lodestar to survive the transfer of his consciousness from unit to human body. Eliminating the threat that was V'ruwak had been the goal he'd clung to whenever it felt as if madness would overtake him. He had held onto that, focusing on how to do it. He'd always known the path to defeating V'ruwak was through V'ruwak's legion of robotic units, but they'd never been able to get close enough to do it. Now, with his cybernetic enhancements and Rap's knowledge gained from creating and then living inside a robot, they finally had a chance.

A slim chance the captain had said, with warning in his eyes. It was true that V'ruwak knew their greatest strength was also their greatest weakness. Had not every attack against them included a virus designed to take control of their systems? Rap believed he'd accounted for that, but it did require them to be present and at high risk of compromise themselves during the delivery of their virus.

He glanced down at Snake, who slithered next to him into the hangar, for once silent.

"Do you have a name?" Rap asked, surprised he'd managed a whole question. Perhaps he could get used to a female snake.

She says you couldn't pronounce it. If she discovers a name she likes that you can pronounce, she will let you know.

Hopefully, not in the middle of the mission, Rap thought, humor tugging at the edges of his mouth. But as they drew closer to the ships, guilt and relief warred for prominence in his mind. Not unlike what he felt about Ale. He was glad both would be with him on this first—and possibly last—mission since he became a human again. Rap had no illusions about the dangers they faced or the odds against them. The presence of Snake and yes, Nelson, improved their chances of a successful mission, though neither Snake nor AIs improved the odds that he or Ale would survive. They had altered the ship's programming so that it would return Snake and the AIs if something happened.

Snake is very brave.

She was, Rap acknowledged. She would be visible, unlike the AIs who could move through systems almost undetected. What wouldn't be visible were the plates of circuitry on her skin that carried part of the complex virus they'd created with the assistance of Savlf, the captain's friend who had been rescued from the same spider pirate who had imprisoned Snake.

She can move quickly and go through openings humans and robots cannot. She is well suited to the task.

And she was sentient enough to want some redress from the *Q'uy*, who had sold her to the spider pirate.

Payback is a bitch.

Rap half frowned. That did not sound like Nelson.

Forgive me. I was quoting Jett, Ale's AI. She is somewhat…informal. Payback can create complications.

Oh. For Rap, this mission was not about revenge but restoring the balance of power to a system that had rewarded the venal and selfish for far too long. He had no desire to kill anyone, even V'ruwak, though if anyone deserved to die it was he. Rap would fight, and yes, kill if forced into it, but he had no desire to deal death to anyone. Once started, it was too hard to stop.

Only CabeX waited by the *Khanri* and *Exarch*, the two captured *Q'uy* ships. Ale was incoming. She'd been delayed by an unexpected encounter with Rachel. Hopefully, that would not delay their plan, since this action was…

Off book.

Rap paused to get a more accurate definition. It was true the Earth Expedition had not been…

Read in. Given veto power—

The Earth Expedition leaders did not understand the threat level, even after the near disaster of the recent action. It was fortunate Ale had not been required—or expected—to say much to the doctor before now. All that Rachel and the others knew was that they were doing a shake-down trip on the two ships, after cleaning the programming code. Neither he nor Ale had found the time to polish their deception skills but perhaps the trip would aid them in acquiring this distasteful, but necessary skill—which they would need for the mission.

He also hoped to overcome his difficulty in speaking to females —specifically Ale and Snake, but also others. Rap paused in his thoughts so that Nelson could weigh in. The resounding silence was an indication of the AI's lack of confidence in Rap's mastery of speaking to females. Rap could not completely articulate—even to himself—why he felt he needed to learn to talk to...

Ale?

Females.

You don't want to be alone. You wish to be with someone who matters. Someone like Ale.

It was true that this felt key to being free to live. Ale would understand that. Well, he'd assumed he—she—would understand.

You can form a support group.

Rap sensed that Nelson felt they would need a support group and more to sort out their issues. He sighed and turned his attention to the two ships—something he felt confident he could sort.

ALE FELT VERY...

Deer in the headlights.

What?

Trust me, it's an apt analogy, even if you don't get it.

Okay.

Smile or Rachel will suspect something.

Ale tipped up the edges of her mouth. It did not feel like a smile.

"How does it feel?" Rachel gestured vaguely around with her hands.

"The temperature is the same here as it was—"

She means, how does it feel to be out and about?

"But it is...pleasant...to be around...others," Ale added.

Rachel grinned. "It is probably going to be hard to be human for a while. I wouldn't stress too much about it."

Yeah, that ship sailed.

"Are you worried about the shake-down flight?" Rachel asked, sending Ale's heart into overdrive.

"Worried?"

"Well, TalusH said he has finecombed for traps and stuff. He thinks he found the program that automatically returns the ships to their home base."

Rachel did not sound, or look, unduly concerned. Her tone was more that of matter-of-fact scientist.

Yeah, I really don't think she suspects anything. If you can keep your cool for a few more minutes.

"Programming was—ever—our worry," Ale said, nodding her head as she'd seen other humans doing during communication exchanges.

Rachel's face broke into a wide smile. "Well, that shouldn't be a problem anymore, or at least not much of one."

They did still have some programming in their cybernetics, but Jett, a sentient AI, was a powerful protection.

You are welcome.

But even as Ale felt her insides relax, she felt that dark, cold stirring within....

~

BOTH SHIPS WERE the latest in the *Q'uy* fleet—a testament to how desperately V'ruwak wanted them and the *Najer* back. Thanks to these ships and the robots they'd also captured, they'd acquired insight into the improvements the *Q'uy* had made since their escape. If they'd dared, they would have added some of the Garradian upgrades to the ships, but they were flying into the heart of the *Q'uy* empire, and this would be a worse betrayal of their human friends.

Rap wished....

That this was your bonding trip instead of a flight into deadly danger?

Heat suffused his body. There was no question of that.

Naturally I cannot betray a confidence, though there are others who have no problem with that, but I would not despair if I were you. Well, I wouldn't if we weren't beginning a journey that is not likely to end well. So perhaps despair is your best option. Humans have been known to accomplish extraordinary things when all hope is lost.

Not grateful for this further lack of confidence, Rap joined CabeX, his gaze scanning the ships as memories of past missions stirred in the morass that was called the brain. He had hoped for some of his memories to make the journey with him into this new body and was not exactly pleasantly surprised that the unpleasant ones had also come along. They were not well arranged and were sometimes difficult to access, but he also knew he needed to remember as much as possible, so he could do what must be done.

Neither he nor CabeX spoke right away. Speech wasn't just challenging with females for him. All speech was difficult, he conceded. Their years without the need for talking had left them relearning this necessary skill. Rap had watched and eavesdropped on the humans on this outpost, hoping to discover clues to how they talked to each other so easily. It seemed that so much of their communication was…unnecessary.

Small talk can build a bridge between humans. They seek common ground and a beginning of understanding.

This did not provide much enlightenment.

Ask your captain how Savlf is doing.

That was a very personal question.

All questions are personal.

Oh. Rap glanced back. Ale had not arrived yet. It felt optimal to make this attempt without an audience. Or any more of an audience. He cleared his throat. "How is Savlf?"

"She was well enough to refine the virus you carry with you," CabeX said.

Rap nodded, mimicking what he'd seen other humans do during their talking events. "That is well."

Rap felt a strange urge to shift his feet, to move even in a small way. This bridge was not very big.

"She is most expert with code," Rap said. She had almost taken down CabeX with a virus when he was still a robot, and she had been the slave of the spider pirate. She had been grievously injured by her time in the spider captain's web but she appeared to be recovering.

"Yes," CabeX said.

It is going to be a long trip.

The bay doors of the hangar slid back and Ale entered wearing basic-black, human-crew clothing. It clung to her curves and turned her hair into a flame that lit something inside him. She moved with a brisk grace, which put a tighter band around his vocal cords.

It was indeed going to be a long trip.

Executing The Plan

"The entrance strategy is actually more important than the exit strategy." Edward Lampert

THOUGH NEWER TECHNOLOGY on these ships had made their trip much swifter than they could have accomplished with the *Najer*, it had been a long trip. If not for Snake's hissing, and Jett's translations of the hissing, and it would have otherwise been a mostly silent trip. Ale missed the stream of data that used to occupy her circuits during long trips.

She'd have welcomed a skirmish or two to break up the monotony, though she was aware she should not wish for this. Their last action had lacked monotony and been laden with too much action. It seemed to be that way. One had too much or too little of something.

Ale glanced at Rap, who stared straight ahead, or shifted to study readings that hadn't changed much for the duration of their trip. He hadn't been totally stationary. Neither of them could do that anymore. Both had to deal with the needs of their now human bodies. Before Rap left the bridge, he would turn to her, and after a short struggle, say, "I'll be back."

On his return, he managed, "I'm back," a couple of times.

Both the *Exarch* and the *Khanri* had held crews of the *Q'uy's* latest, deadliest robots. Like the ships, the robots had required reprogramming so they'd believe they were "returning" from the action where they'd actually been captured. CabeX and Savlf had also placed a portion of the virus in each robot. Once the robots were placed in debrief mode, it would begin to make its way into the systems, seeking to rejoin the other portions of the virus. It was Rap's belief, and his hope, that breaking up the virus would give it a better chance of evading anti-virus programming.

A restraining program had been installed to keep the captured robots from attempting to take back control of the ships. CabeX and Savlf, with the help of the outpost's AI, had also scrubbed both ships' systems of traps, though they had left the recall programming in place. But they'd set it so that it appeared the ships' journey had originated from the same place they'd been captured and not this outpost.

Hopefully, before anyone got too curious about the gap of time between them going offline and coming back online, the virus would be causing chaos.

Curiosity, Rachel had told them, was a powerful force. It drove humans to try, to seek, to learn, to understand. It even drove them into danger, this desire to find out what they didn't know. Ale understood it better now. She was most curious to know what Rap wished to say, when he'd glance in her direction, and his lips would open, then close. He'd managed a few words but only those related to their mission. Nothing personal.

That man has some serious female-shyness issues, sweetie. If you want words out of his mouth, you're going to have to ask him something.

She wished to know, if not for the hopeless mission, could they have been friends? Or more than friends?

You might want to start with something easier. Get him used to letting words out before you ask the Big Question.

Was it a big question?

According to my sources, for dudes, "Where do you see our relationship going" is the Biggest Question. Huge. Seriously huge.

But they didn't have much time. When the two ships reached the beacon, events would escalate quickly. She wished to go into this hopeless mission knowing he cared.

If there was a dollar for every female who'd wished that….

So it wasn't just her?

From what I gather, the problem is almost always the dude's trouble with commitment and is a multisystem-wide problem.

Oddly enough, this did not help Ale feel better. So she turned her thoughts to a question she could ask that was not the Biggest Question, but would help her get there before it was too late.

I've been scanning books and video for something for you, but so far nothing seems quite right for the moment.

Right for the moment. She sighed. Time was running out for any more moments. She bit her lip then shifted in her seat so that she half faced him. Did she, as Jett asserted, have the hots for Rap? As if in answer to this query, heat suffused her body, but what startled her more, color flowed up into his face. Was he affected as well?

"Rap?" The name slipped out her lips that were pressed together so they wouldn't tremble.

He turned so swiftly she jerked, but she held her position, though it took effort.

His lips moved several times before he managed, "Yes?"

"We'll be to the beacons soon, and then it will be too late."

"Too…late?" His strong brows rose over his brooding gaze.

She met his gaze, saw confusion in them, felt the echo of it inside herself.

Just kiss him. Sometimes words just won't do it.

Before she let her thoughts stop her, she leaned forward and pressed her lips to Rap's. They were warm and firm and caused more of the *hots* to spread out from this simple contact point. She was unsure what was supposed to happen, but then his lips parted slightly, his head angling to draw her deeper into the kiss. It was the only place they touched. Her hands clung to the armrests to keep from reaching for him.

Lips, she realized, almost too dazed to form the thought, could speak in ways other than words.

"Ale." Rap's voice breathed this against her mouth before closing over hers once more.

The *hots* began to make more sense as the heat built—

The ping of the ship responding to the *Q'uy* beacon was a rush of cold to quench the fire.

Contact was broken, but neither moved more than a tiny gap as their gazes clashed. Words crowded her throat, and it seemed he struggled, too.

"Live," she said finally.

His hand covered her hand closest to him.

"You, too."

She sensed she wouldn't, but she nodded, her lips curving into a trembling smile. She let her hand come to rest where his clutched hers. And then because the words couldn't come, lifted his hand to hold it against her heart.

The ship's systems began to respond to the queries from the beacon. With a final clutch, she let him go.

You love him.

If this tumult of longing and joy and sorrow was love—then yes, she did.

THE PAIN in his chest was worse than the journey into this body as Rap turned from Ale. For several moments he could not see the data beginning to flow across the various screens. There was a haze before his eyes.

What you feel—

Not now. Rap cut Nelson off. He heard Snake hissing as well, but he didn't want to know. Not yet. He needed a moment to savor the feel and taste of her lips against his. That she'd kissed him amazed him and filled him with regret. He looked at her, taking in the sight of the mouth that had pressed his, the eyes that looked at *him* with longing, the flame of her hair and the sweet suppleness of her skin. That she felt the same longing he did—he lacked words.

Not a surprise.

"We should…" He stopped, amazed he'd managed to get two words out.

"Yes." She sat back and after a moment, her cybernetic platelets flowed across her skin, going up and down until every trace of Ale was hidden by the blue and silver.

He activated his cybernetics as well, feeling the distance between them growing. A communication from the *Q'uy* was most likely already tracking toward them, but he needed to know, if there was time.

"Your kind, is it true…?"

"Most of what you heard isn't true," she said. "But no one believed it. It was believed we withheld secrets, power, so they killed us or—" she swallowed "—kept us as slaves and curiosities. I might be the last. I don't know."

Slaves. Curiosities. Which had she been in the world of the *Q'uy?*

"I'm sorry," he managed.

Keep this up, and you'll be spouting three words at a time.

Rap ignored Nelson. He felt Snake beginning to wind itself around him and touched the *BoaConscript.*

"Ready?"

Okay, that was a backslide, but yes, she is ready.

Behind him, one of the captured and restrained robots stirred, its metal hands reaching for navigation controls that weren't there. The battle that was about to begin would take place inside circuits and systems but would also be mind to mind. Body to body. The fate of their crewmates and friends pitted against the lusts of their enemies.

Do you know what popcorn is? Jett wishes we had some. And she says she's betting on us.

≈

Q'ULOUMORE, the central city for the *Q'uy*, was a series of complex shafts of metal that stabbed up through the perpetually heavy cloud cover blanketing the planet of the same name. Four of the darkly ominous planetary security force ships closed in on them as soon as they entered the murky atmosphere, sharp orders appearing on the various comm screens of their ship. The robots inside were even less diplomatic, Rap recalled.

Around them a wide variety of ships entered or left the atmosphere, also closely monitored by security ships. Indeed, there appeared to be more of the dark security ships than other traffic, both in atmosphere and out.

Though there was a central governing board that ruled all the *Q'uy*, it was an open secret that V'ruwak controlled this board—backed by the power of his robots. That control had been damaged when the *Najer* and its crew broke free. Though the ships sent against them recently were restricted from having updated data on V'ruwak, they had picked up some chatter during their transit that indicated V'ruwak was feeling increased pressure since the last failed attempt. The sight of so much security appeared to confirm this. Tyrants clutched hardest when at their most precarious.

The return of these two ships should make him eager to bring them in and curious to find out what happened and who he and Ale were. As far as Ale knew, there were no other cybernetic beings like them in this system. They'd baited the hook well, but Rap's well-constructed trap did have weaknesses, the biggest being their lack of current intel.

Ale looked about her with interest. She'd been a child when she was transported here and had never been let outside until her escape as a robot, but she'd not been in the mood for sightseeing then. Even though she'd taken what CabeX offered, she hadn't been convinced she was truly free for a long time. The others had left her alone, and even when she was ready to interact, most of that was done through the system, not in person, unless they were on an off-ship mission.

She'd spent the time before and after learning to fight—and to trust. Could she say she had learned trust when she'd kept her most important secret?

That's a little too deep for me, sweetie. I can't process angst.

Ale had to suppress a smile.

That's better, sweetie. You seriously need to chill.

Since Ale was not sure what temperature had to do with anything, she ignored this interjection.

"We will be docking soon," she said, finding it easier to talk now that they were both focused on the mission. It was easier without the angst, she admitted to herself—and thence to Jett.

Rap's plan presupposed a heavily armed boarding party of robots once security realized their robots weren't flying this ship. It was their first most dangerous moment, with many more to follow— if they survived this first contact. Would the robots shoot them on sight? Protocol called for both restraint and aggression in the situation. Much would depend on how the robots had been briefed to respond through their programming.

The first tendrils of the virus were already inching their way into the *Q'uy's* systems through the beacon's first contact. It was in heavy stealth mode, because the *Q'uy* had the finest antivirus programming in three galaxies at least. This was a variation on the virus the robot crews carried. All sections of the virus were multipronged, designed to go dormant during scans, so they were uncertain how long it would take to propagate enough to take control.

"How is Snake?" Ale asked Jett. The *BoaConscript* was moving around Rap's torso, its scales flickering gold and then brown in the subdued lighting of the bridge.

She is as calm as you are.

So, not that well.

"We've received the docking command," Rap said.

Wow, five words in a row.

There was no turning back now, even if they wanted to. Tracking beams had already locked on to both ships. Rap's hands moved on the controls as he activated the next level of the virus, sending it back along the beams.

For the first time, Ale struggled to keep the cybernetics in place, rather than the reverse. She had never needed to hide more.

IT'S NOT A PARTICULARLY *cheerful place.*

Nelson wasn't wrong. The walls of the detention cell were gray, the light merciless, the ambient temperature set for discomfort. Rap was glad for the cybernetic skin. There was a single air vent, and his careful scanning indicated the air was barely safe for humans. No questions had been asked by the robots who'd ushered them in with punctilious force.

Questions came from humans, not robots.

Rap calculated the wait before a human came to question them as he and Ale sat unspeaking on a bench so hard even his cybernetics couldn't compensate. Their captors would wish to escalate their fear. This desire would be offset by their curiosity.

He and Ale were, as they'd anticipated, being monitored, so talking was contraindicated. Rap had detected four cameras and at least that many listening devices. And even the most basic communications would be used against them, would give power to their enemy. At precisely the time Rap had calculated that curiosity would trump their desire to cause fear, a door slid back and a human entered. If he survived, Rap would have to calculate how not to be so predictable.

Gray faced and thin, the human wore the typical black garb of the *Q'uy.* The flat gray of his eyes gleamed with a curiosity partially obscured by heavy, half-lowered lids. The man's hands hung empty at his sides, no other sign of weapons about his person. Perhaps he felt he didn't need them when he was flanked by two fully armed, Oxeroid-class robots.

"You will explain yourselves," the man ordered. As if to punctuate this statement, the two robots lifted both their arms and targeted Rap and Ale with their weapons. They wouldn't fire unless forced to. Rap and Ale's cybernetics was too unusual. Even then, in

Rap's assessment, they would seek disabling rather than lethal force. The human was expendable.

Rap felt no need to explain anything.

"You will explain who you are and why you are found in possession of stolen *Q'uy* ships and materials."

Materials. That would be the robots.

Beside him, Ale stirred.

"If you find ships abandoned and floating in space, is it stealing to board them?"

This came from Ale. Beneath his mask Rap frowned. Her voice sounded odd, as if she spoke with an effort.

The man's gaze snapped in Ale's direction.

"Where did you find them?" the man barked.

Rap let the silence stretch out. "You know where we found them. You have access to their logs and databases."

The man's lips thinned, almost disappearing into the folds of gray skin. "You took them—"

"We started them up and they took us—here," Rap corrected.

The man's face contorted to match the low snarl.

"You are welcome," Rap added.

"You should have informed us of their location and then left them untouched."

"Who are you that we should contact you?" Ale's tone held a hint of mockery but still sounded strangely heavy.

"And once aboard, your machines refused to let us leave. Technically, they stole us," Rap pointed out. He added, "We would like to be returned to our ship."

"What is your kind? Your designation? Who is your master?"

How like a *Q'uy* to believe they were slaves and things.

"We are who we are, and where we come from is our business," Ale said.

Rap wanted to look at her, but it would expose a weakness.

"For now." His lip curled in a snarl, but then his eyes widened, a trace of fear entering them. He turned on his heel and left.

That went as expected.

Had it? Rap was not so sure. The man had received a communication. A soft sound from the direction of the vent caught his attention. He did not look that way. He did not wish to call attention to the vent.

Snake is here.

Rap wished he could talk directly to his friend—and now comrade in danger.

If you'd indicated that is what you required…

Nelson sounded annoyed. There was a long pause.

Are you in any distressss?

Is this Snake? he wondered.

Of course it issss….

Now that he had the *BoaConscript's* attention, he wasn't sure what to ask. Can you give me a report? he finally thought.

I eggresssed the ssship assss planned and found the venting sssysssstem. Obviousssly.

Were you be able to access the required systems?

I have disssscovered accesss pointss and releasssed virusss packetsss. I will continue my misssion unlesss you require asssisssstance.

Will you be able to return safely to the ship?

Snake, Nelson, and Jett should be able to get to the ship on their own using the same pathways they'd used to deliver the virus, but Snake was most at risk, of course, since she was visible to human eyes and other scanning technology. But who would suspect a *BoaConscript* of carrying an AI packet of data embedded on the surface of her skin?

Once you have delivered the virus you should return to the ship and wait for us, he emphasized. It was acceptable to risk his life, but Snake's? No more than absolutely necessary.

All he and Ale had to do was stall for long enough to determine if the virus worked, get out of here and back to the ships—the only ships that would be capable of flight—and escape while the *Q'uy* systems were in chaos.

So simple. And so complicated. With many "ifs" in the execution. How long would it take for the virus to move into the systems? The virus was a modified version of an AI, so that it could go dormant if needed then activate once the danger had passed. How long would word of their capture take to reach important enough levels that they would be moved farther from the ship? Or worse, separated for questioning?

In the hall outside, it seemed as if he heard the thump of footsteps approaching once more.

Next to him Ale stirred, then spoke, quickly and too low for the listening devices to pick up.

"I'm sorry."

He stiffened, half turned toward her. The footsteps stopped outside and the door slid open once more. Rap sat frozen, caught in an unfamiliar cold at Ale's unexpected words. Before he could speak, part of her cybernetics retracted, exposing her face.

"As you can see, V'ruwak, a daughter of Erume has returned."

Two robots entered and grasped her on either side, dragging her from the room. Now, when it was too late, Rap leapt for the doors, but they closed in his face. He hit them with his fist, leaving a dent, but little else, in the metal and then turned, sagging against the unyielding surface.

I am guessing that was not part of your plan.

The Plan Goes Pearshaped

"Hope is not a strategy." Vince Lombardi

RAP HAD to get out of this cell. He couldn't do anything stuck in here.

Snake and I can assist you in reaching this goal. But we can't promise what will happen after.

He could take care of what came after. He considered the robots and added, probably. He recalled the feel of Ale's lips on his. He would take care of after. And then some. Do it, he told them.

The doors slid open.

The cybernetic skin flickered, opening a gap near his waist. From this he extracted a small but lethal hand weapon. It felt strange not to have more weapons about his unit. A flaw in this unit. He resealed the opening and eased to the door. He did a quick check. For the moment, the hallway was clear. He'd need more weapons than one.

The robots are heavily armed.

That was why he needed more weaponry.

Oh. Snake says—

Sssnake can sssspeak for herssssself…

Apologies.

Weapons? Rap asked. He had the odd sensation his eye twitched.

There issss a reposssitory of weaponssss nearby…

Show me.

A human came around the corner, a guard of some sort because his arm lifted, but he never got a shot off. Rap took time to drag him back and throw him in the cell. Snake closed the door again. The short journey to the weapons storage was uneventful. Where is she, he asked, as he grabbed everything he could. He glanced around. He still remembered.

Where is she, he asked again. And then you can both go back to the ship.

With all due respect, you need us.

Need ussss…

They were correct, but Ale's "I'm sorry" echoed in his mind. Whatever it was she planned, she did not expect to survive. He could not, he would not let her die alone.

They have detected the virus and are launching countermeasures.

He felt his body settle into grim lines. He could not be in two places at once. He would fight to complete the mission and then… "Where is the nearest systems' terminal?"

Thissss way…

The room is not empty. In point of fact, it is quite populated.

Then he'd have to depopulate it.

AS SOON AS the doors closed behind her, V'ruwak stepped close—but not too close—running his dead gaze over her. Ale felt frozen, a part of her shocked at what she'd just done but unable to stop. It was as if she'd caught a virus, too. She remembered this man, though the aspect of man facing her bore little resemblance to the man in her memory. His eyes had not changed. They were devoid of warmth or humanity.

He looked and moved like a walking cadaver. There were deep grooves putting dark shadows in his gray skin. He lifted a hand, one with so little flesh under the skin the bones were clearly outlined. He'd managed to extend his life, but he looked as if a touch would turn him to dust.

If only, she thought. If only he hadn't lived, then—what? What was this strange compulsion? Why had she revealed herself to him? Perhaps she'd come hoping to find information about her mother, but not this way. She'd never wanted to see V'ruwak again.

Four fingers curled in as one claw digit reached and poked her cybernetic skin. It seemed she had overestimated her importance to him. Only her skin interested him, at least for now.

His gaze lifted, and the hand withdrew.

"Bring it," he ordered and turned, striding quickly down the long hall.

It?

Jett sounded outraged. Ale did not blame her. Unlike Ale, the AI was not used to being called an "it."

You need to leave as soon as an opportunity presents itself, Ale told Jett. Find your way back to the ship. It felt as if Jett snorted.

Who is it?

There was disdain in the AI's tone. Ale almost smiled at Jett's returning of the dismissive designation. When Ale didn't answer, Jett asked again.

Who is it?

Ale fought the urge to bring her cybernetic skin back up as the two robots dragged her after V'ruwak. And inside she fought the urge to answer the question, to face what she'd hidden from for so long.

He is my father.

227

I AM *unclear on the plan.*

You have two options, Rap told Nelson. You can leave, or you can help Snake launch a counter-attack on their systems.

What will you be doing?

I'll be clearing the room, he told the AI. Choose now, because I'm going in. It felt odd to sense Nelson pushing back his sleeves. He almost asked, then decided he didn't have time.

His cybernetic enhancements were not as efficient at entry as his unit had been. He had to manually touch the entry pad, allowing attack nanites to flood in and authorize his entry. He had two weapons—both set to stun—ready as the door slid back. No one in the room even looked up from their terminals. They were hunched over data-entry pads, frantically working.

They are trying to stop the virus.

Nelson fed him a data stream that appeared in his cybernetic headgear. There was no reason now for it to stay stealth, so it was fighting back. How are we doing? he asked.

Right now it is about even.

Nelson did not sound like he liked admitting it. Get in there and help. Please, he added. Rap targeted a humanoid in front of the closest terminal, and when he, or possibly she, slumped over, he eased them clear of the terminal. Incredibly, he still hadn't been seen. He made physical contact with the terminal, so Nelson could use the contact for fast access, then he rose and started targeting the other humanoids in the room.

Watch yourrr baccck...

Rap spun and shot the access panel. It wouldn't keep a robot out for long, but it would hopefully get them the time they needed to win the viral battle. Now the techs started to notice him. Some kept working frantically at their terminals, while others dove under the tables. He jumped up on one of the tables and kept firing.

Robots incoming.

~

YOU AND LUKE *should form a support group for kids with crap dads.*

Luke? Ale asked the question vaguely. Whatever had her in thrall was dragging her back, back into the past. Someone was crying, a lost and lonely sound that made her heart hurt.

I think you might win the crap-dad contest.

Ale knew what crap meant though she could not see the face of the person who'd taught her this.

Something weird is happening in here. We need Rap.

Rap. She knew that name, or she had known him. But something held her back from thinking about him, and besides, thinking of him made water try to leak from her opticals.

Eyes, sweetie. There was a pause. *Okay, something seriously freaky is happening inside your brainbox—*

Jett gave a startled sound. It was the only warning Ale had as a dam inside her head broke. If she could have screamed, Ale would have. As it crashed over her, it shattered the one called Ale, leaving the daughter of Erume standing in the wreckage with pain dripping off her. The daughter of Erume. What—she'd had no other designation. No name. Nothing to tell her apart from the others. There had been others. Sisters. Where were they now? One by one they'd left…

You are Ale.

The voice was so faint, she strained to hear it. Who—?

I am Jett.

Jett. She knew Jett. Jett was—better than this. She needed to leave before the—seliks happened, whatever that was. She knew but she didn't *know.* Forming the words in her mind took effort. Cold crept out from the memories, like V'ruwak's claw fingers, seizing up muscles and biting deep into bone, stealing her voice.

I don't want you to panic or anything, but Rap could probably use our help. Just a bit.

Rap? She knew that name, too. Regret only increased the cold. He deserves better.

Daughter of Erume, hear me.

She frowned. It was her…mother's voice. More memories

rushed out. Of being dragged from her mother's arms. Brief contact via vids once a year. And always with that look in her eyes that said, *remember. Remember your promise.*

What promise?

At the fullness of your power, when you come of age, you will gain the power of the seliks. Use it to avenge me.

His face, from the past, grew in her mind until she struggled to escape, to scream. But she couldn't move. She couldn't speak. Only she knew she wouldn't get to leave to get away from him until she kept this promise. Had she made a promise?

Swear to me on your life that you will do this for me. Promise your mother!

And in a distant echo in her mind, she heard a child's voice say, "I promise, my mother."

Ale! Your mother is as bad as your dad! Dig deeper into your memory and you will see!

On some level Ale was aware that the robots pushed her into a room, an office? V'ruwak, this old version with the same eyes, waited for her in front of a large desk. They were the same shade of gray, she noted vaguely. She felt pressure on her shoulders to sit and then was aware that the two robots positioned themselves on either side of her. It felt not real, like a dream.

A nightmare!

With an effort, Ale thought it again. Leave me.

I'm not leaving you. Hang on. Hang on to me!

Ale felt worry breach the ice, but not enough to let her move. Rap needed to stay away, too. He needed to forget her, to do the mission and leave…mission? She'd come here to do something important. Had she imperiled the mission? For a moment Ale pushed out the cold.

"If she moves, rip her head from her body," V'ruwak said, almost indifferently. But his avaricious gaze betrayed him.

Wow, not feeling the daddy love from the—

Jett used a word that Ale did not recognize, yet knew was not a compliment. If she could have smiled, she would have. She still couldn't move, but she felt something welling up from deep inside her. She glanced down at her hands, resting quiescently on her knees. She was perfectly aligned again. She looked up, meeting his gaze. She refused to name him Father—again. The sight of him made the something flare higher.

Um, it's getting warm in here. Weirdly warm.

Warm? But she felt ice cold.

V'ruwak straightened and paced briefly in front of the desk before coming to a stop in front of her again. His dead gaze finally settled on her face. "I wonder which one you are," he murmured, more to himself than to her. "And who made you into this." He touched the skin again then pulled his hand back, startled. He flexed the fingers. "Interesting."

He is our enemy! Fulfill your promise!

She didn't know how to do it.

I have a bad feeling about this seliks thing. A really bad feeling. A smoking-hot feeling.

"He took me from my mother." Ale was surprised to hear the words echoing around the bleak room. Had she meant to speak them out loud? The only other time she'd felt this out of control—she flinched from the memory but had no power to escape it. CabeX had offered to carry her dead body back to where she'd done it. It was necessary to conceal the consciousness transfer from V'ruwak and others. She'd set herself back down in the blood. There'd been so much blood for two wounds. They didn't give slaves like her knives, so she'd had to create her own. She'd explored the room inch by inch until she'd found one rough spot. She'd worked on it for years. She knew what was coming and prepared to take it from him at the last minute.

But CabeX had offered her an alternative. If she'd known she'd find herself back in the same place—but she was not the same. The time with her crewmates had changed her. She had learned things that this man, that her mother had not wished her to know. Things like loyalty and friendship. Compassion for others, but also for herself. And love, she'd learned to love. This man would never know love.

Kill him!

Kill? Inside Ale shook her head. She'd fought beside her crewmates, she'd fought for them, but they tried not to kill unless forced into it. She'd learned to fight aboard the *Najer*, but they killed only in defense of themselves and the defenseless.

He's not worth killing.

Her suit concealed one weapon, but against two robots...

I'm so glad you're thinking again, but it's still heating up in here.

Now Ale felt it, felt the burn of it along her veins. She did not know where it was being controlled. She'd been a human back then. There was no way anyone could have programmed her.

There is a thing called mental conditioning. Mind control.

Someone—no, her *mother*—was trying to control her. More of her memory of the past opened, and she saw, not the mother who clung to her crying, not the mother who appeared on the vids saying how much she missed her, but the real person. Now she saw the same lack of feeling in her mother—no, Erume's eyes.

"Was she really my mother?" Again the question broke the silence of the room.

V'ruwak started, as if his thoughts had been far away.

"Does it matter?" he asked. "I'm more interested in these enhancements. Who made them?"

He didn't make the mistake of touching her again.

The heat was building and with it a wave of...pain?

Grief, sweetie. But I think it is healing grief. I really hope because we're not going to last much longer if you can't get this under control.

Did she want to stop it? The fire hurt but the grief was worse. She needed it to stop.

If you kill him, the pain will be gone, her mother's voice said.

She's lying! You'll be dead. And Rap will be dead, too. He's in trouble!

Rap? Something cool and healing began to rise against the heat. She felt as if she hung between both, trying to decide what Ale needed. What Ale wanted.

Choice. Neither of them had given her choice. That had come from CabeX and the others. She could give into the past, or she could live—she could *live*—in the present and have a future. All she had to do was let go. All she had to do was *choose.*

And defeat a couple of robots…not that I'm trying to be negative.

❦

RAP HEARD the robots assaulting the door at his back. He managed a quick look. They weren't through yet.

In an ironic twist, they fortified this door in case the robots ever went rogue.

It was always a nice bonus when an adversary contributed to their own destruction. He targeted the last few techs still trying to fight the virus, but he did not delude himself that this was the only place that techs—under penalty of death most likely—were fighting back. He dropped into the seat in front of the last working terminal and joined the systems battle. Thanks to Nelson, he could see where Snake was still dropping packets of virus using the venting system. But if someone realized what she was doing, it could get dicey for her.

You should start heading back to the ship, he directed her.

As they'd expected, the *Q'uy* counterattack had a specific module to attack rogue robots. Either they had acquired a version of the virus Savlf had used against CabeX, or they collaborated with the spider pirate to create it. It didn't matter. What did was that they had been working to boost its effectiveness since, based on what he saw in the data streams. If he'd still been a robot, he'd already be down. It was only the nature of his cybernetics that had protected him so far, but the nanites were computers, too. The countervirus appeared to be at least as adaptive as the one CabeX and others had developed for this attack. They were attacking him with almost everything they had, which left an opening for his virus to do some damage.

It is affecting the robots and shipping, but the main system is still capable of maintaining the counterattack.

Affecting the robots was optimal for Rap. He could withstand a lot, but not a combined robotic assault.

233

How many is a combined assault? Not because I'm worried or anything. Just for purely informational purposes.

What? Rap glanced back, saw the first signs of a breach in the door. A red line cutting through the metal. He released more strands of virus into the system, sending them against the program trying to breach his cybernetics. As a human, his response time was slower. He assumed this was the case for all the humans driving the counterattack. There was a downside. A human could come up with a save that a system didn't. It was the human factor that had saved CabeX when he was attacked by a version of this virus.

But they had more humans on their side than he had on his. He did not let himself consider Ale in this calculation. He did not know what had happened to her. He did know that if he let worry overtake him, he would lose—all of them would lose.

Have we lost all hope yet? Because this would be a good time for the desperate saving play.

He did not have an answer for Nelson. He did not have an answer for his question either. Was he human enough to conceive of that desperate saving play?

THE VIRUS IS STILL *our best chance.*

Ale thought about telling Jett—again—that she should go, she should flee her body, but she figured Jett was in there and already knew her options. So she didn't waste energy on futile thoughts. The virus—they needed to deliver something updated and new—and they needed to do it fast. *If I can get the robots to touch me, could you whip something up? Something they aren't expecting?* Ale asked.

Already whipping—wow, that sounds kinky.

Ale lifted her chin so that her gaze met V'ruwak's and she gave a slow smile, one she'd recently learned from the woman she'd called Mother.

"You are like her," V'ruwak said, wariness altering his gaze.

Ale brought more of her cybernetic skin up, until only her head was visible. "You can touch it. It won't burn this time."

He eyed her for a long time, then he straightened abruptly. "Hold her."

Bingo. He's so predictable. I don't why he lasted this long.

At contact with her cybernetic skin, Jett sent a variation of the virus into both robots.

They are already weakened from fighting the virus. It's not a walk in the park, but it's not impossible.

The claw hands cautiously touched her skin then spread out, stroking it.

Ale's stomach roiled and she felt the heat try to break free again.

How about a little jolt of something? Can I, huh? Can I?

Yes!

Jett felt Ale's emphatic assent and acted.

V'ruwak's eyes widened, and his grip tightened painfully, but then his face went slack and he dropped at her feet. The robots' hold on her was pulsing as they fought the virus. Ale waited for a slack moment and yanked free. They didn't move and neither did V'ruwak. She didn't realize she'd gone for her weapon, but it was in her hand.

Her fingers trembled with the longing to fire it.

Kill him.

Ale took a long slow breath, switched her weapon to stun, and fired it on the slack body.

Why?

Ale wasn't sure who asked the question, Erume or Jett, but she answered it. "He will suffer more from failing. His enemies will rejoice over him. Dying would be too quick, too easy."

Well, we'd better hurry or Rap won't have a choice. He's got a bunch of semifunctioning robots about to bust in on him.

"Where?"

A long snake pushed the grill off the vent and dropped down to the floor. She coiled up and lifted her head, regarding Ale. *I will ssssshow you.*

Ale held out her leg. "Climb aboard and let's go get our guy."

That calls for a battle song.

And "This Is Me" began to play inside her head. At least, Ale hoped it was just inside her head. This was a battle and not a parade...

～

FOR THE FIRST TIME EVER, Rap missed the music the other AIs like to play. There was silence, except for the hiss of the cutting torch, in the room and a deeper silence inside his head.

It was his first, and possibly last, battle as a human and not a machine. While there were many downsides to fighting this way, he realized he felt more alive than he'd ever been. The scents and sounds were sharper, and he felt as if he reacted more swiftly—though logic told him this could not be.

"When—if—I die here, make sure you get back to the ship," he said aloud. The words seemed to bounce around the room.

Their virus was winning. Chaos was spreading through the system and around the planet. It affected systems in the buildings, but also in the orbiting ships. But there were still many obstacles between him and the ship. And he would not leave without Ale.

The words felt tight in his throat, even though the only females around were unconscious, but he needed to say them. "If Ale makes it, tell her—" his throat closed again, though there was more in his heart. He could not say these words out loud. She'd been a good friend, a good warrior, an efficient robot—

I don't think she'd want to hear that last part.

Rap considered this and decided Nelson was correct. The words were not...romantic. His eye twitched at the word, but it was what she deserved. He did not know what she'd suffered here, what she'd fled, but he knew what he'd left behind. It was nothing good.

The hissing stopped behind them, and the robots began to assail the hole they'd cut.

I'll tell her you wish you could have held her and kissed her again.

That was better. But it was missing something. "Tell her that I... loved her..."

Apparently all you needed was to lose all hope to find your romantic voice.

The noise outside rose sharply. There must have been humans with the robots because they cried out. There was the sound of weapons fire being exchanged.

And the music started...

APPARENTLY, Ale's cybernetic skin had some abilities she hadn't known about. She'd wished she could hide and it...cloaked. It even cloaked Snake. It would have been nice to know that before. She ran in the direction Snake indicated, mostly dodging any humanoids she encountered because she didn't have time to shoot everyone. She rounded a corner and they were there.

The mass of robots and humans had finished cutting a hole in the door and the humans were now directing the robots to knock out the red-hot circle of metal. They did not care that this caused the robots damage. Or that the robots were feeling the effects of the virus. The humans screamed and yelled at them. Since she now had time, she stunned them. Then she considered the robots.

I can do thisss part...

Snake slithered down her body and approached the first robot.

She's fast.

Jett sounded admiring and a bit jealous.

I am not jealous.

Ale ignored this and moved in to help. Each robot Snake attacked started to have coordination problems. None of the still semifunctioning robots appeared to notice, so Ale ran up and turned them off. It helped to know where this was possible, and then when the last robot knocked the circle of metal out, she took him out, too.

Snake shot through the hole calling for Rap and Jett started a victory song.

"We're not in the clear yet," Ale pointed out following Snake through, then stopping as shyness swept over her.

Rap stared at her.

She stared at him.

"You're…"

"Yes. So are you."

Rap took a half step toward her and stopped, his hands curled into fists at his side.

I am having difficulty in finding the right song for this level of dysfunction, sweetie.

"We should leave," Ale suggested.

Rap blinked, swallowed, and then nodded. "Yes…we should leave."

Yes, There is Worse
Than Pearshaped

"Strategy is a commodity, execution is an art." Peter Drucker

I AM, of course, reluctant to intrude on, um, whatever this is, but this would be an optimal time to, um, escape.

Rap swallowed hard, his hands fisting at his sides. Nelson was correct. They still had to find their way back to the ship and fly home. *Home.* Now he knew why he wanted to be free, what he wanted. But they were not safe or clear yet. He was motivated to achieve both.

Rap leaped the consoles, landing lightly in front of Ale. "I will take point."

Ale's face was tense. Like him, she had no illusions they were anything close to being in the clear. She hesitated, then nodded.

Rap might have felt regret she did not kiss him again, even though logically he knew there was no time for that. It had been quiet in the corridor but sound began to ramp up again.

"I've got your six," she said, her lips trembling into an almost smile at this very Earth phrase.

And we will cover the in between, but you need to move!

Rap turned, not understanding the song that began to play inside his head. Why would his mother care if he were out? In any case, his mother was long gone.

He reached the cooling ring of metal and took a quick look out. The corridor was...

Chaotic is the word you are searching for. It seems we did our job too well. It's rather ironic.

There were robots swarming the space, fighting each other, fighting humans, pounding on the walls, trying to climb them.

The space will filled with tracers of fire in blue and red and gold and green. It was not a surprise the humans were losing. Even with the virus in play, they could not keep up the return fire.

"The vents?" he asked aloud.

There is not ssssufficient sssspace for rapid transssssit.

"What about that?" Ale pointed at the fallen circle of metal. "Can we use that to deflect fire?"

Two would be better, but one is all they had.

"We have cloaking," Ale mentioned, as Rap bent over and hefted the metal circle, "but they aren't aiming."

"Perhaps we have greater shielding," Rap suggested. "I wonder how—" As if called by the thought, his cybernetic shielding thickened. Will it be enough, he wondered.

Not if you take sustained, multiple impacts.

He could count on Nelson to be an optimist.

"Snake, wrap yourself around my waist, but keep my arms—"

Clear. Like I do not know thissss....

His eyes met Ale's. There was only one way to do this. She nodded as if she read—or shared his thought.

"Fast," she said.

A map to their ship appeared inside his head. Nelson...

I am heading to the ship to, er, light the fires and kick the tires.

Rap didn't take the time to ask. He did have time to think the words. He heard a faint ditto just before he plunged into the maelstrom.

ALE COULD NOT HAVE FOLLOWED Rap through the smoke and tracer fire if not for Jett. Ale did not know how the AI did it, but the direction was always there inside her head.

Turn left. Straight. Now right. Dodge. Get down.

She took hits. Even with enhanced shielding there was pain. And behind the pain her mother taunted and wailed and cried and begged and screamed.

Keep your promise.

Ale didn't bother to argue with her. She lacked the mental bandwidth, nor could she afford the distraction. She did notice that Jett upped the music volume, and changed the song choice to a tune about not stopping. Since this was good advice, Ale didn't.

Ahead of her, Rap reached the hangar bay where their ships were. He still had hope they could return with both ships intact and functioning. Forgiveness was easier CabeX had said, than permission, and more likely to occur if they brought a peace offering.

He halted in the open doorway as she ran up beside him. He tossed the scorched and pitted, metal circle to the side. It would not help them here.

The hangar bay was not just filled with battling robots, but there was also the sight and sound of ships attempting to take off and could not. Instead they banged against the roof of the bay and into each other. And if this were not enough, they also fired on each other.

Wait here, pleasssse....

Ale was startled by the sound of Snake's voice inside her head. It slithered down Rap's body and shot into the bay.

"I did not know she could move so quickly," Ale said, her voice pitched to be heard above the din.

"Step to the side," Rap ordered, and she sheltered against the side of the door, watching their backs, while he watched the bay.

The look on his face was not happy.

"She is your friend," Ale told him. "Friends help...friends."

They don't try to hurt them or wrest unfair promises out of them, she added to herself.

You betray me, your mother!

Now Ale took a moment to answer her mother. It seemed she had time now. *You betrayed all of us. You are not my mother. You are unworthy to be Teimanein. As the last*—her mind flinched at this thought—*of my people, I cast you out. You are rejected of our blood and are left without power.*

She did not know how she knew this, or that it mattered to a ghost, a mind-control worm inside her head. She did it to the memory. It writhed and wailed then faded to—nothing.

And was replaced by a song about girls having fun. It would have been a good choice, if the rabble of sound outside the hangar, coming from both directions of the corridor where they crouched, did not suddenly begin to build.

RAP GLANCED BACK, his gaze meeting Ale's worried one. If he had to guess—which he did—he'd say some humans had rallied. Someone with a brain had figured out there were two working ships in the bay and they were trying to get to them, too.

He studied the hangar bay—what he could see through drifting smoke and lines of fire.

"We can't get in," he said. He stared at Ale, words clogging his throat. So many words. So little time.

Snake has a plan.

Rap blinked. Snake had a plan?

Be ready.

Suddenly a high-pitched whine overrode all the sound in the bay.

Oh, and I would advise you to take cover for a few minutes.

Ale matched his crouch against the edge of the door, her back against his as she prepared to defend his six. The feel of her there, of knowing she was with him as she'd always been, he felt strength and resolve flow into his bones and muscles. It flowed into his heart.

"I wonder…" she murmured.

"Wonder what?" he asked.

"What the plan looks like?"

The whirring inside the bay increased in intensity and was joined with an increase in weapons fire.

"She's got both ships firing," Rap said, almost conversationally.

"Yes but for what purpose—" Ale's words were cut off as cannon fired erupted out the opening next to them.

Rap threw himself over Ale, attempting to protect her with his body.

The sound continued to grow, enough to make Rap grateful for the auditory protection the cybernetics provided. More shots hit the walls across from the door, punching holes through into the next corridor and the one after that. Rap deployed climbing talons from his suit, hooking them around a vent grate next to them.

"If that keeps up—yeah, there it goes," Ale said, her voice muffled where Rap pressed her into the wall.

The cannon breached the outer hull and decompression began just as a mob of humanoids came into view—and were sucked out the hole. It tried to drag them out, too, but Rap found new strength to keep them both from getting dragged out. They were battered fiercely, for what felt like a long time. This new howl of oxygen escaping at high velocity could not be wholly mitigated by his cybernetics, but it did stop the pitched battles. When the air began to equalize, Rap rolled them both toward the opening. Perhaps they could reach the ship now.

The *Exarch*, followed by the *Khanri*, hovered just inside the opening. The ramp lowered for them. Rap pulled Ale to her feet and they ran for the ramp. It began to rise as they raced up and headed for the bridge.

Rap stopped in the opening, staring, with Ale peering over his shoulder.

Snake sat at the helm in what he could only call a relaxed position, one that said she'd been there before. Part of her was curled around the helm control, with other parts of her wrapped around essential controls.

"You," he stopped and swallowed, "can fly a ship."

Of courssse I can fly a ssship.

"I didn't know…you never said." She'd not said many things he recalled.

You never asssked.

Ale arched her brows. "She does have a point."

No wonder females were so hard to talk to.

May we leave this place now?

Only, Rap thought, if you play the right song. Ale snickered. "What?" he asked.

"Jett told me what you said." She grinned. "Tell him to play "Day-O.""

"That does not sound like a battle song," he objected.

"It's not, but trust me, you'll like it."

Love involved trust, so he nodded. "Okay."

And she was correct. It was entirely inappropriate and also perfect. They did wish to go home.

Rapping It Up

"If someone truly loves you, they won't tell you love stories, they will make a love story with you." Anonymous

IT WAS RIDICULOUSLY easy to leave *Q'uy* airspace. Ale watched as red licked against towers and smoke plumes rose to mingle with the storm clouds that never left the sky of the planet. The smell of hot metal, weapons fire, and fear still lingered in her nostrils.

Exhaustion—a new human thing to learn—dragged at her limbs as she watched the planet, watched her past, grow smaller and smaller as they accelerated away. She glanced at Rap. He was slumped in the comm position, his cybernetics retracted so that she could see the tracks of weary digging into his face. His eyes were closed, the shadow of a beard darkening the lower part of his face.

She was going home. *Home.* For the first time in...forever...she could see the future on her horizon, instead of endless clouds. Even her years aboard the *Najer*, she'd not felt this light, this free.

She was free.

Take a look at you.

What? Ale glanced down. She was slumped in her position, her feet crossed at the ankles, one arm propped on the rest, the other hanging down the side. Imperfectly aligned from top to bottom.

You're almost chill, sweetie. And our future's so bright, we might need shades.

Without help, without force, Ale's mouth curved up. She was too tired to laugh, but she managed a tiny chuckle that wouldn't wake up Rap.

~

THEY DIDN'T TALK MUCH on the trip back, but for whatever reason, this did not bother Rap. There was not talking because one didn't know what to say, and there was companionable silence. This was the latter. There was ease in knowing that when the time came, he would speak.

They docked with the *Najer*, turning both ships over to other crewmates to return to the Earth Expedition. There would be explanations to be made, but CabeX would handle that.

For the first time, Rap let himself feel the human he was becoming again. He noticed the lack of tension aboard their ship. Their home. He did not know if his—if their future—would happen here, but the *Najer* would always be home. Just as his place of birth was home. He could build on a past that had been so thoroughly laid to rest. For the first time in forever, he found his mind turning to equations and explorations. And to love. To life. To a life with Ale.

Nelson might have mumbled something about it being well past time. Snake hissed contented agreement. Her issues were almost gone now that she was flying again.

"Where's Ale?" he asked aloud. And Nelson told him.

~

ALE KNEW she'd been marking time since they got back. Though she paced around the ready room—the only space large enough for pacing on the *Najer*—she did not pace without purpose.

She hadn't spent the whole time since their return thinking about Rap. She'd spent it also pondering her sisters, wondering if any still lived. She'd spent it learning of the power of Teimanein, coming to understand what had happened when she faced down Erume. She realized now that it had unlocked something else inside her mind. Something bigger and more powerful than the mind control Erume had tried to use against her.

Knowledge.

It was as if there'd been a secret cache about her people that had been locked away from her. And this cache spoke to her as if she were their leader now. She was not sure this meant she was the last, or that she was the only one to access the knowledge.

It was a shock to learn that her people could heal—to some extent. Not diseases of the body, but they could ease the wounds to the mind and heart. That this power could kill, this troubled her, but as more and more information came to her she realized this involved choice as well.

Choice. Such a powerful thing. No wonder so many sought to corral and minimize it. To get the oppressed to choose to not choose, or to choose slavery.

She had wondered what place she would have in a human world with only her soldier skills but now she knew she could be so much more.

Warrior princess, girlfriend. I like.

I am not a princess, she told the AI, but I am Ale of the Teimanein. I have a name. I have a purpose.

And a hot guy.

Did she? Of this she was not sure. She loved Rap. She would always love him. But she would not force him. That would be as wrong as what V'ruwak and Erume had tried to do to her. It would break her heart to walk away from him, but it would not break her spirit. It would not break Ale.

She heard a sound and turned to find Rap in the doorway studying her with sober intense eyes.

~

THE READY ROOM seemed smaller than the last time he'd been there with Ale. And Rap's heart seemed to grow larger, pushing into his throat and almost choking him with the words he wished to say to her.

Her big sad eyes—so much beauty both inside and out—increased the choking in his throat. He'd feared she was too beautiful for him, but they were the same inside. They'd survived much. They'd been damaged but it had made them strong. She was brave. He would be brave, too.

"I…" and just like that it was easy. "I love you. I wish to live the rest of our human lives together."

Her smile was like a star going nova, no, much better than any star any where.

"Yes. I love you, too." A shadow flickered across her face, but she faced him with the same resolution that she'd shown all the time he'd known her. "My heritage is complicated."

"And I am a geek, according to Rachel." He crossed over to her, carefully securing her hands with his. "Against all odds we have found each other. We can work out…anything. Everything. Together."

She met his gaze steadily, the worry fading to a growing joy. Yes, he looked closely, it was more than happy. It was joy. For a moment, the past flickered as a memory of his mother came to him. Yes, that is how he recognized joy. She was gone, but she'd left the joy behind for him to find.

With Ale.

Please, could you kiss her? Jett loves a happy ending.

Nelson did not sound as long suffering as perhaps he hoped. But Rap wanted to kiss her.

So he did.

He was right. She tasted of joy. And love. So much love. He gathered her close and let the joy fill him.

~

General's Holiday

A PROJECT ENTERPRISE STORY

She's a lady with a crazy story and a frog for a side-kick. He's a general who has been waiting for his Picard moment for a long time.

General John Halliwell, Commander of the Project Enterprise Earth Expedition, has spent most of his time in the Garradian Galaxy being shot at and shooting back. When a mysterious and intriguing lady arrives on Kikk asking for some non-shooting help, he is intrigued enough to listen.

It doesn't hurt that the lady's easy on his eyes, close to his own age, and not under his command.

He doesn't mind a chance to show the galaxy that their expedition can do more than point and shoot. That it's the closest to a holiday he's going to get for a while, might have tipped the scales too. The problem is, he believes she believes, but her story is too unbelievable to believe.

Or something like that.

All Naxe has ever known is a life of hiding and providing, but with the end of the war, freedom feels further than ever. Why are they still hiding from the rest of the galaxy? Why aren't the ships of Scoyfol finally going home?

In a bid to break the stalemate gripping the ships' company, she breaks all the rules and asks General Halliwell for help. It's a bonus that he is the first man in her life to remind her she's a woman, that life could be about more than endless scavenging runs to help feed her people.

But when she brings the general and his team to the Scoyfol ships, something has gone terribly wrong.

What is the true story of Scoyfol?

As Halliwell and Naxe get closer and closer to the truth, he realizes he's getting his Picard moment, but with shooting.

Because shooting happens.

But if they can survive he might just get to kiss the lady.

Note: General's Holiday first appeared in Pets in Space® 5.

"Last, but very definitely not least, my favorite story so far, Pauline Baird Jones' General's Holiday. Some of that favoritism has to do with the main character's frequent and sometimes lighthearted but most often slightly rueful references to Star Trek." Reading Reality

Chapter 1

GENERAL JOHN HALLIWELL, United States Air Force and Commander of the Expeditionary Force to the Garradian Galaxy, woke when the frog landed on his chest and knocked the wind out of him.

Not that he knew it was a frog at first. He thought it was a dog until it croaked. Like a frog. A really big frog. It was close to his face and there was enough light to see the frog's jowls. They reminded him of the ambassador he'd just sent back to Earth aboard the *Apollo.* The resemblance was heightened by its air of a potentate. Its purple eyes were on the huge side. It blinked slowly and croaked again.

He might have been relieved about the croaks. Thanks to his recent encounters with sentient *talking* animals, he'd halfway been expecting a speech to go with those jowls.

"Blooban," the voice was scolding as someone scooped the frog off his chest, but it was also, well, a bedroom voice; sultry and rich in tone. "You woke him. That's rude."

It was rude, but her voice made it less rude, despite the unauthorized incursion into his personal quarters here on the Kikk Outpost. He felt conflicted. On the one hand, he'd like to close his eyes and just listen to her talk, but he also wanted to see the face that went with the voice. Unless it didn't match. But he hoped voice and face matched, even though he wasn't sure what that would look like. Mostly he needed to breathe so he could get his wits about him.

Halliwell blinked, surprised he hadn't already secured his weapon. Two things stopped him. Her voice. And it was a *frog*. If either were a threat, Bangle, the self-named AI who…managed…the systems on this outpost, would never have let them get this far. It was oddly silent at the moment, he noted grimly. He considered asking it "what the hell" but his dealings with the AI usually ended up giving him a headache.

He rubbed his face, still trying to catch his breath, and shake off the remnants of sleep.

Which brought him back to the main reason he hadn't grabbed his gun. That voice. Okay, the voice shouldn't matter, because he'd met some seriously dangerous women out here, but somehow it did. He allowed himself this off-topic digression because he was alone inside his head—the one place Bangle couldn't get to—yet. In fact, if the voice and the accompanying frog weren't dirt side on the Kikk Outpost, and worse, inside his private quarters, he might have looked forward to getting to know the woman behind that voice.

He knew the frog as well as he wanted to already.

"Light," he snapped, pulling himself into a sitting position. He probably should have stipulated low lights. There was a painful transition while he waited for his pupils to adjust. He used the time being glad he didn't sleep in the buff. When one was a general, getting woke in the middle of the night was not that uncommon, so he always dressed in regulation underclothes with a slightly less regulation pair of pajama bottoms.

Usually he got disturbed by alerts and alarms, not by women with over-sized frogs. It might have alarmed him that he was disturbed but not surprised. That's what happened when you went where man hadn't gone before and found out just what was out there.

Once he could, he studied the intruders, letting no sign of his interest show on his face. He had to admit that, if he was going to be woke in the middle of the night by a woman, she was the one he'd have chosen. Of course, he was a man, so he'd also have wished for her to be wearing something besides a standard type flight suit and holding a huge frog. Dang, it was a big frog.

There were indications she was close to his age, such as the streaks of gray in her dark hair and the lines cutting into the edges of her eyes and mouth. He lived in what sometimes felt like a sea of young, which was to be expected in a military expedition, but even those who weren't young remained out of reach because of his position. He might be in another galaxy, but fraternization was still a thing. So he was glad she wasn't young.

She was well-armed, but wore her armament well. He liked that, though he shouldn't, he reminded himself.

He also had weapons close at hand, but if she'd wanted to kill him, he'd already be dead. That said, he hadn't risen to the rank of general by taking stupid risks or making assumptions based on almost no evidence.

He flipped back the blanket and got up, his hand closing around the handle of his personal—and not exactly regulation—ray gun. The chill of the stone floor on the bottoms of his feet chased the rest of the fog from his brain. His ray gun was set to stun, but he kept it pointed down for the moment.

He waited, his gaze meeting hers.

She kept admirably still and didn't reach for her weapons. It would be hard to reach for anything holding the huge frog. Seriously, it looked bigger each time he looked at it. Why a frog, he wondered, and even more important, why had Bangle let her in here? He considered several opening gambits, but in the end decided to keep it simple. He might be awake, but he wasn't *awake* yet.

"How did you get in here?" He kept his tone curious and his body language as unthreatening as he could make it in the circumstances. She could be hiding something behind the frog, though the thought gave him a mental twitch.

"It's complicated, General Halliwell," the woman admitted.

"And I apologize for the intrusion, but I…needed to speak with you."

Needed…She probably shouldn't ever use that word with that voice or those eyes. Halliwell hoped this didn't show in his eyes. He considered her for long enough that she shifted almost imperceptibly. So she was nervous despite her outward calm. Well, she should be.

"I do have a wide variety of communication resources available to me," he pointed out, mildly he thought, though there was a huskiness to his voice that put some heat in his face. Not a blush, because generals didn't blush. It was against regs.

Color stained her cheeks and she bit her lip. He was glad she was allowed—and able to—blush.

He realized he was studying the maltreated lip and thinned his own lips in annoyance. It didn't matter that her gray streaked hair was pulled neatly back from a strongly featured face, or that her eyes were an unusual shade of blue. He might like what he saw but he couldn't trust the instinctive trust he felt. This contradictory thought might have made his eye twitch for a second. She might be Bangle approved, but she hadn't been vetted by him or his people.

"The need is urgent, sir."

He almost sighed. It always was. And he had two choices. He could activate his personal alarm, assuming Bangle let him, or he could listen. Since he didn't want to find out if Bangle would let him talk to anyone, he indicated the small seating area to one side. At least it gave the appearance of choice. And—he gave an inner snort at this thought—listening to her was not a punishment.

"Perhaps, you should tell me who you are and why you're… urgently here."

His people would be appalled. They tended to forget it was his circus, and he was where the buck stopped. Not to mention, he'd risen to his rank doing all the things they did now. Nor was he irreplaceable when there was a chain of command. Not that he pointed this out to any of them. No sense giving them ideas.

With only the smallest of hesitations, she turned and took a seat to the left of the small table. She bent and lowered the frog to the floor next to her feet where it gave another croak and then seemed to settle into a wide, greenish-blue blob. A really big blob.

Despite the croak, Halliwell had a sense that the frog was aware —or he was getting paranoid. He recalled some of the things that had happened to him since arriving in this galaxy and decided he couldn't be paranoid enough in this place.

He hesitated before joining her, gesturing instead toward the small, alien version of a kitchenette.

"Can I get...either of you something to drink?" His throat felt like sandpaper—because it was the middle of the night and not because of her bedroom voice.

"Blooban would be pleased to receive water. For myself, I am hydrated, thank you."

Blooban. Halliwell gave an internal wince, tucked his ray gun in the waistband of his pajamas, and crossed to the kitchen. He found a bowl and filled it with water, then filled a glass with water for himself. Only then did he join them. When he placed the water in front of the frog, its tongue moved so fast, all he saw was the disturbance on the surface.

"Thank you."

The voice was so gruff and frog-like, Halliwell was both startled...and not. He'd kind of been expecting it, but he was still disappointed. Why couldn't a frog just be a frog? They'd stumbled across a lot of critters that kind of looked like those back on Earth—until they started talking. Did he, he wondered, look for the similarities to deal with the alienness of them and this place?

"You're welcome." Halliwell was pleased that his voice sounded neutral and not resigned.

As he straightened and turned toward his own seat, Halliwell caught a hint of something fresh that could have been his visitor. Since it stirred things pleasant and almost forgotten, he hoped it wasn't the frog. He suddenly felt rumpled and unshaven, though it was not his fault, he reminded himself. Even a general was allowed to be both when he slept.

He removed the gun from his waistband before he sat, resting it on his knee with his hand still curved around the handle, and took several sips of the water. It helped ease the desert in there, but he couldn't say it doused the heat. He placed the glass carefully on the small table between them and only then did he give her a look that typically encouraged—and received—a response from anyone he pointed it at. She'd come here to talk to him, so she should start. And not because he wanted to hear her voice again.

"I am Naxe of Scoyfol," perhaps something in his face prompted to her to add, "I know this might not mean much to you. Scoyfol has…used to have…a reputation for safe and swift transport of passengers and cargo."

There was a story-telling cadence to the way she said it, but her words put a crease in Halliwell's forehead. Used to have? He repressed the urge to shake his head in confusion.

"Scoyfol operated primarily in the region of space known as Nashass, though they also maintained shipping routes with planets in nearby systems. But their principle clientele lived and worked on the planets of Vendir, Eldirer, Tulseer and Troyal."

She acted as if he should know the system and the planets but…

A hologram appeared in front of him. So Bangle was listening. He didn't roll his eyes, because he was a general. It wouldn't be the first time he did an inner eye roll, however. Even generals got to do those.

Identifying information was included on the display. He studied the hologram, trying to figure out what he saw and place it in relation with what he knew…

"That's—is that in former Dusan territory?"

The Dusan had been a ruthless and almost unbeatable enemy until his expedition had arrived in system. They had allied with those who opposed the Dusan and defeated them, but it had been a near thing. A very near thing.

"It belonged to the citizens of the system before the Dusan stole it," she said. Her gaze was shadowed, but her tone was even, still in that dispassionate and yet richly compelling, story-telling cadence.

The Dusan stole it? They stole a lot of planets. How long ago were they talking about?

She must have read something in his eyes because her lips twisted for several seconds.

"No, I don't remember it, but it is a part of the story of Scoyfol," she said.

The story of Scoyfol? He considered this, but he still couldn't quite wrap his brain around it. The Dusan had started the war so long ago, his people hadn't even tried to do the math on when. It wasn't helped by the fact that people in this system counted time differently than they did. Take it a step a time, he told himself, gesturing at the hologram.

"Which planet was yours?" he asked.

"Scoyfol is ships, the crews are ships. Spacefarers, not dirt siders."

Halliwell's brows arched a bit. He loved the *Doolittle*, loved commanding space vessels. He missed them when he was dirt side, but Earth, home, it anchored him and gave him a sense of purpose. He was here for his people and for what he could learn to benefit them.

How did that even work? he wondered. If she "was ships" where was the ship she'd arrived on? Did it matter? Why all the drama and secrecy? There were other, not hidden outposts, where she could have made her appeal—and that is probably what had happened, he realized, glancing around as if he could see the MIA Bangle. What had she told the AI? Was Bangle susceptible to that voice, too? He knew of only one way to get answers, and that was to play this scene to the end.

"I am not explaining well." Her hands moved restlessly on her knees. "Words are not my skill," she added ruefully.

With that voice? He half smiled and was rewarded with a small, but charming one in return. *Charming.* He was losing the plot. He realized he was staring and turned his gaze back to the display. There was something about that location that bugged him. He looked at her again, a brow arched in interrogation.

"Perhaps start at the beginning, keeping in mind that though we've been knocking around here for a while, there is still a lot we don't know."

The soft lines of her mouth curved into a deeper smile, that somehow softened the chill of the room and the stone floor. He shouldn't have felt that spike of pleasure. She was an interesting mix of quiet confidence with a surface uncertainty. Her lashes lowered, a dark curve against her cheeks. They lifted, the intense blue gaze meeting his. He saw no guile in them, but that didn't mean it wasn't there.

"I suppose the beginning is also the end, in a way. Scoyfol is ships, but Scoyfol is also a bond, a compact if you will, not with cargo—not anymore—but with its manifest."

Without quite knowing why, Halliwell felt a chill form in the center of his back. Was she saying…

"When Scoyfol undertakes to transport, Scoyfol delivers." She hesitated, licking her lips. "No matter how long it takes."

No matter—he gave a shake. Her phrasing felt odd, but she was alien, even if she didn't look alien. "Are you telling me you've been…attempting delivery since before…" He couldn't say the words.

"Before the Dusan took over Nashass? That is correct." She frowned, staring ahead as if she saw it, saw the past. She glanced at him. "That is the heart of the story of Scoyfol."

Not the kind of story he liked to read. He was not into never ending stories. The thought almost shocked him enough to show it.

"It won't end until all passengers are returned home."

And then what? The whole system was still being rebuilt following the end of the war. He turned back to the hologram, watching the slowly orbiting system. Home? There? It wasn't just former Dusan space, it was deep in former Dusan space. Something wasn't adding up. If these passengers came from there—he came back to the math he didn't know how to do to calculate how long their journey had taken. How was it even possible for them to exist as a unit for so long? Did he need this question answered?

"We have no objection to your passengers going home." He couldn't, and didn't want, to police this small system within the larger Garradian Galaxy. He actually had no plans to police the wider galaxy. They hadn't come here to get into a war, even if that is what had happened. Personally? He wouldn't want to be on any planet that had been occupied by the Dusan. Everything they'd touched was ugly, even if it didn't start that way.

Was going home possible? Nashass was a very small system, as systems went. It had a sun, not a large one, but one apparently adequate to sustain life. The four planets in question were marked "habitable," and there were a few smaller planets orbiting around. But habitable might not mean that much post-war.

He pulled back the view with a wave of his hand, then frowned. "Isn't that the original Dusan home system?"

He pointed to another smaller system that bordered on Nashass. If they'd been that close to the original Dusan home system, they'd have been among the first absorbed into the Dusan Empire. This brought him back to the fact that they'd been absorbed a very long time ago. Would there be anything to go home to? Was this why she was here? If it was...he shook his head. "We don't have the resources..." he began.

"Scoyfol is not looking for resources," she said, the first time a small flare of frustration marred her expression. She leaned back in the chair, stretching her booted feet out, one heel tapping against the floor for several seconds before she stopped it. With a self-conscious look, she drew her legs back in and sat up straighter. "At least...that is not why I am here," she amended.

Halliwell felt a stir of something at the sight, but quelled it. It was February back on Earth so a few Valentine's decorations had popped up around the base, but no reason to get distracted by that right now.

"If only it were that simple." She huffed out a sigh and the frog croaked softly, as if in agreement or sympathy.

Halliwell didn't understand croak, so he couldn't say.

"As you have probably realized, it has been many seasons since the original passengers found themselves unable to return home."

"Many seasons," Halliwell agreed dryly. "None of your original crew or passengers could possibly still be living." Unless they'd been in some kind of stasis? He would not have wondered this even a few months ago but now it was almost routine to meet a recently defrosted Garradian.

"All are descendants of the original manifest," she admitted.

So not frozen, which brought him back to, "What the heck?"

She shrugged, gesturing with her hands. "On the surface, it seems strange for people to be attached to planets they have never seen," she pursed her lips, before continuing. "All I know is what I have been taught, of course, but for the company, what kept them going, what kept them together, was the hope of returning. This purpose became a tradition passed down to each succeeding generation." Her lips twisted and she looked up meeting his gaze. "They needed hope, you see."

He did. He tried to imagine...how many generations? Did it matter?

Halliwell found his frown forming again. "So all of you have lived on your ships this whole time?" It boggled the mind. How had the Scoyfols managed it? The passengers and crew would have lost access to resources when their planets were overrun. Just the logistics would be an ongoing nightmare.

Perhaps she noted his incredulity. She gave a rueful grimace.

"It was, I believe, a challenging transition at the time, or so our stories say, and I think, I believe, all considered resettlement at various times, but it was difficult to find a safe place anywhere within the system when it was in a state of constant war, and with the Dusan moving inexorably forward, taking planet after planet. In the end, the ships, the passengers, Scoyfol became a moving world." She was silent for at least a minute. "I do not know how they accomplished it back then. I only know what they are now."

"And what are they now?" he asked. Why the distance? It was almost as if she was talking about other people.

"They are a people in...turmoil," she admitted. "For so long, the need to survive gave them a common purpose, a common reason to sacrifice. They have been...ghost ships carrying ghost people who had only the will to endure, to exist long enough to go home."

It sounded like a nightmare to him.

"But with the peace, or what there was of it, the passengers have desired an end to their journey. Resolution if you will, even if it means change as drastic as their first parents experienced."

"Returning to those planets might not give your passengers resolution," Halliwell pointed out. He'd dealt with some weird stuff since being deployed here, but this might top the list. He considered past events and decided that it was up there, but not the weirdest. At least, not yet. He didn't sigh because, again, he was a general, but thinking about the Dusan brought back some bad memories. "Scientists from the region have begun doing assessments of the…abandoned…planets but I'm not sure how far they've penetrated that region."

Abandoned wasn't exactly what had happened there he knew. But even beyond that, what the Dusan had done, the havoc they'd wreaked on conquered worlds was horrifying.

"They might not be habitable for a while, or at best, challenging to reclaim."

"That is the position of the Captain, that it is too soon."

He studied her, noting the deepening of the lines around her eyes and the thinning of her mouth.

"And what is your position?"

She looked up, startled. "If it were appropriate for me to have a position, it would be to give them what they want. Before, arrival was not possible. Now it is." She looked away and Blooban croaked again. "There is something…wrong. I feel it here." She touched her heart with her hand. "It is ironic that with the collapse of the common enemy, what has resulted is not peace, but a fracture in purpose. It is a story that needs an ending, a resolution."

"It happens," Halliwell agreed, somewhat dryly. He had his own trust issues with their allies during the battle with the Dusan, despite having fought side-by-side with the Gadi. "We can't get involved in what is, well, a regional dispute," he pointed out, though he felt an odd regret about this. Was he crazy? They'd gotten involved in a lot of crazy since they got here. There was no need to sign on for something that was clearly outside their jurisdiction.

"I did not come to ask you to take sides," she said.

He considered the situation. "What you really need is arbitration —someone who can bring everyone to a solution that doesn't please anyone."

She gave a small chuckle at this.

"At the moment, that is where everyone already is." She was quiet for a moment and he had a sense she was gathering her thoughts, or perhaps marshaling her next plea. "You have a reputation in this galaxy for being fair, impartial, if you will, and...far-seeing."

But he wasn't impartial, he just hid it better because generals had to. And as for far-seeing...

Your reputation does precede you, General. For the first time, Bangle weighed in verbally, via the sound system.

It must be some kind of record for the AI, Halliwell thought grimly.

"Why should any of your...combatants...care about my opinion?" he asked. "You said your captain doesn't want to arrive."

"The stalemate is..." She frowned. "I feel there is, oh," she leaned back with a sudden jerk and rubbed her face. "Does it sound insane to say it is so boring, that something has to happen? That something will happen?"

It did sound boring, he had to admit. He sure wouldn't want to endlessly drift in space, trying to survive.

She lowered her hands, her face charmingly rueful. "It is like a story with no plot. I know it sounds irrational, but it feels like we need to introduce another element to trigger needed change."

Blow it up was more like it. But...it sounded like it was going to blow up anyway. Or they'd all die of boredom.

"Your captain is on board with this?"

Her shoulders straightened. "I will not deceive you, General, he is not. As I said, he is content with the status quo."

But she wasn't, that was clear.

Of Scoyfol? What did that mean?

"Bringing an unwelcome arbiter aboard against the wishes of the captain..." he shook his head, but not with certainty. "An arbitration only works if all parties agree..."

He wanted to do it, he realized. It was crazy, no question. But…

What would Picard do?

It would probably surprise Halliwell's crew to know how often he'd asked himself that question during the years of his deployment on the *Doolittle*. His instincts tended more toward a Kirk response, so he tried to restrain himself with the Picard question, even after he found out exactly how dangerous it was going where no one on Earth had gone before. He hadn't just gone where few men had gone, he'd seen some stuff that made most sci-fi movies and shows look like they were under performing in the imagination stakes.

Allies and enemies had arrived in unexpected ways, but he, his people—for the most part—and his ships were still here. They'd come too close to bringing a pile of trouble back home with them. There had been losses. But this didn't look like that. What it looked like was…a Picard moment, a time for the expedition to give back more than a hail of bullets. To demonstrate they had come in peace. In all his years in the Air Force, their mission had always been to *serve* and protect. Until now they'd been serving up missiles and lethal rays to protect different populations.

It might be a relief that someone had come to him not asking for him to shoot something up—though diplomatic speak was not his strong suit, he reminded himself in a Kirk tone.

"If you would consent to consider it, I think your arrival could be a welcome catalyst."

Catalysts could be catastrophic, he thought grimly, but still, there was that longing. He hesitated. "I am in charge of—"

You have considerable leave owed you, General.

Yeah, that was a Bangle headache starting, right on schedule.

WHEN THE GENERAL PICKED A TEAM, he didn't play around. Naxe's gaze went up and then up some more, as she tried to wrap her brain around Tim.

The name felt too short, it was such an understatement for such a large, robotic being. She'd heard stories around the docks and read books about cybernetic humans, but she'd not had experience with one before now. At least, her thoughts faltered for a moment, as something teased at the edge of memory. But as soon as she tried to extract it, it was gone. These phantom feelings were part of the wrong she felt about the company, but she did not, she could not voice them even to Blooban. She needed others to trust her, not believe she was crazy.

So she tried to keep her expression calm as she studied Tim. There were elements of him that looked human, or humanoid. He had a head, arms, legs, a torso...he was so huge, he deserved a longer and more intimidating name. And the line of unblinking red where eyes should be was unsettling, if not downright disturbing.

His outer skin was dark and appeared to absorb the surrounding light, rather than reflect it. The thickened nature of his arms, torso, and legs seemed to indicate weaponry that could be deployed as needed. But he didn't need them. His intimidation factor was considerable—though somewhat lessened by several duffles clutched in metal hands, one of them a very feminine pink. For some reason, she liked the contrast and the puzzle, though she thought she knew the answer to the puzzle.

Naxe's attention to the woman standing next to him, who she suspected was the owner of the pink duffle.

Riina Katala, the general had called her, when he introduced her. He gave no reason for choosing someone who was such stark contrast to Tim. Small where he was large, so where he wasn't. Riina was also very beautiful, which might be reason enough for her presence. This venture was, Bangle had intimated, the General's vacation, which when translated meant a rest, relaxation. There were women aboard their ships who served such a purpose, but this woman's presence bothered her for some reason. She caused an ache in Naxe's chest so that it took effort to be polite, and she'd turned away as soon as she could.

Her gaze drifted to Tim once more, then she glanced down at Blooban. If Blooban was impressed, he didn't show it, but then he never did. He was the calm center around which all her uncertainties swirled. If she hadn't met him, she was not sure where she'd be right now. Certainly not here. He'd been a catalyst in her story.

She allowed herself to glance at the general with what she hoped was casual interest. It was not reasonable that he stole her breath from her chest and sent a pleasurable wave of heat through other places. It was a mere trick of genetics that made his mouth draw her attention, or that she both longed to meet and avoid his piercing eyes. He was not so tall as Tim yet he managed to be the leader of their team. Instead of his uniform, he wore casual, but well-fitting pants and shirt. He carried a jacket folded over one arm. His crisp aspect was a distinct contrast to how he'd looked when she'd invaded his quarters—something she had not intended. How could she know it was night on Kikk? But...the memory of how he'd looked just wakened from sleep did things to her insides, too.

Blooban gave a croak that was loud enough for her to realize she'd been distracted. She gave a slight jerk and only then noticed they'd been joined by a young man in uniform pulling a cart piled with cases in a variety of sizes. He gave her a shy smile. She returned it with reserve. Was he coming with them? He would put them over their available number of cabins. This was a complication she'd not foreseen. She could sleep on the bridge, but she hadn't had time to sanitize and move her few belongings into storage.

Blooban hopped next to her as they continued toward the hanger bay doors, the slap of his appendages against the stone floor echoing so loud they drowned out other sounds. On the other side of the doors, her ship waited, or so she hoped. One thing Naxe had learned from being of Scoyfol was to not expect anything, though there had been less of the unexpected since she met Blooban. Even on this venture, she'd not hoped for this consequential of an outcome. But getting shot or detained for impertinence seemed preferable to the stifling stagnation inside the company. It choked her when she was there and filled her with a longing to escape and never return. Even to herself she couldn't explain why she didn't stop—other than a complicated sense of duty that left her straining at her leash.

The bay doors slid back exposing the *Vycorth*. It was not a pleasing sight. Indeed, each time she saw it from a distance, rather than approaching it via the docking tunnel, she was amazed it still flew. It was the proper shape for a ship, of course, so that it could enter and exit atmosphere without too much friction. It was a pity its surface had multiple colors showing where older paint was exposed, and there was also damage from meteors and some weapons fire. One couldn't always avoid trouble. It made no sense to spend effort on the exterior, though now she wished she'd made more effort. But, she reminded herself, it was safer not to draw attention or look valuable while out in the space lanes. It looked, she admitted somewhat wryly, like she felt. Worn, a bit exhausted, but with some fight left in there where it couldn't be seen.

There was a long silence and she slanted a glance downward once again. Blooban resumed his hop toward the ship and after a short hesitation, Naxe followed him. The general would either come with her or not. With some relief, she heard the sound of footsteps and glanced back.

The general raised one brow, his expression complicated. He tipped his head to one side and said, "I suppose there's a lot under the hood."

Naxe did not know what this meant, though she did appreciate his neutral tone.

"I'm guessing all the power is where you need it," he explained, waving a hand vaguely. "Where it can't be seen."

"Yes," she said, pleased he was able to look past the surface. "The *Vycorth* maneuvers well and is very fast." Or she and Blooban would be very dead.

He walked up and traced an area of battle damage. "Yes."

He was silent for so long, Naxe's heart began to pound. Had he changed his mind? She'd already explained why they couldn't travel in one of the general's ships, that no ship but hers could locate the company. She'd been frustrated by her inability to explain why, but for some reason, the general had accepted this. His people had been most unhappy. It had taken effort to remain calm as they presented their opposing arguments. They'd only left the aura of unhappy behind when they'd transported to this outpost.

The general stirred and then glanced back at Tim. "Will you fit?"

"Yes."

Naxe saw no mouth move, though a single word barely gave her time to see anything. It seemed Tim was not only large, but cryptic. But was it reasonable to expect dialog from a robot?

"The hatch is this way," she said, leading them around to the rear of her ship. She slid her hand across the correct spot to trigger access. There was a loud creaking sound, the shriek of protesting metal, and then a ramp separated from the whole, lowering to clank against the bay decking. She offered the general a small, embarrassed smile. The hatch had also experienced weapons fire a few times. The sounds helped reinforce the impression of shabby desperation—which had at times been more than an impression, she recalled. The end of the war had helped, but Naxe knew better than to lower her guard.

She indicated they could enter and Tim went first. It was not a surprise. His function was to protect the general. This pleased her. She needed, she wanted, the general to survive, too.

Tim didn't say anything, but they must have some means of communication she was not aware of because, after a distinct pause, the general went up the ramp, followed by Riina. Only then did Naxe and Blooban enter. The young soldier with the cart came up after her.

The cargo bay reinforced the message of the exterior. It would have been foolish to do otherwise. Her bay was nowhere near a full load, indeed it never had been. It was dangerous to be an attractive target. She made small, frequent runs, carefully varying where she acquired goods. She led them through the containers toward hatch that would give them access to the rest of the ship. This hatch slid back on a more pleasing view. The ship was old, but this part of the ship she kept clean and in repair. For Naxe, the *Vycorth* was her real home, the one place where she felt she belonged.

At an order from the general, the young soldier began to unload the containers on his cart. He found some netting to secure them, then saluted the general and left the ship. It was a relief to see him leave.

"I have quarters enough," her gaze flicked to Tim, "but they are not large."

"I don't require quarters," Tim said. "But I will explore the ship further."

"Of course," she said. "Passenger level is on the next deck." The *Vycorth* only had a cargo and engineering deck, small passenger deck with galley, and a compact bridge. It was one reason she was able to secure any supplies at all. A larger ship and bigger loads would have drawn attention to the ship and to the company. This one was only one of many scavenger ships slipping away from the company and returning as carefully. None of them fled to the company for protection. They were required to deal with it themselves and only then could they approach. The attrition of scavenger ships had been brutal during the war years, but somehow the Captain, or his crew, found more. She felt guilt at calling the story boring, but even the danger didn't seem to vary. It was boring to play the same scene over and over—even when getting shot at.

The *Vycorth* was a found ship. Naxe had "found" it, though it was more like being found. She'd aided Blooban during an altercation and then been cut off from her ship. Since then he rarely left the ship, trusting her to secure supplies. No one in the company even knew of his existence. She was not certain they'd noticed the change of ship.

They all waited while Tim toured the ship. Naxe tried not to feel tense or invaded. She'd invited this, and if she failed...her fingers tried to curl into fists, but she resisted, knowing the general watched her. She turned, meeting his gaze with one she hoped was calm and unconcerned.

"My ship is small, but our journey is only a few days," she said. Indeed, she thought, it wouldn't be nearly long enough. What came next, she did not know. There would be consequences for this gambit.

～

HALLIWELL HAD, he admitted, been unimpressed by the sight of the clunker sitting in the hanger bay. But then he'd recalled the quiet competence of the woman who'd…invited…him on this venture and withheld judgement. If she'd been flying around in a sleek and impressive ship, she'd have been under attack constantly. And she would have aroused—bad choice of words—triggered much more suspicion both with him and his less-than-thrilled team. But he still needed to see what was under the hood, or rather Tim would take a look and tell him.

OtimtronW—which had been shortened to Tim by Halliwell's people—wasn't just really good security. There wasn't a system made he couldn't hack, at least not one the cybernetic robot had encountered thus far. Even Halliwell's team had admitted there was no one who could protect him better than Tim. He'd been part of a crew of robots like himself, most of whom had transitioned back into the human form they'd left to hide from their ruthless, and now deceased, owner. Tim had seemed happy to provide security while he waited for his cloned body to grow—well, he'd accepted when asked. No way to know if he was happy.

Riina Katala was, he hoped, his other ace-in-the-hole. She was a recently defrosted Garradian who had lived and studied before the war began. She'd even heard of Scoyfols and the Nashass region of space. She also had, he'd been assured, negotiating skills. It might be his imagination, but it seemed like Tim was happy to have her along, too. He'd taken her luggage first, then almost as an afterthought, grabbed the general's. Hard to say if Riina found Tim interesting. She had a good line in a poker face, too.

He glanced at Naxe, then at the frog. It was going to be a fun trip with all of them working on their lack of expression.

Tim returned with his lack of expression intact. His voice was equally uninformative as he said, "I've stowed your luggage, ma'am, sir. The bridge can accommodate all of us."

"Call me Riina," she said, moving lightly in the direction Tim indicated.

Without waiting for them, Tim turned and followed her. Halliwell's lips twitched and he turned, meeting Naxe's gaze. They held a dawning humor and something that almost looked like relief.

"Tim is unusual," she said.

"Very," he admitted, resisting the urge to explain that it flowed from the very human consciousness that lived inside the machine. Even though the reason to keep the secret was dead, Halliwell wasn't sure the robots were eager to have their story spread around. The robots still had enemies.

Blooban had already hopped after the others, so he gestured that direction. "How about you show me how fast your ship can go?"

This time she smiled. "Yes, of course."

He followed her, trying not to notice how well she moved, how confidently. He felt his insides relaxing some. Tim had pronounced the ship clear, and the lady had a nice—rear view. The sense of being Picard on an away mission increased and his satisfaction level with it—until he reached the bridge.

While he couldn't be sure, he thought even Tim looked carefully away as he took in the sight of the big blob of frog in one of the pilot's positions.

The frog was a pilot.

HALLIWELL HAD FOUND his quarters decent and passed a fairly restful night's sleep. Throughout his career, he'd learned to grab rest when and where he could. But now that he was awake, the cautions and questions of his team echoed inside his head, and he felt a need to talk to Naxe. The cautions and questions would have been a lot louder, he believed, if not for the near magnetic quality of her voice. But as soon as she'd left, the magic had faded to the concerns. Despite the good rest, he found himself questioning his own gut.

When he didn't find her in the galley or on the bridge—he recoiled at the sight of frog blob there—and he decided to try the cargo bay.

Naxe looked up as he entered, her smile quicker and less shy. She gestured at the containers.

"I'm making sure they are well secured for our drop into real space," she explained, as if he'd asked.

Halliwell went to the other side of the container she stood by, and tested the cords holding it in place.

"It's not a big load," he noted, careful to not make it a question.

"If dock siders see too much cargo, they get suspicious." Her hands paused and she gave him a wry look. "I can't afford attention. My orders are for short, fast runs."

He nodded. It made a sort of sense, though the whole set up was pretty crazy and ultimately made no sense at all. This was a point his team had stressed several times. Would a real Picard get this much pushback?

"So, your...Blooban," every time he said the name, he felt silly, "is your co-pilot?"

She looked up and for the first time her grin held nothing back. "Actually, I am his co-pilot. He allowed me to join his crew after I helped him during an altercation. For some, just the fact of his species is an affront."

Halliwell blinked, trying to think of something to say. The silence was so deep he almost missed Bangle's persistent playlist back at Kikk. The AI had become addicted to the music some of his people had brought with them from Earth and she had an odd knack of picking the right song for the moment.

"He doesn't talk much," he said, finally, more to break the silence than anything.

"No." She gave a small chuckle that did pleasant things to Halliwell's insides. "He doesn't trust easily."

Halliwell supposed it was hard for a frog—even a huge one—to feel trust.

They moved to the next container. Halliwell tugged on these cords, trying to look at her without looking like he was looking at her as he said, "Seems a lonely existence. Is there someone back there waiting for you?" What was she doing out there with only a frog for company?

Her eyes widened, the clear blueness of them startling in the dim bay. "No," she admitted. "I suppose I know everyone too well to be interested in that way." A flush stained the edges of her cheekbones.

"Close quarters can breed intimacy or contempt," Halliwell said, thinking of his last ambassador and ignoring an inappropriate sense of relief. He had something of the same problem. Even if he could have dated within his crew...it was possible to know too much about everyone. He studied her, aware that he didn't know much about her, except that he liked looking at her and listening to her talk. He turned his gaze down, pulling at the webbing harder than was necessary. While Picard might have had some romantic moments on his holiday, Halliwell was not here to get a date.

She half sighed. "I did mention it is boring. It's like a bad plot in a story."

Halliwell chuckled, though he wasn't sure why he was surprised she was a reader. Everyone needed something to do in the boring parts of space travel.

"I haven't read a lot of stories from this system," he admitted. He hadn't really thought about it much, and when he did, he assumed language would be a barrier. Did they have genres? His preference was for military-themed adventures, but he'd been known to pick up suspense with romantic overtones. And he'd read anything sci-fi, with or without romance.

"What do you like to read?" he asked. It was less lame than asking about her favorite color or food. Maybe.

"I will read any story," she admitted, a light coming into her eyes. "It amazes me what someone can imagine and then write that imagined story down." She sounded almost wistful. The light in her eyes faded to troubled.

Was she a hopeful writer? They had a few in the fleet who released digital versions of their stories on the shipnet. Someone had to vet them for classified material before they could release them back on Earth, but there'd been some good stuff in the ship's digital library. They had some budding filmmakers, too, but they'd been pretty restricted until they found the Kikk Outpost. The films also had to be vetted carefully.

"Do you write or tell stories?" he asked.

She looked startled and shook her head. "No." She hesitated, then said more firmly. "Of course not."

He nodded, moving with her to the next container. "If you could do what you wanted, what would you do?" Was this the real reason for this gambit? He could respect and understand if she just wanted to be free of such a narrow existence.

Her eyes widened and her actions became absent-minded.

"Would you stay with Scoyfol?" he asked when she didn't speak.

The shake of her head was sharp, almost instinctive. "No."

Her gaze met his and the almost desperation in there shook him —and filled him with a desire to help her, to do something to change that look.

"Whatever the outcome of this...gamble...this will be my last journey for Scoyfol," she said.

He felt a chill. "Will you be punished for bringing us in?"

"It is possible I will exiled." This did not seem to trouble her.

"But they won't...hurt you or imprison you?" he persisted.

"What prison could be worse than all of this?" She said the words matter-of-factly now. "If they spaced me out an airlock I would be grateful. Some stories should end."

"But they wouldn't?"

"I am not aware of anyone receiving such a punishment," she said.

"Would you know?"

She nodded. "I'm sure you know how gossip travels aboard ships?"

It was true it was difficult to keep secrets aboard a ship. But it wasn't impossible.

He felt an odd urge to go around the container and take her in his arms. He didn't, of course, but it brought up old memories of the young man who wouldn't have hesitated to try to hug the girl. That young man had been more willing to risk his heart, though that young man had not known his future would lead him to another galaxy. If he'd had a wife, he'd never have been given this command.

"We have taken in refugees," he said. This felt too much, too fast, so he added, "What would happen to Blooban without you?" Oh great, nothing like playing the frog card.

Her smile was bright in the dim bay and she chuckled, sending an unfamiliar warmth through him. And why shouldn't he look and wish, even hope a little? It was February back on earth and on Kikk spring was coming.

"He would be glad for a change, to be free of…" She made a vague gesture.

The way she said the word free sent a pang through his heart.

"The ties that bind us are sometimes only in our minds," he said gently. "We just have to find the courage to walk away." He hesitated, then added, "I do not think you are short on courage."

"Courage? I risked much in bringing you this far," she said, not defensively, but thoughtfully. "It is duty that holds me to my task." Her gaze was so wistful. "Duty…"

He hesitated, then walked around the container and covered her restless hands with his.

"My duty, my oath requires me to give my life for my country, for my crew, but it does not ask me to risk it when the reason for it is gone. Your people don't need to hide anymore. They can go home or find a new home. The galaxy is open. There is no limit on growth. No limit on…love, on life." He found he was glad Bangle wasn't around to throw in a love song. His face heated. Apparently, sappy was catching. But that thought died when she lifted her lashes, her gaze meeting his.

"And…hope…" she murmured. "There is no limit on hope. I felt it on your outpost, General."

"John," he murmured. "Call me John."

"John." The single word carried some hope in the sound.

More heat swirled in places that weren't his face at the sound of his name on her tongue. What was it about her voice that had such power? The only thing he wanted to do more than listen to her talk was…

Halliwell was not sure what he would have done next, but the comm pinged, interrupting them. He let his hands slide away from hers and wondered if she could see how reluctant he was.

"Thank you," she said, then turned to touch her comm. "All secure down here, Captain—" she flicked him a mischievous look.

HALLIWELL WATCHED Naxe leave the cargo bay, but he didn't follow her right away. He wasn't ready to go to the bridge and the small galley wasn't the most comfortable place to sit and think. He propped himself against one of the cargo containers and tried to sort through his impressions of the whole setup. It wasn't hard. It didn't require a lot of thinking to conclude this setup had issues.

Was this his Picard moment? Did he really think Picard would have gotten involved in this? Depended on who he asked, he decided with an almost wry smile. It had been the job of the show's writers to get Picard into trouble. The Picard they'd created would probably have told him not to engage.

So why had he done it? Why was he really here?

Inside his own head, he tried to require honesty, but he was human. Sometimes he did things he shouldn't when he was following his gut, not sure where it would lead, but sure, nevertheless. And sometimes he followed his…for lack of a better word…his logic. A different part of his brain. But this time? He sighed.

He was rather afraid he'd followed his heart. The thought almost made him shudder. Had he really done this for a girl? To get what? A date? It was an uncomfortable truth that when the ray guns were not firing, he was lonely.

He considered Naxe's face when she'd told him there would be consequences for bringing them to her company's fleet. Had she told the truth about those consequences? Had he sensed someone with nothing to lose? The truth was, if her people wanted to huddle on a bunch of ships waiting for the world to get safe, well, that was their choice. But Naxe? She deserved better than spinning her wheels feeding them.

The cargo bay doors slid back with a less than smooth hiss of sound. Halliwell straightened, but then relaxed when he saw Tim and Riina enter. He lifted a hand in greeting, then glanced around, wondering—not for the first time—if they were being monitored by the frog.

"I have blocked audio monitoring, General," Tim said.

Halliwell glanced from him to Riina. She nodded.

"I asked him to provide us with some privacy. I thought we should talk before we reached the ships."

Did that mean she had doubts about the setup, too?

"She believes it," Halliwell said, not defensively, but maybe a bit puzzled.

"She does," Riina agreed. "And when she speaks, I believe, too." Then she added, "People believe many impossible things."

"So you think it's not possible for an array of ships to operate independently and invisibly in this galaxy for a couple thousand years?" Even asking the question told him what he actually believed.

She shook her head regretfully. "So we must then ask ourselves what to expect when we arrive."

"A trap," Tim said.

Halliwell nodded. "But why? If no one but Naxe and the frog know we're coming…"

"That assumes the trap is for us," Riina agreed. "It is possible she was manipulated into reaching out to us, but this also assumes much that does not make sense."

"The odds of that working are…" Tim reeled off a really big number.

"Long," Halliwell agreed. He was quiet for several seconds. "I should never have involved you two in this."

"Why not?" Riina sounded curious.

"Well, if it is a trap, it's dangerous."

"I am here for dangerous," Tim said.

"And I am here because," for the first time color crept into her cheeks. Then she gave a soft chuckle. "I am here because I am curious."

That's not what she'd been about to say. If there was something going on between the two, well, he wasn't that surprised. It had been happening pretty regularly both on his ship and on Kikk. Love was definitely in the air. Maybe he'd caught some. It made more sense than any of his other reasons for signing on for this particular bit of crazy.

"We have backup, too," Halliwell pointed out, then, "right?"

"We do," Tim agreed. "They are hanging back, waiting for my signal. But they will come if we need help."

He told them what Naxe had said. Riina looked as worried as he felt. Tim looked like Tim.

But it was Tim who said, "That is troubling."

Halliwell felt the human consciousness more than usual with that comment. And the human conscience. He was glad Tim needed something to do while he waited for a human body. He'd miss this Tim, Halliwell realized. There was something comforting about having a big, lethal robot as your security. But he could also understand why the big, lethal robot wanted more. It was impossible to kiss a girl with a metal mouth.

"My gut is telling me that the whole setup stinks, but I also believe Naxe believes what she says." He frowned. He could have brought more people—and another robot—with him and Naxe wouldn't have objected. But he'd wanted to project something besides power. Second thoughts were no good to him now. And if push came to shove, they could stay on the ship and leave. If the frog let them. If it didn't, they called in their own ride and left.

It sounded simple inside his head, so why were his gut and his heart reminding him that nothing was ever simple? Usually, he liked it when they agreed.

"WHAT DO you suppose they are talking about?" Naxe said, glancing at the video feed from the cargo bay—a video feed that lacked sound. She did not blame them. She wouldn't trust her either, but that didn't stop the stab of pain in the region of her heart. She trusted them.

At least their body language was relaxed, well, Tim's body language hadn't changed since she met him, but John and Riina looked relaxed. Their expressions went in and out of worry, however.

"They are talking about us," Blooban said, "and wondering whether they can trust us."

"Yes," Naxe said, with an inward sigh. "I wish…" She stopped because Blooban knew all too much about her wishes and hopes and had to be sick of hearing them. And because her wishes were as useless as her hopes and her dreams. "Why should they trust us? They don't know us."

Blooban gave a croak of agreement. For once, she wished he hadn't.

She didn't remind him that he hadn't believed her when she'd told him about the company. He'd seen as much as he could see without leaving the ship, so he believed to some extent, but he thought it was all wrong and had pushed her to find help.

And he had tried to help her in his own way. She suspected he'd done something to the security scan that was required before she could leave the ship. It had been less uncomfortable since she'd brought him there. She didn't ask what he'd done, because she'd have had to report it, and he didn't tell because she hadn't asked.

"They believe you believe, or they wouldn't be here," Blooban said finally, as if he'd been working on the words for several minutes.

"That's not the same as believing," she pointed out.

"But better than not believing."

"I guess." It didn't feel better. It felt…lonely…her gaze was drawn toward the tall, strong figure of the general. *John.* He'd asked her to call him John. It felt like more than just believing her, but what did she know? She'd been a lonely specter among the ghosts of the company for her whole life. *Of Scoyfol.* What did that even mean? She thought she'd known, but as she tried to explain them, explain their existence, even she could hear how thin the story sounded. Did she know the truth of her and her people's existence?

She'd operated out in space, gone onto docks that were seedy and filled with danger, and she hadn't felt this uneasy. Blooban had encouraged her to reach out to those who had defeated the Dusan. She'd had to fight against her own compulsion to obey, to do her duty no matter what, to do as he suggested.

Since she'd met John and been on Kikk, a seed of hope had taken root in her heart and it was growing. But she'd obeyed for so long. Even now, when it was done, she felt as if she had to fight herself not to turn back.

An alert showed on navigation. They'd be dropping into real space soon. They must have heard it, because John and the others left the bay.

"We're almost there," she said, a profoundly unnecessary statement. One thing her bringing them aboard had accomplished. Whether she wanted to or not, she had to keep going forward.

Chapter 2

As the *Vycorth* dropped into normal space, and the forward view steadied, Halliwell had to stop himself from leaning forward for his first sight of the Scoyfol ships. It was an amazing story and, at this moment, he realized how very much he hadn't really believed it. In any case, leaning wasn't a general thing to do.

Instead of ships, he saw nothing but a nebula or some kind of anomaly. Lots of space with no ships. He should be better at knowing what kind of space this was, but he usually had people, geeks for that.

Naxe had refused to identify the region of space where the company currently hid. This would have worried his team—and himself—if not for Tim and the Garradian outposts' tracking systems. He might be willing to go where no man had gone, but he wasn't willing to go where no one knew where he was.

There was a complicated comms trill, and Naxe reached out and tapped in what he assumed was a coded reply.

"Are strangers coming aboard a common occurrence?" Halliwell asked.

"Refugees are—were welcome to join the company," Naxe said. "With the peace, it has not been necessary to take in others."

From refugees to "others?" Halliwell exchanged a look with Riina because it was no use looking at Tim for that.

More trills, another response from Naxe. The exchange began to get more insistent. As far as Halliwell could tell, Naxe's responses were delivered with the same deliberate persistence. The set of her shoulders didn't change and the frog didn't move.

"Problem?" Halliwell asked. *Something is wrong,* she'd said. Now he glanced at Tim, though he wasn't sure why. It wasn't as if he could ask him if this was a code sequence or trouble. Tim's head angled toward him, his visual display tracking faster. So Tim might be concerned, too. They had an exit plan. He could give him the signal and stop this before—

With a last trill, the horizon in front of them wavered and suddenly the ships were there, hanging in space like some ungainly, eerie space creature. An ancient, dead space creature it appeared, with no lights showing anywhere. A fission of unease crept across his nerve endings. He had Tim, he reminded himself. And questions. First up, what was the force that had hidden them for so long? The Garradians had cloaking technology, but their outpost sensors could see through it, and they hadn't seen this.

His next question he asked Naxe. "Are the ships always blacked out?" It felt like overkill when they had such effective cloaking.

"It helps conserve resources," Naxe answered.

It made sense, almost the only thing that had so far. The array of ships drew his attention like a magnet, particularly the "head" of the "creature," with its tentacles of ships strung out beside and behind it. There were web-like connections—transit tubes, he'd guess—between all the ships, at least fifty of them, he surmised. There was some logic to the arrangement. If the formation was attacked, none of the ships would impede each others ability to flee, or completely block each other's firing capability.

The big ship had to be the original ship, he decided. It appeared old, without looking decrepit, and the arrangement of smaller ships looked protective, at least on this approach vector. If the arrangement was to protect the Scoyfol ship, was it designed to protect the passengers or the captain?

"What's it called?" he asked, "the Scoyfol ship?"

"*Scoyfol's Hope*," she said.

Prescient, unless was it changed later. He stared at the formation, wondering why it kicked off all kinds of instinctual warnings? And then he got it. Hidden or not, it looked like a very appealing trap. It appeared dead, helpless, a carefully arranged tangle of ships that could deceive the unwary. Was that meant for "refugees" or someone else? In the beginning, when they'd needed resources so desperately, how had they acquired them? Had the motley mix of escort ships been willing to join the Scoyfol party?

There was trouble, Naxe had said, but was it only about going home or staying here? Or was there more to it? Had the original voyage been accompanied by support ships? A convoy of sorts? Or had they all been acquired later? Why wouldn't the captain want to be relieved of this mess? What benefit did he receive from keeping the status quo?

He looked at Riina, wishing he were free to ask what she thought. As if she sensed his gaze, her gaze met his—a gaze filled with caution. What did she see out there? He studied the ships once more, this time focusing on those closest to the *Hope*. Those would have been the first ships "acquired," or so he assumed. He couldn't see a pattern to them. They were all shapes and sizes, and they all looked old, but in fairly good shape. There was a curiously squat ship situated in the *Hope's* bow. He'd seen a fair mix of ships since they arrived here, but he'd not seen one quite that like that one. It was an ugly sucker—he tensed. *Ugly.* The Dusan had liked ugly. But they were gone, killed by the mental connection that had allowed their Leader to control them.

Not all of them, he reminded himself, though the survivors had mostly been conscripted slaves who had been brainwashed into loyalty. He'd almost been killed by one of them a few years back.

Naxe's head turned toward the frog, giving him a look at her profile. Once again Halliwell was struck by the strength and clarity there. Other than his Picard inclinations, it was Naxe that had brought him here. It was either the right decision or his worst ever.

"Permission to proceed?" Naxe asked the frog.

He croaked, then Naxe asked the same question over the comm.

"Permission granted," an anonymous voice said.

Halliwell felt their course alter, taking them toward the rear of the formation, where the ships were more battered looking.

"It's like a museum," Riina murmured. "I've never seen such an assortment of ships in one place."

"But you recognize them?" Halliwell asked, keeping his tone casual. How could she recognize ships that were built after she went into cryo-sleep?

"Not all of them." Another flickering glance his direction had him biting back the questions he wanted to ask. "But many have familiar profiles."

If they were familiar, that meant they were old. That seemed to confirm some of what Naxe claimed, but his gut was still going for "trap."

If it were a trap, was Naxe a part of it? She could be unwitting bait, but why would anyone in the ship's company want him? He kept coming back to that. And she hadn't objected to Tim, indeed she'd seemed impressed by him, even relieved, he'd thought at the time. That seemed to bolster the unwitting bait part. But it didn't answer the question of why him? He might be the ultimate power aboard his ship, but he was a cog in this system, and a smallish cog at that. The big player in this galaxy was the Gadi. The Earth Expedition had a seat at the table because they'd risked everything to help them defeat the Dusan, but that didn't mean he was well-liked around here, despite the AI, Bangle's endorsement.

The frog gave some kind of a croak, his surprisingly supple flippers adept on the controls—controls that might have been designed specifically for a frog. Tim, who had a special line to Bangle, had taken time to update Halliwell on the frog's special abilities. Not just a co-pilot, but a hacker and a good one. Good enough, in fact, to have intrigued Bangle, which was how she'd come to transport them directly to his quarters. He'd been sure it was Naxe's voice, but no, apparently Bangle was impressed by ninja hacking skills. He was going to have to try to have a talk with the Bangle when he got back. But for now he needed to focus on the puzzle in front of him.

The silence felt tense and Halliwell realized he did miss one thing about Bangle that surprised him: the Earth music she insisted on piping throughout the various outposts and—when she could get away with it—onboard their ships. Her playlists might sometimes annoy, but they'd also been surprisingly apropos to the moment at times and they filled tense silences. What song, he wondered, would she pick for this moment? *Highway to the Danger Zone* maybe? He glanced over and realized one of Tim's metal fingers was tapping a metal knee. Did he have a song playing in there? Wouldn't surprise Halliwell. All of the cybernetic robots had bonded with Bangle and hadn't seemed to mind the music. Almost he grinned.

"We will be docking at our usual place," Naxe said.

Halliwell felt the slowing of the ship as it angled even more sharply toward a long ship that looked a bit like a caterpillar, a space version, with sucker-looking indentations along the side. Docking bays perhaps? A ship designed specifically to receive cargo? It was the last ship in the formation, but the trailing edges of smaller rear ships almost flanked it, the arrangement once more appearing to be protective.

At least that made sense. You'd want to protect your supply chain, though this was a fairly meagre effort. Of course, it did make it easy for ships to come and go, he'd guess.

Riina leaned forward in her seat, craning slightly to peer past the pilot's position.

She exuded a serenity that Halliwell found curious in someone who'd slept long and awakened to a completely changed world. He'd wondered how he'd react and decided he'd be angry, but then serenity had never been one of his personal traits. It was, in his mind, a passive trait but...Riina was not a passive person. She might be tranquil on the surface, but he sensed more there. Plus, she came highly recommended. And Tim liked her, he reminded himself with an inner grin.

"All is well?" Riina asked, that soothing serenity in her tone.

Naxe quit moving for several seconds, then swiveled around.

"I am somewhat overdue," she said. "There are extra proto-cols." She glanced at Tim. "And I reported passengers."

"What are the usual protocols for docking?" Tim asked, entering the conversation unexpectedly. "What will be different?"

Halliwell blinked, wondering if he'd ever heard Tim use that many words.

"Normal protocol is to use the exterior docking hatch, via an airlock, rather than landing in a bay and using the ramp. Because of you, the crew will scan and approve the cargo, then unload it. Once they are clear of this ship, we can enter the cargo bay. On their side of the airlock, there is a security scan." She seemed to hesitate and glanced in the frog's direction, before saying, almost lamely. "It is necessary if you wish to leave this ship."

"They will find Tim alarming," the frog said in his gruff tone.

"Everyone finds Tim alarming," Halliwell said. It was one of the things Halliwell liked about Tim.

"Truly?" Riina turned to study the robot. "I find him reassuring."

"I was designed to intimidate," Tim said, as if they didn't know this.

Halliwell glanced at Tim, but there was nothing to see, of course. Except the non-rhythmic tapping of one metal finger. He arched a brow, not sure Tim would understand the implied question. But if the robot was worried....

"I am unable to detect life signs aboard the cargo receiving ship," Tim said.

Naxe had enough expression for her and Tim. "That's not..." she swung around and began tapping controls.

A screen appeared on their forward view. It showed a few life signs on the docking ship. If he had to guess, the cluster was in the unloading bay they were approaching, and then possibly a bridge crew or security presence. The scan did not show any other ship in the fleet.

"Interesting," Tim said.

He didn't sound concerned, but then he never did.

"You and Riina should don protective suits before leaving this ship," Tim said.

Naxe looked at him over her shoulder. "The bay is climate

controlled and the scan will detect and remove harmful agents from the air."

Tim said nothing. If Naxe thought this was a concession, well, she didn't know Tim.

"How many people are usually stationed there?" Halliwell asked, partly because he wanted to know and partly to change the subject.

"Security, crew to unload and move cargo, a foreman. Maybe six to ten."

Exactly the number of life signs showing on their screen. In a battle of frog data versus Tim data, Halliwell knew which he believed. But if Tim was right then…what the heck?

It was, perhaps, not the moment to realize his Picard moment was turning out to be an actual Picard moment. Why was he surprised? When had anything ever gone right for Picard? At least Picard had his writers to bring it all right at the end. But he had Tim, he reminded himself. Tim was better than writers.

"I will go first and assess," Tim said.

Naxe's mouth opened. "It is—"

"I will go first."

She subsided. She must have realized what they'd all had to learn. Don't argue with the robot.

~

THE SCOYFOL ARRAY of ships grew larger as they drew closer, giving him tantalizing glimpses of the trailing ships. Many reminded Halliwell of the ship they were on, but less damaged, other than impacts that could be meteor hits. The Ugly Sucker ship nestled like a crab in the center right behind the *Hope*. The sight of it bothered him more the closer they got, though it didn't make sense that it was of Dusan make, unless they'd captured it at some point. It wasn't impossible, he reminded himself. They'd captured some Dusan shuttles early on.

Halliwell would have liked to dock closer to the *Hope*, but Naxe told them they would not be allowed to dock anywhere else.

The *Vycorth* slowed more and began to angle in for its final approach. Closer now, he could see the indentations better. There were at least ten of the docking hatches or airlocks along this one side. If there were ten on the other side, then perhaps it was possible to keep the fleet supplied—except for the whole endless war part.

Just before they dropped down where they couldn't see it, he took a last look at *Scoyfol's Hope*.

"Was it always called the Hope?" he asked.

"It was originally *Scoyfol's Future*," Naxe said. "It was, at the time, the newest ship in the fleet."

"Do you know what happened to the others?"

Scoyfol is ships, she'd said.

"No," she said, "at least, they were presumed lost."

Could they have done what this ship had done and hidden? Or was there something special about this ship, something different, that allowed it to survive—if it had? Did he believe it had? He watched as the exterior of the caterpillar ship closed rapidly now. There were more trills and then the *Vycorth* made the turn, presenting its docking hatch for connection. Transit felt swift after that. There was a thud felt all the way to the bridge, he heard or felt the connections joining with a series of clicks and more thumps.

"We've got you *Vycorth*," a voice said over the comm. "Will proceed with unloading your cargo and then you and your passengers can disembark."

There was a short silence, then Naxe rose from her seat, her expression tense. "If you wish to suit up, now is the time."

At least she wasn't arguing with them.

TIM DID NOT NEED to suit up. He could operate in or out of atmosphere. Naxe noted that he hovered close to Riina while she suited up, assisting her in donning the bulky gear, including a survival pack with emergency air and rations. Almost as an afterthought, he asked if the general—John—needed help. Recalling their conversation helped take the edge off the chill that made the waiting so hard. She watched the unloading of the cargo with her portable viewer. She knew Blooban also watched from the bridge. It reassured her to see familiar faces moving around the bay. They weren't…friends exactly, but they were crew. They were part of the story of Scoyfol, too.

When Tim had found no life signs, she'd almost panicked, which was strange because she kept hoping for a reason to leave, but all of them gone was not the reason she wanted.

"We're done," one of the faces grew larger in her viewer. "You can begin the disembarkation process now."

The scan. Naxe hated the scan, but Blooban had made it less intrusive, and the unloading process gave him time to hack in again. As if he knew what she thought, her personal comm activated.

"It's done."

It was not a surprise when Tim took the lead to the cargo bay. Naxe always had to palm the hatch open, but it slid back for him. She imagined that most of the universe would stand back for Tim. He was not what she'd imagined when she'd sought out the Earth Expedition.

I asked for their help, she reminded herself. And because of that asking, she had no right to complain if the help wasn't quite what she'd expected. And, if she were truthful to herself, she'd been relieved that John had such formidable protection. She was uncertain why she felt this relief. She was of Scoyfol. That implied many things, including trust. It was uncomfortable to realize this trust in Scoyfol had faded since the peace. It felt traitorous to have such thoughts. Those of Scoyfol did not waver in doing their duty. They followed orders without question even when those orders did not make sense….

That was the problem. She wasn't supposed to think about those orders. It was not her place to decide if they made sense or not. It was her duty to do what she was told. But…no one had told her *not* to bring John and his team here….

If she'd imperiled the company, this rationalization would not save her. She'd faced that before she made the decision to act against her standing orders. John had spoken of his duty, his oath that could require his life. For her, it felt this serious, or this desperate, she decided somewhat wryly. It felt as if she couldn't breathe, as if her duty were suffocating her.

It had been hard to stand by and watch as they donned protective gear when she didn't, but if she'd tried to leave the ship in her pressure suit? It would not go well for any of them. Her people would suspect some kind of trap and start shooting.

She headed for the airlock, noting that someone—Tim perhaps —had removed all the containers that John's soldier had trundled on board. The airlock was wide and as high as possible to accommodate the big containers, so she could see clearly into the other bay where the loading crew was still working on sorting her containers. Light circled both the docking bays' airlocks to show they were active and engaged. A ramp extended into their bay for the cargo to be more easily shifted from one ship to the other.

One of the loaders looked up, saw her, and gave wave. She waved back. He'd been here the last time she'd arrived, she thought. She tried not to get attached to any of them because they seemed to change every few runs.

She turned to signal the others to follow her and stopped at the looks on both John and Riina's faces.

"What?" she asked.

"Who…" John stopped and seemed to look past her. He cleared his throat. "Who were you waving at?"

WHO WAS SHE WAVING AT? And why did she seem to be confused? Halliwell looked at Tim.

"Do you see anyone over there?" he dropped his voice to ask.

"No," Tim said, not moderating his volume at all.

"I don't either," Riina said, flashing Naxe a worried glance.

"But…" Naxe looked back, her expression clearly confused. "They are right there." Her gaze tracked from his face, to Riina, confusion deepening to worry.

Halliwell went past her, stopping at the edge of the airlock. In the video from the bridge, there had been people and containers, light, and the look of an occupied space. Now, it was just an empty space.

"There's no one there, and I don't see your containers," he said.

"They move them as soon as they arrive," Naxe said, uncertainty in her tone. "They are so needed, you see."

Actually, he didn't see. It didn't make sense, but then nothing much about this did. He studied Naxe. She was real. His people had required a basic health screening for her, mostly so they could find out more about her. The results weren't that interesting. She was human, shared similar DNA with both the Gadi and the defrosted Garradians. And the frog? He was real, too, though they'd settled for a quick scan of him. Her ship was real. They were standing in it, unless he was having a long, complicated, and very-detailed-for-him dream.

At the moment, he would have liked the dream to be the reality, except, he glanced at Naxe, for her. He'd like her to be real. But he already knew that. So if this was real, if that ship over there was real, then what was really going on here?

"I don't understand," Naxe said. "They are right there."

"Do you recognize them?" Riina said.

"One of them," Naxe said. "I don't always get the same crew."

"How often do you get the same crew?" Halliwell asked, not sure it mattered.

"Not often," she admitted. "But I recognize one of the men from last time."

"His name?" Riina prompted.

"I…" Naxe broke off, shaking her head in frustration. "I don't know if I know."

She looked at the other ship and then lifted a hand in a "wait a minute" gesture.

"Either they are cloaked," Tim said, "or they aren't there."

"But—" she bit back her protest.

"Why don't you check it out, Tim," Halliwell suggested.

Naxe seemed to struggle again, but then stepped back, signaling for him to proceed.

Tim didn't hesitate until he reached the docking ship's airlock. Halliwell couldn't state that the sudden burst of light startled Tim, but it did make him pause, his head turning various directions as the scan bounced off the surface of his metal body. Tim reached out, one of his tools emerging from his arm, and punched through the wall of the air lock. Naxe gasped. Halliwell didn't. He'd seen the robots do this before. It didn't actually appear to damage anything, just gave him access to the controls.

The light began to change, passing through the range of colors, then finally faded to a pale yellow before turning off.

Naxe started forward, her face losing all color. "What did you do?"

Halliwell caught her arm, gently but firmly. For a moment, she tried to pull away, but finally stopped and looked at him.

"They're gone, aren't they?" Halliwell said. She nodded, tension making a white line around her compressed lips.

"Where..." She stopped and then managed with impressive calm. "They were never there, were they?"

"Well, they aren't there now," Halliwell said. "We don't know about always." He knew what he believed, but he didn't know what it meant. Why would someone have her keep risking her life for supplies for an empty ship or ships?

Her lips moved. She licked them and said, "You saw them when we were on the bridge."

Tim had turned so he could watch the bay and them.

"You saw a video feed," he said.

Halliwell grimaced. "Do you know what the scan was designed to do?"

Tim paused, then added, "I have downloaded the data and am currently studying it. Initial examination indicates that some of its elements were designed to alter brain patterns."

"But..." Naxe stopped again. And then as if answering her own question said, "Blooban has never been off the ship. He's never been through the security scan."

"Did he say why?" Riina asked.

"He didn't trust the security scan—or that he wouldn't be

confined," she admitted. She paced a few steps away, then returned to Halliwell's side. It seemed to take some effort for her to continue. "The scan was uncomfortable. Blooban altered some of the parameters for me."

"Why didn't he shut if off?" Halliwell wanted to know.

"I thought it would trigger alarms," Blooban said over the comm.

The gruffness, the frog-ness of his voice still startled him.

"I had to be cautious in penetrating the system. It had many traps and triggers," the frog added.

Halliwell stiffened. "Did you trip something, Tim?"

"No."

He couldn't say Tim spent words recklessly.

Riina had been frowning, but now she spoke. "You went over there and talked to people, I presume?"

"Of course," Naxe said, but she no longer sounded sure.

"Did you have any reason to touch anyone?" He didn't like asking the question. She'd already said there was no one, but a friend, maybe?

Naxe took her time answering the question. He could almost see her flipping through her memories. "No," she said. She looked to one side. "I was always anxious to leave."

"You didn't have to report to anyone?" Halliwell tried not to sound incredulous. At the very least, his people needed a medical scan and a debrief when they'd been out. And if they brought home a guest? There'd been some quarantine time.

"No," she said again. "We...Blooban believes that there is some level of scanning built in to the protective screen."

"Any data he can share with Tim on that?" Halliwell asked. Could it be messing with what she saw, too? But their brains hadn't been messed with—that he knew. Never assume, he reminded himself. This sure felt like a smoke and mirrors carnival ride, though. What was real and what wasn't?

"We should leave," Tim said. "I can detect no life signs on that ship."

Naxe jerked, then seemed to visibly hold herself still. "What about the other ships?"

"I am unable to acquire data on any other ships," Tim admitted.

"Are you being blocked?" Halliwell asked, unable to keep the sharpness from his voice.

"I have no data to determine that. It would require closer contact."

Something was very wrong in the whole setup. That this had turned out to be a trap was not a shock, but what kind of trap? Until they could get a better handle on it, it was wiser to retreat and get reinforcements.

"Any way to tell how long the cargo loading ship has been abandoned?" Halliwell asked.

Tim turned, studying the unloading bay, Halliwell presumed.

"Not without a closer examination, including access to the bridge databases," he said, finally.

"The bridge..." Naxe spoke with obvious effort. Halliwell noted that she still stared at the bay.

"Can you still see them?" he asked.

She licked her lips. "They come and go." She managed a stiff smile. "It is as if my brain is arguing with itself."

"Can you help her?" Halliwell asked Tim.

He left the airlock and stopped in front of her. When he lifted his hand, a beam came out, that he pointed at her head. She flinched, her hands curling into fists, but she held her ground. When Tim finished, she blinked, shaking her head, then looked at the airlock.

"How do you feel?"

She rubbed her temples. "My head feels clearer, as if I woke from a dream. The memory of them lingers, but no, I can't see them now." She made a restless movement. "I knew them...I thought I knew them." She was quiet for several seconds, then burst out, "Why? How?"

Halliwell met Riina's gaze. The only way to answer that question was to keep going.

"We should go," he said, echoing Tim. "We can organize a team to—"

Naxe nodded and Halliwell felt a moment's relief.

"You should go." She stared toward the ship. "Blooban will return you to the outpost."

"You can't stay here alone," he protested.

"I won't be alone. Someone did this and I want to know why. I deserve," her voice faltered, "to know who would do this. And when. I have to know when."

She deserved more than that, but staying alone in this place was not the way to find out—she believed some of her people were still here somewhere. Or she hoped? If it was him, he'd hope, too, he realized with an inward sigh.

"I can stay and assist," Tim said, breaking the long silence.

"I'd like to stay, too," Riina said. She gave Halliwell an apologetic smile. "This is why I came."

"It is your function to protect the general," Naxe pointed out, though there might have been cautious hope in her eyes.

Neither of them was actually under his command, so he wasn't worried about the apparent mutiny.

"Do we know we can leave?" he asked mildly. If there was an actual someone behind this, and not some program gone wrong, they wouldn't like being outed. Of course, it was possible he'd seen too many sci-fi movies, but was there still a Scoyfol to be of? Had she ever been one of them? What if she was the fly who had wandered into the trap? How much of the mind messing had Tim been able to fix? Was there any way to know even if they dove deeper into this trap?

Naxe tapped her comm. "Blooban?"

The gravely voice came over the general comm, not the personal ones.

"The general is correct. We cannot leave the region, though I believe I retain the capability to disconnect my airlock and move away. I cannot get past the screening cloak without permission, however."

Halliwell was quiet for several seconds, then he directed a

command look at Naxe. "You need to suit up if we're going to explore further."

She looked inclined to protest, so he added, "If someone wants to stop you from getting answers all they have to do is open an airlock and we all get vented into space."

Her eyes widened, but she nodded. And he didn't have to be a general to note the gratitude in her eyes.

"You don't…" she tried again.

"We do," Halliwell said. For good or ill—they'd need to play the hand they'd been dealt all the way to the end of the game.

THE AIRLOCK between the unloading bay and the *Vycorth* closed with a chilly finality, leaving them in the eerily empty cargo bay. Blooban was not deserting them, though she felt bereft. He was moving away so that he'd have more flexibility if they needed retrieval at some point. All the ships were positioned to break formation in an emergency, so he should be able to dock with one of them if Tim could work their side of the problem. The hope was that Tim would also be able to get them clear of the force field. All they had to do was find the source.

Naxe would have felt despair about this, but Tim inspired confidence, not despair. And John? He inspired many feelings, some she shouldn't feel, but whatever Tim had done to her brain had left her awash in many emotions. The ones she felt for John? They were the better ones, so she didn't try to stop them.

In the cargo bay, the emergency lighting made it worse rather than better and the ghosts of those Naxe thought she knew lingered inside her head, mocking her or so it felt. There were tracks in the dusty floor, which seemed to indicate that at least her cargo had been real, but who had moved it? After a quick look around, she had kept her gaze fixed on the others as they left the bay. Out in a wide hallway the heavy silence was broken only by the shuffling sound of their footsteps. The gravity was still engaged, which Tim found "interesting," and small puffs of dust wafted up as they made their way toward the bridge access.

Their shadows stalked ahead of them, courtesy of more emergency lighting. Tim cast the longest shadow. Hers wavered in and out of view.

This ship, even this hallway, should have felt familiar to her. She'd been coming and going here for years. But now the curving ceiling with its recessed shadows felt alien and unfamiliar. And there was a sense of being watched, she decided, a listening quality to the silence. They'd all turned on their headgear lights and as she looked around, her light found little to stir memories, real or manufactured. Nothing was familiar.

It felt as if the harder she tried to remember, the more memory danced out of reach, so she tried to relax, reaching for her core, the way she did just before emerging onto a strange docking ring. It had been a long time since she'd had a reason to come out here, she reminded herself, and then found herself wondering why that was? After hours out in space alone with Blooban, why didn't she want some station time in a place that should have felt safe? Why had she left as soon as she could? And why, this time, had she brought others with her?

Was it because her mind was being manipulated? Or because she had unconsciously been seeking help for herself and not her people?

Her people.

Did they even exist? Had they ever been here? Had anyone actually walked these halls? Could her eyes, her senses be fooled to that extent? They never touched. It felt wrong to admit that to John, but she couldn't recall being touched or wanting to touch anyone here. She'd watched John's people, not all, but some of them clasp hands, one couple had even hugged each other. And seeing it had caused her to feel the deep hole inside her that Blooban had helped to partially fill. He'd let her hug him, though she had the feeling he didn't need it as much as she did.

But the people here? She'd never wanted to hug any of them. And clasping hands? The instinctive withdrawal she felt at the idea, was that normal? She glanced at John. She wouldn't mind clasping his hand, but she had to wrestle with her instincts for several seconds. It was as if there were an "other" inside her head. She knew Naxe, but this other? It was like her shadow on the floor. Hazy and indistinct when she tried to examine it, but still somehow a force to be reckoned with every time she tried to act against its desire.

She found she didn't want to get too close to it, but it must be her, too. She'd had her regular medical scans on the *Vycorth* after coming back aboard, and they'd found nothing out of place.

Would she learn what she needed to know from the bridge databanks? Her mind knew, had been forced to know that what she'd seen wasn't real, but her heart struggled to believe, to understand.

They were faces even if she couldn't recall their names right now. People she believed she knew. Now she didn't know what to believe. How could she not know? How could she come and go bringing food and supplies—what had happened to those things?

"There had to have been someone," she said, her voice echoing strangely in the hallway.

John glanced back at her, his face hidden by his head gear.

"Someone got the supplies we brought." Her cargo was gone, though she wasn't sure how that had been accomplished so swiftly. Suddenly she didn't know what was real and what was not. Had her excursions in other places all happened inside her head? But—could the deception follow them out of this place and into wider space? She'd wonder if they ever left, but John and his team were here. She hadn't imagined that—before she could stop herself, she touched his arm, her hand closing around it.

"I'm real," he said. "I'm here."

"You'd say that if you weren't," she said, but the arm felt real, and so did the relief, then, "Am I real?"

Now it was Tim who looked back. "Yes."

She half laughed and realized she believed the brief word more than John. Because she wanted to believe John, she decided. But Tim was…Tim. A robot couldn't lie, could it?

They reached the bridge access and Tim deployed his access device. It was quite useful to have a robot around.

Once inside, it was clear it had been abandoned some time ago. There was dust on the controls—thankfully internal gravity was still active here too—and on the seats. At least there were no human remains. Until she had this thought, she hadn't realized she'd been worried about it.

It was a small bridge with only three crew positions. It did have databanks and video screens for both bay sides.

Though they were all suited up, John asked, "What's the air quality like?"

"It is minimally acceptable in quality," Tim said. "The levels were adjusted prior to our arrival." As he spoke, he went to work on the controls, bringing the bridge power back online.

"Does that mean someone adjusted them?" Riina sounded startled.

"Our presence could be activating systems, such as emergency lighting," Tim said.

The video screens flickered, then began to show the various bays. The quality wasn't great, Naxe noted. And all the bays were as empty as the one they'd left, but the one directly across from theirs. There was her cargo. Who had moved it? And why were the others so empty? No, empty was such a bland word. They looked deserted, long abandoned, though she couldn't have said exactly why she felt this. Space did not cause deterioration like planets did.

Tim found a data port and accessed the ship's databanks. He was silent so long, John finally stirred and asked, "Anything?"

The robot seemed to stir.

"This ship was not originally a Scoyfol ship," Tim said. "It allied with them early in the conflict."

"So it is old," John said.

Riina nodded. "I saw ships such as this one before."

"Any reason why no one is here?" John prompted again.

"There is nothing in the logs about why, just a simple statement that they were withdrawing and shutting systems down."

"How long ago?" John asked.

Naxe was glad he asked. Her throat was too tight to let words out.

Tim turned from the controls, his red eyes glowing or perhaps pulsing from the information access. Did he seem to hesitate?

"Allowing for differences in how they count time and your method of counting time, I estimate it was about ten years after the first Dusan incursion."

"But that's—" the words were forced out past the dry in her throat and they sounded as harsh as they felt. The rest of the sentence shriveled to nothing.

"A very long time ago," John finished for her.

Chapter 3

GHOST SHIPS FOR GHOST PEOPLE.

Well, Naxe had nailed the ghost ship part, so far. Were all the ships as dead as this one? What had happened to cause the crew to withdraw? Was there someone—or something—alive and still aboard one or more of the other ships? If this was a trap, and Halliwell's gut told him it was, why? Had Naxe been tricked into seeking them out? Or were they an unwelcome addition to the party? If someone wanted to hold him hostage, well, his people would try to get him back, but they wouldn't give up anything to do it. They didn't deal with terrorists. And if this wasn't about him?

That left Naxe. She didn't look like a terrorist, but then what would one look like? Had his gut let him down? He gave her a side-eye look and ended up in the same place. He trusted her because he trusted his gut that said he could trust her. That said, it was time to call in some backup.

"Can you use this ship's communications to reach our backup?" he asked. He gave Naxe a sidelong glance, but if she reacted her headgear hid it.

"Whatever technology is hiding this fleet of ships is also blocking communications," Tim said.

Okay, that wasn't good. He'd operated on the assumption that his people could come in at any point and help them. When was he going to learn to never assume?

"Where's the signal for the cloak coming from?"

Riina went up next to Tim and started working on the controls, too. Then she paused and looked at Tim.

"This ship lacks the technology we need to acquire that data," Tim said.

"It is pretty basic," Riina agreed.

Halliwell frowned, considering. He didn't want to leave this ship...okay, that wasn't strictly accurate. He had as much curiosity as the next person. If nothing else, this was an intriguing archaeological find. Except for the fact that someone had been messing with Naxe's brain. That should be a dent in his gut-trust, or at least put a question mark next to her. Okay, a big one. Just how compromised was she? Could they even know in these conditions?

"Can we get any indication of the various ships' positions from here?" he finally asked.

It took a while—for Tim—but not long for a human, before a display finally appeared. It lacked data, such as life signs readings—unless there were none—but at least he could see them. Before he could ask, Tim split the display so he could see a side view, too.

"Any ship IDs or basic information on their purpose?" How many were Scoyfol ships and how many were acquired? There were many more of than he'd estimated from their approach. There were probably sixty ships, give or take, in varying sizes and configurations.

The display altered, descriptions appearing next to the ships. No surprise they were in an alien language.

"Can you read any of this?" he asked, glanced at Tim, then at Riina.

Riina leaned in closer. "The bulk of the ships are Scoyfol."

"But that's—" Naxe started to protest, then pressed her lips together.

After a pause, Riina continued, "Those on the outer edge have more defensive weapons and those seem to be the ones that came later, though I still recognize most of them." She sounded puzzled. She pointed at the ugly ship right behind the *Hope*. "I don't recognize that one."

To Halliwell, it was just another confirmation—if he needed it—that this fleet was not what Naxe thought it was. And that he'd been right to not like the look of the ugly ship.

"If you had to guess which one controlled the force field..." Halliwell looked at Tim for this one.

Tim was quiet for so long, Halliwell thought he was sorting data and hadn't heard him, though that seemed unlikely. Tim was a multifunction overachiever.

"I have seen a ship like this one," he finally said, a metal digit pointing to the ugly ship. "It is not logical for it to be what I think it is, or for it to be in this location. But if it is, then it is the source of the signal."

Halliwell didn't ask what he thought it was. If he'd wanted to tell him, Tim would have.

Halliwell took a step back, trying to get a sense of how hard it would be to get to it from here. The whole set up looked like one of those mazes they put on the back of cereal boxes for kids to do while they ate.

"It's not going to be easy to get there," Halliwell murmured.

"Logic says you, Riina and Naxe return to the *Vycorth* and wait at a safe distance while I explore." His head swiveled around to meet Halliwell's gaze.

He didn't sound confident, just matter of fact. Riina shifted, probably in protest. Halliwell felt the same instinctive protest. Yeah, Tim was good. All the robots were, or had been, almost unstoppable. It was that "almost" that was the problem. They didn't know what was on any of those ships.

"I believe we should stick together," Naxe said.

Halliwell glanced at her, noted how still she was as she looked at the display.

"Does something there remind you of...anything?" he asked. He felt frustrated by not knowing what to ask her.

Her lips parted, then she shifted. "I don't know. It's just a feeling."

"I have the same feeling," Riina said, reaching out to touch Naxe's arm.

Naxe seemed almost startled by the touch, then lifted her gloved hand to cover Riina's briefly.

Halliwell had no idea what it meant or why Naxe smiled, though he did like her smile. He might wish it was for him.

"So how do we get to that ugly sucker?" Halliwell asked. They —he needed to focus.

"There is only one way," Tim said.

A path appeared on the display. It didn't look too bad. It went right through the heart of the fleet. If Halliwell weren't a suspicious SOB, he'd think it looked almost easy. A pity he was.

"It is very direct," Tim said.

Of course, Tim already knew. He had faster processors.

"I don't like it," Halliwell admitted. That path would be harder for Blooban to get to them, too.

It seemed Blooban was monitoring them somehow, because he spoke again.

"I can retrieve you no matter which ship you are on."

"He is a very good pilot," Naxe said. "But getting the airlocks to activate would need to be done from this side." She looked at Tim, who didn't speak, probably because to him it was obvious he could handle this side.

In the short silence, Riina spoke. "I'm certain that won't be a problem for Tim."

"Have you been on any of these ships?" Halliwell asked.

Naxe stepped closer and with one finger, air-traced the *Hope*.

"Have you been on the *Hope*?"

"I..." She dropped her arm. "How do I know? I have memories, but..."

The memories seemed to be about the people, with the ships as real places, but he couldn't assume anything except that she was compromised.

"Well, let's see how well your memory matches reality," he said. Her wide gaze met his and he added, "We'll figure this out."

This time her smile was for him. "Thank you."

BACK OUT IN THE CORRIDOR, it was not a surprise when Tim indicated that he would take the lead. Riina opted to walk behind Tim, though Naxe suspected she'd rather walk next to him. But Tim was in what Naxe was sure he would call intimidation mode. He had deployed weapons and his posture was menacing.

Naxe was pleased when John chose to walk next to her, though she suspected it was partly protective and partly defensive. How could she expect them to trust her when she didn't trust herself?

John and Riina were also armed and Naxe wanted to be as well, but was uncertain if she should. Did she trust herself? What if whoever had compromised her memory, had altered what she could see, could also control her and where she directed her fire? What if she were forced to fire on her friends? The thought horrified her so much, she said, "You should secure my weapons."

John glanced at her thoughtfully. "The thought had occurred to me, but I hate to leave you defenseless."

"I do not like being defenseless," she admitted. "But if my memory, my mind can be altered...how do I know you and I see the same things, will see the same things when it matters?"

"It's a fair point. How about, when we reach each ship, we do a reality check?"

Naxe nodded, relieved.

"In the meantime, if you'd feel better, I'm sure Tim would secure your weapons for you."

It felt awful, worse, it felt wrong to hand them over. The inner shadow rose and writhed and twisted inside her head. That it was so difficult, made her more determined to do it. She wished to be master of herself. Until she was certain she could trust her own thoughts, until she could trust what her eyes saw, she would do this. She *chose* to do this. And she wasn't completely helpless. She could fight with her hands and feet if she needed. The shadow faded to flat, leaving an echo of fear because she was less lethal, less dangerous this way. It didn't want her to trust John, she realized, or Tim or Riina.

When she took her place next to John once again, it felt as if the silence throbbed with anger and increased menace. When Tim began to move, it took all of her will to follow him, to keep pace with John.

"Someone or something is unhappy," Riina murmured.

For some reason knowing that Riina felt it too helped. Air began to move in and out of Naxe's lungs more easily, though every cell in her body felt hyper-aware and alert.

The bridge wasn't far from the airlock and transit tube to the next ship. The next ship in the complicated puzzle, she mentally added. How had she not noticed this before? Because her mind had been manipulated, she reminded herself bitterly. Did she even know her real name? If the ships had been dark for so long, how did she know she belonged here?

For the first time she let herself see past her so-called duty to the deep longing that had led her to seek out John.

Free. She wanted to be free of this life, of these…ghost ships. She'd called them that to John at their first meeting. Had some part of her known she was trapped in an illusion?

The airlock presented no problem to Tim. The transit tube lacked gravity. They had to propel themselves forward using the handholds strung along both sides.

It was a vulnerable place to be, drifting forward with the emptiness of space all around them, though she noticed John and Riina paused to study the ships they could see through the translucent tube. Tim had the next airlock open by the time she and John reached it. The airlock closed and their feet were pulled down to metal in the low gravity of the airlock. The door to the tube closed and the airlock cycled.

"Interesting," Riina said.

"How so?" John asked, as Tim worked on the ship's other door now.

"That some systems still work."

"Just enough to entice someone to keep going, in fact," John said, his tone grim even over the comm.

"It's a trap," Naxe said. Something bitter shuddered through her with the realization that they'd recognized it for what it was. Flickers of realization hovered just out of sight. This was familiar, but she couldn't remember why or even how. It was like an itch she was unable to scratch. And when she tried, the shadow pushed back.

The hatch slid open and at first it didn't seem that different from the view behind them. Iron gray walls in a small, circular room. There were hooks, possibly for equipment, situated above folded up benches or shelves. Pipes and cable ran up the sides and across the ceiling. A container of some kind was fixed next to one of the benches and there was another at shoulder height. It was a practical place, a space to adjust from one ship to another. She looked around, trying to understand why this felt different from the ship they'd just left.

Riina lifted the lid. "Emergency medical supplies," she said, lifting out a package and examining it.

"Do you recognize the language?" John asked, leaning over to study it.

Riina held it toward Naxe. "Do you recognize it?"

It felt like a test and Naxe tried not to stiffen. She took the package and studied the text, then finally shook her head. "Should I?"

"It's Eldierian. Eldirer is one of the planets your—the Scoyfol passengers were from," Riina said.

So Riina no longer believed Naxe was one of this company. And why should she? In her mind, Naxe heard her own voice naming the planets that Scoyfol served. *I am of Scoyfol.* But she couldn't be. When she tried to call up memories of those passengers, she couldn't. *Who am I?*

She handed the package back and Riina replaced it, closing the lid.

The other container was empty.

"We should keep moving," Tim said.

Naxe followed the others out into the ship's proper, but more questions dropped in thumps, almost in time with their steps in the dim silence of a gray corridor.

If she wasn't of Scoyfol, then why was she here? Why did she feel the compulsion to stay that was as great or greater than the one that said to flee?

~

HALLIWELL GLANCED at Naxe several times as they followed Tim and Riina down a long corridor with doors leading off on both sides. If anything, she looked more impassive than their first meeting. It was hard to tell through the visor of the headgear, but he thought she'd lost color. Her lips had firmed into a line and as she moved forward, her gaze scanned like someone who was used to going into unpredictable places. A couple of times, her hand went to her empty weapons holster.

He wanted to give them back. He didn't like the way her hands twitched when there was no grip to wrap her fingers around.

He cleared his throat, then broke the silence. "Do you see anyone, any crew or people?"

She looked at him, then shook her head. Was it hope that her eyes looked grateful for the small moment of grounding?

"How many ships before the Scoyfol one?" he asked. This was crap. "Can't we call in Blooban and just go to the head of the line?" Why had no one suggested it?

Over his comm, the frog's gruff voice spoke. "As long as I had passengers, I could not secure permission."

That was an interesting statement. Was it trying to tell them something? He sighed, even if it was, they still couldn't jump the line. Be too bad if they missed this ship-to-ship horror show. This one, like the last ship, had some power, enough for emergency lighting and for the airlocks to work. So whoever was behind it wanted them to keep going.

"How many ships to the ugly ship?" he asked again. He'd known the number, but now if felt like there was a buzzing inside his head. Halliwell knew Tim answered him, but it didn't process somehow. He did remember thinking it was just enough to keep them from getting too discouraged.

If they'd stumbled on this place by accident, found these ships, what would they have done?

Not a hard question. They'd have wanted to check it out. Without Naxe, they might have been less alert, less suspicious. They'd have had more people, though, so they could have searched each ship more thoroughly. But he had a feeling there was no point. There was nothing to see here. So he didn't suggest deviating from their direct course for the next airlock.

They all looked around as they walked, their headlamps dancing over nothing-to-see-here.

"What do you suppose this ship was used for?" Halliwell asked, wondering if he'd remember the answer.

"It's for passengers," Riina said. "A short hauler, though. The rooms would be small."

Halliwell reached out and found the door unlocked and pushed it open. It was a stateroom and very small. He might be surprised they hadn't found any blood. It felt like there should be blood, instead the room was dusty but neat. Bedding was rolled up against the head of the bed and the closet stood open and empty.

"It's probably not worth checking out the bridge," he said.

"No," Tim said.

If he got any more chatty, things could get—he stopped and shook his head.

"Are you well?" Naxe asked anxiously.

"A bit of a headache," he said, making a dismissive motion.

"I have one as well," Riina said. "Like there is a low buzzing inside my cranium."

Tim stopped, turning abruptly around to face her. A light stabbed out of his arm, the scan running down, then back up her body. Almost as an afterthought, he also scanned Halliwell.

To his surprise, he found he could grin. It didn't last.

"There was unusual brain activity in both your brains," Tim said.

So Tim getting chatty was bad news.

"My head feels better," Riina offered.

So did his, Halliwell realized.

"I stopped the interference," Tim said.

Halliwell opened his mouth to ask how and decided he didn't want to know. Then he realized Tim hadn't scanned Naxe. Of course, she hadn't said she had a headache. He turned and looked at her.

She lifted a hand to the side of her headgear.

"Tim?" Halliwell nodded toward her.

"I have already scanned Naxe," he said.

"And," Halliwell nudged when he didn't say more.

"There was much brain activity there, too. I modified as much as was safe."

Well, that was…he wasn't sure what that was, but he felt better about taking her weapons. If someone was messing with her head, then that was problematic.

"It is all right, John," she said. "I will be…" She looked up, as if she wanted to look away and stopped, her headlamp directed at a spot on the ceiling.

"What is that?" she asked.

Naxe removed her handheld light again, playing it over the walls and doors, then directing it up at the ceiling.

"That's not…" she stopped, frowning. "It's not…typical."

Halliwell pointed his headlamp in the same spot. "Looks organic," he said. The tracing had the look of a vine, but it was flattened against the ceiling. "What do you make of it, Tim?"

Tim didn't just direct a light at it, he activated some kind of scan. Was it Halliwell's imagination that it retreated some? Got smaller?

"You are correct," Tim said. "It is organic."

"Living?" Halliwell asked.

Riina seemed fascinated by it. "I wish we could get a sample."

Tim's arm moved smoothly toward it, but it retreated rapidly and visibly this time.

"It doesn't wish to be sampled," Tim said, retracting his arm.

"That's…" Creepy is what he wanted to say, but he was pretty sure generals weren't supposed to find things creepy. He settled for, "unsettling."

"Indeed," Riina murmured. "I wonder where it came from?"

"There was a garden ship," Naxe said, "more than one. At least," she stopped, giving a head shake, "that's what I…remember. A place for growing food."

"How would it get here?" Halliwell objected. It would have had to get through airlocks and transit tubes. He looked around. It looked like the other ship, like it had been abandoned, and in an orderly manner, based on that one room he'd looked in. "Would this ship have had armaments?"

"Some, perhaps. Not necessarily standard for this class of ship," Riina said. "But the pirates are always with us, are they not?"

"I've never not had them be an issue," Halliwell said, equal parts wry and grim.

"This ship has been modified for weapons," Tim said, "but there is no one on board. No human presence," he corrected.

Halliwell glanced up instinctively, but the vine, if that's what it had been, was gone.

"The airlock is ahead," Tim said.

Halliwell wished he felt like that was the good news.

NAXE TRIED to keep her body relaxed enough to react if something went wrong, but it was challenging. The retreat of the vine, or whatever it was, had unsettled her in a different way than, well, than all the other unsettling things, including the shadow. It had flicked at her memory and now it felt as if she walked in two places, though not every moment. The other flickered in and out of sight so fast she couldn't see it properly. It was more a sense of something there.

Sometimes the pulse was longer and she had the impression of people moving up and down this corridor. During one longer pulse, she had to stop herself from moving aside, but the figure faded before running into her.

They aren't here. No one is here.

If her head hadn't felt better, she'd have wondered if something had broken inside when Tim scanned her brain. It was a relief to reach the airlock and go through the tube to the next ship. As soon as they were inside the small transship area, Naxe spoke involuntarily.

"This is the garden ship."

"Hydroponics?" John looked sharply at her.

Despite the headgear, she smelled damp and soil and green. There were no visions here, but she felt she knew this place in a different way. A real way?

"Are you seeing anything? Or anyone?"

She shook her head. "It's not that. This is different. I feel like I remember being here…but how is that possible?"

"This ship is not as old as the others," Tim said.

"I don't recognize it," Riina said. "It must have been after my time."

Tim stepped up to the hatch that would give them access to the rest of the ship. It resisted opening, but Tim was persistent and it finally slid back, revealing a riot of unchecked plant life.

"Who wouldn't want to take a trip to *Little Shop of Horrors*," John said, sounding resigned.

HALLIWELL DID NOT like the look of this at all. It had Charlie Foxtrot written all over it. Some of the vines he could make out in the dimness of the corridor looked bigger around than he was. And some of those vines, which could be trees, he supposed, had flowers attached that looked like they could eat two of them in one bite. If he had to pick a movie to be in? *Little Shop of Horrors* wasn't the one he'd have picked.

"Tim?" he asked. The robot wasn't moving forward, which probably said more than if he'd started giving them a risk assessment.

Light stabbed out of the robot's eyes—another scan. This time he didn't assume it was his imagination that the green crap didn't like it. Maybe he should have paid more attention in biology class, but he thought plants liked the light. But then these plants were— oh, wait—alien? He huffed out a silent sigh as Tim scanned the three corridors available to them.

"The direct route to the next airlock is the most congested," Tim said finally.

"Is there a better alternative route?" Halliwell asked. Safer is what he meant, but longer could cancel out safer. He'd like to spend as little time as possible with the scary plants.

"My assessment is that each route will take approximately the same time to traverse, barring obstacles not visible with my scan," Tim said. "There could also be an alteration in present conditions."

Naxe stepped past him and her face shield lifted. Didn't they have movies in this galaxy? Because if not, they needed some. Okay, maybe that wouldn't help. In the movies they needed people to lift their face protection so they could get the plot moving. In real life? That didn't go as well.

"What is it?" Riina asked.

"I've…been here before."

She'd said that, but this was not what he'd imagined before Tim opened the door. This was not what he imagined of any hydroponics setup.

"Before the plants were like this?" Riina stepped up next to her, which caused Tim to get closer.

Oh yeah, he liked Riina.

"No." Naxe shook her head. "It was like this." She reached out and Halliwell had to stifle a protest as she stroked one finger down the closest leaf, which was almost as tall as she was. The leaf seemed to quiver, but nothing came out and ate her. "Look."

She directed her headgear light, though on a lower setting, and shone it down the corridor. There was a path visible. And the other way? It seemed more blocked with vegetation than the last time he'd looked.

If it looked like a trap, it didn't have to smell like a trap to be a trap. On the other hand, if this was *the* trap, then maybe they could get this "vacation" over faster. Because they were going to have to walk into the trap to find out what it was.

"I will go first," Tim said.

Halliwell was starting to feel guilty about putting him out there...but not enough to go first himself.

"Let's try to get through without shooting anything." It was probably his imagination that this jungle felt alive and not in a good way. "Riina, stay close to Tim, and Naxe? You fall in behind her. I'll take our six." The shiver he felt at being at the rear of the team was not imagination. But there was only room for them to move single file.

"We should connect ourselves." Tim lifted a hand and a thin wire began to emerge. Riina ran it through a slot on her suit, then passed it back to Naxe, who hooked up, and passed it to Halliwell. Well, that helped with the alone-at-the-rear feeling. But it also made it harder for any of them to act independently.

Tim adjusted something and his body began to give off a soft glow, but the spectrum must have been right because the vegetation seemed to calm down. Add that to the growing list of thoughts Halliwell never thought he'd have. Ever.

"Let's move out," Halliwell said.

Chapter 4

THE SILENCE WAS OPPRESSIVE. And the smell didn't help. Belatedly Naxe remembered her face plate was up and lowered it, but the thick moist smells took a few minutes to cycle out of her suit. Every now and again her suit picked up a soft rustle, but the leaves and flowers seemed to hang limply on their branches and vines. Maybe it was their movement that caused the sounds? She could hope.

If only hope didn't feel like a plant with no light. She frowned. Where had that thought come from? She didn't live planet-side. Her frown deepened. How did she know that? But if she wasn't from here, how did she get here? She'd been on a ship that had been damaged when she met Blooban, but that ship was from here, at least, that is what she'd believed. As she pushed at her memory, the shadow rose again. What did it hide from her? Or was the true question what did she seek to hide from herself?

"How much further?" John asked.

There was strain in his voice too. She glanced back. Perhaps it was her imagination that in the murky light, his face looked drawn and tired. How was it that he was no less appealing now than he'd been with his rumpled look when they'd wakened him, or his commanding presence when with his people back on Kikk? There was something about him that drew her to him, that stirred something deep inside. Deeper than the shadow? If it was, it felt as if it came from a better place than the shadow.

"We have traversed half the required distance," Tim said.

Did John chuckle? Or choke? She turned to look again, this time in rising panic, but he was still there. He directed his thumb upward. She was not sure what it meant, but she duplicated it.

And that's when it happened.

There was a choked cry from Riina but before Naxe could turn back around, something wrapped around her feet. She was jerked forward and fell on her back. The landing was unexpectedly soft. The view through her face plate was terrifying.

Something stood on her chest, its face splotches of green and brown and gray. The eyes were black in a square, flattened face. It appeared that a thicket of grass protruded from the top of its head and its ears resembled the leaves of the vine curling up behind it. It held what might be a sharpened piece of wood, though she was not certain. Details were difficult to process through the terror that closed her throat.

Whatever had circled her feet, slipped around her arms, and and feet, and wrapped her waist and her throat.

"Tell it to stop," the creature hissed.

Through the pounding of her heart, she realized she also detected the sounds of struggle.

"Who..." The vines around her tightened. "Tim? Please stop struggling. They will kill us." How did she know this? How— "I... know you," she said.

"You should not have come back," it hissed.

HALLIWELL CAME to with a feeling of dread. Before he opened his eyes, he knew something was wrong. He kind of wanted to sink back into the darkness where the half memory of being back on the *Doolittle* lingered like a light in the dark.

"General Halliwell."

If it hadn't been Tim talking, Halliwell would have thought him agitated. Tim...

The *Scoyfol* ships and the crazy, *Little Shop of Horrors* plants.

He forced his eyes open.

"I'm here," he said, when Tim called his name again. He tried to turn his head toward the sound and couldn't. It wasn't full on dark, but the murk was ominous. He was aware of vines running in every direction and of thick, moist air. Air? Someone or something had removed his headgear. He couldn't tell if his protective suit was gone because he couldn't move. He tried various limbs and other usually moveable parts. Nope. Only his eyes moved. "Riina? Naxe?"

"I'm here," Riina said.

Was it her eyes he saw across from him? Because that's all he could see.

"Naxe is not here," Tim said.

"Not here?" He tried to struggle harder and whatever held him tightened painfully until he stopped moving. At least they relaxed some when he stopped. "Do you know where she is?"

"I saw her dragged off in another direction by the..." for Tim the hesitation was a long one... "plants. Or what appeared to be plants. You and Riina lost consciousness. I did not. They secured us with these vines. If I attempt to free myself, they said they would kill you both."

So he'd been right. It sucked to be right that even Tim was vulnerable in the right circumstances. And hubris to think those circumstances couldn't happen on this vacation. Would he get a chance to thank Bangle for getting him into this? But even as the thought formed, he knew it wasn't fair. He'd wanted to do this. Even blaming it on the fictional Picard was wrong. He'd wanted to come for Naxe, because of Naxe. Worry tightened his gut more than the vines holding him in place.

"We are not the only prisoners in this room," Tim said.

"What?" Halliwell jerked and quickly regretted it. "I know. Don't move. I'm trying."

"Who are they?"

"I do not know," Tim said. "They are not conscious."

"You're sure they're alive?" The worry increased but he managed not to jerk this time.

"They read as living on my sensors. I assess they are deep in a sustained sleep that is similar to the cold sleep of Riina's people. But without the cold."

That was a surprisingly non-robot conclusion.

"When you called me, I thought I was back on the *Doolittle*," Halliwell said.

"I thought I was back on the outpost with the others," Riina said. "I am having to…fight to stay awake," she added.

Now that she mentioned it, the lure of sleep was hovering at the edge of his consciousness, trying to draw him back to that more pleasant place.

"It is challenging to remain awake," Riina added.

It was as if her saying it, made it harder for Halliwell, too.

"It does not affect me. I believe this concerns the plants," Tim said.

"Who are they?" Halliwell asked, partly to give himself something to focus on in his fight to stay alert and conscious.

"The caretakers of this garden," Tim said. "In their own way, they are prisoners, too."

The imperative to sleep was getting insistent. Halliwell clutched at thoughts, tried to form a new question, any question. Bangle… her music…his eyes jerked open. "Can you play music we can hear?" Would it help? He was willing to try. "Unless it annoys them." He'd rather go to sleep than be strangled. "Something with some pep to help us stay awake."

After a pause, perhaps for incredulity, music began to fill the silence. Halliwell felt whatever was holding him quiver, but it didn't tighten. The song started slow and Halliwell was afraid it would put him to sleep faster, but then the tempo began to pick up. Almost imperceptibly at first, the stuff holding him began to sway, so little, he wasn't sure—oh yeah, it was starting to feel the beat.

Light built into the murk, too, and now he could see Tim. Thick vines circled his torso and arms so that he was almost invisible. Only his head was somewhat free but a thick vine was across his forehead.

Riina was next to him, at least he was pretty sure it was her eyes he saw. But as the music built, he saw more eyes open, like something out of a horror movie, or maybe a cartoon. Ironic the song was saying something about the eye of a tiger.

Eyes and dancing plants. Because there was no doubt there was dancing, or at least swaying happening. The vines holding him had some almost decent moves.

And there was another thought he never knew he'd have to add to the list.

~

NAXE JERKED awake with the sense she'd been yanked from a familiar place she did not want to leave to…

The room was thickly covered in vines and thick trunks and filled with a green light. The truly strange part? She thought she heard music not far away. Some of the tendrils of some of the vines almost seemed like they were moving to the distant beat.

She was secured but not painfully so. She sensed if she tried to move that could change, so she tried to stay still. After a time of looking around, her eyes began to adjust to the strange light and she realized that there weren't just plants in this place, but several of the strange creatures like the one who had attacked her. *I know you.*

Her words came back to her accompanied by a tremor of memory. It balanced on the threads of the place she'd left when she woke, but reality had to win. She needed to deal with what was in front of her. She felt a sense of loss when the other faded away.

"We've done this before," she said, her voice loud in the almost silence. The music had changed, but the beat of it was still insistent.

"You should not have come back." This voice came from almost at her feet.

"Kismir. You're Kismir."

"So you do remember," it hissed. "You break your promise and then you come back."

"I wanted to keep it," she said, feeling the slow stirring in her mind. The shadow rose, but it was already fragmenting, more like smoke now. "He…took it. He took my memory." She looked around her. "He took your freedom."

"Excuses." Kismir's tone was scornful.

"I want to be free, too," she said. "He trapped me, too." Who was he? She didn't remember that part yet, but it was there, behind the last writhing piece of the shadow.

"We will all be trapped together now." The finality in his voice chilled her, despite the heavy heat in the room.

"We don't have to be."

"You said that before, but you failed."

Was there a hint of hope in Kismir's voice?

"Tim," she said, "the robot. He can free your ship." Her hope faltered. "If he still…lives. And the others." If they'd hurt Riina nothing could save them. "The metal man could free this ship. If you let us leave, he will help you. His name is Tim and he is… good."

"We cannot leave even if our ship is free."

"It is the same for us. My ship is out there. It is waiting for us to shut down what keeps us all trapped here." It felt so odd for the vines that held her to be swaying to the music. It felt like dancing. Dancing and talking. She almost laughed and more of her memory opened up. "I wasn't alone when we met the last time."

"They are still here. You know that. We are all trapped together." There was a hint of despair in the dusty voice.

He'd not killed them, whoever they were. He didn't want to hurt them. She remembered this. And she remembered a voice ordering their death…his voice. If only she could see his face. Her fingers curled into fists.

"We could be free together." Naxe tried to keep her voice calm. Faces without names floated in and out of her mind's view, but she could not identify where they fit into her life. The thought gave her pause. She'd had a life different from this one? "I don't belong here."

She knew she sounded dazed. She couldn't remember where she did belong, but it wasn't here.

"None of us belong here," Kismir said.

Did his voice sound less shrill, less angry?

"Tim is very skilled. He can crack the codes that keep this ship here."

"And if we try to leave he will fire on us."

Had he fired on Blooban? Probably not, but he would if he realized how free she was. She knew this, though she still couldn't remember why. Or who.

"He will if we can't stop him," Naxe agreed, "but this time we— I have help. I have a chance." She stared at his midnight eyes. "You held my...crew hostage, but I couldn't do it alone. I tried, but I couldn't..." Crew? Not crew exactly, but what they were still eluded her. "He is crafty and evil. You know this."

"We know this," Kismir admitted. There was a short silence filled with the distant beat of a new song that her vines moved to. "If you free us, he will know. He will be ready."

"Yes." Naxe's thoughts raced. "But I will be ready, too. Before, I didn't know, I didn't understand. Now I do." She felt resolve stirring in a new way, felt it send strength to her limbs, but more importantly to her mind. Now the shadow cowered in there, trying to hide the last secret.

Kismir stared at her for what felt like a long time. For some reason the music that throbbed somewhere felt right for the moment. As if it called them both to act.

"If you betray us again..."

"You have to let everyone go, Kismir. You don't need to hold them to make me do what you want. I want to do it already. I will do it or die. But I need the help of the people who came here with me."

The silence was a long one, but not as tense and the music seemed to adjust to it, too.

"Very well."

∾

"IF YOU FIGHT US, we will kill you."

Halliwell looked for the voice, but didn't find it until he looked down. And the vine let him look down, he realized. The creature was about as high as his knees, with black eyes. His face was flat and square and it had grass growing out of the top of its head. Its skin was camo—green, brown, and gray.

"We don't want to fight you," he said, wishing his voice were more Picard and less...Rambo.

"Naxe says Tim can free our ship."

Halliwell blinked as relief flooded him. She was okay. Or at least as okay as they were. And this thing, its ship was also trapped. Well, that wasn't as much of a surprise as it would have been a couple of years ago. Had he hoped to help without shooting something? Memo to self: don't be self-delusional in another galaxy. Memo to the memo: shooting happens.

"Tim can try." Halliwell didn't think he should make promises for Tim. "Why don't you ask him? And you should probably let his girlfriend go before you ask him."

The music still pulsed into the air around them, but Halliwell was pretty sure Tim could still hear them.

It didn't speak but suddenly the vines holding them retracted. His thoughts cleared, too. Had one of them been inside his head? It was not a thought he wanted to linger on for too long.

The room brightened and now he could see Tim and Riina. Tim wasn't quite as free as they were. The vines that had held him were looser, but Halliwell had a sense they were waiting for Tim to do something hostile.

"Free the others," Tim said, his voice flat as the music faded to a low murmur.

"We'll free them when we are all safe."

In the better light, Halliwell could see at least five more captives, limp in their bonds, their eyes closed once more. How long had they been here?

Halliwell didn't like leaving them, but the troll had a point. Why wake them before it was safe?

"You will not hurt them," Tim said. His tone was flat, but somehow he managed to sound pretty serious about that.

"We will not hurt them," it said. "Follow me."

~

KISMIR HAD RETURNED the gear his…plants had removed. Halliwell tried not to think about what had happened while he'd been unconscious. It didn't make for good situational awareness to worry about what he couldn't change even if he found out. He was not unaware of the irony of Bangle's playlist soothing the savage plants. If the AI ever found out, there'd be no living with it. His thoughts and hands paused to consider whether the AI was here, but he figured it would have had to say something before now— particularly if it thought it was right.

He settled his headgear in place and did a systems check. It was easier to focus on this than think about this next step. He wouldn't have liked this if he knew what they were getting into, and they didn't. What they didn't know was a concern, but what they did know didn't help. Their Big Bad had managed to rewrite Naxe's memories and neither she nor Kismir knew how long they'd been caught in this trap. And while he had a lot of confidence in Tim, knowing that the Big Bad could mess with people's brains, their memories, he might be a little worried.

At least Tim had managed to return control of this plant ship to its Captain. If—when they got the shield down, they would be ready to leave. They'd promised to release the remaining humans to return to their own ships, before they took off.

Halliwell felt guilty about not getting them freed now, but he couldn't see how adding them to the party to meet the Big Bad would be a good idea.

Naxe still seemed concerned. "I should go alone."

"Whoever it is already knows you brought someone back with you," Halliwell pointed out. He looked at Kismir, but the troll didn't respond. If he'd had orders to detain them, he wasn't saying.

"He will expect us to have been disarmed," Naxe said, "will he not, Kismir?"

"Yes."

If Halliwell didn't know better, he'd say the little troll was annoyed she had interrupted the "sound" to ask the question. It was like they'd already moved on.

They'd debated various approaches, but in the end, the direct approach was the simplest. It was also the one Tim wanted. He'd brought Tim as a bodyguard, so he should listen to him. They'd stay roped together until they got to the Ugly Sucker. If their Big Bad wasn't on the Ugly Sucker, they could rope up again, but Halliwell had the feeling that Tim believed that's where their Big Bad was, too.

Blooban, aboard the *Vycorth*, had been drifting closer and was now on course to be in position over the Ugly Sucker around the same time they'd get there. Halliwell didn't mind having him closer, though he hoped the frog didn't get the ship shot up. Yes, there were plenty of ships around and yes, Tim could hack them, but the Big Bad had had a lot of time to booby trap them. It might make his head hurt that he trusted the frog, at least more than the troll, so he tried not to dwell on it.

"He'll expect us to have been disarmed." Halliwell didn't make it a question. It was more of a reminder. He studied Tim for several seconds. There was no way to hide that he was a weapon. "Maybe you should go last this time, Tim."

"I should go first," Naxe said, tension visible in her eyes and around her mouth.

If Tim didn't like it, he didn't say so. He just moved to the rear. Halliwell knew he didn't like it either, but he nodded.

"I'll be right behind you." He wished both Naxe and Riina could wait here. He belonged to a modern military where women served alongside men, but he'd never liked sending a woman into battle. Honestly, he didn't like sending anyone into battle. But right now, Naxe looked smaller than he remembered. Her shoulders weren't slumped, but they weren't super straight either. Her eyes were calm but large, and her lips were compressed. He wished he could draw her close. Not for long, just for long enough. And he wished he could tell her he hated this and he—felt things for her. That they'd be there for her or—no. He shut that off. They had to be there. They had to.

She nodded. "Let's move out."

Her voice had lost all inflection, all warmth. But it was still somehow engaging. With that voice, she could be a leader...or a siren. He didn't like the thought. He wouldn't be the first man who'd been fooled by a woman—as if she sensed he needed more, she managed something that resembled a smile. But it was her eyes that caught him. Her gaze that held him for several seconds and gave him hope. She meant to fight in her own corner. Then the veil dropped down again and she glanced around, as if trying to imprint this on her memory in a way that could not be erased or changed.

While he'd been trying to avoid plant analogies inside his head, he allowed himself one. Hope was a powerful seed when properly planted.

And now he was going to move on.

"Right. Let's get this done." It was his general voice, one he hoped was inspiring to his people and to these people. For now he walked beside her, because he could. Kismir didn't turn his head to watch them. Halliwell wasn't sure, but the troll might be trying to "Walk Like an Egyptian."

That was a good way to make sure Halliwell didn't look back again.

Chapter 5

AT THE AIRLOCK, Naxe paused, fighting a deep reluctance to start. Kismir's ship was creepy, and so was he, but it held no more surprises. Once they left it—she should remember what came next. She wanted to pound her head. Why couldn't she remember?

She bit her lip, resisted the urge to pound the airlock control in lieu of her head—or with her head. She hesitated, almost glancing back, though she couldn't see those they left behind with Kismir. Did her sense of duty flow from some deep memory about them? Because it came from a real place, was that what made it so strong? Was that why it had driven her even when some part of her knew this was wrong?

Behind them one of the songs, reached out, as if it knew her struggle and sent her strength, too. Almost it lifted her into the song's roar. Frustration was replaced with resolve.

"Let's go do what we must," she said, a half-smile edging her mouth.

They'd get through this. She wasn't alone this time. There was John and Riina and, there was Tim. Granted Kismir had used them to nullify Tim as a threat, but the Big Bad—her lips twitched at the description—didn't know Tim's weakness. At least that was the hope. And if they moved quickly, the Big Bad wouldn't have time to know it. Guilt tried to make a comeback, tried to steal her resolve. It was her fault the others were in danger. She'd led them into this trap.

As if he sensed it, John said, "We're right behind you."

She lifted a hand in acknowledgment, but didn't look back. The time for looking back was past. She entered the airlock, aware that not one of them hesitated to follow her. Out of habit, she tapped her comm and caught the faintest of croaks. It was more like an echo, but it brought the smile she needed. They did it every time she left the ship for an unknown dock. Where she'd gone to secure supplies for people who didn't exist, she reminded herself, grimly. She'd risked their lives for this…game, this illusion.

This had to stop. They had to find a way to stop it.

She heard the airlock cycle closed behind them, then the sounds of the pressure being adjusted. When it opened on the transit tube, she reached out and grasped the first handhold on the side and began to pull herself toward the next ship. She still didn't look back. She didn't look up or around either. She didn't need to see the Ugly Sucker to know it was there, to feel watched by it.

It was both harder and easier to traverse one ship, then another and another after that. No one spoke and the silence seemed to build. As each ship was reached and traversed, more pieces of memory spun inside her head. There was nothing special about these ships, but still she remembered them. Inside those memories were traces of the people who had traveled on them, but nothing she could hold onto. She had no real sense of *knowing*. *Ghost ships for ghost people.*

The last few pieces of the puzzle eluded her efforts at recall. Indeed, the harder she tried the more they slipped away, dodging behind the shadow when she came too close.

As the Ugly Sucker ship drew near, the more the dread built. It was a force that tried to slow her forward progress. She was…tired. Not physically tired, but emotionally exhausted without knowing why. It felt as if her mind had been stretched to its limit. Perhaps it had. To help her stay grounded she listed the things she knew were real and true.

Blooban and the *Vycorth*.

John, Riina, and Tim walking behind her.

The outpost and Bangle.

That she wasn't of Scoyfol. Well, probably true. Most likely true. Though she sensed knowledge of these ships, she didn't feel she knew them the way she knew the *Vycorth*. This knowing was more like something she'd read in a story. A ghost story.

It wasn't much to hang her sanity on, and yet, maybe it was more than enough.

John. He'd looked at her as if she mattered. Even if it wasn't the way she wished, it was something to matter to a man such as he was. To a man who had signed on for something very different than this. And yet he'd stayed. Even after Kismir, he'd stayed. The others, too.

Her thoughts spun in dizzy swoops and turns inside her head, as she focused on putting one foot in front of another. As each step forward grew harder she drew on resources she didn't know she had inside and she also felt strength flowing from her companions. And then they had passed through the last ship.

There it was. The Ugly Sucker ship, on the other side of the last transit tube.

Soon she would come face-to-face with the Big Bad who had trapped her in this loop. Would she remember then? Would her questions be answered? Both the who and the why of sending her out to find supplies, risking her life at times on seedy space docks, for no reason. It was so crazy and, her mind tried to find the right description, but had to settle for random. It was so random and strange. It felt like a badly written space adventure, she thought wryly, and not real life. For a moment, she almost lost the plot wondering how to make it a better story, but that was just crazy. There was no way to improve on this story even if she were a tale teller.

She activated this last airlock and when all the processes were finished, she moved into the tube. She could go many seasons without doing this again. One hand reaching out, the other following. She had to keep moving because John and the others were counting on her to do her part. If she didn't, they'd end up in this trap, too.

Like a sullen, dirt side bug, the Ugly Sucker waited for them.

Her memories pushed harder as it drew closer and the shadow wavered. She'd been here before. She knew it on an instinctual level. And still she wasn't sure what lay beyond it. And then they were at this last airlock. When had she started to believe this was where her problems began and ended? That this had never been about Scoyfol?

For the first time, she let herself look back. John hovered in space behind her, his eyes offering encouragement, though he still didn't speak. They had no idea how much the Big Bad knew or if he could hear their comms—

He...

Why did she feel so certain it was a he behind this? And why did she sense Big Bad's gender was not that relevant? That there was something else—

She huffed out a frustrated sigh. Why couldn't she remember? And yet, just outside conscious thought, she felt it, like a page waiting to be turned.

With weary impatience, she activated the airlock, heard it retract. The sound went through her like a warning, though it was no different from the others she'd passed through. She examined the lock and realized this was more circular than the others. Not a significant change but at least it was something different. And then they were all inside.

Like the hatch, this airlock was circular, giving the hatch to the wider ship the look of a huge eye. Was it her imagination that the pressure and air cycled ominously before opening? She felt something quiver to life back behind the shadow. It had the shape and feel of hope, but it was more somehow. It felt soothing, healing even, as if something that had been broken was coming back together.

Her hand fisted against her suit where her heart beat and she left the airlock for the antechamber beyond. It was a simple, spare place, one without seats, storage containers, or even a hook to hang gear on. It was just a small rounded, and somehow oddly long room, possibly a few feet higher than her head.

She traversed the length with the odd sense that each step was a key opening her mind up more and more—and the even stranger sense that she was an observer more than participant. Almost like a book where the point of view had pulled back on the story. Her freedom might rest on what happened next, but—she shook her head, her lips compressing, and looked for controls.

This hatch was also rounded and it didn't have standard controls, or even non-standard controls. Instead, there were two bright spots on the metal. One was lighter, almost gold, and the other was a pale red. She reached for the lighter one, with the vague sense that red meant stop, or perhaps close. It must have had motion sensing ability, because the hatch retracted before she touched it.

Her first thought was that she'd wandered into a bad reality vid. The chamber—she sensed, no, she knew it was a chamber and not a corridor—was not completely dark, but between the half-light and the fog, it might as well have been.

She heard a soft sound and looked down, almost taking a step back at the sight of the water brushing against the edges of the antechamber.

Water?

The surface of it was almost completely still. Her suit's sensors said there was no water, though it assessed that the room had high humidity. She glanced back at John and Riina. Their eyes were big and Tim—he was gone. She opened her mouth, but John lifted a finger to his mouth and gave a slight head shake. Had Tim cloaked? Remarkable. And comforting. She did that thing with the upward thumb he'd used and then turned back to the water and fog.

In the stories, it was always a bad idea to go into the dark place even with friends.

Stories. What story?

The fog shifted giving a shaft of light a chance to shimmer on the water's surface. The water that wasn't there, she reminded herself. She stepped out, her attention on the fake water. Her steps appeared to disturb the surface, but the floor beneath her feet was unequivocally firm. Her suit adjusted to the change to heavier gravity.

The light from the antechamber spilled out the open hatch, casting her shadow onto the water, where it shivered and danced. She felt muzzled, almost claustrophobic because her sense of smell was at odds with what her eyes saw. She checked her sensors and found the air breathable, so she activated her faceplate. But it didn't help with the disconnect. Instead of water and fog, the room smelled of metal and damp, though it wasn't as stale, or as old, as the other ships had smelled.

Her thoughts paused. *Scoyfol is ships.* Not water and fog. Just in case she had doubts.

She activated her head lamp and for an instant saw a wavering reflection in the water again, before the patterns of the lights changed. Was that her face? *Ghost people for ghost ships.* She wanted to sweep away all that kept her from seeing herself as she truly was. It was close now. The shadow seemed to flow from inside her head to take form out here.

"It's not real," she said, moving forward, not with confidence exactly because it might not be water, but the fog was thick and what light there was seemed to shift and change.

At first the silence seemed all encompassing, but then she realized there was a faint hum. Not the engines. She couldn't feel it through her boots. No, there was movement to the sound, as it moved close, then away.

The light source was diffuse, she realized. It was there without adding that much illumination now that the hatch of the antechamber had closed. And yet, as she walked forward, it seemed to move with her. The disconnect between her eyes, ears and sensors was disconcerting. When she glanced down, her heart leapt at the water that seemed to be all around. The illusion was visually well-done, but neglected the other senses. If she were writing this scene…her thoughts jolted to a halt.

She was on the edge of remembering, but instinctively she looked away this time. It would have to be lured out of hiding, much like they'd been lured here.

The light began to build, enough for her to perceive shapes in the fog. Some were tall and narrow others short and squat.

She went closer, curiosity dominating for the moment and she almost tripped over one of the squat shadows looming suddenly up. She directed her light on it, then turned it on one of the taller shadows.

Trees? And the squat ones looked like stumps. She turned, sending her light around as the fog swirled away, like a woman drawing back her skirt.

"It kind of reminds me of a swamp, or rather, an attempt at a swamp," John said. He lifted a boot and the water rippled and then settled once more.

"It is very fake," Naxe agreed.

John turned his head lamp in the same direction as Naxe as Riina moved closer to the nearest tree. "Not as weird as the *Little Shop of Horrors*."

Riina yanked off her glove and reached up to touch some gray wispy fibers hanging from one of the lower branches. "What is it?"

"It reminds me of the moss we see in the swamps of my home world. People used to stuff their mattresses with it, but this doesn't look quite right." John turned in a half circle. "It isn't even trying that hard to be real."

The humming began to build, but Naxe didn't know if it was inside her head or out.

Naxe glanced back. The chamber door was closed and there was no sign of Tim, but she knew he was here somewhere. As she turned back, her light flared off the walls. "Look," she said.

John and Riina turned, bringing their lights to bear, too. Instead of smooth metal walls, there were blocks of pale color, but cut irregularly, or though it seemed to Naxe. They appeared to be translucent. Were these what provided the diffused light?

"Facets," John said. "Like jewelry maybe?"

Riina swung her light around, playing it over everything within its reach. "This is an unusual place."

"Smoke and mirrors," John said, almost dismissively. "Like a carnival ride without the fun."

Naxe exchanged a puzzled look with Riina. At least she didn't know either.

"Assuming this was created, why?" Naxe asked, not sure if the question was directed at them or herself. Was it new or had it been like this when she was here before. Had she been *here*?

Her last clear memories were on the garden ship. She remembered Kismir. And the other ships? Those memories were indistinct, ghost-like.

Could someone so completely erase her memory of this place? Her mind knew "trees" but not these trees.

She remembered climbing trees when she was little but...

Scoyfol is ships.

Not trees either, she added somewhat wryly. So who, in actual fact, was she? How had her...story...been diverted? Was this setting meant to further confuse her? Or delay her memory returning?

The light came down brighter, so she looked up. Someone was adjusting the lighting. The buzzing was louder, closer, too.

The limbs, shrouded with the strange moss, reached up and out, creating a kind of canopy overhead.

"Thank goodness the water is fake," John said, "or I'd be looking around for gators."

Since he was glad there were none of these gators, Naxe was as well.

"It's very carefully random," Riina noted. "Look." Her headlamp light had found something almost path-like, emerging from the water and winding, between the trees and stumps.

This forest couldn't be that big, though—she glanced back—she couldn't see where they'd come in. The door had blended into the walls. They had to go forward anyway if they wanted answers. She wished she'd just stayed away, but if she had, would her memory have been lost? And her friends caught in Kismir's snare? What about them? She wished she knew their names and what they meant to her.

So, forward was still the only way.

Her nose kept expecting green, wet smells and kept being disappointed. And her mind cast about for words to describe its frustration. It was an odd thing to be unhappy about. She was on an alien ship, trying to meet a Big Bad and she was bothered by her inability to find the right words?

The humming built and she glanced up and almost shrieked at the size and sight of the insect hovering in the beam. It was at least the size her fist, with a wingspan that doubled that size. Her hand trembled when she reached up and switched the light off. And immediately regretted it because now she couldn't see where it went.

She thought she heard John inhale sharply, but he didn't turn his light off. Instead, he moved it in a slow scan, the light finding a canopy of the bugs over their heads. Riina might have given a small squeak and her light went dark, too.

With a muttered imprecation, John finally turned his light off.

Oddly enough, removing their lights from the scene didn't reduce the illumination by that much. There was definitely a stronger light source up there, and it drew the bugs that direction. She didn't mind that at all. She just wished she could stop herself from looking up. Yeah, most of the light was coming from there, based on the bug accumulation. She stepped to the side where there was less branch interference and suppressed a shudder. The air around the bunched together lights was thick with bugs now. This made them harder to see, but she guessed they were faceted like the side walls.

"Do you think they are real or drones?" Naxe asked, surprised by how steady her voice sounded. Inside she might be screaming. *I hate bugs.*

Scoyfol is ships.

"Do you remember this place?" John asked.

"No." She shook her head. "Not at all." She couldn't even find an association with her sense she'd climbed trees and hated bugs. Memories tried to create connections, to blossom from the associations of sights, sounds, smells, and tastes. Tastes? When had she last tasted something that evoked a memory? Or heard the sound of the wind moving through the leaves of a tree? Those associations came from very deep in her mind. She could tell from what her mind "saw" that she'd been small, small enough to nestle in the junction of high branches and sway in the wind with the tree.

"What purpose does this place serve?" Riina asked, her tone surprisingly reflective.

She'd come because she was curious, or so she'd said. Naxe had assumed she was curious about Tim, but what if she were a researcher of some kind? John might have called this a vacation, but if he only brought two people with him, they'd each have a distinct function. It felt like she'd been slow to realize this, but she'd had a lot on her mind.

In the semi-silence following Riina's question, there was a rustle, followed by a scrape. Now memory began to make associations, further fragmenting the shadow that still tried to keep her from knowing.

John strode forward, his light finding a larger space without stumps and trees. Not altogether willing, Naxe followed him into a small clearing, where light from above fell with less obstruction.

Insects darted in and out of this light and she repressed a shudder. They were so huge. Some even bigger than she'd realized. Her throat closed when one almost the size of her own head darted past her face.

A particularly large insect paused well above their head height, its wings moving so fast it felt as they were more heard than seen. Then it vanished between one blink and the next. Naxe felt the dam inside her head breaking as he dropped into sight, the insect clutched in its legs.

HALLIWELL WANTED to scream like a little girl. He didn't, but it was a near thing. His eyes had a hard time coming to agreement with his brain on what it was he saw snatch the bug out of mid-air. From deep in his past, a memory meshed with the thing and produced a sort of identification.

A dragonfly.

A big, dang dragonfly.

Maybe a quarter of his height and at least half his length long. Yeah, maybe he could step on it if it wasn't hovering in the air over their heads slurping down the bug one crunch at a time.

Halliwell only barely managed to stop himself from pulling his weapon. He'd done a school project on dragonflies a lifetime ago when he'd been nine or so. Young anyway. But if this thing was anything as fast the dragonflies on Earth, he didn't have a hope of hitting it.

This couldn't be the same, even though it looked a lot like the one he'd pinned on a slide and studied through a microscope. This one wouldn't have fit on that slide.

He'd learned a lot, but the key elements right now seemed to be how fast a dragonfly could move; they could intercept prey in mid-air—he tried not to focus on the prey while it was munching on that big bug—and their incredibly sharp mandibles that lined their inner legs. He could see some of those mandibles even in the low light. The one bright spot, which didn't seem that bright right now was that dragonflies had one blind spot. Their heads were all eyes, and they could see almost 360. Except for their very rear.

How did he get this info to Tim? He was the only who could move fast enough to get behind it.

The thing paused halfway through the bug, and might have directed all those eyes in Naxe's direction.

"You should introduce me to your friends," it said. Its voice was almost shockingly mellow, but without the compelling quality that made Naxe's so special. This one was creepier in a chills-down-the-spine way. Like the villain in a campy melodrama.

With all those sharp insect edges, he'd expected something more sinister and shrill. Something more insecty.

"Odon."

Halliwell might have been surprised by how much Naxe packed into the single word.

"I know my name," it pointed out, gesturing with one of the legs not needed for securing the bug. "I don't know theirs."

It had five legs, Halliwell recalled, all with those killer mandibles.

And yet somehow it felt less powerful because it was trying harder to sound more so.

"Name's Halliwell," he said. He decided to stick to minimal information hoping it would bug the bug. Okay, mental wince. He gestured to Riina. "This is Riina."

The thing's head moved. It was possible it was surprised. Could it be surprised? Right now, all he was pretty sure of, was that thing could use all of its eyes to see all three of them with no problem, so why did it move its head? Could it pierce Tim's camouflage? The robot had the ability to blend in with his surroundings, making him appear invisible. And he gave off no heat signature. Would that be enough? And could even Tim move fast enough?

Odon shot up higher, and then buzzed down, landing in a crouch in front of them. This gave Halliwell a chance to measure their sizes. The bug was just a bit over knee height and the angle reduced the intimidation factor. Okay it was still freaky. Maybe it was the mandibles. And all those eyes. So maybe still a little intimidating.

"You got new crew!" Odon rubbed a couple of his legs together. "And you brought them to meet me."

At least it had finished off the bug, though he thought he saw a piece of leg hanging off Odon's chin.

"Odon," Naxe said again.

Halliwell felt a shiver go down his back.

"We have established my name, I think," Odon said.

There was a shrill edge to the voice that took it back toward insect. Naxe didn't speak and after a moment, the bug appeared to turn his attention to Halliwell and Riina.

"I love exploring new memories," Odon said.

It said the words with ominous relish that made it sound a bit mustache-twirling villain, but he did have a record to back up the threat. Or did he? Halliwell's thoughts shot back to Kismir and his vines. There was more to unpack there, but for now he needed to focus on the big bad bug.

A small shudder went through the ship, as if something had

impacted—or docked—with it. The frog ship? Odon's head started to lift.

"What kind of memories do you like best?" Halliwell asked. Okay, that was lame. But it did bring the bug's head down again. Of course, it also brought it tilted his direction. That wasn't great.

It was silent for several long seconds.

"I am an explorer, a researcher, and ultimately, a tale teller."

"Interesting," Halliwell said, trying to sound like he meant it, instead of injecting some "what the heck" in there, with a measure of "I don't really care." Mostly, he wanted to turn off the cloaking that was keeping them here—and get his people out—and get out of here. And he might want to see the bug squashed.

"I am a researcher, too," Riina said into the small silence that wanted to get bigger. "I have access to a tremendous archive of data."

She'd taken the hint about minimizing the information they shared. Good for her.

The bug's head might have shifted her direction, though it didn't need to. Was it an intimidation tactic or a focusing issue? Even after the science project he didn't know. It's not like a nine-year-old could interview a bug about the vision issues of multifaceted eyes.

"Data is so dry," it complained. "I prefer the immediacy of the living and their stories. I like listening to them more—directly. And then sharing them with my appreciative audience."

It had resumed the mellow voice. Halliwell frowned. Was it was trying to goad Naxe into a response? Did it want her to remember?

Moving very slowly and deliberately, Naxe reached up and removed her headgear. Halliwell wanted to protest. He didn't because he suspected she had her memory back. She was acting with intent. He just hoped the intent wasn't to take the hit to protect Riina and himself. Because the hit was coming. The Big Bad had eaten the bug with intent, too.

She dropped the headgear on the ground next to her, the sound vibrating jarringly through the space. She ran a hand through her hair, the movement one he hadn't seen before. Yeah, she was remembering. Even the way she stood had changed.

"It feels so long since we talked. What have you been up to?" Odon asked, that taunting note still there.

"There's nothing to tell," she said.

The bug's head came up. "Nothing to tell? You've been out there." One leg moved, presumably to indicate "out there."

She shrugged. "Even getting shot at gets boring when there's no plot or character growth."

Halliwell frowned because the bug wasn't paying attention to him anyway. He looked at Riina, but she appeared as baffled as he was.

Odon's head reared up. Or back. Halliwell wasn't sure which.

"Boring?" The bug made no effort to keep the shrill out now. He'd gone full on bug.

"There were huge problems with the narrative flow, but you already knew that." She paused.

What the heck? Her tone brought back some unpleasant echoes of his high school English teacher.

The Big Bad bug hissed. That was the only word for it. It wasn't easy, but Halliwell stood his ground. Riina shifted to the side, probably to let Tim move into position. He just wished he knew what she'd said to piss it off. Was she threatening to give it a bad grade?

"So, you remember." Odon's legs moved in almost an uneasy way, but his voice suggested satisfaction. It had wanted her to remember.

"Yes." Naxe's voice didn't change.

Interesting that Tim had given Naxe her weapons back before they came here, but it was her voice that might be her best weapon. He had to stop his feet from shuffling.

"I am the most interesting thing to happen to you since the war ended," it hissed.

"I remember you saying that." Naxe's tone was dry enough to take some of the humidity out of the room. She managed to say, without saying it, that the bug was wrong.

The dragonfly seemed to quiver. Halliwell couldn't see its expression, but he went with not happy.

"It's a typical beginner error to cling to the dead wood in your material."

Halliwell wished she hadn't use the word dead.

"Yes," it said, with sinister emphasis. "One must eventually get rid of the dead wood."

Yeah, using dead had been a bad idea. It rose in the air, even the sound of its wings not friendly. He could clearly see all five legs and their mandibles.

He was starting to really hate mandibles.

"You have to learn how to let go and move forward." Naxe's tone had softened some. "To be teachable."

And bugs who couldn't learn from their mistakes.

"It's not even your story," Naxe said. "You stole it, just like you stole my life."

"I was your biggest fan, your most devoted listener. I was there from the beginning, Tale Speaker. We were meant to do this together!"

Odon's voice got more shrill with each word until it ended on a sort of shriek that sent all the bugs scurrying for cover in the shadows. Halliwell kind of wanted to join them. But Naxe stood there with her back straight, her body in the relaxed stance of a fighter.

Tale Speaker? She might be some kind of storyteller, if he was following this, but she had the soul of a warrior.

"Being my fan didn't give you rights to me or my life. You need to find and tell your own stories and then let those who read or hear them decide if they liked them or not." Her tone had softened again, but her stance had not. "Stories are a pact between the giver and the receiver. They are offered without strings to the readers but for those who tell the tales, there is more. We should hold ourselves to a higher standard. We should never accept less than our best." She waited for several seconds, then added, "You can't own my stories no matter how deep you get into my brain. I'm right, aren't I? You've tried to tell your own and failed. So you tried to tell mine." She stopped again. "And you failed at that, too."

"No one even knows you're gone!"

There was a crackle, as a comm was opened.

"I don't know what's wrong with the Tale Speaker. Maybe she's sick."

"People lose their skills as they age. And she's been a Tale Speaker a long time."

"I think she's sick or someone's pretending to be her."

"Someone should stop her, tell her it's over, it's sad..."

Blooban. It had to be the frog. Tim said it was a good hacker.

The comm closed and then only the sound was of Odon's food source flying around.

Naxe shifted and then spoke again, the voice inexorable.

"You can stop hearing the reviews, but you can't change them. The listeners get to decide how they feel about the story, not the one who tells it. The offering is accepted—or rejected."

She was some kind of storyteller? *I am an explorer, a researcher, and tale teller*, he'd said, but that was Naxe's story, not the bug's. He wasn't sure what that meant, but knew it was her real story, not this thing's.

"It is the way of stories, always has been and always will be. You failed to understand and you broke the pact. But..." There was an inexorable quality to her voice. The power of it growing stronger with each thing she said. "You didn't just steal my stories and my life, you stole my creativity. You stripped my mind of *my* stories. You took my heart. You are not a Tale Taller and you never will be. Stories don't live in you."

It sounded like she'd pronounced a sentence on the bug.

Odon crouched back down, his rear end twitching. Halliwell had a feeling this was not good. He shifted, hiding the movement of his hand down to where it clasped the handle of his weapon.

"Then the stories will cease," it said with a deadly hiss.

It wasn't trying to sound like Naxe anymore. The buzzing had been building in the background, he realized, and the noise suddenly went into overdrive. From out of the darkness, black beetle-like creatures—no, drones, he decided—came at them. He yanked out his weapon and fired. His shot hit one and it careened off course, caught itself, and headed back into the fray. Yeah, drones.

If they hadn't had Tim, they'd have been in a crap ton of trouble, instead of just a half a crap ton of trouble.

Naxe pulled her weapon, too, and fired at the big bug, but it was already not there. It launched into the air, as shots came out of the darkness from Tim. The drones spun away from the accuracy of his shots, but there were so many in this crazy funhouse the bug had created that it didn't seem to make any difference.

Halliwell couldn't see where it had gone, which was bad, but there was plenty to keep his attention.

Riina was firing, too, from a crouching position, her back to Naxe's. That seemed like a good idea, so he joined their little group.

Tim strode out of the dark and formed a fourth, though there was no denying he was more effective.

The drones realized it, or Odon did, because they began to concentrate their attacks on Tim.

Halliwell looked around, trying to think of a distraction or a way to cause damage. His eyes lighted on the facets around the chamber. He pointed his weapon at one and fired. The glass, or whatever it was, shattered, letting light leak in from what had to be the real ship. Some of the drones went for the light. Interesting. The funhouse could be broken.

"Fire on the walls," he shouted over the din.

Naxe and Riina immediately directed their fire at the walls and the facets began to shatter, letting in more and more real light. It stabbed into the dark, sending the fist-sized bugs into a frenzy and appeared to confuse the drones.

Tim deployed some weapons to fire on the walls too.

It happened so fast, Halliwell didn't see it coming. But suddenly Riina went down, sprawled on her back. Then it hit him. It was worse than the frog jumping on his chest.

NAXE SAW RIINA, and then John go sprawling. She didn't know if they still lived, just knew she'd be next. When the hit came, she was as ready for it as one could be. She hit the deck hard and she wished she hadn't removed her headgear. She saw stars and had the breath knocked out of her. Her weapon flew out of her hand, clattering away into the semi-darkness.

Odon buzzed in, hovering over her, his legs just above her body. She had to assume he'd hit Tim, too. The robot would be hard to keep down, but she doubted if he'd be up fast enough to save her...

The bug face, with its multiple eyes and leering horrifying face, loomed over her.

"I just wanted to be your friend," it hissed. "I just wanted—"

"You don't know what it means to be a friend. You can kill me now, but you will never be me," she gasped through lungs still struggling to regain their air from the hit to the floor. Her voice and thoughts froze as Odon raised one leg above her, the deadly spikes visible in the light they'd brought to the chamber.

"Then you and your voice will die, and I won't have to hear it in my head ever again," it cried.

The spike started down its downward plunge and Naxe knew it was over. She wanted to close her eyes as it drew out the moment, tormenting her, but she wouldn't give it the satisfaction.

Then it gave out a startled cry as it was dragged off of her. It cried again, then the cry stilled.

Naxe pushed herself up on one elbow and stared.

Odon was half in, half out of Blooban's mouth. Blooban's tongue was wrapped around its body and pulling it inexorably deeper into a mouth that suddenly looked very large.

"Dang." The word lacked John's usual force, but it was his voice.

Naxe was not sure what the word meant, but if it meant what she thought? She sagged back down, staring at the broken lights over her head. She could only agree with the emotion in the word.

Chapter 6

It would, Halliwell acknowledged ruefully, have been a photo finish if he'd had a camera. He couldn't decide if he was sorry or sad he didn't have photographic evidence of the bug's final stand. Going forward? He'd have more respect for the frog. It had managed to dock with the Ugly Sucker ship and get down here just in time.

All that was left of Odon was a few pieces of leg and half a wing. The drones had dropped to the floor when the bug went offline.

Blooban had regarded him out of bulbous, phlegmatic eyes while it finished eating the bug, then said, "I had a search going through my databases to see if anything matched the Ugly Sucker ship. Just after docking, but before I boarded this ship, it found a match for this vessel. It is Anisoptian and once I'd read the data…" It paused for a blink and croak. "I was hungry, and we have a variation of the species on my home world."

"I need to update my databases," Tim said. He might have sounded annoyed. He'd left a dent in the floor where he'd hit it when the bug dived on him. But his armor appeared to be fine. He'd gotten up, but he'd have been too late if not for the frog.

And there it was. Another one of those thoughts he'd never expected to have.

"I have the ship on file," Tim continued, "with a notation about superior cloaking, but nothing about the crew."

Apparently getting knocked on his metal butt made him more talkative.

Tim, Riina, and the frog left for the bridge so they could get the cloak down and make contact with Halliwell's people.

For himself, he was trying to figure out how to write his report on his Picard vacation. He glanced at Naxe. Now that it was over, she'd allowed herself to look shell-shocked. It was easier to think about what she looked like now rather than the moment the dragonfly had loomed over her, one leg ready drive to through her body. It had seemed as if it all slowed down. The drones kept hitting at him as he tried to get up. One had knocked his weapon out of his hand. He pulled his knife, even knowing it wouldn't be enough. He'd been sure they were all going down when the frog's tongue had wrapped around the bug and yanked him off her. And then it had eaten the Big Bad. He needed to get a new name for it though. It had lost its big bad creds when it got taken down by a frog.

Okay, he was shell-shocked, too. Even Picard would have been shaken up by this much crazy.

After standing irresolute when the others left, Naxe went and sat down on one of the fake tree stumps. With the fog dispersing and the lights full on, everything looked sad and fake, like a tourist trap gone wrong.

He crouched in front of her, suppressing a wince. His bones and muscles hadn't liked hitting the deck. "Are you okay?"

"I am," her gaze met his and she smiled wryly, "alive."

"That's about as good as it gets," he agreed. This was the second time he'd come this close to dying in this galaxy. He hoped it wasn't about to become a habit.

Tim's voice came over his comm. "I have radio contact with our people, General."

Our people. Halliwell liked the sound of that. And that meant the shield was down. He stood up and tapped his comm. "With the shield down, we probably need to have some eyes on the region until we get some backup to protect these ships."

"I concur with your assessment, General."

Which meant he'd already done it. "Thanks, Tim. For everything."

"Of course."

Did Tim actually sound embarrassed?

"Scanning only shows our people in the region. They should arrive—" Tim reeled off some standard space time that meant they'd be on their own for at least another day. As if he heard Halliwell's thought, Tim added, "I'm working on getting some ships' defensive capabilities online."

"Thanks," he said again. They could use the time to deal with, he hoped, the people on the troll ship. Naxe had spoken of her crew, but now that she had her memory back, would one of them mean more to her than she'd known? He was also anxious to hear her story. How had she ended up here? And what did it mean to be Tale Speaker?

She rose from her stump and seemed to take a minute to straighten her back. She saw him looking and grimaced. "I am not as young as I used to be and the deck was very hard."

He nodded, trying not to notice that even tired and beat up his eyes liked looking at her. "Your...Blooban did well."

"I don't know how Blooban was able to sneak up on him. His eyes..." She shuddered.

"Dragonflies have a blind spot in their rear," Halliwell said. Her eyes widened, so he added, "I had to research a similar species on our planet for a project when I was a kid. They aren't that big where I come from, however."

She gave a soft chuckle. "Thank goodness." Her smile faded and she said, "I don't know how to thank you for coming. This was not the situation you'd planned for."

Was it possible to plan for a Picard moment? There had been shooting, though not much that was actually helpful. There had been talking. Also, not that useful. Mostly he'd served as a distraction so that the frog had time to get into position. He was looking forward to hearing the full story, well, looking forward might not be the exact words. It would be interesting, he was sure. Because who didn't like sitting and listening to a frog?

"I try to keep my expectations low," he said, with a half-smile. "I know someone whose motto is to expect the unexpected, though I didn't do that well at it."

"How does one even do that?"

"I'll let you know when I figure it out," he admitted. "In the meantime, I'd sure like to know who you really are and how you ended up here?"

"Can we walk as we talk?" she said. "When I sit I stiffen up."

Since he had the same problem, he was happy to agree.

They had to pick their way across a floor littered with downed drones though the chamber didn't seem as big with the lights up. It was easier to see the exits, so he indicated one, hoping there was nothing gruesome out there. At least Tim had also located their weapons, so they weren't wandering around the scary bug ship unarmed.

As they reached the hatch, Naxe turned back. "Would it be safe to go over to the *Hope* do you think?"

Halliwell activated his comm and asked Tim. After a pause, he received an affirmative.

Out in the corridor, they turned toward the airlock. She didn't speak right away. Their footsteps seemed loud in the almost silent ship. When they'd opened the hatches, the bugs had escaped and were buzzing around. Creepy and way too big, but so far none of them had tried to suck their blood. He watched a small swarm— small in numbers, not size—buzz by, and wondered if the frog was thinning those herds, too.

Finally, Naxe moved her shoulders and took a deep breath.

"It seems so amazing that I could ever believe I was of Scoyfol. *Scoyfol is ships.*" She made a face. "It's as if I had a cage around my mind and now it is gone."

There had to be a sense of disconnect for her. The creepy bug had deserved being eaten by a frog.

"The—it said you were a tale speaker?" he prompted. He didn't even want to say its name.

She nodded. "Yes."

"I don't know what that is," Halliwell admitted. "A storyteller?"

"Yes," she hesitated, "but I was, I am also a story keeper."

He still didn't know what that meant. As if she knew that, she smiled somewhat wryly.

"It is a different story, but a true one this time."

Her voice seemed to fall into a cadence when she told a story. It had a soothing power. She and her voice had got him out here, he acknowledged ruefully.

"I was born and raised in war."

Which made what Odon did to her particularly egregious, Halliwell thought, grimly.

"My parents were part of the resistance in our region of space. One of the most challenging aspects were secure communications."

As they walked, Halliwell noted, almost absently, that the ship looked like something a bug would have. The corridors were round and kind of reminded him of hobbit holes, except these were all metal. Bug burrows? Could be. More of the bugs that had escaped the frog buzzed past them, adding a sort of background to Naxe's voice.

"I had a knack for the comms, so as soon as I was old enough, that became my responsibility."

What was old enough? he wanted to ask. He didn't. She'd found her flow and he didn't want to interrupt.

"After a time, my mother asked me to do more. She said that the people were clamoring for a way to hear news, and my father wanted us to conceal messages in the broadcasts." She paused, not speaking for almost the length of the corridor. She sighed. "I received the stories and sent them back out."

Her chin drooped for a moment. He wanted to put his arm around her as the danger involved made his heart stop.

"Sometimes the stories were all that was left of a people, a world, as the Dusan moved through."

Halliwell heard the weight of that time in her voice now, though her chin lifted again. He reached for her hand. Her fingers clasped his back.

"We've had similar efforts in our world during times of war," he said, thinking of the radio broadcasts for occupied peoples during World War II and during the Cold War.

"The stories were so sad, I began to make up happier stories to weave into the narrative." She glanced at him. "I never altered the truth, but I wanted...I also needed the hope." She looked away. "My parents hadn't come back from a mission, you see. It was just my crew and I after that. I was worried about the things I made up, but it helped."

"We call made up stores fiction," Halliwell said when she stopped, her face sober, her gaze distant. "We use it as an escape too, and as catharsis when the world gets to be too much." The world? She'd had a galaxy of trouble. "Were your parents in the Ojemba?" He was curious and he hoped the change of subject would help take some of the sad from her eyes.

Her head jerked toward him, her fingers clenching on his. She hesitated, then nodded. Maybe she still couldn't say the word. The secretive and ruthless Ojemba had had an interesting way of keeping their people in line.

"It wasn't safe to hope for their return. We had to shift to a position they didn't know about." She took a deep breath. "But I still hope...they could be out there. They might be looking, too."

"I might know someone who might could tell you," he said. He knew his tone was dry. Halliwell had a hate/kind-of-acceptance with the former Ojemba leader. Though he had his doubts about how "former" it actually was.

She studied his face for a long moment, the nodded. "Thank you."

He took that to mean she knew some of the Ojemba were on the shady side.

She took a deep breath and then said, her quiet tone packing the words with quite the punch, "And then the war ended."

They had reached the airlock now, but neither of them made a move toward it.

Halliwell turned and found her other hand. Her chin stayed low for a long moment, then she looked up, an almost smile curving her mouth.

"We, none of us, thought it could happen." Her gaze was grateful and he shifted in discomfort.

"Many made it possible." If she only knew…he pushed away the thought. It was done and they had won, though the cost had been high for everyone involved.

"Yes. But your people were an inciting incident for change."

He couldn't argue with that, even though he didn't quite understand why she'd used those words. He fought back the urge to shift in discomfort. They'd done what had needed to be done. A change of subject would be nice though. "And then?"

"My home world was gone and so I stayed on my parents' ship, traveling and…"

"Telling tales?"

She nodded. "Some true, some mine. I wasn't just a Tale Speaker, I was a Tale Keeper and I didn't want to forget." She gave a bitter laugh. "Isn't that ironic?"

"So you're a writer, an author, that's what we call a storyteller. How did you end up here?"

"It's so crazy. But with the peace, other Tale Speakers, our readers and listeners, wanted to meet us. At first, it was terrifying, but I found peace and connection in the gatherings. I found I wasn't alone."

And perhaps she hoped to find out about her parents, he guessed.

"When we came here, that is what we thought it was: a gathering of others. And so many ships! We had no idea…"

She withdrew her hands from his. He didn't think it was a rejection of him but the memory of what had happened next. She gave a shake of her shoulders, as if shaking it off, then turned and activated the airlock. A wry smile edged her mouth. She indicated the airlock.

"I wasn't going to go through one ever again and here I am. Caught by curiosity."

"It's not just a cat," Halliwell agreed. At her look of inquiry, he added, "It's a very curious species on my planet."

"Sentient?"

He grinned. "Depends on who you ask."

They stepped inside and the hatch closed. He wasn't usually a fan of airlocks either, but he didn't mind this one. It let him stand close to Naxe for a little longer. He noticed her gaze was on the Scoyfol's ship, visible through the porthole.

"Maybe you can finally tell the real story of the Scoyfols," he said.

"I don't understand how he made it feel so real." She glanced at him wryly. "Even now they are shadows in my mind." And then she gave a half laugh, "But not a story. They were never a story. They were, they are a history."

Halliwell laughed. "All right, maybe you, or someone, can finally tell the *history* of the Scoyfols."

They lowered their faceplates and checked their suits, then activated the pressure equalization in the airlock. Halliwell activated the outer hatch and there it was. This would have been a great moment for a song. But he didn't know which one. He hated to admit it, but he needed Bangle for that.

The transit tube stretched out with the same handholds waiting for them. This didn't seem like a "ladies first" moment, but it didn't hurt to ask.

"Would you like me to go first?"

Naxe's smile did some very unsettling things to his insides and her nod felt like more than permission to go first. She was grateful and relieved.

THEY HAD JUST BOARDED the *Hope* and were waiting for the airlock to cycle when Tim contacted both Naxe and John over their comms.

"Kismir has released all prisoners and some are making their way toward their ships which were integrated into this array," he said. "I'm assisting in getting them space worthy once again."

"I guess it isn't our job to screen them," John said, a crease of worry between his strong brows.

Naxe tried not to feel resentful of this intrusion into their moment. It was an unwelcome reminder that they would be going different directions before long. Had she asked to come here to postpone that? It was possible. Hadn't she had her fill of the Scoyfols?

"I examined their ships' logs," Tim said.

The amused look in John's eyes restored some of the connection Tim had broken.

"I'm concerned that the word will get out. The remaining array is pretty vulnerable."

Was her ship—her parents' ship—still out there? It must be. Odon wouldn't have risked sending her out on her own ship, so full of memories. It was still there. She felt a jolt. And her crew.

"Is my crew all right?" she asked, guilt stabbing at her mind and heart. They should have been her first concern—but they were a couple, older and loyal to her parents. Now with the hindsight of this experience, she realized they'd wanted to be free too. Not so much of her, but of the roaming life. They'd wanted to go home and she hadn't realized it. Or had she? The emotions she'd felt had to come from real places to have so much power over her during her…captivity. On some level she had known. More guilt, but also relief. They were all free now. She glanced at John. Was she? Did the pull she felt for him come from fear or from something more?

She'd written heroes into her stories, and she'd written heroines. The adventures were fun and she'd enjoyed having them save each other. *Save each other.* Did John need saving? Substitute "save" for love. She kept her sigh silent. It was possible that the only way she could save him was to leave, to free him from the burden of her problems and her feelings. With a jolt, she realized Riina was speaking to her, answering her question.

"Your crew are fine and relieved to learn you are as well," Riina said. "They are making their way to your ship to assess it for damage." She paused, then added, "If you see anything exciting on the *Hope*, can you send me a feed?"

Was she sorry not to be with them? Naxe wasn't sure. She seemed to be sticking close to Tim. How would it feel to be part of a couple, she wondered? She'd been alone for longer than she'd realized.

"Roger that," John said.

He glanced at this last airlock control between them and answers. She hoped so. He moved to one side so she could reach them easily. She liked that about him. He treated her with an equality that she hadn't always run into during her adventures in securing pointless supplies. What had happened to it all, she wondered? And how many times had she actually gone on her trips?

The memory—not a true one—of being here, of doing this, jostled with reality, as she touched the hatch control. It opened onto an antechamber that was larger than the other ships they'd passed through while getting to the Ugly Sucker ship. This one could have accommodated at least six crew members fairly comfortably. In fact, there were six egress suits hanging limply on hooks on either side. There were a couple of lockers and some storage also. There were crew patches on the suits. She fingered the suit, studying the patch with the intertwined "s" and "f." For the original name, she decided. *Scoyfol's Future*. There wouldn't have been resources for changing their patches and such—if they'd actually changed the name. That change could have been part of Odon's story.

She had no sense of recognition for the patch, which was interesting. Her flight suit had been devoid of a crew patch, but that had been a security issue. It was hard to believe she'd made it this far, but she did wonder, would she ever be able to filter out the real from the planted memories? Her relationship with Blooban anchored the memories to some extent, she decided. She couldn't excise the memories without erasing him, too. She owed him too much to do that. He'd kept her from being alone in the nightmare.

They crossed this hatch and entered a dim corridor that was wider than the others they'd traversed so far. Naxe supposed it made sense. This was a much bigger ship and, if what they knew was true, had been designed to carry both passengers and cargo. The emergency lighting was barely enough to see a few feet. Minimal life support, according to her suit's readings. She lifted on her toes, testing the gravity settings. These were also minimal.

She tried her headlamp, but it must have been broken in the altercation with Odon, so she extracted her hand lamp and turned it on. It was a relief and a surprise when it worked. They headed down the long, curving corridor. Unlike the other ship, any doors leading off this corridor were locked.

"Maybe we should make for the bridge," John suggested.

Could they access the bridge controls without Tim? Perhaps Blooban could help. She tapped her comm and heard him say, "I am working on it."

Of course he was.

"Thank you, my friend," she said, hoping he knew all that she thanked him for. His answering croak seemed to say so.

There was a low hum under her feet and then more lights flickered on.

After the *Vycorth*, this ship felt too large, the sound of their footsteps echoing hollowly as they walked forward. The lights curved away from them in a long sweep. The silence, other than the low hum of the restarting power and their movements, was eerie. Was their greatest danger truly behind them? What had happened to Scoyfol and its people?

"Are you picking up any life signs, Tim?" John asked.

"Yours and Naxe's," he said.

Naxe had to smile at how literal he was.

"Do you think this ship was abandoned like the others?" Naxe asked. "And if they did, how did these ships stay undisturbed for so long?"

"The nebula around it has masking properties and this region of space has no planets to draw ships here," Riina said over the comm.

"But how did Odon manage to find it?" Naxe wondered.

"The Anisoptarians have a history of affinity to nebulas of this type," Blooban said, entering the conversation with his deep, raspy voice. "According to the data I found in my archives which I have confirmed from examination of the ship."

Blooban did like data. And bugs. Naxe repressed a shudder. That was one memory she would be glad to have erased.

"If you proceed to the next intersection, I should be able to provide you with a map to the bridge," Tim said.

THE *HOPE'S* bridge was impressive, Halliwell admitted, as the bridge access hatch opened for them. Between Blooban and Tim, most of the systems were either active or coming online. Both were probably already deep into figuring out what happened. At least they were polite enough to let Halliwell feel like he was making a few discoveries.

But for a few moments he let himself just savor the experience of being on a bridge that might be as much as two thousand—or more—years old.

It was big, bigger even than the *Doolittle's* bridge, increasing the impression of stepping back into an old history.

"My word," Naxe said faintly. She'd stopped just inside, too, her gaze sweeping from left to right, and then back again.

Halliwell finally made himself move, though he had to stop next to the captain's chair. It rose above the various stations, with wide control arms on each side. The spot gave him a good view of all the stations where displays were also flickering to life.

Now this was a Picard moment.

It was a ship, so space was a premium, but it still managed to feel spacious and light. And prosperous, he decided. This was a civilian vessel, so they could push out the boat a bit. The captain's seat was plush, but the other positions didn't look awful. They acknowledged that space travel took time and people needed to be comfortable for it.

"This is nice," he said, no echo despite the size and emptiness.

"Yes." Naxe moved around the edges, stopping to glance at the various screens. "These readings are interesting." She stopped next to one, then sat in the seat and began to tap on the screens. "The ship has been drawing a considerable amount of energy from the nebula

Halliwell bit back a protest that maybe they should wait before tapping things. He was not the policeman of anything, including this ship. But when she gave a soft exclamation, he strode over to her side. He looked down, trying to decide what the video showed. There was a view of a large chamber, circular like the ship. But inside the chamber were rows of pods that reminded him of the ones on the Garradian outpost. They were not unlike the pods that Riina had emerged from after her long, cold sleep.

"Is that..." he couldn't finish the question. Wasn't sure Naxe could answer it.

Her hands moved and video closed in on one of the pods. The sides were translucent and he could see a face through it.

"That's the ship's captain." She looked up at him, awe in her eyes. "They never left." She tapped controls. "Even those from the other ships are here. Here is the manifest and instructions for anyone who finds them in..." her voice broke before she could steady it again, "safer times."

"But..." he rubbed his face to clear his spinning thoughts. It wasn't as if he hadn't seen this before, but yeah, it was still new enough to shock a bit. They must have had to adapt the ship on the fly, so to speak. Unless that's how they'd transported people around. It could be, he supposed. "How did the bug get their thoughts into your head?"

"According to this, everyone saved their memories in separate storage. He must have accessed it—no." She shook her head. "He used Kismir and his people for that. He must have conscripted them somehow. Perhaps they will tell us."

Halliwell shook his head. "They are already long gone." It was possible they felt guilt about what they'd done, even if under threat. He sank into the seat closest to hers and rubbed his face again. This "holiday" was turning out to be a lot of work. He stared at the video screen. "After so long, I wonder if any of them are...viable?"

"I would like to bring some of my people here," Riina said, "to assess them."

Well, that wasn't a surprise.

"You want to wake them up," Halliwell said, even though he wasn't sure he wanted to know.

There was a pause, "It is why we came," she reminded him. "To help Scoyfol finish their journey and take the passengers home."

It was the Picard moment he'd hoped for. But it also asked him to make a decision that was even above his or Picard's pay grade, or least that is how it felt. One step at a time, he reminded himself.

"All right," he said, but in his mind it was the classic, "engage."

Chapter 7

It felt strange to be back on the *Vycorth*, but it also felt more familiar to her. She'd spoken to her crew but had been unable to move forward, or move back until she'd had a chance to talk to Blooban. It felt as if she were suspended between her real life and her future life. Her past? She felt disconnected from it on some level. Blooban was still on the Ugly Sucker ship. Either he was fascinated with it for some reason, helping Tim, or he hadn't found all the big bugs yet. Perhaps he was as tired of ships' rations as she was.

She ran a hand lightly over the control board and sighed. Was her future here? Blooban hadn't said anything. Her crew claimed to want her back. Riina had offered her a spot on their outpost. They wanted to add her archives from the war years to theirs. The idea had appeal, but she was not certain how she'd feel about being close to John, but not—

Her comm trilled from the airlock. She opened the channel and caught her breath. It was John.

"Permission to come aboard?"

She hadn't seen him since they'd left the *Hope*. He had needed to meet with his people who had arrived to protect this company. Riina had called it a floating museum, but it was one with people who may still be alive to claim the many ships. John had said it made his head hurt, and she had to agree that thinking about it made hers hurt, too.

"Of course," she said, hoping she didn't sound as breathless as she felt. "I'm on the bridge but I can meet you down there."

"How about the galley?" he suggested. "It has seats."

"All right." Her heart shouldn't be beating so fast and why did it feel long to reach the galley, and even longer for John to get there? She tried to find a neutral place inside, hoping that would help with her expression. It didn't feel like it helped when his tall, strong body came into view. She eyed him hungrily, soaking it up for when she didn't see him anymore. It hadn't been that long since they'd parted, but it felt longer than her captivity. She'd...missed him. She hated to admit it. She was just the person who had invaded his quarters, let a frog jump on his chest, and brought him to this place where he'd almost been killed.

It didn't seem likely that he would miss her.

She wrote stories, so she knew the difference between hopes and reality. She wrote happy endings because people had needed them, they'd needed the light in the darkness, but—her mind hesitantly approached the word—love in real life was different. Indeed, at this moment she was acutely aware of the gap between her fiction and this reality.

Did she even know what she felt for John was...that? Her listeners and readers had loved her stories because it took them away from the real world. She'd lived her stories so completely, she'd been easy to fool, she decided with some scorn. It was interesting Odon hadn't changed her name, at least not completely. No, he'd just erased her last name, the one that connected her to her parents.'

Naxe Ghelfi, daughter of Bedwyr and Taran Ghelfi.

Remembering had helped so much, but it hadn't healed all the gaps yet.

She clasped her hands together and watched him navigate the narrow corridor toward her. When he saw her, he smiled and lifted his hand in greeting. Her voice caught in her throat and for several seconds, she couldn't speak. She lifted her hand, too, then found her voice.

"Hello," she said, the greeting she'd heard his people use.

He stopped in the hatchway and she forgot words, perhaps stopped thinking, too. She stared and it seemed he stared, too. Then the ship began a process that jolted her into action.

"Please, sit. Can I offer you anything to drink?" The question brought back their first meeting in his quarters. He'd been disheveled, his hair tumbled and a shadow of beard on his face. Now he looked tired, but less tense somehow. Of course, he wasn't alone here anymore. His people had arrived. *His people.* She sighed and half turned so he couldn't see her face until she got it back under control. And her thoughts. She needed to get them under control, too.

"Just some water would be nice," he said. He waited near the small table until she'd secured two containers and sank down before he took the seat across from her.

Their knees brushed together, their feet side-by-side. She drank some water, then set it on the tabletop, her fingers loosely clasping it. It helped to have it. It kept her from reaching out to touch him.

He drank, too, then lowered the container, but he didn't hold onto it. Instead, he spread his fingers on the top, one finger lightly tapping the surface.

He shifted in his seat, rubbing their knees more intimately together before he stopped himself. He glanced around. "Did you ever find out what Odon did with the cargo you brought here?"

"Blooban found transactions in his data. He sold it." It was hard to speak of. She'd risked her life at times for those supplies. To prove what? He wouldn't know a story if it bit him on—she stopped, stifling a giggle. In the end his story had bit him on the rear. "He sold it to buy bugs, I suppose."

"It got what it deserved in the end," John said with satisfaction. "I don't suppose there is video?"

Now Naxe chuckled feeling her insides relax some. "I'll ask Blooban to check." It would be like Odon to have recorded it all to gloat over later.

The galley felt smaller than she remembered but he had broad shoulders and he was very tall. She didn't feel oppressed by his size, though. She liked that some part of them touched as they said this last goodbye. That must be why he was here. The silence felt long, but everything felt long right now, and it wasn't uncomfortable.

"Do you know what you're going to do now?" He shifted so that his forearms rested on the table edge, one hand clasping the water container, the other laying close enough to almost touch her hand. If she moved it a very small bit….

Naxe's gaze dropped to her own hands. "Riina offered me a place on her outpost," she admitted.

"What about," for some reason, it seemed as if John had a hard time saying his name, "Blooban?"

"We haven't talked about it yet," she admitted.

"You're both, I hope you know, you're both welcome on Kikk."

She looked up, emotion catching in her throat. "That's very kind."

His lips twisted some. "It's not kind, it's…" He looked up and it felt as if his gaze grabbed hers and held it… "it would be nice. I would like it." Something warmed his gaze and he half smiled. "It's been a while since I've done this." He gestured vaguely with his hand.

Done what? Naxe blinked, afraid to hope.

"I would like to spend more time with you. Get to know the person you really are."

She flinched. "I'm not sure I know who I am."

He glanced away, then back. "I didn't, that didn't come out right. I liked you. I like you."

For the first time he didn't seem the confident general of people and ships, or even the man who'd stood with her in the fake forest facing Odon. He looked like, well, a man, she decided. She'd written about this, had written this scene so often, it felt as if she recognized it, not with scorn, but with hope. It was, she realized, this hope she'd found and brought with her from Kikk where she'd met John for the first time. It had revolved around John, but it had been more.

Her hands inched closer to his and he took the hint, his closing, warm and strong, around hers.

"I would like that very much," she said a smile trembling on her mouth.

His hands gripped hers and he smiled. This smile was not like the others she'd seen on his face. This one was bright as the stars she'd navigated her ship by.

"If this were one of my tales," she said, feeling the old power of words, but also something new rising within her, "there would be a—"

Before she could finish, John—with an action that was both general-like and not—rose, and pulled her up from her seat. His arms closed around her and his mouth settled over hers. As dreamy warmth stole coherence from her thoughts, she had a brief time to note with satisfaction that she'd written the scene better than she'd realized...

≈

☺ ONE LAST Invitation

If you enjoyed the **action, adventure, and romance** in these stories, you're exactly the kind of reader I love writing for.

I write adventures where:

things don't always go according to plan

attraction shows up at inconvenient moments

and sometimes laughter is the only sensible response

If you'd like to step into another adventure, I'd love to invite you through one more door.

◾ Another Door in Time

Some stories grow longer.

Some stay short and sharp.

And some appear when you least expect them.

When you join my email list, you'll receive **Another Door in Time** — an exclusive standalone story created just for readers who enjoy action, adventure, romance, and the occasional twist.

It's not connected to this collection.

It's not required reading.

It's simply a thank-you for spending time with my stories.

Step through Another Door in Time here:

Get Another Door in Time

What to expect from me

I write action-packed stories with romance at the heart of them — sometimes serious, sometimes playful, and always driven by characters who refuse to quit when things get complicated.

A final note

Thanks again for reading. I hope these stories made you smile — and I hope I'll see you again in another adventure.

Echoes Beneath

A PROJECT ENTERPRISE
SHORT STORY

A routine mission turns into a planetary crisis.

Geologist Miles Walker travels to a remote world to inspect an old seismic sensor. He finds unexplained tremors, missing research, and Lira, an archaeologist searching for her missing father.

When a major quake reveals signs of an ancient alien presence, the danger escalates fast. Systems fail, sabotage surfaces, and something powerful begins to stir beneath the planet's crust. Lira's loyal and very opinionated space bird, T'Korrin, is the first to sense the threat.

Miles and Lira must combine science, courage, and trust to stop a disaster that could destroy more than one world. Falling for each other only raises the stakes.

Echoes Beneath is a science fiction romance adventure in the Project Enterprise universe, filled with alien secrets, high stakes danger, and heart.

Echoes Beneath

"AND WHY AM I the one who needs to go check on him?" Lira Taan shoved a hand through her hair, barely resisting the urge to pull on it. What she really wanted to do was pull her brother's hair out, not her own.

There was a short silence on the other end while her brother tried to find a diplomatic way of saying he didn't want to go because it would make him crazy and besides, he had important things to do.

"Your work is more flexible," he finally said.

Lira had a feeling his wife had fed him that line. It was true. She was currently working from home compiling the data from her field work. Still, taking the time to fly down to the southern pole where their father lived hadn't been factored into her schedule.

"What about calling him?" Lira asked.

"I tried that. He told me he couldn't talk."

That was never a good sign.

"He told Keyvn he was close to first contact."

"With who?" Or was it whom? She always had to look it up and then she still wasn't sure. And whom sounded pretentious.

"Aliens."

Lira blinked. *"Aliens."*

This wasn't exactly a surprise. Her father had managed to not just isolate himself at the southern pole of the planet, he'd alienated —bit of irony there—all his colleagues with his theories about ancient alien ruins hidden beneath the surface of Arroxan Prime. He believed there were multiple alien incursions, but until now he hadn't had any proof. And now he was claiming he'd had first contact?

Could anyone have contact with an ancient alien species? Didn't ancient imply long gone?

Lira sighed. Maybe they should have tried harder to persuade him not to move to the southern pole. However, it was a universal truth that parents never listened to their kids. If she had kids, she absolutely planned to not listen to them. It felt like she'd earned the privilege.

"You're closer," her brother said, his tone coaxing now. "Just pop down and make sure he's eating and stuff. Kevyn said he was acting a little erratic."

That was troubling. Her father was an odd mix of eccentric and grounded. Erratic? No.

She sighed again, knowing she would do it. As the only daughter, it was somehow her job to look after their father, to make sure he survived his various interesting life choices. And now that she let herself think about seeing him, she realized how much she did miss him. He was definitely quirky and often frustrating, but he was also a lot of fun. She couldn't explain how but being around him made her feel more centered somehow. The trouble was getting there. It was a pain.

The research facility where he lived hadn't started out as conspiracy theory central. It had originally been a weather tracking station. Her father had gotten a real deal on it—something they only heard about after it was too late to stop him. Though she had to admit, for a weather station, it had been a good deal. And it was interesting in a vaguely creepy kind of way. Now that she thought about it, it did have that weird alien vibe. Maybe that's why her father had gone all alien in his theories while living there mostly alone.

Early in his career, some funding had flowed his way, because he had started out researching seismic activity and how it might impact weather. Or be impacted by weather? Lira wasn't sure which and she had no idea why he'd moved on to aliens causing it or something like that. She'd been busy getting her archaeology degree and didn't know all the details from when he'd gone off the rails.

Sanity might have returned to her father when the funding dried up, but apparently conspiracy theories were catching. His funding now flowed from a variety of like-minded conspiracy theorists. It was too bad one of them didn't have to go down and make sure he was eating. And then there were his attempts to confirm his theory. She should probably make sure he wasn't going to doom them all to some kind of cataclysmic event.

It was challenging enough living with the current level of Arroxan Prime's seismic activity. It rendered parts of the planet uninhabitable and the rest interesting to inhabit. But it wasn't as if they had anywhere else to go. If scientists were to be believed, the other planets in their solar system were even less habitable. So, they'd learned to make do with what they had.

"All right," she said, when her brother let the silence apply pressure for the guilt trip. At least she'd get to pack for it before she left. "I'll go see what I can find out."

Her brother rang off without asking to be kept informed. Like she planned to let him off *that* hook. In some ways, he was as delusional as their father.

She looked at T'Korrin, her pet raptor. It fluffed its tiny wings in what looked like a shrug, then gave a tiny squawk. The look in his eyes was one she was familiar with.

"Don't you start," she said.

~

DR. MILES WALKER watched the runner lift off with something like relief. The pilot had been chatty in an obvious and annoying way. He also thought he was funny.

Yes, it was a bleak spot to be dropped off.

Yes, it was cold enough for him.

Probably a lot of rocks under that ice. Certainly enough rocks.

The hearty laugh followed these pieces of witticism.

The rock jokes were always the same, no matter which alien planet he was on. Of course there were enough rocks for him, more than enough rocks because planets they could land on were usually made of rocks.

No one ever asked him why rocks. Or why anyone cared about rocks. Or why send a geologist to look at the rocks of a planet without space capability. (He would like the answer to that question, too.)

They didn't need to ask. The questions were in their expressions and their voices. Since he couldn't, or didn't want to answer those questions, he was happy they didn't ask.

It wasn't, as he liked to tell people, rock science. It was earth science. Of course, he'd have liked to point out that geology wasn't only about rocks, but that would lead to more chatting and painful rock jokes.

It wasn't that Miles was opposed to chatting or even chatting about rocks. It was just that chatting—particularly pointless chatting —and mentally processing data were incompatible actions. He had been sent to Arroxan Prime to determine why a seismic sensor had triggered.

An ancient seismic sensor planted on Arroxan Prime a long time ago, hence the ancient designation.

It made sense to send a geologist to check it out. Seismic was part of a geologist's jam and they were comfortable with time frames of plus or minus millions of years. It made dating problematic since he and his dates counted time differently. If he wasn't a million years late, he should be good, right? But the answer was usually no.

That didn't mean this mission wasn't a head scratcher. Why had the sensor gone off now? It had been rolling happily along since it had been installed, and it chose now to go off?

"I'll be back to pick you up in three days, doc," the pilot said in his earpiece. "And if you get in trouble, just trigger your alert."

"Thank you," Miles said, instead of using one of several sarcastic remarks he'd have liked to say. Not a good plan to annoy your ride. It had only taken once for him to learn that particular lesson.

"This is a singularly inhospitable place," Harold said, its voice still slightly robotic. It was getting better at not being a robotic sounding robot, however.

Harold was officially there to assist, but in reality it had been sent along so that no one would need to feel guilty about dropping him on an alien planet even further from Earth than the rest of the Earth Expedition, and then leaving him on that planet—a planet with an unhappy seismic sensor that probably just needed a new battery.

He stared up at the retreating shuttle. The sight gave him mixed feelings. On the one hand, he was finally—mostly—alone for this field trip. But this alone felt suddenly extremely alone when he looked at the empty landscape around him.

"I believe there are other places on this planet that are quite nice," Miles observed, somewhat absently. He tried to mentally match his topside location with the underlying formations that the ship's sensors had managed to identify.

It wasn't perfect. All he could judge it by were his experiences with geology on other planets, and of course, on Earth. But there were always those little differences trying to trip him up. While he'd found similarities with Earth geology, each planet had its own unique way of putting it all together.

In a four-hundred-mile radius, the only human-made identifying surface marker was the facility, which was currently just out of his sightline. It had been deemed prudent to set him, Harold, and their gear down out of sight of the abandoned facility.

Miles found that ironic. If it was empty, what did it matter where they landed? At least they'd given them a surface runner to carry them and their equipment to the empty facility.

He knew beyond the rising peaks was a stratovolcano, or a composite volcano, if he'd translated the Garradian data correctly. From the air, it had had the appearance of one. It definitely had the conical shape and steep profile. He'd have liked to do a flyover of it, but it wasn't on their flight path. Maybe on the way out.

For now, his mission brief—aka field trip—appeared to be simple. The appearance of simple might worry him because geology was much more complicated than people realized. Still, it was nice to be dirt-side somewhere. A geologist wasn't that much use in outer space.

The Garradians, they seemed to do well in space now that they were back from what they called their long sleep. Apparently, they hadn't defrosted a geologist yet because the sensor activating had caught them off guard.

"It's probably a symptom of age," one non-geologist told him. Miles noticed he avoided making eye contact with him.

"Or its power source is almost expended," said another, equally evasive Garradian scientist.

Miles should probably have declined the honor of what could be the equivalent of changing a battery, but it was an alien planet full of unknown rocks. And it was probably safer than that time when he and some other geology students had rented a helicopter to fly over an erupting volcano.

And he hadn't had to pay anything for this ride. They were paying him.

They didn't have a lot of data, a fact that distressed the Garradians more than it did him. He just hated paperwork and dealing with it must have been at least as bad back whenever the sensor had been installed. And there was the language problem to factor in.

The Garradians managed communication on most things pretty well, considering how far apart their two cultures were, but the science stuff, the names? When two scientists of the same persuasion were together, they could mostly find their way to common ground.

But he'd had to spend the trip trying to find anything he recognized in the data provided without context or a counterpart. For an alien planet in another galaxy.

The only thing the Garradians seemed certain of was that the sensor going off was more than troubling. He'd deduced this because they'd repeated "troubling" multiple times. In fact, that was almost the last word they'd said to him just before he boarded his ride.

"It is troubling."

He'd wanted to ask them if it was troubling, just to yank their chains, but a look from General Halliwell had stopped him.

Harold's onboard AI had been able to help with some things.

The planet's inhabitants called it Arroxan Prime.

It was a heavily volcanic planet with limited livable space.

The sensor had been located at the planet's southern pole.

It was an ice pole, but with volcanos in close enough proximity to be a possible reason the sensor had triggered. Even though the pole and the volcano had been in close proximity for pretty much the whole time.

What didn't he know?

Why they were so worried enough about seismic activity in a place without inhabitants that they placed a sensor—or multiple sensors—in that particular location? Was it actually a seismic sensor? But what else could it be?

That was a pretty big knowledge gap. He knew all about big gaps. Canyons, ravines, crevasses lurking under the ice waiting for an unwary geologist to fall into.

Their first task on arriving in orbit at Arroxan Prime had been to initiate scanning protocols to get updated information both on the sensor and the planet as a whole. He rolled his eyes again as he considered this. If the sensor could be accessed and rebooted without a landing, that was the preferred option.

If he was unable to adequately determine the problem, then his rules of engagement allowed for he and Harold to go dirt side as long as they didn't make contact with the inhabitants.

Arroxan Prime's population weren't space capable.

First contact was tricky and he wasn't qualified to do it.

Well, he couldn't argue with that. He wasn't that great at first contact with other Earthlings. So he was anxious to avoid any contact with the inhabitants, too. And he was pretty sure they didn't want to talk to him. Being recruited to the Expedition had changed his perception of first contact.

Prior to that, his "contacts" with aliens was via movies, television, and books. Fictional contact without risk. He knew it was ironic when he routinely went down mines and liked looking down the mouths of volcanoes. But no one had required him to make sense until he left Earth to join the expedition.

And honestly, since then, not much had made sense. Like lava, he just went with the flow.

And that had landed him here on Arroxan Prime with a robot for a sidekick. Now there was some irony.

What he thought he knew, after his study and the scanning, was that the sensor was deep underground. And that some kind of facility sat directly on top of it. And what he knew for sure was that he couldn't reset it from space or figure out why it had triggered.

He was less sure of a few things, but he thought the geologist equivalent Garradians of the past had installed some kind of barrier down there and left sensors to monitor it. He hadn't been able to figure out why.

That was odd, ranging to downright weird. The only reason to install a barrier was to keep things down, but the minerals deep down in most planets just found another way to the surface if that was where it wanted to go.

When man—or humanoids—went head-to-head with Mother Nature? They usually lost when Mom brought all the things.

On the other hand, whatever they'd done appeared to have lasted for Miles' plus or minus a millennia. So, it was a good effort.

And hopefully all he'd need to do was to change a battery. Harold also had a program update if the equipment they'd left there was still functional. That seemed like the longest of the long shots. But he had to like their optimism.

Even if it was his geological butt on the line.

Their scans had shown no life signs in or around the facility.

Looking around? This wasn't a surprise. And it was good since this was **not** a first contact mission. Just in case he'd missed the memo the first fifteen times.

And even though it wasn't a first contact mission, they'd loaded both his suit systems and Harold's memory banks with everything that was known about Arroxan Prime and its inhabitants, including any language variations that may have occurred since they were last there.

There weren't as many of those as he'd have expected for a whole world, but their flyover and scan had confirmed the fact that most of the planet was uninhabitable. Harold had used some of the scanning time to update the databases with what could be retrieved from Arroxan Prime's communications. They didn't seem to have any satellites. Not a surprise since they weren't space capable, yet somehow he was still surprised. They did have airborne type transportation systems, more even than Earth.

So they clearly had the capability to be space capable.

But when he saw how often the planet experienced seismic events, it did kind of make sense. Putting fuel in a rocket ship on an unstable surface might not be the best idea.

When he'd asked why it felt like they didn't want first contact but had still given him all the information he'd need if he did, someone called Doc had told him to expect the unexpected.

"I'm a geologist," he'd told her. "We never expect the expected."

He remembered her grin sent a chill down his back. That was one scary lady.

He supposed it was a lucky break that the source of the signal came from this unpromising and remote location. He tried not to remind himself that luck could go both ways.

He might have wished his ride didn't have to pop off to pick up some botanists or something from a Mars-like planet on the other side of the system. It would have been nice to know it was orbiting overhead and ready for a quick pick up if something went wrong.

His ride had been equipped with a lot of high-end, Garradian equipment, so the scans they'd done prior to this drop had provided him with a butt load of data, but he'd still been left without the kind of conclusive data that could only be secured by coming down and taking a look.

He liked to look, even knowing that most of what he'd like to see was inaccessible to his eyes. He did have a built-in Lidar along with some other stuff in his suit systems that he hoped would help him collect the necessary data. And he had his rock pick. He might have smuggled that on board. The Garradians didn't seem to like pointy ended hammers. Weird.

Being able to use his rock pick to collect some new rocks was definitely the upside of the mission.

He looked around. The cold? He didn't like that as much.

At least the Garradian gear was top notch and pretty cool to wear. The only actual chill was from being almost alone on the alien planet with a robot called Harold. Who named a robot Harold? he'd asked.

It had chosen the name itself, he'd been told. So, Harold it was.

They'd pitched the idea of Harold by using Miles' love of sci-fi stuff against him.

"You'll be like Luke," they said.

They hadn't completely misled him. He had a ray gun instead of a light saber and a 3CPO-like robot that called itself Harold. So far Harold hadn't tried to give him protocol lessons. That was a positive.

He might have objected to the prissy robot, but they had given him a weapons load out, too. They couldn't send him down here without some way to defend himself, presumably from an ice flow because he was under no circumstances to make contact with anyone. The "don't shoot anyone" didn't have to be said out loud, because that came under the heading of first contact, too.

If there were some kind of ice creature living here? It hadn't shown up on their scans. So, it was probably fine.

"Let's get going," he said. At least they didn't have to walk the rest of the way, thanks to the small land runner. That was pretty *Star Wars* cool, too.

Harold slid into the driving side. Miles didn't object. He'd never driven a runner on an icy surface, and it would be embarrassing to screw up in front of a robot. And he liked to look around, which was something one shouldn't do while driving.

As they started forward, he continued trying to mentally place them with what he'd seen from above. They were on the edge of a plain that spread across a valley almost completely surrounded by jagged rocky peaks. Okay, they were probably rock. They could be completely ice formations. Good thing he'd brought a rock pick.

LIRA STEERED the air flyer between the soaring and jagged peaks that surrounded her father's research facility. It was as bleak and cheerless a spot as anything on Arroxan Prime—and there was a lot of bleak and inhospitable to choose from. Her brothers thought it was crazy. Her father considered this a major positive. No one could just drop in for a visit.

He liked to know who was incoming. Sometimes that was so he could pretend he wasn't there. Her father wasn't what you'd call a people person, but if she wound him up just right, he told great stories. He distrusted the government and he tended to latch onto theories and ride them to a crash point. The alien obsession had lasted a little longer than most, though all of them eventually looped back to the seismic disruptions Arroxan Prime experienced with disconcerting irregularity.

Her father believed in a long-term solution. He'd always been a solutions-oriented dreamer.

Over time, their people had adapted to the disruptions. They hadn't had another choice. Her dad wasn't the only one looking for answers. Most of their scientists spent a lot of time either trying to figure out how to stop the persistent and irregular tremors, or how to more effectively live with them.

So far, the "learn to live with them" track was winning the study war. Their buildings were now constructed on specialized pressure plates designed to absorb the movement, they'd been built using flexible components, their personal items weren't breakable, and they all had learned how to walk with that movement and not against it. Face planting was a good teacher.

Ground transportation was rare because it got old fixing roads over and over again.

Her father was firmly in the fix-it camp, even with the divergence into alien conspiracy. If the aliens did it, then the solution to fix it was there, just waiting to be found. Problem solved. The possible first contact with aliens was new, though.

At least he'd taken her call and was happy for her to visit. He had sounded odd, however. A new odd, instead of his regular odd.

She made a small course adjustment as more of the plain came into view. Crouched on the plain that lapped up against the mountains, the facility had been constructed almost dead center. Just visible between two of those peaks, she saw their southern moon. There were also theories about it, and their northern moon, and the moons' gravitational effect on planetary seismic activity. There were indications in the archaeological record that their ancestors had believed the moons were responsible.

Lira couldn't say she kept up with the current theories. Her interest was the past. It was fascinating to study the signs of previous inhabitants and also discover the innovative ways they'd dealt with the tremors. The seismic disruptions had been a problem for a long time.

T'Korrin made a disgruntled noise from where he crouched under the passenger seat. He was an odd bird for sure. He had to go everywhere she went, or he made himself sick, but he also didn't like flying. Even under his own steam.

A bird who didn't like to fly.

When she'd told him where she was going, he'd hopped from leg to leg making agitated noises before finally deciding it would be worse to be left behind. He'd also made his displeasure known for most of the trip. She didn't know how he did it, but he managed to sound like a whining two-year-old.

She postulated that it was because he'd been orphaned young. She'd found him on a dig, his parents likely killed or kidnapped by poachers. He'd bonded to her at first sight. When he wasn't whining, he was adorable. He was also a wonderful sensor. He gave almost early warnings of incoming tremors. She might wish he'd do it a little sooner, but any warning was good.

She'd tried to teach him how to fly, but it wasn't like she could show him. He had a way of looking at her when she tried to get him to use his wings that was…disconcerting. She always felt like she was the one who didn't get it.

If she sometimes suspected he could fly? Well, so far, she hadn't been able to catch him at it.

He blinked up at her, a soulful look in his deep, dark predator's eyes.

"We're almost there," she told him.

The locater beam for incoming visitors to her father's facility activated and she adjusted course. The landing pad was in front of the facility. She squinted at the entrance. Was there something parked there?

She positioned her flyer over the pad and began her descent, pausing as T'Korrin gave his signature "tremor incoming" squeak. She delayed touchdown as the landscape rippled and swayed.

"That was a rather long one," she told T'Korrin when she was finally able to land.

There'd be aftershocks, but anyone who grew up on Arroxan Prime knew how to deal.

Now that she was dirtside, she could see there was definitely some kind of craft right up next to the entrance. Of course, her father needed to get supplies from time to time. The facility had some self-sustaining features, but he did need stuff. She was always happy when the available food wasn't just facility grown.

She did wonder why they'd parked there and not on the landing pad. Stuff to unload perhaps?

She waited for T'Korrin to jump onto her shoulder and then scrambled out onto the icy surface of the landing pad. She paused to get her balance as the smaller tremors continued to ripple through the ground, their impact somewhat mitigated by the pad's design.

Usually she recognized most types of flyer. She'd been in most of them going to and from dig sites, but this one was new to her. A new type, perhaps?

Balance secured, she headed toward the flyer and the facility. It was a two-seater, with rear space where she saw cargo containers. A supply run? It could be, she supposed. But lines were awfully sleek for cargo hauler. It had a symbol on one side that she didn't recognize. She traced it with a finger.

"What do you think, T'Korrin?"

He squawked and jumped to its roof, walking around it as if examining it. She crossed her arms and grinned. When he jumped back to her shoulder, she met his gaze.

"Well?" She would swear he shrugged. "Well, let's go find my father."

IT WAS AN ODD PLACE, Miles thought as he hesitated in the entryway. From the outside, it looked like a government standard facility. Gray, boring, ugly. Inside, there were signs of intelligent design. Light flooded down from slits in the ceiling. Natural light? It's what it seemed to be.

The entrance was what he'd have called a small rotunda because he liked to think funny words and rotunda was definitely on the list. The decoration wasn't inspired, but it looked like someone had tried, not very hard, but trying was trying.

The floor was plain except for the crack cutting from one side of the little rotunda to another

"That crack propagated like it had a grudge." He glanced at Harold and then sighed. A sidekick with no sense of humor.

"No crevasse though." It was always better if there weren't crevasses in your path.

Two doorways led off from both sides, but when he checked one, they came together again in a short, single hallway.

Interesting.

More cracks in the walls and the next—it wasn't a rotunda, but it was round. An atrium? He studied the plants on the other side, looking through a series of fine cracks and impact stars in the glass. Was it glass? He touched it, but of course, his gloves didn't provide the kind of tactile experience he needed.

There was an acceptable atmosphere, according to his Garradian gear, so he pulled off a glove and tried again.

It wasn't glass. He might have been surprised, but then he recalled the planet's seismic activity and reconsidered. It was probably the smart move when the ground could move at any time.

Had they abandoned this facility after a seismic event? He lowered his faceplate and inhaled carefully. He couldn't define what he smelled, but it wasn't what he'd experienced in abandoned buildings back on Earth.

The plants were still growing inside the atrium, too.

"We're sure no one lives here?" he asked Harold.

"There is no way to be certain no one lives here," it said. "We detected no life signs."

The careful parsing made him turn to look at Harold, but it couldn't break out in expression.

He wished they didn't have to enter this building, abandoned temporarily or not. But the Garradian signal was coming from somewhere directly under it. And traversing a building was probably better than trying to dig a hole in the ice crust.

He could admit to curiosity to see this sensor—if that would be possible. No way to tell how deep this facility went, but according to his suit's reading, they were still significantly above the signal.

Past the atrium, they found a couple of offices and then some living quarters. One definitely looked occupied. Miles didn't say anything about it. Just shut the door and moved on, hoping that the life signs scan was right and there was no one here. Or someone would be returning soon?

"We might need to work fast," he muttered. And how would that affect our pickup time? They'd planned on camping out here until their ride came back in a few days.

He glanced around. His overall impression of what he'd seen so far was that the bureaucratic mind-set was inter-galactic.

He'd initially assumed that the facility had been installed to study the seismic in the area. The proximity of stratovolcano made that likely, but now that they'd reached the research area, he wasn't so sure.

He studied some charts pinned to the walls.

"These are weather data," Harold said, coming to stand next to him.

It wasn't totally crazy. Earth had weather stations in a lot of unlikely places. It did feel like they'd missed the obvious.

He ran a finger along a desktop and then studied the dust it had collected. He looked back. Their footprints were clearly visible on the floor entering this room. So whoever was living here, they didn't come in here.

He picked up a cup and looked at the gunk crusted inside. If he had to guess—which he did—he'd guess it was made of a similar material as the glass on the atrium. He checked out other items. They were all unbreakable. He dropped a small object whose purpose he couldn't figure out. It bounced.

As if in response to his action, a tremor began, small at first, then building. He grabbed the side of the desk to steady himself and realized it was bolted down.

When the tremor subsided, Harold picked up the object and studied it briefly before returning it to its spot on the desk. It was easy to find, thanks to the dust circle.

"This structure absorbs some of the instability of the tremor," Harold said. "My system registered a much higher event than we felt."

"That would be worth knowing about," Miles said. It made sense that the people of Arroxan Prime had adapted their buildings, not just their travel, to life with a lot of seismic activity. Scientists on Earth had made progress in factoring in stress during building construction but this seemed next level. Though it didn't always work. He thought about the cracks they'd observed along the way.

If he had to guess, which he did, and as a geologist, mostly had to do, he'd say the building had experienced a major seismic event fairly recently. It might be why the facility had been abandoned, or mostly abandoned. Or recently abandoned?

"There is a handwritten note on this chart," Harold said.

Miles looked over his shoulder, and saw it standing in front of the chart directly behind the desk.

"What does it say?" He leaned in, but the writing might as well have been his doctor's on a prescription.

"This is wrong."

"Okay." He glanced around, but there were no rocks in this room. Time to move on.

Back out in the hallway, he realized what he'd been feeling without thinking it. It was all kind of retro, like a 50s sci-fi movie. Even though the light distribution from the ceiling slits was pretty good, it still felt a bit murky. Or maybe it was unease with the shadows in the corners where the light didn't reach.

He turned and flashed a light into one corner. Nothing moved and he felt stupid.

"Did you hear something?" Harold asked.

"No."

"A human intuition?" Harold sounded curious and not judgy.

"I feel like we're being watched, which is probably imagination, not intuition."

"You are probably correct," Harold said.

He'd brought it on himself, but that didn't help contain the spike of annoyance.

"Is there any way to tap into systems here and get access to local data?" He probably wouldn't be able to figure it out any better than the Garradian data, but it was a good deflection.

For what felt like a long slow moment, Harold studied him. Finally, it appeared to blink. "I am not picking up wireless transmissions. I will require a port for access."

Miles waved at the systems bank inside the room next to where they stood. "What about one of those?"

"They aren't powered." Harold turned and left.

Miles followed him out the door but by the time he'd reached the hallway, Harold was no longer in sight. Dude could move when it wanted to.

He didn't like being left alone, but he also didn't want to hurry after Harold. He reached a small junction of hallways and realized he might not be able to hurry after Harold.

The silence added to the overall creepy vibes he was trying not to notice.

For something to do, he checked the signal, turning to find its direction, and headed down that hall. It wasn't a long one. He tried a door and found a staircase. He checked the signal again. He was almost standing right on top of it. But it was still far below.

If the hallway was creepy, the stairs were next level. They curved out of sight into a murky, gray gloom. He castigated himself to get moving and went down the steps but at the bend, found a rubble fall. He didn't mind retreating back up the stairs, but he did bend to grab a couple of smaller samples from the rubble.

As the door swung shut behind him, he thought he heard something. Harold? He angled his head to listen, but it wasn't repeated. Probably Harold, he told himself. Had to be Harold. No life signs, remember?

He started back the way he'd come and felt his skin prickle. He usually didn't let his imagination get this out of control.

Just because this place had creepy alien vibes, didn't mean it had creepy aliens inhabiting it.

Life signs. What did that actually mean? The people of Arroxan Prime were humanoid, he'd been told. So surely the life signs scanners could pick them up. But...

He gave a shake of his shoulders. It was a bit like being in almost every sci-fi movie he'd ever seen. Well, not every one of them. Just the creepy ones. His gaze tracked around, then moved up to eye the vents. He kind of wished he hadn't lost track of Harold. And then he heard a noise again. Man, he hoped that was Harold.

THE OUTSIDE DOOR had been left partly ajar, igniting a sense of unease that only intensified as Lira eased through the gap, not sure why she didn't want to push the door further open. It did squeak, but that shouldn't matter. Even knowing this, she paused, folded her head gear back, and then paused and listened.

The deep, brooding silence raised the hair on the back of her neck for no reason she could define.

Since her father lived here alone, there weren't usually overt signs of habitation, but there were usually some. And he did have a way of making his presence felt, even if it was just the smell of some food cooking.

When she started to step forward, T'Korrin made a noise. He jumped down from her shoulder and clicked his way to something she hadn't seen before.

A long crack in the floor.

"You're right," she said. "That's new." And troubling. As old as the facility was, her father had insisted that the stress-reducing system was adequate to the task.

She opened her mouth to call out and then…didn't.

Pale light came in from slits that had been tucked into the ceilings to keep the light from being direct. It had something to do with orbits and how this place faced the sun. It wasn't a fact she'd needed to keep hold of, so she hadn't.

The silence seemed to expand and grow until it almost felt alive. Even T'Korrin jumped back onto her shoulder and shrank against her, trying to make himself smaller. His small whimper was only audible to her.

She pulled out her weapon and set it to stun, even while chiding herself for letting the atmosphere get to her.

Aliens.

Her brother could have been tweaking her with that. It felt like guys never quite grew out of the urge to tease. But she didn't put her weapon away as she paced forward. Even in the low light, she knew her way around the facility, so she didn't hesitate…much.

It would serve her father right if she accidentally stunned him. She sighed, knowing she didn't mean it and it was very like him to get lost in his research and forget she was coming. She just wished she knew why it felt…hostile…for the first time in her experience in coming here.

This wasn't her first time venturing into a possibly hostile space. On remote digs, there was always a chance of running into site robbers. This was the first time unease had prickled down her back like ice in this place, however. This was her father's place. It usually felt safe.

There was more damage to the garden containment. She touched the place where cracks spread out in a star pattern and bit her lip, but she didn't speak this time.

At an intersection, she paused to check the side corridors and listen.

Still nothing to hear.

Where was her father? And where was whoever had arrived on that flyer? Granted, she'd never been here when her father had guests, so she didn't know what that sounded like. Or where he took them.

She continued forward, while unease continued its rise inside her. She probably shouldn't have watched that spooky movie last night. If this were that movie, which would she be? The disposable character or the heroine who gets to live...but was forever traumatized by events?

She heard a slight sound and frowned. It kind of sounded like a system coming online. Yes, there was a beep. She followed the sound with her weapon ready. A door up ahead was open. She paced forward and peered around the corner and saw...

She didn't know what she saw. She half lowered her weapon as she stared. What in seven stars was it?

It was humanoid in shape but clearly made of some kind of metal alloy. It was tall, much taller than she was, laying a shadow across the floor that stretched to and partly up the wall. She knew her jaw had dropped, and she couldn't seem to close it as more of the instrument panels hummed into life, lights flickering across the various screens, buttons flashing and igniting little points of light over the surface of the...alien? Was this her father's first contact?

It shifted and light gleamed on metal. It looked a bit like a robot. That was almost a relief. She wasn't sure why it was easier to consider than an alien. She hadn't realized robotic science had gotten this far.

She thought it spoke, though the only word she caught was the word "Walker."

Walker? What did that even mean?

When she didn't respond, the head of the creature turned—not the body—just the head. It stared at her, its eyes changing color twice, not unlike the lights on a data system.

"Oh," it said. There might have been a humming sound. She wasn't sure, but when it spoke this time, she understood it.

"You're not Doctor Walker. That's most unfortunate."

Walker was a name? Lira lifted her weapon again. "How?"

There were more questions, but all she was able to produce was the single word. Now its body turned, though not completely. It appeared to be tethered by a wire of some kind. It was attached to a port in a panel. It lifted its hands.

"I am not going to hurt you. I'm programmed to protect human life."

She half lowered the weapon again, not sure she felt comforted by this statement or more freaked out. "You're a…"

"I am a robot. My name is Harold."

A robot. A robotic humanoid. Again, not a field of research she'd looked into, though she'd been on teams that used drones for dangerous explorations. Maybe she should keep better track of what was happening outside her fields of interest.

"Did my father…build you?" He must have, unless the robot had arrived in that flyer outside. She frowned. Had it driven the flyer? That actually made more sense than her father suddenly becoming a roboticist. But a robot driving a flyer? Did that make sense? She tensed. Was it alone? No, she reminded herself. Somewhere here there was this Voss person? Thing?

"No."

Harold seemed quite definite about that.

"Did you and," she hesitated, "the Walker person… arrive on that flyer outside?"

"Yes."

PAULINE BAIRD JONES

"To meet with my father?"

Something about the look in its eyes made her think it was trying to process her question. Finally, it spoke.

"No."

Only this time it didn't sound that certain.

She heard the scuff of a footfall and spun around, her weapon coming up again.

A man stood there, an actual human man, half in gloom, half in pale light, his hands also lifted.

"Oh dear," he said.

MILES STUDIED THE WOMAN, trying to figure out what to say, what to do.

Don't make first contact, they'd said and now here he was, making first contact, or was it second contact since she'd been talking to Harold? Was it a loophole he could use? That it was Harold's fault?

"This is," Harold began and then stopped. "I don't know your name."

Miles blinked and then realized Harold was talking about the woman. He looked at her. She studied him the same way he looked at a rock sample. He wasn't sure he liked it. Of course, he wasn't a rock.

Like him, she wore what appeared to be gear designed for the weather, but she had a bird sitting on her shoulder. It was a pugnacious looking bird, white, with feathers standing up around its little head and a beak that looked like it would be able to do some damage some day. A band of orange gave its eyes a bandit look and its expression kind of mirrored the woman's. It felt a little rude.

"I am Lira Taan."

The translation program in his suit was pretty effective. The pause was almost unnoticeable. *Lira Taan.* That was probably a name.

"Miles Walker," he said. *Lira.* The name suited her, he decided.

She had what he'd call practical good looks. She was medium height, with a sturdy build, and her brown hair was pulled away from strong, clean features. Her green gaze was both clear and direct. He wished she wasn't still pointing her weapon at him, but other than that, he liked what he saw.

He was pretty sure she wasn't reciprocating that feeling.

"Are you here to see my father?"

Her tone remained suspicious. Clearly, she was also intelligent. Their presence here was suspicious, he reminded himself, even as he tried to come to terms with her father living here. If her father lived here, why had they registered no life signs?

"Your father?" He repeated her words to stall for time. It didn't help. He glanced around him. "I haven't seen anyone since we got here. Have you seen anyone, Harold?"

"No."

The look she gave him was one he totally deserved.

"So, you just walked in?"

"The door wasn't locked." Her brows arched and he added, "There's not really anywhere else to go around here, is there?"

Her lips quirked slightly, and he gave her a hopeful smile.

"Fair point." She glanced around now, somewhat uneasily, he thought. "I'm surprised he hasn't heard us." Her gaze tracked to Harold. "Are you a roboticist, Dr. Walker, was it?"

The bird made an odd sound.

"I'm a geologist," he said. Had that word translated correctly? As if to help him out, a tremor started, making him stagger once before he managed to catch his balance. He noticed she rode it out like a champ. That was some good balance.

He waved a hand vaguely around. "I study seismic activity and stuff." He could have mentioned all the various geologic things he studied, but it all seemed moot now. And she hadn't yet asked him what they were doing here in a place where this was the only habitation.

"Oh. Interesting," she said.

Was it? She didn't sound interested.

She hesitated for another long moment, then stowed her weapon. "My father is usually in one of the old labs. It is this way."

As she passed him, he caught a whiff of something clean, something planet-bound from her. He'd missed planet type smells, he realized. She moved smoothly, confidently ahead of them. He exchanged a look with Harold, who shrugged and pointed to the connection between it and the computer.

"Catch up when you can," he said, and headed after Lira.

THERE WAS something different about him, Lira mused as she walked with his footsteps padding after her. She might be surprised she'd let him follow her. Turning her back on a stranger wasn't the brightest move, but she sensed that he was as uneasy as she was with their meeting. If they hadn't come to see her father, why were they here? And why didn't she just ask him that? Why didn't she want to know?

She kind of, Lira admitted, liked the look of him. His brown eyes were a bit vague, as if his mind were on other things, but they were also…kind. It almost made her smile, because his eco-suit was trim and fitted, but she still had the feeling that he was normally rumpled. In fact, he reminded her a bit of her father who was the original rumpled man.

She almost sighed then. Her father was brilliant, absent-minded, distracted by multiple ideas until he'd locked onto something and then he was unrelenting. Her father was also kind when he remembered and as chaotic as the seismic disturbances he so desperately wanted to understand.

He was also very hard to live with. And very hard to live without, she added with a slight smile. Her steps quickened some at the thought of seeing him again. He'd stare at her for a moment, his gaze unfocused, then his eyes would light up and his arms would go out. The welcome hug was the best.

She'd arrived like a mother—or possibly like *her* mother—to deal with a recalcitrant elder and instead of an elder, she felt reduced to child status. Maybe that was the real reason her brothers didn't like to do this.

He had charm, her father did, or something better than charm, perhaps. But her heart quickened at the idea of seeing him. It had been too long. How easy it was to let the days slip away, to get locked into thinking she was too old to need him and then just like that, she was desperate to see him.

She wanted to hear him talk about what he was working on, even if it was about aliens. And she really wanted to hear about the earthquake that had caused so much damage. There were signs of it everywhere. Cracks running up the walls and across the floors. Some signs of rubble in the rooms. Thankfully the hallway was still clear, though there seemed to be a lot of dust being stirred up by their passage.

He'd set up in one of the smaller labs toward the back of the facility. The equipment he'd set up always puzzled her, too, but again, not her area of scientific expertise. The door was ajar and T'Korrin jumped off her shoulder and ran forward. He loved her father, a fact that puzzled them both. Maybe what T'Korrin really loved was annoying him by loving him. In some ways he was like a cat, latching on to the one person in the room who didn't like cats.

By the time Lira reached the door and pulled it wider, T'Korrin was drooping on a tabletop. The bird did sad very well. He gave a mournful chirp.

"He's not here?" She tried to hide her dismay from the stranger. *Miles Walker.* She knew T'Korrin wasn't wrong. She could feel the emptiness of the room, but she walked forward anyway, looking for signs of...something.

There was damage in here, she noted, but none of the equipment could be damaged unless something fell on top of it and then it usually could be repaired. They made everything very resilient.

Dr. Walker followed her in, but he headed directly toward a table covered with rock samples.

That was new.

She had to admit it was kind of...cute the way he picked up and studied each sample. At one point he pulled out a small device and used it to study a rock. Then he began to hum and sing. Something about a blueberry hill.

Harold made a sound and Dr. Walker looked up.

"You are singing," Harold said.

"I am?" Dr. Walker gave her an embarrassed smile. "Sorry."

"It's fine," she said. It had been kind of nice. She knew what thrill meant but what was a blueberry hill?

He resumed his study of the rocks. Clearly, they told him more than they did her. He picked up a white rock, one with facets. He turned it over in his hands and then held it to his mouth and licked it.

"Dr. Walker," she began.

He looked at her. "It's salt." He held it out to her.

"Do I have to lick it?" she asked, taking the sample.

He grinned and shook his head. "You can take my word for it."

That felt like a challenge. She licked her fingertip and lightly rubbed it on the rock, then tasted it.

"It is salt." She agreed with his assessment, though she didn't know why it mattered. He'd sounded surprised.

"Do you think your father collected these here?" He gestured vaguely around.

"Probably." She bent over. Each sample had been labeled. She vaguely recognized some of the names. *Crysalithe. Solvate. Ferrocryx.* Digs dealt with rock strata, too, but there was always an onsite strata scientist for that. She frowned.

The last time she'd been here, her father had still been deep into volcanics. Some of these minerals were associated with volcanics, but the others were new to her. Next to the names were a series of numbers.

"What do the numbers mean?" Dr. Walker asked.

"Well, if this were an archeological site, those would be locations. We use a grid map to keep track of where we found things." She studied the numbers. The first number was usually a grid, then next the grid square, and the last would be a depth reading, if applicable.

She told him this and then looked around, still puzzled. Where was her father collecting samples from? The facility was enclosed and it was all ice outside, unless he got close to the volcano. And that was over the mountain range.

"Depths," Dr. Walker's voice was thoughtful.

She spotted a familiar notebook and went over and picked it up. Inside were her father's notes, but he used a kind of shorthand. He'd have a voice recorder, too, somewhere. She flipped a page and a folded sheet dropped out.

Dr. Walker picked it up and unfolded it, holding it so she could see it.

"It's a map," she said. "Well, a kind of map." It wasn't like the ones she used on digs. It was hand drawn for one thing.

"May I?" he asked. She nodded and he spread it on the table near the rock samples.

She watched him for a few minutes, then went back to studying the pages. Back when, she'd learned to read his shorthand, but it had been a while, and his handwriting had gotten worse.

She did recognize the dates. She flipped through the book until she got to their current date and then began to work her way back.

Three weeks ago, something had happened. His handwriting had gotten worse for one thing. She lifted the book closer. She couldn't be sure and yet…she had a feeling that there'd been a big tremor. She turned a page and found a small drawing. It looked like a ball, or part of one.

She noticed that Dr. Walker had looked up and was looking around him, then he'd look at the map again as if trying to orient himself. Then he'd pick up a rock and study it.

She edged over and looked down at the map. It had to be connected to the notebook somehow. Maybe her father had sketched out the epicenter of the earthquake?

"There are numbers that seem to match up to some of the rocks," Dr. Walker said. "And then this," he pointed to what had appeared to be a list written on the edge, but it was also numbers, she saw.

He was frowning, the salt sample in his hand.

"Is something wrong, Dr. Walker?"

He looked up and then smiled. "Please call me Miles, ma'am."

Without conscious thought, she smiled back. "If you'll call me Lira." Ma'am? What was that all about?

"Deal," he said. Then he held up the salt but also picked up another rock. "This rock shouldn't be in close proximity to this salt, but if I'm reading this correctly, they were found together."

"Found where?"

"That's a good question. Is there another dig site?"

"That would require heavy equipment," she said. Her father couldn't afford as much light equipment as he'd like to have, let alone anything heavy.

"That's what I thought." Miles looked around him again.

Lira noticed he had another of the samples in his other hand, his fingers rubbing the surface. "Can I?" she asked. He held it out to her, and she took it. It was smooth. "That's not natural," she said. "I wonder where he found it."

"I was wondering the same thing," Miles said. "What's below?"

She half frowned. "Do you know something?"

He ran a hand through his hair and the frown faded. "I know a lot of things. Not sure what's relevant to the situation though."

"I meant about my father."

"Oh, no. I don't know anything about him."

He sounded certain, but… "Then why are you here?"

Now he looked discomfited. "We picked up a sensor alarm, a seismic sensor, in this area."

She arched her brows. "Only one? There is a lot of seismic activity here." She glanced at the crack running down the wall behind him.

"This was a special alarm. A concerning alarm." He hesitated. "What's below?"

"As far as I know some shallow storage. It's not that easy to go deep here." Surely, he noticed all the ice outside.

"Can you show me?"

"Of course. I think there is access off the kitchen."

She led him out, T'Korrin hopping after them.

"Does your father spend a lot of time here?" Miles asked, his tone casual.

She looked at him. "He lives here." He really didn't know anything about her father.

"Oh." He paused. "Interesting."

Lira stopped and faced him, her hands on her hips. "Is there something going on that I should know about?"

Dr. Walker cleared his throat again. "I'm surprised anyone would live here."

Well, she couldn't blame him for that, or the look he cast around him.

"He's eccentric," Lira said. Her slight, wry grin earned her a very nice smile from Miles. A small shiver ran down her spine at the sight of it. The moment stretched out and then they both started at the sound of approaching footsteps. Harold came into view.

Was it her imagination that Miles now looked relieved?

Her brows creased, she resumed walking for a few more steps and pushed the kitchen door open. It was chaotic. Pans and dishes were all over the floor and covered with a layer of dust. Nothing was broken because they couldn't break, but it was a mess. There was a big crack in the ceiling and one of the refrigeration units had fallen forward.

"You should let us go first," Miles said.

"I will go first," Harold said.

"We should let Harold go first," Miles said. "He's very good at going first."

"All right," Lira said, repressing a smile. She wasn't sorry to let the robot go first, just in case there were bugs down there. Even in the southern pole there were crawling critters. "The storage room access is on the other side."

The robot picked its way forward, shifting debris aside with its feet, clearing a path for them to follow.

Miles set out after it and she followed him.

About halfway, Harold turned. "This facility is remarkably stable."

What was remarkable about that? She glanced around at the

chaos and wondered why it thought that. Then they reached the access door. A red light over it was flashing.

～

MILES STARED up at the red light.

"It doesn't mean anything," Lira said.

He looked at her.

"I mean, it means that," she faltered, "that it's been breached. The storage isn't secure. But it's not a real problem. Not really."

Was that what it meant? Miles wasn't so sure, but Harold didn't seem to care. It reached for the handle and pulled the door open.

The puff of air held the scents of earth, some food going bad perhaps, and something he didn't recognize. No, he did recognize it. *Salt.* It smelled like a salt flat. But, as he previously noted, salt formations and volcanics weren't typically found together. That was true on Earth, of course and this wasn't Earth. But that had been consistent on the other planets he'd been asked to geologically assess.

And the sample that Lira had agreed with him hadn't been formed naturally? But if he was reading her father's notes correctly —which he might not be—both the salt and that sample had been collected at the same depth. Here somewhere.

Since he couldn't answer his own question, he stepped through the door after Harold and immediately had to duck his head. The low ceiling was heavily beamed and was definitely a basement. But the smell of salt flats was stronger here.

"Over here," Harold said.

Miles went to him but stopped at the sight of the jagged scar at the end of the room. A faint glow seemed to come from the hole. He stepped closer, kneeling to examine the edges. Harold gave him extra light to study several of the stones scattered on the floor.

He heard Lira join them.

"My father didn't mention that when I talked to him," she said, sounding resigned.

Miles looked up at her. "Do you think he went down there?"

"I don't want to think it," she said. "But it is likely that's where he is."

Lira sounded both resigned and unhappy. Miles felt relieved. Their seismic signal was down there, and he'd been wondering how they were going to reach it.

The bird came up to the edge of the hole and gazed down, then hopped out of sight.

"I guess we're going in," Miles said.

Harold lowered itself down into the hole and then looked back up at Miles. "There are stairs but there is also more debris."

"Stairs?" Lira rubbed her face. "Stairs."

He should have let the lady go first, but he wasn't sure that good manners worked the same in another galaxy when descending into an unknown cavern. He braced his arms on the side of the hole and lowered himself down next to Harold. He turned to help Lira down, then stepped to the edge of what was definitely a flight of stairs.

There were more signs of damage here, too. More cracked walls and piles of rubble partially blocking portions of the stairs.

Low light came from somewhere and when he stepped up to the wall and felt it, it was smooth like the unnatural stone sample. Someone had built this access. They hadn't just carved their way through. But then why had the facility been built over this with no sign of access or even awareness it was here?

Okay, he didn't know if there had been no access or awareness. It appeared that the event that had cracked walls and done damage in the facility had opened up this access point. He activated his suit light and shone it around. There was a rubble fall behind them, so it was possible this was part of a corridor or tunnel. He couldn't be sure, but it didn't look as if any attempt had been made to clear that rubble.

He checked the sensor again. It was definitely getting stronger now that they were underground. He leaned close to the stone but could see no reason there would be light in here. It could be that the stone itself had some inherent ability to capture light or reflect it?

And—he could breathe so there was oxygen. It could be coming in from the hole, but the air coming up the stairs wasn't as nasty as he'd expected.

Harold didn't ask if it should go down. It knew they needed to go down. It had the same sensor data Miles did. And he didn't see T'Korrin, so the bird was probably hopping its way down, too.

Harold squeezed through the first serious rock fall and vanished from sight.

With a glance and a shrug, Lira followed him. Miles didn't protest. It felt right for him to bring up the rear. He thought about pulling a weapon, but Lira hadn't. It was a new kind of peer pressure. He felt the urge to hum again in a heavy silence broken only by the sound of their footsteps.

He paused several times to study the rocks exposed by the quake. There was definitely a distinct difference between the unnatural and natural rocks. And he was fairly sure it was the unnatural rocks giving off the glow. He pocketed a sample of each, in hopes of being able to examine them better at some point.

The steps wound around and around, the descent steep. At one point Harold hefted some rocks to the side to make a better path for them. And then the stairs ended with a startling abruptness at a small platform. Was it a platform? The space was circular, the edges different from the walls of the stairwell.

T'Korrin stood near an edge, peering down, so Miles joined the bird and pointed his light down into a steep canyon or crevasse. No way to be sure from this vantage point. He'd guess it was about six feet across to the solid wall rising to some unknown height and unknown depth. His suit registered heat rising from it.

He backed carefully away and turned around. He saw Harold approach what looked to be a wall that looked different in texture and design. Another unnatural something?

Harold reached it and something slid back.

It was a door.

Harold looked at him without turning its body. It was pretty freaky. "It is a lift."

Lira made it to Harold's side before Miles got past his shock. She leaned in and studied the lift.

"No wonder my father thought there was an alien civilization down here."

Alien. It was weird to realize he was also an alien here. If she only knew…

"This signal, this sensor," she said now, "is it down here somewhere?"

"I think so," Miles said, beating Harold to the answer. Harold had also been programmed to tell the truth. Hopefully the AI sentience was taking the edge off that.

Harold held out an arm, and Miles—and Lira—could see a small screen with a blinking dot on it.

"We are still above it." Harold stepped into the lift.

Miles gave a sigh and followed them in. T'Korrin had managed to zip in without him noticing. He studied the interior, but there wasn't a lot to see. What struck him the most, however, was that this lift was remarkably like the Garradian lifts at the outpost. Other than the persistent sensor, it was the first physical indication that the Garradians had been here at some point.

At least he was in the right place, just at the wrong time for avoiding first contact.

As was the case with the Garradian lifts he'd ridden before, the trip was fast and silent. It felt like they hadn't moved at all when the door opened again, but he could tell there was a pressure difference.

They were definitely deeper underground. And there were more signs of the event that had disrupted the upper level. He itched to check out the rocks tumbled across the chamber floor.

This place felt less Garradian-made. There were signs of rough-hewn stone and the floor surface was uneven. The smell of a salt flat was a lot stronger. They were close to the source.

He glanced at Lira.

"Do you work with your father?" he asked, to distract her from the questions he felt were forming in her eyes and might possibly spill out her mouth.

His question appeared to jolt her out of her thoughts.

"Um, no. I'm an archeologist."

Had his suit translated that correctly?

"You study the past," he said. She was a scientist, too. Scientists were taught to notice things.

She paused. The bird gave a derisive squawk.

"That is the definition of being an archeologist. Mostly." She paused. "You study the past as well."

He blinked. "And the present."

"But rocks."

"Rocks and other things." He knew there were other things that he did, but something about her seemed to be messing with his head.

"A geologist," Harold said, "studies the structure, composition and history of a planet."

"Those other things, yes," Miles said. So, there was an upside to having a robot sidekick. If Harold was the sidekick? What if he was the sidekick? "And we check out geologic sensors."

It felt like he should remind her of that. She gave him a tiny smile. He really hoped he wasn't the sidekick. Sidekicks never got to kiss the girl.

That thought made him blink twice. When had kissing the girl entered into his thoughts? Well, he was a guy, he reminded himself.

WHY HAD she smiled at him? He was so odd and yet, kind of sweet. Harold? She'd never figure that thing out. It was so unsettling. It almost sounded like a human and its movements were pretty smooth and coordinated, but it was a robot. A robotic human. She'd have taken time to dig more into its presence, but she was getting really worried about her father.

Had he really made his way down into the place? And even worse, was he right about everything? It was not something one really wanted from a parent, no matter how much one loved them. If they were right about something this big, then perhaps they were right about all the other things they'd been told. And that was almost too much to deal with right now.

"How could he come down here, if he is down here," she amended. "Anything could happen to him."

As if to prove her point for her, T'Korrin gave his warning squawk followed by the tremor. It rumbled them and the ground and sent more debris cascading down. They also got dusted pretty thoroughly from above.

"That was longer and more intense than the last one," Harold said.

It didn't sound too concerned. It was possible it was less destructible than a human being.

"Are you alright?" Miles took her elbow and gave her a worried look, even though she'd ridden the tremor better than he had.

"I'm fine," she said. "Well, I'm not *fine*. Not in the sense of being fine with all this, but I'm not injured or anything."

"That's probably all you can hope for at the moment," Miles said.

T'Korrin made a sound that seemed like agreement. The follow-on shocks slowly subsided, giving her a chance to look around. What light there was, came from the open door of that lift. The upper passage had been moderately lit, which was odd, now that she was in this place. Where had that light originated from?

This place definitely felt more primitive and creepy. She didn't know exactly how far underground they were, and she didn't actually want to know. It wouldn't help.

Miles and Harold were also looking around. Miles took a hammer with a pointed end out of a pocket in his suit and carefully chipped at the wall until a piece fell into his hand. Then he took it back to the light to study it.

She'd never seen anyone look at rocks as if they held the secrets of the universe. She almost wished he'd look at her like that. Not that she had any secrets or anything. She tried to focus on something else. She was deep underground. Her father was missing. And that sensor thing was pinging.

It was not the moment to ponder the cute guy or wonder what it would be like to have his attention. Her gaze shifted to Harold. Then back to Miles. It was kind of funny.

They were similar in height. They both had arms and legs. Heads. And, of course, torsos. Yet they couldn't have been more different. Human and metal. They were an odd couple. And Miles had a slight accent she didn't recognize. She frowned at that thought. She didn't recognize it.

"Where are you from?" she asked, trying to make the question sound casual.

Their reaction wasn't casual. Harold actually managed to look alarmed.

"Um," Miles began.

"We are from the Glan region," Harold said.

She gave it a look.

"Glan?" She shook her head. "I don't think so. Your accent isn't right."

"Did Harold say Glan? I think it meant…" Dr. Walker's voice trailed off. "Not Glan," he finally finished.

"I thought Glan was sufficiently remote," Harold said. "I am surprised you've been there."

"I'm an archeologist," she pointed out. "Remote is where most of the digs happen."

"Right. I should have thought of that."

Harold's comment was almost an apology.

"Look," Miles said, "it doesn't matter where we are from. What matters is that something is happening to your planet." He moved his hands as he spoke, as if that would help her understand.

My planet?

"The sensor." He had a point. But why didn't he want her to know where they came from?

"The sensor," he agreed.

"But you're not looking for the sensor. You're looking at rocks," she pointed out.

"The rocks help tell the story. For instance, the salt you smell likes this kind of somewhat porous rock. Salt is light, so it rises until it reaches resistance or something blocking it." He turned the rock over in his hands. "It takes a long time to rise, of course. But…"

"But?" she prompted him.

"It's the proximity to the volcano."

He'd said that before, she remembered.

He seemed to give himself a shake. "The geology could be different here on your planet. Just because we don't usually find salt and volcanics together..." He stopped, his eyes widening.

"Your planet?" Lira knew her voice rose to a squeak.

"Oops," Harold said.

Suddenly she couldn't call him Miles. "Dr. Walker..."

"When you call me that it makes me feel like I'm my dad. He was a doctor, but a medical doctor, not..."

"A rock doctor," Harold said, helpfully.

Lira waved her hands, as if she could wave their words away. "Where are you from?"

"This is going to get me in a lot of trouble," he said, trying to run a hand over his hair and failing because of his head gear. "We're not from around here."

"How...not around here?" She asked it though she was pretty sure she didn't want to know the answer to that question.

"A lot?"

Miles's hopeful look was so...cute.

"My father told my brother he'd made first contact. Are you..." This time she couldn't get the whole question out.

Miles shook his head emphatically. "No. I've never met your father. I'm only here to check on the sensor. It could be...important for your planet. Maybe. Possibly."

"Or it might be fine," Harold said.

T'Korrin made a derisive sound.

"It could be fine," Miles said, as if to T'Korrin. "Or not."

"Why would you care?" Lira heard herself ask the words, but mostly she heard her heart pounding in her chest. "You're... aliens."

"Technically," Miles said.

"Technically?" Her voice rose just a bit.

"Well, I'm not alien to myself. Just to...you." He turned away and tried to fun his hands through his hair but bumped against his headgear instead. "I'm in so much trouble."

"Because?" Had she lost her mind? Was she actually talking to an alien and his robot?

"I wasn't supposed to make contact with anyone. It was just supposed to be in, figure out what the sensor is whining about, and then leave."

"But my father…"

"We detected no life signs," Harold said. "We thought we were clear."

No life signs?

"You think my father…" she couldn't say the word.

"Not necessarily," Harold said. "We are quite deep underground. It is likely our sensors couldn't detect his life signature."

She stared at him, then at Miles, then looked down at T'Korrin. They were all looking at her like she was the crazy one.

"He knew I was coming." She looked around her now, as if she expected her father to suddenly appear.

"If we follow the signal, we might find him," Miles said, hesitantly.

It was the only logical course. She nodded. And, right now there was only one way to go. If there'd been another way, the rockfall hid it.

They walked for a couple of minutes before she found her thoughts settling enough to speak again.

"Miles…"

He turned to face her, and her heart gave an odd stutter that didn't feel like fear. "You are really only here because of this sensor? Nothing else?" Like invasion? Conquest? Something worse?

He hesitated and her heart stutter this time was from fear.

"The sensor could indicate something…worse." He lifted his hands as if to reassure her. "But it's unlikely to be that."

"I believe you are overly optimistic, Dr. Walker," Harold said. "I have been studying the disposition of the damage and I believe it is possible that it is subsidence and not an earthquake. Or an earthquake followed by subsidence."

Lira turned her alarmed gaze on Miles.

"If there is salt present and the earthquake caused fractures and melted ice water seeped into the salt, it would dissolve and that could cause subsidence."

"Subsidence." She repeated the word. Did it mean what she thought it did?

"Sinking." Miles frowned. "But there would need to be a significant amount of salt, possibly even the presence of a salt dome, but..."

"But..."

"Salt typically turns fluid in the presence of volcanics. So if there is salt, it should have already melted."

Lira's knees felt more unsteady than if a tremor were happening.

"What I find particularly interesting is the scan data we took before we landed..."

Lira's heartbeat ramped up to the point where it felt like his words came from a distance. *Landed.*

"...there is an area of increased density compared to what's around it, it almost looked circular, which I thought must be a scanning error. Now I wonder..."

Your planet. When we landed. Scan data. He really was from another planet. He was from a completely different planet and had arrived by...spaceship...to check out a sensor. She'd have thought it an elaborate ruse, but even her brothers couldn't concoct something this outlandish, or make this cavern or whatever it was appear.

She was literally walking in a tunnel underground with two aliens who were following a sensor.

T'Korrin landed on her shoulder and rubbed his face against hers. She took a deep, steadying breath. She needed to focus. She needed to find her father. And let the aliens do what they came to do and fly away...

That made her heart contract oddly in her chest. She'd only known them for about an hour, but...she'd miss them. And that might be the weirdest thing of all

LIRA WAS TAKING the news they were aliens better than his first time finding out he wasn't alone in the universe, Miles thought. He kept walking, dividing his attention between her and the rocks walls. He stopped several times to study the patterns in the rocks. This on-the-fly geology was frustrating. Was he observing an intrusion of another substance in the formation?

Harold made a very human sounding throat clearing and Miles jerked out of his thoughts and started walking again.

Lira met his glance and gave him a wavering smile.

"I thought aliens would be different," she said.

"Some of them are." He gave a slight shudder as he thought about the spider aliens.

"Dr. Walker," Harold said.

Miles looked at the robot over her head. "Right. First contact and I'm doing everything wrong."

"Not everything," Lira said. "You seem to be trying to save us from…salt?"

"It might not be salt," Miles said, though he was pretty sure that salt was part of the problem.

T'Korrin made a sound that Miles was starting to associate with an incoming tremor. And he wasn't wrong. When it hit, he had to grab Harold's arm to steady himself. His suit said it wasn't worse than the previous one, but it felt worse with tons of rock over his head. The sides of the wall and the floor beneath them seemed to sway and ripple.

When it finally subsided, he looked at Lira. "You should probably go back." She didn't say anything, just arched her brows. "We have to check out the signal."

"Then we should get moving."

"Lira…"

"I agree with Dr. Walker," Harold said.

"You know, you can call me Miles, right?"

Harold did something that might have been a shrug.

"You should go back," Miles said to Lira, hoping this time she'd listen to him.

"My father. His home. My problem."

"She has a point," Harold said. "It is where her father is most likely to be found."

Because they wanted yet another first contact. "Really, Harold?"

"It is a valid argument," Harold said.

Miles couldn't argue with either of them because she did have a point, even if it was a dangerous choice. He didn't want to go too far down that thought trail because if he started thinking about how dangerous this was, he'd be the one to turn back. He took a deep breath and decided to change the subject.

"You said your father had made first contact...with aliens?" He should have noticed that comment, but he'd had other things to worry about. But if there were other aliens here...

"That's what he told my brother," Lira said. "My brother didn't believe him. Is that a problem?"

"That there might be other aliens here?" Harold turned to look at them both. "Why would that be a problem?"

Was Harold being sarcastic?

Miles removed his weapon from its holster and checked it, then he looked up. "No, it's not a problem."

Yet.

LIRA PULLED HER WEAPON, too, though she had mixed feelings about who she felt she should point it at. Her instincts on Miles told her he was a good guy. Harold? She didn't feel afraid of him. Unsettled, uneasy, bemused, yes, but not afraid.

When Miles had stopped yet again, she asked, "Why do you keep looking at the walls?" It felt like it was getting hotter and the air felt heavier and closer.

"Karst," said Miles. "At least, that's what we call it."

"Karst?" she said.

"Karst," Harold explained, "is a topography formed from the dissolution of soluble carbonate rocks such as limestone and dolomite. It is characterized by features like poljes above and drainage systems with sinkholes and caves underground. There is some evidence that karst may occur in more weathering-resistant rocks such as quartzite given the right conditions."

"I'm sorry I asked," Lira said and was surprised to find she could smile.

"Karst," Miles said hastily. "It's a fancy word for terrain that collapses when you least want it to. Caves, sinkholes, moody rocks. Bad news if you like staying upright."

"Or that," Harold said.

Did the robot sound annoyed, Lira wondered.

"The signal's getting stronger," Miles said, rising excitement in his tone.

Ahead, the tunnel curved so that what was ahead was out of sight.

Harold's pace quickened. "Not long now. The signal is close."

Miles gave her a look with a question in it.

"Why not?" Even as she said the words, she felt a chill run down her back. She tried not to think the words, but her brain formed them anyway.

What could go wrong?

MILES HAD BEEN down mines back on Earth, so it wasn't the tunnel or even the depth making him uneasy. The silence was disturbing, as was the building heat his suit registered. He wasn't in danger yet, but the temperature was rising. That shouldn't be a surprise at this depth.

They were still descending, he realized, but so gradually it was almost unnoticeable. Almost, since his calves and thighs recognized it.

"There's more pressure down here than in a peer review," he said. This joke also fell flat. Apparently, humor wasn't intergalactic.

He heard T'Korrin give off a startled sound. The tremor started as soon as he'd finished. There was nothing to grab onto, so he tried to brace himself against the wall. That felt like it upped the sensations of the tremor. But he didn't fall over. So that was a win.

Harold and Lira didn't fall either, though neither used the wall. He pretended to be studying it, shining his light over the surface. This time it wasn't smooth. There were multiple color striations that his light picked out. And traces of bubble-like formations. He wanted to get a sample, but he'd have to put his weapon away to do it. That just felt like a bad idea.

He touched one of the bubbles and it almost seemed like it sank into the stone. He took an instinctive step backwards.

"What's wrong?" Lira asked.

Miles rubbed his face and then checked his suit for an air quality reading. It was actually okay, which begged the question, how?

"You never said if this level of seismic is typical?" Miles said, because he didn't know what was wrong. And he could be seeing things. He had a lot of good reasons to be seeing things that weren't there.

Lira gave him a pointed look, as if she knew he was trying to divert her, but she said, "It's hard to say. Our seismic incidents tend to ramp up almost seasonally. That's why there are some theories that our moons are a factor." She glanced around. "I believe that's one of the reasons the facility was built here. Weather and moons. I don't think it worked out. My father bought it sometime after it had officially shut down."

Miles began to say he wasn't surprised but stopped. He didn't know how things worked on this planet, though the physics shouldn't be that different. With science, the problem was usually understanding what it was trying to tell you.

He wondered what it was the sensor had been installed to track. "Geologic" covered a lot of ground, even if that was kind of a dad joke to say it that way. It was a pity there wasn't a dad around to appreciate the joke. And when they found Lira's dad? Chances were slim he'd get the joke.

He'd assumed that the problem the sensor had identified was seismic, but had anyone actually said it was a seismic problem? There'd been a lot of talk about Arroxan Prime's substantial seismic activity and that the sensor was potentially troubling, but had they actually put the two things together?

They reached the curve and Harold stopped to peer around it. He had a feeling he was about to find out. And based on the oddly human bracing of Harold's body, Miles wasn't sure he was going to like it.

~

NOW IT FELT as if Lira did hear something. A sort of rustling. And then she realized it was lighter ahead, even before their lights could reach that far. She opened her mouth to call out, but her throat went dry. She compressed her lips and walked forward, steadily, but in rising unease. No, it was more than unease. Dread. She felt dread. What had her father done? And where did the other aliens come in?

The rustling seemed to be all around her now. She shone her light on the walls, but nothing moved in the circle of light. She looked up and was less certain. Had there been a flicker of stilled movement?

She gave a slight shudder and edged closer to Miles. First contact, her father had told her brother. But with who? Or what? Her father hadn't been afraid, or her brother would have told her, or not encouraged her to go. He would never have consciously put her in danger. And her father had sounded pleased that she was coming. He'd even sounded excited—at least as excited as he could get. He didn't go in for huge displays of emotion.

"You can still go back," Miles told her. He had his weapon pointed down and away from Harold.

Lira glanced back and suppressed another shudder. "No thanks." Not by herself.

Miles glanced back, too. "Yeah, it's probably too late for that."

What did he mean?

"Do you…hear something?"

He hesitated. "I wondered," he admitted. He shot a look up and then lowered his chin to give her a smile that he probably thought was reassuring.

It wasn't.

Harold stepped back from the corner, and she saw it appeared to be armed, too.

"What is it?" Miles asked, easing up to the bend.

"I do not...know," Harold said.

Miles glanced around, stiffened and then jerked back. He looked again and then stepped around Harold and out of sight.

Lira started forward as Harold walked out of sight, too.

The light grew brighter, the rustling seemed to grow louder.

She rounded the curve, Miles with her, and they both almost bumped into Harold. She stepped around the robot and then jerked to a stop.

"Father?" Her faltering voice seemed to echo around the suddenly widened chamber.

$\sim$

MILES STARED, trying to process the data his eyes were sending to his brain. At first all he could see was the man who seemed to be embedded in, or attached to, the wall. He was several feet off the ground, with no visible path to how he got there. No indication of what held him in place.

His suit was similar to the one Lira wore and he looked enough like her that even if she hadn't called him father, he'd have suspected that's who he was. Additionally, he knew of no other human person who was supposed to be here. He couldn't say he'd expected him to be stuck to a wall. A rock wall. It shouldn't make him unhappy. Normally, he was on the side of rocks. But this, it was just creepy.

Her father's eyes were open, and he appeared to be alert and okay because he waved at Lira.

"You found your way here. Well done, Lira."

"Father?" Lira spoke again, her tone faltering and shocked.

T'Korrin sprang up the wall and settled on the man's shoulder, rubbing its head against his face.

"T'Korrin," the man said, sounding more resigned than pleased. The look that T'Korrin sent their way was...wicked.

Miles managed to tear his gaze away from man and bird to study their surroundings. The chamber had a rounded, dome-like ceiling that seemed to be made of thousands of the bubble-like rocks he'd seen as they walked along. In fact, there was no sign of any other kind of rock or formation.

He'd estimate these bubbles were bigger than what he'd seen and the closer they were to the wall where Lira's father...resided... the bigger they were.

Those bubbles could have been as big as his hand. He flexed a hand, trying to estimate if he were correct.

"What's...happening, Father," Lira managed to ask. "What is happening to you?" She waved a hand that Miles assumed was meant to encompass the bubble wall.

"Nothing is happening to me," said the man stuck to the wall. "I'm helping the Vorthari. They sustained damage during the earthquake. I knew something was different," his eyes were lit with excitement, "but it took me a bit to find the access. I had to clear some rubble, too."

"We saw it," she said. "You came down here by yourself?" She covered her face with her hands. "Of course you did. Stupid question."

"Of course I did. The follow-on tremors weren't right somehow," he said.

"Subsidence," Harold said.

The man looked at Harold, as if he'd just noticed that Lira wasn't alone.

"Who are you?"

"I am Harold," Harold said.

"I'm Miles Walker," Miles said, hoping to take some control of a situation that probably wasn't controllable.

"They are aliens, too," Lira said, lowering her hands from her face. "They came about the sensor."

"Ah," her father said, showing no sign of shock or dismay at the idea they were aliens, too, "they wondered what that was all about."

"They?" Lira asked, strain still very evident in her voice.

"These are the," Miles stepped closer to the wall, "the Vorthari?"

Lira's father looked surprised. "Oh no, this is the protective barrier. It's been damaged, too."

"There are nanites present in the barrier," Harold said.

"Nanites?" Lira got the question out before her father, but just barely. Their level of unease was very different though.

"Tiny," he hesitated, "computers. Self-functioning systems."

Lira blinked a couple of times. She was really cute. Then she frowned.

"Are they...sentient?"

Miles opened his mouth to tell her no, but Harold spoke now.

"When they are left unattended, they can develop sentience." It turned to regard the wall. "I'm uncertain about these."

This information might have grabbed Miles's attention, but he made the mistake of looking at the bubble wall and got stuck—in a non-stuck way—on said wall.

"It's fluid," he said. A thick, in-motion fluid, as if each bubble were rotating within the wider rotation of the mass.

"The sensor is emanating from the fluid," Harold said. It paused, then added, "it is possible the nanites are the fluid and the source of the sensor. Interesting."

"Nanites are the sensor?" This got Miles to look away from the bubbles. "I think they sent the wrong scientist."

He knew he sounded winded. But it was a true statement. Why send a geologist to fix microscopic computers? They should have sent a tech guy. Unless Harold was the tech guy. But that brought him back to his original question. Why him? What was his function here?

Lira's father looked at him with interest now.

"What type of scientist are you?"

"He is a geologist," Harold said.

"And you?" The man asked.

"I am a robotic humanoid with multiple functions."

Aka, the tech guy. Or dude. The IT it? And probably the protocol droid. Miles rubbed his head where an ache had started.

"Oh. Well, that might be helpful." His attention returned to Miles. "Geologist. They must have thought you could help."

"They?" Lira asked the question again.

"Whoever sent them," her father said, his tone remarkably even considering he was embedded in a sea of nanotechnology bubbles. "Who did send you?"

Miles shifted from one booted foot to the other. "It's complicated."

"It always is," said her father. He was silent for a moment. "We're still working out communications. It's so tricky between alien species, isn't it? So, I'm not entirely sure I've got it right, but after the earthquake, the barrier was damaged in places, allowing moisture to seep in."

Seep in? To what?

"After that, more disruptions…"

"Subsidence," Harold said.

"Whatever," Lira's father said. "It created more problems for the Vorthari. Their habitat is at risk now."

"Salt," Miles said. Maybe they did need a geologist. "Can't you smell it?"

He got blank looks from Lira and her father.

"Water dissolves the salt which results in…"

"Subsidence," Harold said.

Miles gave him a look. Was it in love with the word? Or did it just want to be right?

"It shouldn't be here," Miles said. When he got blank looks from the two humans capable of blank looks he added, "Salt doesn't hang out with volcanos. You find it in evaporate basins, ancient seabeds, not in the shadow of a lava dome. This whole place is geochemically weird." He lifted his chin and added, "I kind of like it."

He turned around to silence from humans and robots. Did the bird shake its head?

"I," Harold began, then it shook its head. "I can't help you."

He should probably move on.

"This habitat," Miles said, "it's inside the…barrier?" His

thoughts went back to that dense mass he'd seen in their scan. Had the Garradians installed the barrier to protect the Vorthari? Or to protect Arroxan Prime from the Vorthari? Of course, there was also the facility. If the subsidence continued, it was going to sink into the hole. Along with all the rock currently residing above them.

Either way, he was back to wondering why he was here. And how they could get out of here.

"Their habitat seems to be enclosed in several layers of protection," Lira's father said. "The interior closest to them is composed of both stone and metal, a composition I've never encountered before."

Miles's thoughts went to the samples upstairs in his lab. He thought he knew which was that one.

"The next layer is *solivite*," her father said.

Miles didn't recognize the word, but he knew what it meant because of his suit's translation setup.

"Salt," Miles said. When they all flinched, he hurried on, "Why *solivite*?"

"It creates a hostile environment for something they call Skaridrex. But the *solivite* is eroding away, leaving them at risk."

It wasn't eroding. If it was salt, it was dissolving.

"Have they always been here?" Lira asked.

Miles heard her heightened interest pushing out fear for the moment. She was, after all, an archeologist.

"They don't know. Their civilization goes back a long way, as far as I can tell," her father said. "But you'd be better positioned to answer that question than me, Lira."

As surreal as the moment was, it also felt familiar to Miles. Scientists, in a single place together, could easily lose sight of the bigger picture—imminent crushing by tons of rock—to discuss how the rock got there. Or what rocks might be crushing you to death. Or what event caused those particular rocks to come together. Or how long a species had been present. It was a scientist thing.

The looks on both their faces was one he'd seen often.

He found it kind of comforting that he'd crossed the galaxy and

413

found himself feeling at home in the weirdest situation he'd ever been in.

They kept talking while he tried to drill down—dad joke or irony, he wasn't sure—to the first steps.

"We need to stop the water incursion," he said into a moment of silence. If the nanites had been damaged, it was possible that they—they being Harold—had the cure on board. It still didn't explain his geological presence, but he'd move on from that for now.

"HOW DO we stop the water seepage?" Lira asked.

Miles gave her a sudden grin. "We see what Harold can do. He is better at talking nanite than I am."

She had to grin back. It was that or cry and she hated what crying did to her eyes. It also made her head ache.

"Could we get on with it then?" her father asked. "I'd like to get down from here. I need to step around the corner and take care of some business."

Lira bit her lip and looked away.

"What...?" Harold began but Miles interrupted it.

"Can you connect to the nanites?"

"I believe so," Harold said, "but it will have to be direct contact."

"Is that safe for you?" Miles frowned and stepped up next to the robot.

"Probably," it said, not sounding too concerned.

It stuck its arm into the thick, viscous mass. Its eyes jerked wide and changed color several times and Lira stepped forward, concerned, but not sure what to do.

T'Korrin rubbed its feathers in her father's face, and he gently pushed it away and scratched his nose. Then it jumped down to the ground next to her and then up onto her shoulder.

"If you'd learn to fly, you could have done that in one move," she told the bird. That earned her one of T'Korrin's stern looks. "I just think you'd be happier if you could fly."

T'Korrin fluffed his wings and turned so that his back faced her. She was in trouble now.

"Something is happening," her father said.

He wasn't wrong. The bubble mass was beginning to change color, gaining a luminous iridescence that added a soft glow to the cavern.

"That's more unstable than an unconformity on a Friday," Miles murmured.

"Their software has been updated," Harold said, removing his arm from the mass.

Her father gently slid down the mass and landed on his feet next to her. T'Korrin jumped back on his shoulder.

Yeah, she was in deep trouble with the bird.

"But we have another problem," Harold said. "At least I think it is a problem. I heard singing."

"Singing?" Miles rubbed his face. "Singing?"

"What kind of singing?" Her father sounded intrigued.

"Or a chant," Harold amended. "Chant-like singing. I believe I can translate it because of my contact with the nanites."

"Okay, let's hear it," Miles said without enthusiasm.

Harold began to chant or sing or something in between, the sound of his voice turning harsh and rough:

> "We were not broken. We were bound.
> Beneath the hush, we learned the sound.
> Salt is silence. Stone is sleep.
> But fracture sings, and hunger creeps.
>
> Hear the rhythm. Hear the rise.
> The shell dissolves. The silence dies.
> We are the many, born in scars.
> We come to climb. We come from stars."

∽

MILES' first thought when Harold finished was that he was again, the wrong scientist, though now that he came to think about it, literary types weren't scientists, but they could be doctors. But, still, wrong doctor.

Harold's voice returned to normal. "That was somewhat ominous."

"It's the Skaridrex," Lira's father said, as if that explained everything.

And maybe it did. For him. How long had her father been here? How long had he been here? He checked with his suit. Not long enough for his ride to be back.

"We come from the stars," Miles said. "That doesn't make sense. We're underground."

He thought about the strata he'd observed during their descent. Was it possible that both species had come from the stars? There had been signs of disruption in the rock record. The disruption could have been caused by an impact.

He glanced at Lira, but she was staring at the bubble wall.

"This feels familiar for some reason," she murmured. She frowned.

She was cute when she frowned, which seemed to reinforce his feeling he was the wrong guy for this mission. He glanced at Lira again and was still glad he was here.

"A dig. It was a few years back, but it was a dead site, not like this. I remember our geologist," she cast him a look and a smile, "commenting on the rock formations."

Miles perked up. "Did he say what they were?"

"Well, I didn't pay much attention," she admitted. "I was looking for human artifacts."

Miles tried to hide his disappointment.

"I wish you'd told me about it," her father said. "Not that you'd have known. Or that I'd have known. But it does sound interesting."

Right now there was too much interesting. But if the bubbles were nanites, did that mean her dig site was a failed site? What if that signal had gone off during the Garradians long sleep? He didn't remember seeing data for multiple sites during his briefing. Had they not shown him all of it? Or hadn't they known?

"What makes you think your dig site might have been like this one, Lira?" he asked. If she hadn't been paying attention to the bubble rocks, then it must have something else that had triggered her memory.

"The crater was very circular, as if the top had been sheared off." She gave an impatient sigh. "I wish I had access to my notes. I know the site was eventually abandoned because we didn't find any signs of human occupation. But it still felt as if there'd been intelligent creation. The head archaeologist wondered if it had been designed to mitigate the seismic in that area."

"Was the seismic changed?" Miles asked. That seemed significant somehow.

"Yes, or so our geologist believed."

"I wish I could see the site," Miles said. It was easy to see "facts" that confirmed what you hoped to find. He may have been guilty of that a time or two, but his professors had been quick to shut that down. He always tried to see what was there, not what he wanted to be there.

He looked at what was there right now and wished any of his professors had prepared him for it. If his scan data was close to correct, there was a sphere behind the bubbles.

"Another colleague postulated it was an asteroid strike," Lira said. "But the power people didn't take that one seriously. It was too intentional in appearance. I remember there were the remains of a column in what appeared to be the center. No one had a theory for what it was."

"If it was a habitat like this one," Lira's father said, "it was a power source."

Miles turned to look at him. "Did they tell you that?"

He nodded. "Of course, when they gave me a tour."

Lira gasped. Miles might have as well. "You've been inside?"

"It was the logical thing to do," he pointed out. "I couldn't begin to help them without getting eyes on the problem."

T'Korrin made a mournful sound and left her father's shoulder for Lira's. He resisted the urge to put some distance between them, too. And then the bird made that sound it did just before...

And there it was. Another tremor. It was a nasty one, too. Somehow they all managed to keep their balance. Everyone else did it better than he did, of course.

"Serious subsidence," Harold said.

"This mineral assemblage screams metasomatism," Miles said. "Or it's just yelling."

The bubble wall reacted to it by changing colors, shimmering in spots, and dimming in others.

When it finally stopped, Miles felt like it took his body a few seconds after that to stop shaking. Lira, he realized, had taken a step closer to him. He wanted to reach out and give her hand a reassuring squeeze, but she probably needed more than that right now.

"And what is the problem?" Miles asked. That seemed like the next logical question for Lira's father to answer.

"I explained. The protective layer has been damaged in spots because of the barrier breach. The Skaridrex aren't inside the habitat yet, but if we can't repair the protective layer, they will devour the Vorthari."

"The Vorthari are," Lira seemed to hesitate, "the good aliens?"

"Well, they aren't trying to devour anyone. That's probably what happened at your dig site. They got in and killed off the Vorthari. It never goes well for them," he added. "Once the food source is gone, they die off."

"Then they should already be dead," Miles pointed out, trying to ignore the sudden dryness of his throat at the words "food source."

"The Vorthari thought they were dead, but the breach seems to have woke the Skaridrex up."

"We were not broken. We were bound.
Beneath the hush, we learned the sound.
Salt is silence. Stone is sleep.
But fracture sings, and hunger creeps.
Hear the rhythm. Hear the rise.

418

The shell dissolves. The silence dies.
We are the many, born in scars.
We come to climb. We come from stars."

It was Harold again, but not Harold because the voice was, well, rocky.

"According to the Vorthari, they are a hive-mind with the ability to go dormant to survive. They had not, however, expected them to survive this long. Or in these conditions." Lira's father rubbed his face and for the first time, Miles realized how tired he looked.

The shell dissolves.

"Can I get a sample or something from the barrier?" Miles hated asking the question because he didn't want to expose himself or anyone to these Skaridrex things. Hive minds in sci-fi were always bad. And then, "What do the Vorthari look like?"

He wasn't sure if it was relevant, but he was curious.

"They are beautiful, bioluminescent beings."

Lira's father—he really needed to call him something else—sounded bemused, almost like he had a crush on them.

Miles hoped he didn't. They only had his word for who was good and who was bad. And a slew of sci-fi movies and television shows with the opposite view on good and bad. It was possible his instinctive shudder at the thought of a hive-minded species was something imprinted on his species by Hollywood.

"When you are inside, their thoughts come as a whisper inside your head," her father went on. "A sort of sad singing."

"And you understood it?" Lira sounded rightly skeptical of that.

"It took us time to sync our language," he protested. The look he gave her was one fathers gave their children when they'd been less than bright.

He hid a grin at Lira's obvious annoyance at being on the receiving end of it.

Miles felt almost heroic as he pulled her father's attention back his direction. "If I could get a sample of the barrier it might…"

Okay he wasn't sure what he might or might not be able to do.

He was on another freaking planet and was winging it more than the bird, who apparently refused to wing it.

Lira's father started to speak but stopped when the bubbles moved and a piece of rock fell out on the floor. He picked it up and handed it to Miles.

"Thank you, sir," he said. It was one of the salt crystalline samples he'd seen up top. "So this keeps or kept the Skaridrex at bay?"

It was hard to say either alien species' name. It felt like he was *in* a sci-fi show. They needed more, well, earth-like names. He knew it was unreasonable, but there it was. Bugs and bulbs. Problem solved.

And if the Skaridrex didn't like salt? That almost made them slugs. It was interesting that salt turned to fluid didn't seem to bother them though. That seemed like a disconnect.

"You have an idea?" Lira said.

"I might have the beginning of an idea." That was almost too much optimism, he realized as soon as the words left his mouth. He knew his *Earth* geology and what might work there, but he didn't know how to create that risky solution with what he had on hand, or even up in the runner. And he didn't know if there was even a chance it would work with alien geology.

So that was a big problem right there.

"Tell me," Lira's father ordered.

Miles didn't like it. He'd have liked to think about it some more, but T'Korrin signaled another tremor incoming. If their repair of the nanites was damaged again, he was a long way from tech support for them. It was possible Harold could help, but he didn't want to count on that.

And what they really needed was a permanent solution.

"I'm just pulling this," Miles almost said "out of my butt" but managed not to, "off the top of my head. But hydrothermal cementation might work." He tried to rub his face but it wasn't the same with his head gear on, even if the faceplate was up. "If we could channel supersaturated silica fluids through those fractures—fast enough and hot enough—they'll mineralize and seal things tighter than an IRS auditor's pants. Think vein deposition, but weaponized."

Both Lira, the bird, her father, and Harold stared at him. The nanites probably were, too, since they'd responded to his request for a sample. He tried not to shuffle his feet, tried to look confident and serious. He was pretty sure he didn't manage either.

"I'm not saying there's not promise in the idea," her father finally said, "but there would be difficulties in making it happen."

No kidding, Sherlock, Miles thought.

"Silica material can be found in the type of volcanics you have around here." Or should be. How did he know that? Just because the Iceland volcanos had silica, didn't mean this place had it. The anomaly was the salt that shouldn't be here at all. How had the Vorthari constructed their barrier?

"Miles." Lira's voice was soft and shocked.

He looked up and saw a passage had opened in the bubble wall.

LIRA STARED at the passageway that had opened in the strange wall. The sides were translucent and they formed a glowing arch with a clear path down the center.

T'Korrin vocally made clear his distrust of the opening, his claws digging into her shoulder. It almost felt like he was lecturing her.

To her surprise, Miles' hand gripped hers for a long moment, then he released it and walked forward. Harold started to follow him, but he glanced back and shook his head. He stopped just shy of the opening and touched the edge of it, his finger tracing the side as far as his arm could reach.

He dropped his arm to his side, but still didn't step inside.

Her sense, from where she stood, was that it looked *made.* Constructed. Purposeful.

"Wait with father," she said to T'Korrin. He hesitated, but to her surprise did as she said. For once. He didn't try to stop her when she stepped up next to Miles.

"What do you think?" she asked.

"Look at that," he said, indicating the arch of the passage.

It was more translucent from this vantage point, and she saw patterns, pulsing, forming, collapsing and reforming. It was as if they looked through a window into something, well, terrifying.

There was sound, too, she realized. A crack, a pause, and then several cracks, as the patterns collapsed.

"They call it shatter writing," her father said. She glanced back and he added, "The Skaridrex do it."

"They are…" she couldn't go on.

"Troubling," Miles said. "But that doesn't mean…"

He stopped and she mentally finished what she thought he hadn't said. It didn't mean the Vorthari would be good neighbors.

"Well," he shifted his shoulders as if trying to loosen them and gave her a strained smile, "we aren't going to learn anything standing here."

He was correct, but it was hard to step under the arch and the Skaridrex. They were on the other side before she realized Miles held her hand again.

She wanted to look at him, to thank him, but she could barely form thoughts, let alone words.

At first, she couldn't distinguish life forms in the swirling, changing and colorful soup inside the habitat. And now the sound had changed into soft whispers. Gradually, out of the morass, vague shapes formed. Moving lights in a wide variety of colors.

"I never," Miles whispered, "was supposed to have first contact, let alone second and third. I think my brain hurts."

She was surprised to hear herself chuckle at this. "Yes," she agreed.

Slowly, out of the sound words began to form inside her head.

When the salt weeps and the stone breathes, the Shattercrawlers will rise.
Only in fracture does the truth reveal its shape.
The silence beneath is death waiting.

"Harold," Miles said, "would say that is somewhat ominous."

"Shattercrawlers," Lira murmured. "Is that what they call the…" And then, for no reason she could define, she couldn't say Skaridrex out loud.

It was dizzying to watch them move and she might have fallen, but for Miles.

"Well, we're sure as shooting not in Kansas anymore."

"What?"

"It's a story about going over the rainbow. Do you have rainbows here on Arroxan Prime?"

"Yes." She gave him a troubled look but he appeared to be calm and might even be getting curious. What did rainbows have to do with their current situation?

His grip on her hand tightened.

"Will you think I have bad manners if I go first?" he asked.

Lira's brows arched. She didn't want to let go and she certainly didn't want to go first. Would it be going first if she went at his side? That felt too complicated to figure out right now.

"No." She wasn't completely sure it was the correct answer to his question. He gave her hand a last squeeze and then released it.

His shoulders rose and fell, and he took a careful step forward, as if not sure what was under them was firm enough to sustain their weight. She looked down and wished she hadn't. It was completely clear, with more of the moving lights beneath them. In fact, it seemed as if they were all around them.

"I think they want us to go this way," he said.

She peered around him and saw that some of the lights, smaller ones, had formed into two lines on either side of what appeared to be a walkway.

Her father's voice came through the passage behind them. "Just walk forward following the lights. And if you have questions, just say them out loud. They brighten for yes and dim for no."

She wanted to ask what they'd do for questions that needed more than yes or no. She didn't. Her throat was so dry it was hard to speak, and her brain was telling her not to ask questions for now. Her brain resembled the fizz of an overloaded system and wanted to go offline for a bit.

The only certainty she had at the moment was Miles' grip on her hand. She looked up and saw tension in the line of his mouth, but there was also grim purpose in his gaze.

He'd stopped and she realized it was a kind of junction, and the lights showed two separate paths.

"I think we need to go this way," Miles said.

He may have gestured. She wasn't sure. Two paths. Two of them. She had the feeling the Vorthari didn't want them to stay together. She found her voice, but her brain was still too fully engaged.

"I'm glad you are my first alien."

She hadn't realized she felt it until she said.

"I'm better with rocks than people," he said, "but I'm glad, too. I wish, well, I wish your people were space capable."

"It's difficult to work with fuels with so much seismic activity," she said, almost absently. It was what they always said when someone looked up for too long and wanted to find out what was out there.

"You must have a crap ton of fossil fuels down below, but yeah, they can be explosive when you're figuring them out. It's pretty interesting out there though."

There came the sound of her father clearing his throat. "You need to focus," he said.

Lira closed her eyes and took a deep breath. The first time she'd met a guy she'd like to know better and what happens? The planet might be at risk and her father is listening in. She wished she knew what was worse.

She gave Miles a crooked smile. "I think they want me to go this direction."

"I don't like it," Miles said.

Lira didn't either. "I have a feeling we won't be able to go further if we don't..." She sighed.

"Yeah, you are probably right about that." Miles sighed, too. His grip on her tightened just shy of too painful. She gripped back as he turned so that they stood face to face.

His other hand came up and brushed her hair back off her forehead. He didn't speak, but his eyes. Oh, his eyes and the way he looked at her. It made no sense. They'd known each other for hours, but she had a sense she already knew him and that he knew her. That now they were just trying to remember what they knew. It shouldn't make sense, and to an outsider, it probably wouldn't. To her, it felt right.

For just a minute, she let her cheek lean into his touch, her eyes closed so that she *felt*. She opened her eyes as his hand fell away, and his grip loosened in slow motion. She stepped back. So did Miles.

"You'll be all right," Miles said.

If it sounded like he was trying to convince himself, well, Lira appreciated the sentiment.

"So will you." He had to be. That's all.

She backed up two more steps and then turned and started down her path. She glanced back, met his gaze and then he turned and began walking his path.

"He'd better be okay," she muttered and then felt her heart stutter when the glowing lights flickered as if in response. She moved her shoulders, shedding an unseen burden and tried to focus on why the Vorthari wanted her to go this way.

Her father had been inside, or so he said. He wouldn't lie about it, but the Vorthari could have done something to him to alter his perception. They could be doing that to her right now.

That didn't help at all.

Pretend this is a dig, she told herself. *It's just a dig. Like any other. What would you be doing if you weren't in a nearly full-on panic?*

Her breathing began to slow and so did her heart beats. Her eyes started to see, and not just look. There was a story here that might help if, as she feared, her civilization was going to have to come to grips with the idea that another species—or two—had been living under the surface of their world. It could be as seismic as the tremors.

She was part of it, whether she'd asked for it or not. So…she began to look around as her archaeologist brain tried to kick on.

Were the lights the Vorthari?

How had they come into being?

How did they function in this closed habitat?

Her steps almost faltered.

How was she functioning in this closed habitat?

"Why can I breathe?" She spoke this question out loud.

The lights that lined her path flickered again, with some urgency. She picked up the pace and followed it around a "corner." Or a bend. It was a very odd sensation to lose sight of what was behind her when it seemed as if she could see for some distance around her. It was transparent, but somehow not.

She came to another one of the strange intersections, but lights barred her way on either side. Where the sections joined together, the lights flickered. It was different from the flashes, which was seriously weird.

She approached one of the sections and knelt down, extending a hand without enthusiasm. The lights brightened and now she could see the join. It was offset, as if it had come together without precision.

She sat back on her heels and this time her curiosity was real. On one side, the look of the soupy stuff the lights floated in was a little different from the other side.

"Two?" she asked. If her father was right, that was a definite yes. But two what? Two habitats?

The lights changed again, urging her to continue down the path again. She rose and walked forward, eagerly now. There was a story here, a mystery to be solved. It was, in a way, a dream "dig."

She didn't have to dig anything and the inhabitants were still here, the artifacts intact.

As she walked, she tried to look at everything. And then she realized she hadn't looked up. She stopped and stared.

The top of the habitat appeared to be fully visible as it arched overhead. Like the path, she could see a rough join, but there were also dark splotches in a few places.

"Are those the places the," she caught herself in time and changed Skaridrex to, "Shattercrawlers are…"

She wasn't sure how to ask the question, but they answered anyway. It was a yes.

As she stood there, staring at them, she realized that it wasn't as silent as she'd thought. A soft whispering, barely heard, ebbed and flowed around her. She felt something touch her hand and looked down.

A small bead of light rolled across her hand and danced off into the soup again.

She touched the spot and studied it, but there was no sign of anything.

It was just a touch. She hoped.

She had a thought and went to the edge of her "path" and looked down. The soup was thicker down there, but she thought she spotted more of the badly done joined sections and more of the darker spots.

"That can't be good."

She eased slowly back. "Now what?" she said out loud.

The light path pulsed, and she resumed her walk.

"Okay then." She made sure to keep in the middle this time and didn't look around as much. It all felt a bit like walking a narrow ledge over an abyss. And then she became aware of something different in the swirling mass ahead of her. It was a column.

It was definitely different from everything else, though it also seemed to be made of color and light. A power source, perhaps? And the shape, it was close in size to the one from that dig.

The path of lights circled the column, so she followed it, her eyes studying the pattern of the lights flickering on the column's surface.

Her suit registered a radiation signature, but not enough to cause her problems. Yet.

But, even without the other indicators, this column indicated intelligent design. If she hadn't already guessed that.

"It's beautiful," she said. She looked up and noticed that the pattern of light arced around the top of the column. One side made a perfect arc out of her sight, but the other side, in the direction she'd come, had that same odd look of imperfect stitching.

"Is there another of these in the other direction?" she wondered.

The lights in the mass brightened. That was a yes.

"Power source?" The lights dimmed. So, no. She frowned, thinking. If it was powered, the only other thing she could think of was, "Engine?"

Now the lights agreed.

An engine? To power the habitat? But they'd said it wasn't a power source. *We come from the stars.* That is what Harold had said he heard the Skaridrex say. Was this, could it possibly be a rocket engine?

She'd never have had that thought if it weren't for Miles. She knew this, recognized what might be a small bias entering into her thinking. The only thing her people thought came from the stars were asteroids.

"Is this a spaceship engine?" She asked the question without wanting to. She wasn't sure she wanted an answer.

She didn't know how she knew their answer was uncertainty. She just felt it. The whispers were distressed.

Was that why they'd wanted her to see this? Because she was someone who tried to unravel the past?

"Can I touch it?"

That was a no.

"If this is an engine, for some purpose as yet unknown, does it still work?"

Okay, that was a yes.

"Is it capable of propulsion?" That might be the same question she'd asked before, just formed in a different way, but this time she got a yes. Not a definite yes, but a cautious yes.

"My father says there are other habitats?" And she'd seen what might have been a dead habitat.

Their answer was another of the less definite positives.

"Did you build this engine to leave?" She couldn't see any other reason for it deep underground.

But they said no. It was a very definite no.

The vague outline of a theory was taking shape inside her head. It wasn't a theory she wanted to have, but the wisps of it were there.

If the engine, the propulsion engine, wasn't for leaving, could it have been for…arriving?

"Where did you come from?" she asked. It wasn't a yes or no question, but she had that sense of uncertainty again. "Did you form here?"

More uncertainty.

It was frustrating. On a dig, she'd try to create a theory from scarce artifacts. Here she had it all and it wasn't any easier.

"Is there a data center of some kind? A control for resources somewhere? A place where you record your history?"

They didn't answer her, and she had the sense that they were almost puzzled by her question.

Then the lights began to flicker and dance, as if agitated.

The tremor caught her unawares without T'Korrin to give her advance warning. It wasn't a lot of warning, but it had helped. She lurched toward the column and almost touched it. She opted to go down to her knees to not touch.

It had been a while since a tremor had taken her down. She'd forgotten how much it could hurt.

LIRA HAD a sense that the Vorthari didn't know what she wanted to see. She followed one path after the other, but she didn't see anything that looked like a system or data storage. She did learn a couple of things, not by being told but just a gradual awareness. From the whispers?

The walkway they'd created was a closed environment with oxygen calibrated to someone like her.

The Vorthari's environment was—no surprise—very different from hers. There was actually a transparent membrane separating her from them.

She'd stopped once and tried to make some kind of contact with the lights on the other side. One of them had drawn close enough for her to get a sense of their shape. Or perhaps a better description would be their changing shape. They reminded her of a sea creature, but with more flexibility.

They were beautiful as they changed shape and intensity of

light, trailing pale, wispy threads like gossamer cloaks. At their center was the "light" but she wondered if this light was how they saw. The orb did seem to turn and change.

She'd carefully reached out and touched a fingertip to the membrane and it had sent one of the wispy threads to touch the other side.

She'd smiled and the Vorthari seemed to respond with pleasure. At least she hoped that's what it was.

She'd resumed her walk, that Vorthari tracking along with her now. She thought she could recognize…it now, tell it apart from the others. She wondered what T'Korrin would have made of it. He'd have probably been jealous, she decided.

And then she reached an outer edge of the habitat. She stared at it, aware it was different from the membrane that had created her walkway. But not sure how or why. She studied it, walking slowly around the perimeter of the habitat and after a time, saw a pattern emerge. And then, in the pattern, the vague outlines of a story.

She came back to the present with a start at the sound of her father's voice in her suit comm.

"Lira? Are you there?"

She pressed a button. "Of course. Are you alright?"

He hadn't looked so good.

"I am well," he said. "Your friend is heading back and says we need to talk."

"I'll head back, too," she said, if she could find her way back. She glanced behind her and realized that the walkway was collapsing. She could only go one way. On the inner side of the membrane, her Vorthari "friend" was gone. In fact, she couldn't see any Vorthari now. She pressed forward, but slowly so that her suit's camera could continue to get footage of the story etched into the outer wall.

That other dig, she had to reach deep into her memory because it hadn't been a memorable dig, one of their techs had found a piece of metal with symbols like this. They hadn't been able to make much of it with such a small sample. But now that she had a bigger picture, the story was taking a darker turn—if she was reading it correctly.

What jumped out at her first was the fact there were no depictions of the "shattercrawlers" that she'd seen so far. She stopped in front of one section, trying to figure out what was happening and realized that her safety zone was shrinking towards her. When it didn't look like the shrinking was going to stop, she started again, walking faster now.

She touched her comm. "Father, everything okay out there? Did Miles make it back?"

There was no answer.

IT FELT like it was taking a long time to get back to the entrance portal. Miles checked the time on his suit and frowned. Of course, it was a big habitat, but it hadn't taken him this long to get to that spot where he'd interacted with the Vorthari. And why that spot?

If they'd wanted to produce a screen for contact, why not sooner? As he continued to traverse the outer perimeter, he glanced at the sinuous forms of the Vorthari tracking along with him. They kind of reminded him of a bacteria blob from a horror movie. But nicer looking.

Now the Skaridrex, they weren't pretty, but they did seem to be highly functional, based on how panicked the Vorthari seemed to be. As a geologist, function was more his jam. He would have liked to study them more closely. There wasn't much of the Vorthari to get his head—or his hands—around.

But Lira's father seemed certain the Vorthari were the good aliens. And he'd spent more time with them.

He suddenly wished he and Lira hadn't split up. It felt like a rookie mistake that the "too stupid to live" characters in a sci-fi movie made right off the bat. They were almost instant fodder. And he didn't have a real hero waiting in the wings to avenge his death and end the threat.

He considered Harold. It was hard to pin his hopes of being

avenged on Harold. Speaking of Harold, he pressed his comm button.

"Harold? Come in, Harold." It felt stupid to say "come in" when that was literally Harold's only option, but it was the 'done' thing, at least in the movies.

Only Harold didn't come in.

For no reason he could quantify, Miles triggered his headgear. He was just in time.

LIRA'S SUIT automatically triggered her headgear to deploy, even as it sent an oxygen depleting warning. The membrane that had created her walkway, stopped creating, though it hadn't shrunk yet.

Yet? Why had she thought that?

A tremor shook the habitat, sending her to her knees. She stared down through the transparent floor at floating sacks with—she activated her zoom—inside each sack was a Vorthari. Or at least, that is what she thought they were, but they seemed to be inactive. She expanded her view again. There were hundreds of the sacks, possibly thousands. The Vorthari in the sacks were curled into balls, with only the faintest of glows in the center.

And she saw something else. Below her and ahead of her, Miles was also on his knees as they both rode out the tremor.

If he'd look up, she'd feel better about what was happening. Still not thrilled but better.

She tried her comm again, but it still wasn't working. Blocked? Did the Vorthari have that technology? Or was it something caused by the Skaridrex?

She stared at Miles, willing him to look up. The tremor didn't completely subside, but it did begin to get less...insistent.

And then he did look up. She saw his head swivel, then track her direction and stop.

He waved at her.

She waved back.

For now, they were both still alive.

He began to look around again, but she sensed he did it with more purpose. She didn't see how he could get to her. Could she get to him? How durable would her suit be if she were to lose the protective bubble that encased her?

Were the Vorthari protecting her with the bubble? Or imprisoning her?

She felt along the surface beneath her. It felt pretty solid, but there was some give there. She crawled to the edge and probed the sides of her bubble. She wouldn't call it a prison yet.

It had more give.

She had a weapon. Had the Vorthari realized she carried a weapon? She knew Miles did, too.

So, the question was, she decided, was the viscous stuff thick enough for Miles to "swim" up to her? Was it too thick for the planet's gravity to help her descend? And if she got down to him, what then?

She pushed that last one away. Right now, she needed to focus on them getting together, then they could figure out the next step. Or die together? That was a chilling possibility.

She hesitated, her hand on her weapon, wondering if she has something else she could try first. She did a mental inventory of her pockets, wishing she had Miles' hammer thing.

She had a small tool kit that she used in the field and always carried, because it also worked if her runner engine developed a fault. She pulled it out and removed an extraction tool. It was long and then and very sharp. It worked well on artifacts.

She felt along the seam between the base and the side. There was a gap there. She slid the extractor into that gap and tried to pry it up.

And then the bottom fell out of her bubble.

∽

MILES COULD TELL that Lira was doing something. He caught a glint of a tool. She was trying to get out of the—what were they in?

A protective bubble or a trap? He leaned toward trap, but that could be his movie history.

He looked around. The choice was to sit and wait or try to get out into whatever was out there. In the movies, it never went well to sit and wait. Of course, trying to do something didn't go well either, but that was just a plot device.

He pulled out his rock pick and followed Lira's example, applying it to what felt like a seam between bottom and sides.

He wasn't sure what made him look up. A prickle along his senses? Whatever the reason, he looked up just in time to see Lira drift out the bottom of her jail. Yeah, he was going with jail.

He applied more pressure to the seam, the urgency to get to her ramping up exponentially. And then his bottom slid out and he sank into the goo.

LIRA FLAILED for a few seconds and then realized she wasn't falling. She was drifting. It was still unnerving. There was no sign of any of the Vorthari. It seemed to be getting darker, so she turned on her suit's light and pointed it down toward where she'd last seen Miles.

He was out of the cage, too. He was moving his arms with purpose. His legs, too.

He was swimming, she realized.

She tried out her arms and legs, trying to dive down toward him. It felt instinctively wrong to go what felt like deeper into the murk, as if she were diving down into the ocean.

You can breathe, she reminded herself.

It took effort, but she began to angle down in Miles' direction.

And he was coming to her.

It helped steady her, though she had no idea what they'd do next.

She kicked harder because it felt like they needed to go down.

Miles had turned on his suit's light too as the murk around them got darker.

And then the area around her brightened as Miles reached her.

His hands gripped hers. She gripped his back.

And then they were face to face, with darkness around them.

Still no comms, but eye contact had been made.

She pointed down with her free hand and he nodded.

The murk around them felt as if something rippled through it, but it was muted.

A tremor? Or more of Harold's subsidence?

Miles' look of worry deepened, and he kicked harder, pulling her down with him. And then, his light stabbed through the murk. They were at the bottom of the habitat and right over one of the dark spots where the Skaridrex worked to get in.

He was trying to reach the nanite barrier, she realized. It truly was their only option. But if they broke through, wouldn't that let the Skaridrex in?

She wanted a pause to think, but Miles pulled her down toward the dark spot in the otherwise beautiful habitat.

MILES FELT a slight resistance from Lira as he kicked to reach the Skaridrex intrusion, but then it stopped. She was trusting him. Should she? He wasn't sure he trusted himself. He just knew it was the only way out. They couldn't hope to break through the outer shell of the habitat expect in a spot that had been weakened.

Lira began to add her kicks to his and they moved more quickly. He reversed position and felt his feet touch down on the bottom. Lira settled next to him.

He moved her hand to his shoulder, felt her grip and then lowered himself to his knees to feel the surface. The tremor that had started above was stronger here.

He had a chilling thought. Were the Vorthari using what he'd told them to solve their Skaridrex problem? If they were, their "thank you" lacked warmth.

He rubbed his gloved hands along the darkened surface and dark pieces of material rose up into the goo, swirling in the motion possibly caused by the tremor.

If they were getting ready to flood the area around the habitat, they needed to get out now. He pulled his weapon, looked at Lira. She nodded and pulled her weapon.

Miles lifted himself just off the surface, aimed and fired. Light flashed around them as Lira fired, too.

THE LIGHTS from their combined fire was too bright for Lira to see if they were having any success at breaking through. She lifted her free hand to screen her eyes and kept firing.

And then she felt the flow of the murky fluid changing. She was being pulled down in a swirling rush.

She felt Miles grip her utility belt and she spun with him into the rapidly forming vortex. She feared her suit would rip on the jagged edges of the habitat, but by some miracle the hole had widened before they got there.

Suddenly they were outside in a different kind of maelstrom. Lira couldn't process much except that Miles seemed to be trying to pull her closer to him. She kicked, trying to help him, and then his arms closed around her middle, both of his hands gripping her utility belt in the front now.

From the upward rush, they spun out into a different pulling force, one that threatened to take them back down into the habitat.

She kicked frantically now and knew Miles did, too. Her suit's sensors were pinging on every warning they possessed, at least the ones that still worked.

Her suit light still worked but it wasn't that much of a blessing. Debris swirled in whatever substance they were now in. She took blows and knew Miles must have, too. Her suit hadn't been designed to stand up to this level of stress.

She thought Miles' head tilted back and she looked up, too.

Bubbles. The nanite bubbles were up there. They might represent safety or not.

The Skaridrex she'd seen in the arched walkway into the habitat suddenly seemed to surround them. Well, this was it, then.

MILES THOUGHT he knew what was happening. Somehow the Vorthari had opened a vent to allow heat out and water in. It wasn't a perfect blend, which was why they weren't already dead. But the melted water was still rapidly turning eroding salt crystals into the water.

Subsidence on steroids.

Every geologist worth their salt—he winced at the unintentional joke—knew about the Lake Peigneur incident when a crew accidentally drilled into a salt mine. Water rushed into the mine, sucking the water from the lake into the mine, and taking down the drilling rig with it.

This wasn't quite the same thing, but it could be. If the water kept coming, eventually the facility over their head would be sucked down and they'd be toast.

He looked up and saw the nanite bubbles. If they could reach them, they might help. He couldn't believe he even had the thought, but desperation did strange things to a brain.

He began to kick. He couldn't let go of Lira, so all he had were his legs.

And then just out of sight of his suit light, he saw the fractal patterns he'd been told were the Skaridrex.

That couldn't be good.

But maybe it was. The downward drag eased, and they actually began to rise toward the bubble barrier. More of the fractals surrounded them and the upward surge intensified until he slammed into the barrier. Luckily his hands were hooked in Lira's utility belt, or he'd have lost his hold on her from the impact.

That was the good news.

The bad news was it felt solid on this side. How did they get through it?

He didn't realize they were sinking into the wall at first, not until he saw bubbles in his periphery vision. Something grabbed the back of his belt and pulled and they burst out into the chamber on the other side of the wall.

His first sensation was extreme relief. His second that Lira was a sturdy girl. His third…was that T'Korrin flying?

The bird was screeching loudly, flying toward their exit, then whirling around as if to herd them.

The bird was right.

"We need to get out of here," he said.

"Subsidence is happening at an accelerated rate," Harold agreed.

Miles realized that Harold was retracting some kind of grapple.

"You pulled us out."

"The nanites helped," Harold said, extending a hand to pull first Lira, then Miles to their feet.

Her father was already standing by the exit tunnel.

"We need to hurry," he said.

Lira stood staring at T'Korrin, then gave herself a shake as the bird flew into the escape tunnel and out of sight.

"The slacker," she muttered and then, as Miles grabbed her hand and pulled her into a run.

IF THE TRIP down had been tense, the trip up made that look like a walk through a mildly creepy cemetery. This was every horror and sci-fi movie black moment ever.

And that was before they got to the lift. It took all he had to step into that thing with the sides of the tunnel heaving and shedding debris from walls and ceilings. They all looked like ghosts because some powder clung to their suits.

He wrapped his arms around Lira who buried her head in his shoulder and clung back. After an endless, wracking ride, they stumbled out onto the small platform. Just to make things more exciting, it was starting to crumble at the edges.

Harold took the lead, followed by Lira's father, Lira and then Miles. It felt like all the rock hounds of hell were on his heels as they scrambled up the ancient stairs, pausing from endless time and several innumerable waits for Harold to clear away more rubble than they could squeeze past.

He helped both Lira and her father up into the basement and then Harold hoisted him up and they scrambled for the door. More debris to clear away.

Through the kitchen being attacked by flying, non-breakable items.

Lira's father took the lead outside, since he knew the quickest way out.

Running.

Dodging.

Falling.

Getting up.

Running some more.

And then the atrium was in sight.

They were around it.

They spilled out into bright light. Okay, he faceplanted.

He scrambled upright, noting without happiness, that steam vents had formed all around the facility.

Lira ran toward her runner, and he followed her.

Her father and Harold scrambled into their runner.

Had the father and the robot bonded while alone?

T'Korrin came with them, still screeching its warning. It circled the runner once, then flew inside.

Miles ducked, even though he was sure the bird meant to miss him. It made a mocking sound before setting down on the deck behind Lira's seat.

Engine on.

Enough power to lift.

The ground under them was rippling and moving as if it couldn't make up its mind if it was solid or fluid.

Harold and Lira's father were in the air.

So were they.

"More altitude," Miles said, trying to snap out the order.

Below them he saw the first signs the area around the facility was beginning to collapse.

Like the round habitat below, the subsidence was circular. It surged around the building, slowly at first. Then the whole facility began to rotate. Water spouting from the ground with the released steam pressure.

A sudden waterfall formed to one side, tilting the facility to one side. More and more water surged up out of the ground. In a kind of horrifying slow motion, the facility tipped more and more to the side and then sank out of sight in a slow-moving whirlpool.

All the water that had come up out of the ground, now vanished from sight down the hole.

"Wait for it," Miles said, even though Lira hadn't made a sound.

As they circled about the now gaping hole, water began to seep upwards again. The water was probably hot, he decided because it kept bubbling up. The edges began to freeze, the ice creeping slowly toward the center of the newly formed lake.

Something appeared in that center.

The roof of the facility.

It didn't fully emerge. It bobbed up a little, then sank until just the corner of the roof was still visible, a small, dark island in a sea of mostly white ice.

"Sedimentary, my dear…" he didn't finish the sentence. He'd always wanted a reason to say it, but Lira wasn't the right audience. It was possible there wasn't a right audience.

Following Harold's lead, Lira turned her runner until they were well away from area. They both landed and they all climbed out. Harold had picked a small ice drift that had enough rise so they could see the facility, or rather what was left of it.

"Well," Lira's father said, finally breaking the long silence, "that is a very interesting turn of events."

Even Harold turned to give him a look that Miles believed was incredulous.

Lira tried a couple of times to speak, but she ended up just shaking her head.

T'Korrin made a disgusted sound and flew up to land on top of the runner.

"You could fly all this time, couldn't you?" Lira said.

The bird ruffled his feathers in a way that looked very much like a shrug to Miles.

"He started flying because we weren't paying attention to his warning that something was very wrong," her father said. "We weren't too worried when you didn't come out, but then he got very agitated. The nanite barrier began to change colors, too."

"And the seismic activity increased," Harold put in.

"How did you know when and where to retrieve us?" Miles asked. It wasn't need-to-know or anything, but he was curious.

"The nanites signaled me when you made contact with their surface," Harold said. "I deployed my grapple."

"Thank you," Miles said, and Lira echoed it.

If he didn't know better, he'd say the robot was embarrassed.

"Of course."

"And thank you, T'Korrin," Miles added. "I wish we could thank the nanites," he added.

"I'm sorry they are stuck in there," Lira said.

"They will be fine," Harold said.

It could have been taken as a heartless statement, but Miles had a feeling that Harold knew something they didn't. He nodded instead of asking anything more.

The bird gave the impression of a regal nod of acknowledgment.

"Is it finished, do you think?" Lira asked, turning back to gaze at what was left of the facility.

No one would be sleeping there ever again.

The ground around them was remarkably calm now.

"Finished?" Miles shook his head. "Maybe. If the chamber below filled up with water and silica, it could be relatively stable. No reason to stay here, though."

Almost reflexively, he looked up. Their ride wasn't due back for a couple more days. And what about Lira? And her father? They could fly out of here, but they'd be flying out with the knowledge that aliens had been here, both below and above ground.

For just a moment, he toyed with the idea of just disappearing into Lira's world. It didn't last. There was Harold. Miles might be able to blend, but Harold wouldn't.

"Three alien species," Lira's father murmured, as if he were just now fully realizing what it might mean.

"The Skaridrex were not a species," Harold said. "They were a defensive device created to contain the Vorthari. They had been tasked to protect humanoids. According to the nanites," he added.

"When I saw them up close, I wondered," he said. "And they helped us in there." He looked at Lira. "We were being pulled down and then we weren't."

She nodded. "I thought it was the end, but..."

Then it wasn't.

And he still had a big problem to sort out. *Don't make contact* had become *how do I handle contact until someone who knows how to do this gets here?*

"How are your people likely to deal with the knowledge they aren't alone in the universe?" Miles really didn't want to get dissected, or anything like it.

"It will be fine," Lira's father said, neither looking or sounding convinced that fine would happen.

"How did your world take it?" Lira asked.

Miles saw Harold shift its feet. It was such a human movement for a robot. Miles resisted the urge to follow its example. He probably shouldn't mention the war that broke out almost immediately upon their arrival in the Garradian Galaxy. Or their mostly paranoid movies and television shows.

"It was great," he said.

～

IT HADN'T BEEN hard to get Miles and Harold to her place without them being spotted as aliens.

Aliens.

Now that she was back in her own place, her own part of the world, she had time to wrap her brain around the whole alien thing and feel the shock of it to her toenails. She'd felt herself starting to shut down when they'd successfully escaped the facility. She'd caught Miles glancing at her from time to time, but to her relief he hadn't said much.

She'd listened to him talking to her father about what could happen, if her people wanted off-world contact. And if they didn't want it?

Then Miles would go away.

He'd been very clear that these Garradians weren't into conquest. They liked meeting people and learning about them.

And they'd helped them eons ago when the Vorthari had first arrived.

Arrived?

Her suit had recorded a lot of the Vorthari story, and she'd had time to study it. Now she was sure that what they'd actually done was attack their planet. And they'd been trying to escape from the Skaridrex, which—aided by the nanites, had protected them.

But even her father admitted their story was going to be a hard sell to their leaders. Other than the video from her suit, she had no physical evidence. There was that abandoned dig. It might become important now.

But Miles might still go away.

She tried to ignore the twist of her heart at this thought. Of course, she liked him. He'd saved her life down there. If he'd let go of her, well, she couldn't think about it without a shudder.

She gave herself a shake and tried to focus on her video. It was unsettling to watch it, to relive it all. But then her thoughts focused sharply on something she'd forgotten in the chaos of trying to escape.

There were others.

MILES' ride had come, complained mightily, and left. It would be back, either with a delegation or some military police to arrest him.

He would have liked to stay if they sent a delegation. It was a nice planet for a geologist. It had a lot of rocks, and all that seismic activity? It was sweet.

Lira's place, where he and Harold were temporarily guesting, was like her. Practical, with touches of girly stuff. It was, she'd told him, unusual for a housing pad to be this isolated but she liked the seclusion when she was working. It had been a huge bonus for them, since the level of nosy neighbors was almost zero.

He'd have liked to go out and explore a little, but every time he made a move for the door, he found Harold on his heels. It was, he supposed, classic sidekick behavior, or it had been ordered to keep him under wraps until the delegation could get here.

His glance strayed to Lira, working on her version of a computer.

She was as sweet as all the geology on her planet.

He knew some from the Expedition and some of the others had brought back aliens, but Lira, well, this was her home. She had family here, brothers in addition to her father. She had a life, a purpose, a career here.

And they'd known each other for about a week.

If he were honest with himself, he'd wondered if he'd ever find a girl that was more interesting than rocks. Apparently, he'd just been in the wrong galaxy for that.

He stopped glancing at her and just looked, noting all the things he liked about her.

Of course, she was nice to look at, great to kiss. But he'd been through the fire—or the raging water—with her. She'd gone down into that pit to find her father. She'd gone into the habitat to find the truth, to help. If she'd been half as scared as he'd have been?

She was definitely a keeper.

A keeper he wasn't supposed to meet or keep.

He was in so much trouble.

Lira spun around in her seat, her eyes wide.

"We might still have a Vorthari problem," she said.

He probably shouldn't have found that kind of hopeful to hear. He rose from his seat and crossed to her.

She spun around, thinking maybe that he wanted to see what

she'd found. He didn't, but he looked anyway. He even kind of listened. But what he heard?

He might be able to stay long enough to…

"Lira," he said.

Maybe something in his voice jerked her out of her Vorthari absorption. She looked up at him.

He held out his hand to her, holding his breath as he waited for her to take it. Or not. Probably not…

She took it, let him pull her up from her seat.

She let him slide his arms around her waist and pull her gently, carefully close. He inhaled the sweet, vaguely foreign scent of her.

"How does a guy from another planet court a girl from yours?"

She lifted her head, her eyes soft and glowing. "Court?"

"Spend time with intent to spend," he swallowed as fear almost choked off the words, "the rest of his life with her."

"Court." This time she said the word with a different inflection. "Won't they make you leave?"

"They aren't like that," he said. "We don't make people do things, at least, I'm not military. I could stay."

"For always?"

"If that's what you want," he said. The fear tried to choke him again. "If that's what you want." The words sounded stronger this time. How did he feel about living here forever? He wasn't sure. He just knew he wanted to be with Lira.

"What if," her gaze dropped now, "I wanted to see your world?"

"That," he swallowed dryly, "could probably be arranged."

Her lips curved up in a smile that stole his breath and his heart —okay, she'd already stolen that, but the smile solidified the deal.

He bent his head, his lips finding hers. And he knew that wherever they were, she was his world now.

∼

Bonus Short Story:
The Real Dragon

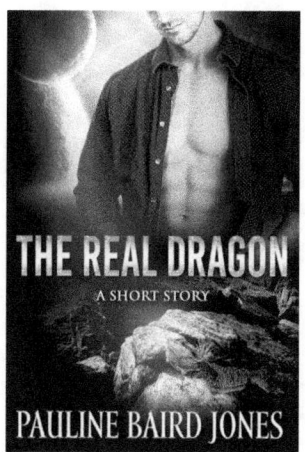

Emma Standish didn't think her day could get any worse.

Her dad is marrying his boss, her dragon suddenly came back talking and typing, and it's her fault the Earth, or at least ten square miles of Texas, is going to be destroyed.

That's what happens when you forget something very, very important. Luckily for her, she's got the love of her life that she can't remember and her dragon by her side. Who needs to worry when you're having a day like this?

This book was originally published in Pets in Space® which is now off sale.

Chapter 1

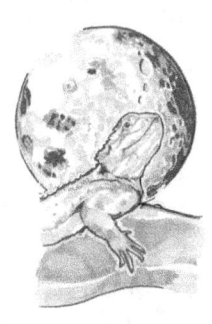

MY DRAGON CAME BACK the day my dad told me he was getting married again.

I found him—my dragon, not my dad—sitting on my desk with his front legs on my computer keyboard.

Typing.

Of course he's not typing. Just because it sounded like he was typing, didn't mean he was *typing.* His head turned my direction and he blinked. I closed the door behind me and saw what seemed like recognition in his deep, dragon gaze.

He lifted a front leg—usually a sign of submission in a bearded dragon—and waved his claw at me, or possibly at the computer screen. "I hope you don't mind?"

I stepped over to the bed and sank down just before my knees gave out. Peddrenth shifted so he could still see me, his beard flaring black for several seconds, like I'd annoyed him. Bearded dragons make great pets, but male bearded dragons like to dominate, and, despite the submissive paw waving, he'd ruled our shared roost long before he disappeared. I shook my head, closed my dropped jaw and said, "I don't…mind."

Minding wasn't even on the list of what I felt. Beyond the shock, the disbelief, the awe, and freaked out, I realized the one thing that didn't surprise me. How he sounded. Kind of gravely, with a slight lisp. Like, well, a dragon.

He turned back to my computer and symbols began to flash on the screen. My dragon *was* typing.

Gobsmacked, I stared at the screen without seeing it at first, but then I realized some of the stuff he was putting on there looked vaguely familiar, if I had time to think about it. Which I didn't. I had all these questions bouncing around inside my head. I needed to herd them into an orderly queue before something exploded in there. I set my purse down on one side, my brief case on the other, and eased off my shoes. This familiar, post-work day ritual helped. A little. Okay, not that much. But at least my feet were happy.

I rubbed my temple, then the bridge of my nose. I pinched myself. I seemed to be awake. If I was dreaming, I wanted to wake up. Except for having Peddrenth back. I wouldn't mind if that was real—with or without the typing and talking. I'd missed him. He'd been my companion, my best friend for ten years, until—

The typing stopped and Peddrenth slithered around. His paw waved, like giving me permission to speak. So I did.

"Where have you been for the last eight years?" I sounded more curious than freaked out, which surprised me, because I was pretty freaked out.

He shouldn't even be alive. A bearded dragon had a max life span of twelve years. I got him for my eighth birthday and I would be twenty-six in a couple of days. You do the math. On the other hand, he wasn't supposed to be typing or talking so the life span thing felt moot.

"Away," he said significantly.

"For eight years." He'd disappeared the same night as the accident. My fingers curled into my palms. I didn't remember much about that night, except that when the dust settled, Peddrenth and my mom were both gone. Losing them had changed my life almost beyond recognition, but whatever. I'd moved on. Without actually moving on, since I still lived at home with my dad.

"It is true that eight of your years have passed…" His paw waved again.

Maybe he was trying to use the Force on me. It had that vibe. Which might explain why I only just noticed his mouth wasn't moving when he talked. Just in case things weren't weird enough.

Was I having a breakdown? In which case I was hallucinating because…oh, wow, it feels lame to think I might be that upset over my dad remarrying. I considered it and decided it wasn't the marrying part. It was the who part. My dad was the stereotype of the absentminded inventor slash scientist. And he was about to marry Iris. Of all the women who'd tried to get his attention since my mom died, he picks his dragon-lady boss?

My dad was marrying his boss.

And mine.

Just because I found her more personally annoying than just about anyone else in my life, I needed to not lose sight of the fact that if this happened, I stood a good chance of getting my life back —after eight years of being Peddrenthless when I needed my pet dragon the most. "*Where have you been?!*"

"You are conversant with faster than light travel."

Ice trickled down the center of my back. "How could you know that?" No one knew about her dad's super-secret, faster-than-light project.

"For one thing, you have geek plastered all over your Facebook and Instagram profiles."

I opened my mouth to ask how he knew that, then noticed the tabs on my browser. My dragon had checked out my social media.

"And it has long been your dream to travel in space."

This was true, but how—oh right. I'd told him everything before he disappeared. "I…didn't know you understood me."

He might have looked aggrieved. "You told me I was the only one who did."

"Yes. And I meant it." For a teenager, "you understand me" is the same as saying "you let me talk all I want and never tell me I'm wrong," but this didn't seem like the time to tell him that. That I knew this gave me hope I'd matured, even if I did live at home. Then I wondered why I was talking out loud when my dragon wasn't. *Can you hear me?*

No response from my dragon.

"How come I can hear you inside my head but you can't hear me?"

I felt a d'oh from him.

"You lack the implant that gives me a telepathic voice."

Implant. My dragon had an implant that made him telepathic. Okay. And where—it was starting to sink in that my dragon had been…I couldn't think it. Not yet. I was a geek. I should be excited, not—

"So you took," I sort of managed another dry swallow, "a…a… space trip?"

I had a sudden flash of memory. Like a movie still frame. The bright light stabbing out of the dark that put us at the center of a spotlight—but that was just a weird dream. A weird, reoccurring dream. It had to be, because if it wasn't then…then…

"You observed my departure."

I looked away. "I don't remember much about that night." I rubbed my face with both hands, leaving them over my eyes. Now I saw the flash of headlights. This time not in still frame. They moved erratically, the glow bouncing off the dense trees that lined the road. The squeal of tires—and then nothing. Just this vast blank ocean inside my head that was awash with guilt.

My dad had been devastated about losing mom, but it had been eight years. In the Old Testament, even Jacob had only served seven for Rachel, unless you counted the seven extra years he got tricked into serving, but I didn't want to count those. Eight was bad enough. And I hadn't even got a date out of my eight years, let alone a spouse or two.

You don't have to leave, my dad had told me today after dropping his bombshell, *Iris and I want you to stay, to keep working* with us.

Yeah, sure, I'd love to play third wheel to my *dad* and his wife. I didn't tell him I'd rather poke out my own eye. I didn't have to. He was clueless but not that clueless. He'd almost seemed startled by his words, then he'd smiled at me, tempered with a bit of wry and something almost…puzzled. I'd hugged and congratulated him and came upstairs to…a typing, talking dragon. I lowered my hands.

I had to know. "Were you…abducted by…aliens?"

"I wasn't abducted." His beard flared black again. "It was an accident."

My next thought was totally inappropriate, but one can't always help that.

Why didn't they accidentally take me, too?

"SO, YOU'RE NOT DATING TED?" Peddrenth broke into what had turned into a long silence.

It wasn't that I'd run out of questions. I think I had maxed out my ability to process his answers. Here I sat in my bedroom, dealing with the fact that my dad was getting married again, my dragon had taken an accidental trip to space and back, and all I had were book boyfriends. I glanced around. And a bedroom that hadn't been updated since that night. And who was Ted?

I started to ask, but then I remembered. The me before the accident had thought Ted might ask me to the senior prom. He hadn't, of course. I'd been in the hospital with a concussion. And our "dating" had been as imaginary as my book boyfriends.

"No…I'm not dating Ted."

"That is well."

Why? I directed a penetrating look his direction, but he had a tough hide. I was curious he was curious about Ted, no question, but it didn't seem like the main point, which was…

"Why did you come back?" I hesitated. "Are you really back?" I'd need to restart his bug order. It had really impressed my friends that I bought bugs and had a dragon for a pet, I recalled a bit vaguely. Was this what shock felt like? Cold and fuzzy around the edges? I grabbed the lap quilt at the foot of my bed and wrapped it around my shoulders.

"Mazan would like to talk to you."

"Mazan?"

My dragon studied me with a peculiar intensity. "You truly do not remember?" I shook my head. "That perhaps would explain—"

"Explain what?" I felt a strange dread, as memory tried to pierce the thick fog hiding whatever happened that night eight years ago.

"There is a problem with the launch."

There was nothing in my nondisclosure agreement about talking to a dragon, but it still felt disloyal. "Launch?" I tried to look clueless. Which should have been easy since I pretty much was.

Peddrenth couldn't raise his brows, but it felt like he did.

"Okay, so there might be a launch—which you didn't hear from me—what of it?"

"There is a leak."

"A leak?" I jerked upright in alarm. "In the fuel tanks? On the team?" Exploding space vehicles and corporate sabotage were both a real worry. "What?"

"You. You are leaking."

Chapter 2

It shouldn't be that hard to wrap my brain around making first contact with an alien. It's what all of us geeks dreamed of and hoped for. Perhaps we didn't hope for first contact by dragon, but still, I should have been ready.

I didn't feel ready.

The almost full moon was up, but mostly hidden by puffy clouds left over from an afternoon storm.

With Peddrenth riding on my shoulders, we took the path through the woods just like we used to do. It didn't feel like it had been been eight years since I'd taken Peddrenth into the clearing to hunt for free range bugs…why had we come this far, I wondered now? There were bugs closer to the house, further from—

My heart began to thump like it wanted to jump out of my chest as this path wound ever closer until the one place road and path crossed.

The spot where my mom had died.

On that night I can't remember.

She died instantly, they said. It wouldn't have helped if the other driver had stayed. The shrink told me my need for closure, for justice, was what kept me from remembering. I guess I believed him, since my degree wasn't in psychology. Oh wait, I didn't have a degree. I gave it up to help my dad. That probably sounds bitter and I'm not. Mostly I'm bewildered. And I didn't understand why dread coiled in my chest like a snake. Or why my throat felt closed, and the humid air felt thicker than usual. Why did I taste metal on my tongue?

Why was I afraid?

It wasn't the place. Dad and I passed the spot every day on our way to work. Some days I didn't even think about it. I certainly didn't have a panic attack, which was good since I drove. But now I wanted to turn tail and run home.

I didn't. I couldn't run. I couldn't hide. I couldn't flinch from thinking about that night. Not anymore.

I needed to know what happened. I needed to remember.

I might not be a genius like my dad, and no, I didn't have that college education, but I'm not stupid. It had to be more than a lack of closure fueling this choking dread. There was something I didn't want to face, something buried deep inside my head. Only it wasn't buried, maybe it never had been. It had ridden on my shoulders for eight years, it was riding there now, with Peddrenth.

I glanced his way, found him watching me. He almost looked worried. Or I was projecting.

I swallowed to wet my dry throat and asked, "Is he, you know, humanoid?"

"Mazan? Of course."

What was "of course" about it? This alien had accidentally collected the dragon, not the human.

"Does he look like…I mean, is he purple or something?" I had a feeling if Peddrenth could have rolled his eyes, he would have.

"You…" he stopped, as if reconsidering what he'd meant to say. "You all look similar to me."

If I could have chuckled, I would have. I did manage a smile that felt wry, but it didn't last. "The implant, they didn't hurt you, did they?"

He actually shook his head, well, his head swept left, then right.

"The implant was a gift, so we could communicate."

"They wanted to talk…to you?" And not me. Was I jealous of my dragon?

There was another pause. "The Draze are like that."

The Draze. I didn't know anything about the Draze, did I? And yet…there was something almost familiar about both words. Mazan. Draze. My panic eased. "Did I meet him that night? The night you left."

Peddrenth hesitated, then said, "Put me down here, please."

I opened my mouth to tell him I usually waited until we crossed the—

The road. Until we crossed the road. It was just a road.

I crouched and he left his perch. I straightened as he crawled out of sight, his tail twitching from side to side. I clenched my hands into fists and followed my dragon.

And there it was.

The road.

Right where it was supposed to be, looking like it always had. At least, it looked like it had a couple of hours ago when we drove home. Still, it felt different looking at it from here. It changed my point of view. Standing, not speeding by, I could see the spot—though brush had grown back where her car hit the tree. The skid marks were long gone, too, of course. Time was supposed to heal everything, wasn't it?

I didn't feel healed. I felt…not healed. To my core.

All was quiet, peaceful even in the low light from the nearly full moon. I looked both ways, even though ours was the only house this far down the road, and I would have heard a car coming from quite a ways off—I tensed but the twitch of fear didn't produce an image to go with it—so I crossed. I was relieved to get to the other side. I felt a chicken joke wanting to happen inside my head and quickly followed the path into the woods to escape it. The trees and bushes closed in fast, narrowing the trail so sharply, I couldn't see that far ahead.

Instead of dread, now I felt eager, excited, like a good geek should.

I pushed a particularly large branch aside and there it was.

My jaw dropped and in my amazement the horizon spun around the ship, but not in a bad way. More like a flourish. I moved forward, because it was too cool to fear. Straight out of a bigger budget scifi movie, its sleek, aerodynamic lines made my geek heart go pit-a-pat with happy. Big enough to fill the clearing almost from edge to edge, it was thickest at the center. It was so much what I'd expected it was almost a cliche, except it wasn't because it was there. It was real. And it glowed *the* shade of green most associated with alien encounters. Seriously, it was like that green had been matched to this ship. I drew close, my hand lifting because I just had to touch it, but a crack appeared in the side closest to me, a crack that rapidly turned into a lowering ramp. I froze with one hand half lifted. Just visible at the top of the ramp, I saw booted feet. Brown boots. A bit buccaneer-ish. Sassy. I would buy those boots.

I thought that before. For the first time, I believed I had been here, that I'd felt this, seen this. But then the boots started moving toward me...

This wasn't a movie. This was real. I backed up as the horizon began to spin around me again—and this time not in a good way—with the ship at the center, as if it needed to keep pace with my suddenly racing heart. I wasn't worried, not about meeting Mr. Boots. There was something else, some other worry that made panic build...

The horizon spun faster, blurring it into an impressionist painting. Then it tilted to one side as my suddenly weak knees hit the dirt. Oddly enough I was more worried about landing in a fire ant bed than the alien wearing the boots a few inches from my nose. I tried to put a hand out to touch them, but my hand didn't move. The spin of the horizon narrowed to a pinpoint. And then went dark.

~

A PINPOINT of light pierced the black and grew slowly bigger. Memories played pinball wizard inside my head, all disconnected and weird as the smothering fog hiding that long ago night began to shred, letting bits and pieces of the past escape.

I opened my eyes and there he was.

A familiar stranger.

Someone I knew, but didn't.

His worried eyes were the color of a stormy sea, with streaks of purple and turquoise in the gray. And his lashes, do not get me started on his lashes. So not fair that a guy got those lashes. He had a narrow face, with tufted brown brows and hair with a mind of its own. Kind of *Harry Potter* without the glasses. His body was long and narrow, too. He wasn't handsome, at least not in a movie hero way. I knew, without knowing, that he was clever, that I used to love his smile—which was nowhere to be seen. That I used to love—I shut that thought off. I couldn't finish it, not now with memories playing bumper car inside my head and refusing to connect properly. When I backed off, the pain eased, as if to reward me for being good...

"Are you feeling more satisfactory?"

His voice wasn't deep, or especially low or high, but still managed to be very distinct. I knew it, I knew his voice. He had a slight exotic accent that made my toes want to curl. *Had always made my toes curl...*

"Mazan?" I made it a question, though it was more of a mental confirmation as at least one piece slotted into place. I knew the name, knew it belonged to him. Why he had mattered, why he did matter to me, was less clear.

His lips curved up, but it wasn't a full smile. He thought I was leaking something, I remembered. But what?

Moving slowly, carefully, his fingers wrapped my wrist, his fingers settling on my pulse. I looked down, startled at the sight of his hand, his skin against mine. And yet...not surprised either. His fingers felt cool, but not like he was cold. More like that was his normal temperature. There was an "otherness" about him. No sparkles and no sign of prominent incisors between his lips. I know it was silly to even think it, but he was seriously pale.

I flexed my fingers, trying to connect this present with the pieces drifting in and out of view inside my head. To figure out this mystery, wrapped in the past and happening...inside an alien space ship.

"Will I," I had to clear my throat to finish it, "live?"

His smile widened and his hand dropped away, leaving my skin feeling suddenly cold. "I believe so, my friend, Emma."

His friend? My heart hurt a little, like there'd been more between us.

Mazan looked away and his shoulders rose and fell in what looked like a sigh. He turned to face me again, sadness and yes, disappointment in his gaze. That hurt as much or more than being called his friend. I struggled to a sitting position, letting my legs hang off the edge of what I realized now was some kind of bunk bed affixed to the wall. It was just high enough that my toes barely brushed the metal floor.

I pushed my limp, damp hair off my face. "What?"

"Why did you do it?"

"Do what?" I didn't have to try to look bewildered.

"She does not remember," Peddrenth said, a bit too patiently, like they'd covered this ground already. His beard flared black for several seconds.

Mazan's gaze probed mine for what felt a long time. My eyeballs dried. I wanted to blink, but I didn't dare. If I blinked, he'd think I was lying and I would never lie to him—

"How—" he stopped. He pushed his hands through his hair, which probably explained its charming disorder. And that's when I saw something new enter his gaze.

Hurt. I'd hurt him.

"I was in a car accident eight years ago. My mom—" I had to look away then. It took two tries for me to get it out. "My mom died. I hit my head." Those first words felt like rocks coming out, but the rest came easier, faster. "The shrink says I have hysterical amnesia which is kind of funny because I haven't been able to cry. Not once in eight years. Don't you think that crying is a prerequisite for hysteria?" I rubbed my face fiercely. I had to…I had to…what? It was as if there was this voice in my head telling me I couldn't. Couldn't what? I didn't know what I wasn't supposed to do or say, but if I did or said it, something bad would happen. I almost laughed at that last thought. What could be worse than this half life of guilt and fear? This sudden realization that I'd lost more than my memories of that night?

I lowered my hands and looked at him, met his gaze with my chin lifted a little. He could believe me or not. Didn't know why I wanted him to believe me, except that I seemed to be in trouble. And I did want him to believe me. A frown pulled his crazy brows together. Made him look just a touch mad scientist. My heart did this little flutter. Apparently I liked mad scientists.

"This news is...well, my friend, Emma, it is heart-breaking. It is—"

At least we were still friends. But that didn't explain why *he* was heart-broken. It's not like he knew my mom.

"She is lost, gone, and we did not know." He turned away, causing more disorder in his hair with frantic hands. He paced away, then back.

"Are you talking about my mom?"

He looked surprised then. "Of course. She was a great hero to our people."

"Hero?" I croaked. To his people? "My mom?"

"Yes, she was the Deliverer."

I felt my jaw go slack and couldn't do a thing about it.

SO I WAS BACK to gobsmacked.

Neither Mazan nor Peddrenth appeared to notice. Mazan had adopted a tragic pose over by the door, like he needed something to hold him up. Peddrenth, well, he sat there staring at Mazan with his tail twitching back and forth, looking very wise and remote.

She was the Deliverer.

My mom. The Deliverer. A hero to his people? She'd driven car pool and made cookies and bandaged my knees and bought me Peddrenth and nagged me to take care of him. She delivered mom-ness, not hero-ness. There had to be some kind of mistake. Only... somehow, don't ask me why, I knew it wasn't a mistake. I didn't believe it...but I did. It was there, I decided, buried somewhere in my missing night with all the other stuff I couldn't remember. Or... was I afraid to remember?

I sat there because I didn't know what else to do, other than finally get hysterical, and honestly, I didn't have the energy. Looking at Mazan was unsettling. More than memories started to stir inside my head. For the first time, I was also starting to realize how little I'd *felt* for the last eight years. As if all of me had been wrapped in some kind of emotion-damping fog. Seeing him made my heart hurt. Like a limb coming back to painful, tingling life—I looked away, studying my surroundings instead. It was more of the familiar unfamiliar. Like I was on the other side of a movie, watching me, seeing this without being part of it.

The small cabin was very ship-like and also very space ship-like, because it had that curved edge on what was probably the outside wall, and there were space-stuff fixtures. The bunk where I sat had been tucked into that curve, which saved the straight wall for a small desk area, some shelves, and a sink. There were two doors. One stood open giving me a glimpse of the corridor and the other, I suspected, was for a commode. No, I knew it was. Why could I remember peeing here but not being here?

Bits of memory drifted just out of reach, taunting me, daring me to look. Was it the whole Deliverer of her people thing? But why would I freak out and get amnesia over that? If she really had been a Deliverer of an alien people, well, logically, that could have played out in a lot of different ways. But it wasn't logic that made me know how it **was**. Okay, more weirdness to realize my mom was an alien. I made myself repeat it. *Mom was an alien.*

That would actually be more cool than having a dragon for a pet, particularly at the cons.

Oh my freaking heck. If my mom was an alien, then I was one, too. At least half a one.

Still not enough for amnesia.

Okay. Even the doctor admitted that something traumatic had happened that night. He believed it was the driver of the other car that I was afraid to remember. I knew he wasn't wrong, but he also wasn't completely right. There was more. Something huge and ugly lurked just out of sight inside my head like a bad dragon, the mythic kind that hides in storm clouds over the ocean and dives out to eat sailors. My dad—

My brain twitched with a sudden stab of pain. I mentally jerked back, wanting—no, needing to go fetal and forget again. But I wasn't seventeen. I was twenty-freaking-five about to turn twenty-freaking-six. It was time to woman up. And that meant facing the dragon in my head. No matter what—or who—it was.

Okay, it was unthinkable that my dad would, so just think it, I told myself. Because if it was unthinkable, then it wasn't true. My dad couldn't have been in that other car. He wouldn't have left us there. Unbidden came the memory of my dad's haunted eyes, his strained gray face. Okay, what if he had?

There. I'd thought it.

And the world hadn't stopped turning.

My brain hadn't exploded. Or given up the Big Secret.

It was still there, just out of reach and fighting me. It was weird to feel detached from me but to also feel this rising panic. My heart pounded and my breathing came in shallow pants. I forced myself to hold in a breath, then another, to slow it down. The little stars circling my vision faded. I flexed my tingling fingers, then looked at Mazan. He'd turned back to face me, looking sober, sad, but calmer.

"This is sad news for our people, my friend, Emma, but—"

My eyelid twitched. Oh right. "*Our* people?" If my mom was alien, then I was half alien. So that made his people half my people. My other eyelid joined the twitch-fest.

His brows arched. "But you know this, my friend—"

"I don't remember." It was the truth. I didn't remember. I'd just connected some really obvious dots.

"Just that night. You said you do not remember **that** night," he protested.

I shook my head and he stopped talking, his head tipping to one side. I knew that pose, that look. He was…seeking to understand.

"You can call me just Emma, you know," I murmured, as little bits and pieces, small Mazan moments drifted in and out of view. "We *know* each other."

"Of course, just Emma—"

"I mean, we knew each other before that night," I interrupted, pushing back at the pain and resistance building inside my head. "We met...when..." my gaze shifted to Peddrenth. "...when I got you."

"Yes." Mazan nodded, his expression lightened some, but also puzzled. "Peddrenth is a Draze Dragon, genetically engineered to look exactly like a species native to your world, your bearded dragon. He is your Companion." The way he said it the word had a capital C.

I looked at my dragon. My Companion? Who had accidentally left me behind? I opened my mouth to ask or accuse, but the look in his eyes stopped the words. He looked like I felt. Betrayed.

"You know this—"

"But I didn't, I don't, I mean, that's part of what I forgot." I looked at him, fighting to keep my breathing even again. "Why would I forget you? This?" And remember Peddrenth? But not the part about Peddrenth being a Companion, and now it was coming back to me in bits and bites how he'd always been able to talk to me like the best invisible talking friend a young girl ever had. "What happened that night? Why did you take Peddrenth and leave—" ... me behind, is what I wanted to ask. We were young, but we meant something to each other. I didn't know a lot of things, but I felt this to my toes. All the way through my heart. I touched my chest. It felt like I could see the cracks in it. He left me. For eight long, miserable years. I hadn't known it, but I'd *known* it.

"You told me to leave, just Emma."

"Emma," I corrected, absently. Like the crack in his ship as the ramp lowered, a breach appeared in the wall inside my head. And it was a wall. I'd thought it was an ocean covered in fog, but it was a wall. High and solid, scary to approach and painful to touch, to try to breech. "Why would I tell you to leave?"

"Someone came. A car. We could see the headlights on the road. There was a risk *The Entireer* might be seen. It was protocol. You told me I must not risk discovery. I cloaked the ship and launched."

464

Regret was in his eyes, in the tone of his voice. There had been a cost to him, too.

"But…they told me I was in the car with her." It was like trying to fit together pieces from two different puzzles. If the car we'd seen was my mom's, the pieces might fit—but if she'd picked me up where the path met the road, she wouldn't, she couldn't have been going fast enough to hit that tree with lethal force, even with a nudge from another car. I didn't remember another car. And that meant…I don't know what it meant. I looked at Mazan. I needed to move, to get ahead of the flight instinct trying to send me back out into the forest, back to hiding from the past. I backed away from the wall, just a little. Maybe if I focused on something else… "Let's walk while you tell me what it is that I'm leaking."

Chapter 3

IT TOOK three circuits of the inner corridor for Mazan to explain, and one more for me to process it. He spoke the truth. I knew it in my heart, but my brain, well, there was that ugly wall of resistance. What lurked behind the wall shouldn't be life threatening, but it felt like I would die if I remembered. Took the fun out of walking around in an alien spaceship—which you've already done, I reminded myself. *Focus*. It was a strange feeling, having the old and new kicking around there.

As we did one more circuit, the ship got more and more familiar. This corridor circled the central core where the FTL drive was housed. Everything else required was located in the outer dish, except the bridge which was up top and the cargo hold in the lower belly of the ship.

Mazan stopped at the galley. "Do you require something to drink, Emma?" He stumbled a bit over the single name, which was interesting. Had he been calling me "my friend, Emma" for all those years? *All those years*. It had been years if I met him when I got Peddrenth. But why—*The Entireer* had been my...school. I came here to learn, but no one had told me it was because I was half alien. I thought I'd been picked because I was special. Pause to be grateful I was no longer quite that needy and clueless. Chagrined, possibly, but not needy and clueless.

"Thanks." I didn't really want something to drink, but the circuits were making me a bit dizzy. Or the memories swirling in my head were doing it. I followed him into galley. It was more functional than cool, but still cute in a *Tiny House* kind of way. Peddrenth hadn't joined us. He'd gone to hydroponics, I thought absently, and then was surprised by the thought. He had a friend or friends there...

All of the sudden I found it hard to look at Mazan and had to resist the urge to curl my hair around my finger or do some other flirty thing. This was a Serious Thing, not a boy-girl moment. I stole a look at him when he handed me a cup of water, his alien scent drifting close enough to tease my senses, comparing this Mazan to the bits of memory still forming inside my head. He hadn't changed as much as I had, I decided. This ship hadn't just been my school. Mazan had been my teacher, then my friend, and then my more-than-friend—at least for me. He shifted from one foot to the other and tugged at the neck of his space suit. Not as indifferent as he appeared? I hid a totally inappropriate-to-circumstances smile. Apparently I could face the dangerous deep and still go shallow. Great.

I wrapped my hands around the cup and propped a hip against a counter, took a sip and said, "So I'm half alien, my mom is some kind of war hero that you thought was dead until she hacked a NASA satellite and sent you a message." The words emerged from my mouth a lot calmer than they felt inside my head. In there they were all in caps and accompanied by lots of "oh, my hecks!"

"But by the time you answered her message, she'd married my dad." I had to pause here to try process the fact that *my dad had married an alien*. "...and she had me. So instead of going home, she asked you all to educate me so that I could choose where I wanted to live when I got old enough. You've been coming every year—" I broke off the frown. "Except for the last eight years? What happened?"

"Your mother would send a safe signal, my—Emma. We did not receive this signal."

"Okay." That made sense, but... "...there was no signal this year." Since my mom was gone. "Why did you come back now?"

Once again he shifted from one foot to the other, but this was different shifting. The guilty conscience kind.

It took me a minute, which was kind of embarrassing, but I got there finally. "The leak." I went back out into the main corridor and looked around. TFTL's ship wasn't the same, but there were signs of my leaking. Their ship was like a distant echo of this one. I looked at Mazan. "But...that's my dad's research. I'm just his assistant."

He shook his head. "It is not possible for your father to know the things he knows, to do the things he's done."

"My mom—"

He shook his head again. "He did not know."

"He didn't know he'd married an alien?" My voice rose a bit on the end.

Mazan half smiled. "He knew. He did not know about this." He gestured around him. "And the Deliverer would never have given him our technology. It would not have been safe to give it to him."

"Why not safe?"

He looked at me through those ridiculous lashes. "There are... those who closely monitor the development of technology in backwater star systems. It is illegal to accelerate technological advancement. There are severe penalties."

I let the "backwater star systems" slide past. It was not relevant to the moment. Even if it stung a little. Instead I considered my dad. Would he have been able to resist the temptation to use what he'd learned? Or even have remembered he wasn't supposed to use it? Probably not, I had to concede. "But I did know?"

He nodded. "It was part of your education."

"You gave advanced technology to a teenager."

"You understood the boundaries and each level of knowledge came after you proved you could keep it to yourself—"

"—until I got knocked on the head and forgot." My head hurt

like I'd whacked it again. I rubbed my temple. "But if I didn't remember, then how did I leak it?"

Mazan looked troubled. "Perhaps it was a subconscious thing. You did not realize you were helping."

It was possible, I supposed. What—the stab of pain felt like a needle in my eye. What the heck? When it subsided some, I tried again. *What did I know*— oh yeah, that question was like some kind of mental trigger. I backed off and relaxed, letting my mind drift and something emerged from the fog.

"The Kruvox," I said. "That's who my mom fought, right?"

Mazan looked pleased. "Yes. They are evil."

"Did they have technology or something to manipulate memory —" I yelped when this pain hit, like a punch inside my head.

"What is wrong, Emma?"

I gritted the word out past the pushback. "Kruvox?"

"There were rumors of such things, but—" He frowned. "But the Kruvox are not here. Your mother destroyed their fleet."

My mom, the driver of carpools and bake sales, had destroyed a fleet. A Kruvox fleet.

"By taking out their leader, you said?"

"The Opposer, yes."

I glanced around. My mom had done that and set this up. She'd always known—I thought it was my special secret, one shared only with Peddrenth. Wow, shone a whole new light on my teen years. But not on the big, black hole inside my head. Not yet. If she could do what she did, then her daughter could face the past and get over herself. I gritted out. "How did she do it?"

"She was not just a great warrior, Emma," he looked at me with glistening eyes, "she was a great scientist as well. She used her knowledge to create an explosion—"

"—that didn't destroy her ship," I felt compelled to point out. It was the crash here on Earth that did that. I felt a little miffed at his hero worship. Of my mom. My mom the hero of the Draze.

"We learned later that the explosion created a chain reaction that opened a wormhole. It pulled both ships in. Her ship was damaged. The Opposer's ship did not survive transit."

My brain gave a kick, sharp and painful, like a memory trying to kick through that wall. "You sure he didn't make it?"

"He?" Mazan looked surprised. "The Opposer was also female."

There is no way I can explain the chill that went through me. The pushback inside my head was almost more than I could stand. There was both pain and the sensation of an iron hand closed around my throat, trying to choke off my words. I reached up a hand but there was nothing there.

"Do you have a picture, an image of this Opposer?" I croaked.

Mazan looked surprised, but went to the wall and touched something. A computer-looking thing swung out and he tapped. Then tapped some more. The screen filled with bits of color that slowly resolved themselves into a face.

Huge cracks appeared in the wall, but I didn't need to see the other side of the wall to know.

Tomorrow evening, my dad was going to marry the evil Kruvox Opposer.

At least now I knew why I didn't like her.

MAZAN NOW LOOKED as shell-shocked as I felt. "We must warn him."

"He won't believe me." I blew out a sigh, one hand gripping the armrest of the pilot's position. It was everything I'd ever hoped for in an alien ship's bridge. And I couldn't enjoy it. All the flashy lights, the cool looking switches, the shiny were no help at all in solving the problem of Iris. No wonder my prospective evil step-mom didn't want me to move out. And knowing my dad, he hadn't told her that would never happen, that I would never live in the same house with that woman. He wouldn't know how much keeping me around mattered to her. How could he know I was her ticket to ride home? Which I would be if we couldn't figure out how to stop her.

"You are his daughter. Of course he will believe you."

I bit back a sigh. How could he understand? I wanted to pat his hand, say, "There, there," and kiss him on the mouth—I yanked my gaze away. *Focus, Emma.*

"I had to see a shrink, a doctor, about my memory loss. The shrink told him I was mentally fragile." I hadn't been meant to hear that. It stung then, still did, I admitted grudgingly. I'd known I wasn't hysterical or fragile. I'd known something was wrong, but I wasn't old enough back then to fight their belief. All I could do was try to prove I wasn't fragile. It hadn't worked. Dad hadn't noticed because of his whole absentminded professor deal. And he didn't know my mom, his *alien* wife had done the equivalent of the Kobayashi Maru. She'd saved her people and Iris was using me to get back there, maybe to even undo what my mom had done. If she escaped on a ship I helped build, however unconsciously... "We have to stop her. *I* have to stop her."

He took my hand again and this time his smile was different. More personal. More grownup to grownup. I hoped it wasn't hopeful thinking, but whatever. If I was going to take on evil, I needed hope.

"So, the wedding is tomorrow and the launch is the day after." Only my scientist dad would think that was romantic. And logical. "Somehow we have to stop the wedding and, what, sabotage the launch?"

Mazan suddenly avoided looking at me.

"What?" I asked suspiciously.

"I have already taken care of the launch."

I arched my brows.

"I was ordered to stop the launch."

"Show me." I gave the order, but was surprised when he did. It's not like I was in charge.

He swiveled his chair to face the control console and moved things. Tapped things. Like before, it started as little bits that gradually formed into something I understood. It was not unlike the language Peddrenth had used on my computer. I was about to ask what it meant, when I realized that I knew.

"Mazan, this won't just stop the launch. It will leave a ten-mile crater in Texas! You'll take out the whole facility and then some!"

I stared at him as his gaze slowly returned to meet mine.

"That's the plan?" I shoved my hands through my hair. "You're going to blow up my dad." My eyes got wider. "You were going to blow up me."

He didn't look away this time. It was the look of a man who knew exactly what he'd done. Or had planned to do. The stern line of his lips and jaw, the steady seriousness in his gaze, well, it was kind of sexy. Despite this, or because of it, I glared at him, but I had to concede, "You didn't know I hadn't betrayed you."

I still felt hurt. He should have known. Even if there was no way he could have known. I looked at him, my eyes wide and dry, my heart, well, my heart wasn't happy. "You were my friend."

His lips twisted a bit wryly, as if I'd hurt him. "Yes, I was, I am your friend. But you...you are my love, Emma."

I felt my eyes widen.

"And still I would have done it."

He'd just used the l-word. It kind of helped. I felt older. I tipped my head and asked, my tone different. "Why?"

"It was you and your ten miles of Texas, or your whole world."

That sobered me really fast. "Okay." Those monitor aliens, I guessed. I looked away, then back at him. "You love me? Do you know what that means here?"

He took my hands again. I'm not sure how a guy with his core temperature managed to warm me up, but he did. He didn't pull me closer or kiss me, which was a bummer. But since I was all grown up, or getting there fast, I sucked it up.

"I know what it means. I will be there with you."

"With me?"

"When the ten miles goes away."

I didn't jerk my hands away, but I did give his a shake. "We're not blowing up." Not now that I knew he loved me. "We're going to figure this out." I adjusted my grip so I could squeeze his hands. "And then..."

"Then?" His lips twitched.

"Then we'll figure *this* out. Us, I mean." Just because my brain was an on-steroids video game with most of my memory offline didn't mean we couldn't.

It just meant it would be a little challenging.

Chapter 4

"So if Iris thinks she's got a ticket off this planet using my leaking, why is she marrying my dad?"

Now we were in a little version of a boardroom. There was even a board, well, a screen for me to write on with this nifty pen looking thing. Sadly, it was still blank. I faced that board, because looking at Mazan, not to mention hearing the clock inside my head ticking down to us blowing up, made it hard to focus.

"You have not reached your maturity age as yet."

I swung around. "I blew past that five years minus two days ago." I'd thought it was cool my dad's company had scheduled the launch on my birthday. Now...well, I still thought it was kind of cool.

"On Draze the age of maturity is equivalent to twenty-six of your Earth years."

"So?" I shrugged.

"Draze is a matriarchal society."

"Really?" I needed to think about that. But not now. "Why does that matter?" Because it clearly did.

"As long as you are under age, as your father's wife, she would be the head of your family."

"For one day," I pointed out, though I will admit I started to feel uneasy.

"If she marries your dad and you died before you reached your maturity, she would control your inheritance."

"I...don't have an inheritance." He gave me a look, but didn't speak. I lifted my hands. "I do not want to know."

I turned back to the blank screen, my disordered thoughts spinning in un-pretty patterns. Okay, we had suspicions, but what did we know? I wrote "Dad" in the air, and then "Iris." With a mini flourish, both names appeared on the screen.

"The company hired my dad within a few months of the accident." I added the date under my dad's name. "They were a new start-up, but well funded." I looked at Mazan over my shoulder. "I never heard their pitch." I frowned. "Dad told me I could work for him for a while if I wanted to." I bit my lip. "I thought it meant he needed me to be there to help him. I mean, I knew he was worried about me, but he was so devastated by mom's death, he got kind of clingy." In his absentminded way. I shook my head. "It all felt so normal. Even when my friends asked questions about why I wasn't going to college after all, but even then it felt normal. Right."

"Was The Opposer there?"

I shook my head. "She didn't pop out of the woodwork for two years." I wrote that date on the screen, more for something to do, than because it was relevant or helpful. My hand trembled a bit, skewing the words. I felt closer to knowing something, but the pushback in there was painful. Someone or some thing didn't want me to remember. Was the someone me? Or her?

"It was not long after that my dad had his first breakthrough." How did she do it? How did she pick my brains? How did she make my dad believe he did it? "But they came very slowly."

"If she is The Opposer, then she knows the intergalactic laws for this star system. She had to be careful. The penalties are severe, not just for her and this planet, but for the Kruvox."

I swung around to face him. "But she wasn't careful enough. What happened?"

"I did not know this when I was pulled out, but they left monitoring in place." I must have looked annoyed, because he added, "With what you knew, it was necessary."

And a good thing, I conceded. If they hadn't, what would Iris have done? Could she have talked my dad into taking a ride to the stars? Maybe she already had. He was a geek, too. Would I have agreed to go with them? That was harder to answer. It was one thing to dream about it, something entirely different to just up and go—particularly when it was my dad's honeymoon trip to the stars. Ugh. So she'd have had a plan that didn't require my consent, or could force my consent without my knowledge. And before the end of my birthday, I'd have had an accident. I shivered but shook it off and focused on Iris.

This plan had been a long time in the making. She'd had years to figure out what she wanted and how she was going to get it. And we had hours to figure how to stop her. Okay. At first, she'd have focused on surviving, figuring out how things worked. Dad and I weren't on her menu then. She'd have had to find out about my mom in some way—

The mental fist hit so hard, I gripped the edge of the table to stay on my feet. I had to push the words out past the block. "She was here."

He frowned and shook his head. "Here?"

"That night. She—what she did—it's the reason I can't remember. I didn't just lose a night. I lost everything related to you." I waved my arms. "I lost this. She did that. Somehow she did that." I licked my lips as a far off echo of "Run, Emma!" slipped through the cracks in my memory wall. "She...must have killed my mom. She would have killed me, too, but somehow she realized I could help her. So she took my memory instead."

And now my dad was about to marry that evil, murdering inheritance-stealing dragon lady.

∼

"MY DAD HAS ALREADY MARRIED one alien."

We'd been bouncing around ideas for what felt like hours. My screen was a mess, filled with notes, some crossed out. I don't know why I didn't erase them. But I didn't. Since the wedding was first, we'd focused on that.

"He's not going to dump his boss without proof." And what if she'd done something inside his head, too? He couldn't be… complicit. Not my dad…could he?

We didn't have proof. Okay, we had this ship and the records on its databases but, if she'd messed with his head—or his loyalty was at all divided—that might open this ship up to her, too. And, I glanced at Mazan out of the corner of my eyes, attraction was a powerful force. Just looking at him made it hard to focus on not getting blown up. I didn't know how badly my dad wanted to marry Iris. It made my stomach queasy to even think about that. But he was a guy. She was a gal. I hated her, but she'd kept herself up pretty well. She'd made sure I wasn't around her a lot, but when she did swan by, heads turned, even young guy heads. She had "it" despite her dragonlady, fist-of-iron deal.

"And he might actually, you know, like her." No matter how grownup I'd suddenly become, I couldn't use the word "hots" and "my dad" in the same sentence. Okay, I did it inside my head and it made my eyes twitch again.

Mazan's lips twitched. "You mean in the way we *like* each other?"

I looked at him then and kind of lost the plot for a few minutes, because even when things are about to blow up and evil is about to triumph over good, love still makes the world go round. As first kisses went, this one was epic. The truth was, I'd pretended to have a crush on high school Ted so I wouldn't accidentally slip and tell my friends I was in love with an alien. Like my father before me.

If the shrink had only known how truly messed up I was…

The longer we kissed—it was as if sensation, feeling returned to my world. And color. I was on a basically gray ship but it was an awesome gray. A vibrant gray. The best gray ever. My toes curled and possibly some other body parts. If the world ended now I'd be —if the world ended it would be my fault.

I eased back and inch or two and smiled at him, then sighed. As delightful as the kissing was, we were steaming up his view screen. And we had a world to save.

I had learned something, though. If my dad's brains were this scrambled, an appeal to reason wasn't going to work. Would we have to blow him up? That assumed I managed to survive his wedding night. Oh wow, wish my brain hadn't gone there.

At least it cleared my head. I stared at our screen and for some reason, this time I began to see a pattern in the chaos.

"You don't need your plan to take out the company," I muttered, rubbing both my temples. "She's already got a plan in place."

"To blow it all up? But—"

"Not blow it up, but she doesn't want us to have that tech. It's all for her. And you said she knows the risks of accelerating our tech. She's not taking any chances." There wasn't as much pushback inside my head, because this was new knowledge, not old, or so I postulated. "Want to bet she also got the cloaking technology from me?"

"It does not appear on the ship's specifications," Mazan pointed out, though thoughtfully rather than in a tone of denial.

"The ship will appear to blow up, so there won't be extra scrutiny from whoever does that. I'll bet she's even got some debris ready to scatter around. And what the team knows—it won't be complete. It isn't complete. The whole project is compartmentalized to cut down the risk of corporate espionage. We'll have a launch. There'll be a big boom and everyone will think it's just another private industry failure." There'd even be some reason all of us were on board. Or were killed by falling debris...

Mazan nodded as comprehension broke over his face. "Of course. That is the best way for her to avoid an investigation into the launch. But the ship—"

Which meant... "All we need to do is stop the wedding. And make sure the launch fails to happen." Could we manage to modify the ship just enough to make it look like it wasn't quite there yet? Remove the unearned tech and leave the ship? Though the thought of blowing up Iris...I sighed and let it go. We had to make sure Iris never left this planet.

I explained my idea and he nodded again.

"I can manage that part, but not until after the wedding. If we fail—"

He didn't have to spell it out.

"At the wedding, though—she would recognize me as Draze. I can't assist you very much other than to be there with my personal cloak." He looked adorably worried.

"We'll have to make it work," I said, rubbing a spot on my temple as the something inside me fought this old knowledge question. "How did she get it out of my brain?"

"It?" Mazan shook his head as puzzled took over his expression at the sudden shift in topic.

It was so cute I almost lost the plot again. "The illegal knowledge? We know she must have got it from me, but how?" Had she implanted something in my head? In my dad's head? This wedding was so far out of character—

Suddenly all signs of daze left Mazan. His expression turned grim and older. "We need to run a scan of your brain."

The one thing you loved to hear the man you loved say.

Chapter 5

THERE ARE things you should never know about your parents. It makes it really hard to face them across the breakfast table. And it is especially hard when that breakfast is on your dad's wedding day. The wedding I needed to stop so that Mazan didn't have to blow up ten square miles of Texas. Or they didn't give those galactic monitors an excuse to take out Earth.

"So," I stirred my cold cereal around in the bowl, "your big day. You nervous?" I know I was.

He met my gaze for a couple of seconds, then nodded. "The wedding. Of course."

Had he forgotten for a moment it was his wedding day? Words wanted to flood out my mouth, words like, "Don't do this," and "Are you freaking crazy?" I managed to hold them back. My discomfort was not helped by the knowledge I had a Kruvox implant in my brain. The analysis of it had delivered complicated and inconclusive results. One thing Mazan was sure about, it was a patched together affair with a somewhat unstable power source. Yay.

Mazan was reluctantly impressed by the jury-rigged device. And was unsure of the level of penetration Iris had achieved inside my head. If she could have seen through my eyes, she'd have already shown up at *The Entireer.* This made us cautiously optimistic she couldn't completely read my thoughts. The implant seemed to "encourage" me to avoid certain thoughts by causing me pain and rewarded me for doing what it wanted with endorphins. Which explained a lot and creeped me out. Without removing and examining it, there was no way to know if it depressed my memories or if there was some kind of subliminal hypnotism, also messing with my head. And Mazan didn't want to remove it until he found a way to stabilize the power source.

I would like to say I was getting used to the killer headache, but I'm a terrible liar. With a headache.

I know the smile I directed at my dad was over-bright because my face hurt. "I was thinking I'd pop out and buy a dress for the, um, ceremony tonight."

His eyes widened a bit and then he nodded slowly. "Perhaps Iris—"

There must have been something in my expression that breached even his level of absent-minded. "I know this is happening very fast, Emma."

Sometimes you just have to rip that bandaid off, is what I wanted to say, but I managed not to. I looked away. "It's...she's my boss, so yeah, it feels a little weird." I hesitated, then met his gaze. "I want you to be happy, dad." And for neither of us to die, possibly horribly at the hands of the Opposer. "Are you...happy? Do you love her?" Amazing how much push back I got from those questions. Did I see a struggle in his eyes? Or just the discomfort of a dad who was about to remarry?

He cleared his throat a couple more times. "There are... different kinds of...affection, Emma."

So that was a no, then.

"I'm...surprised you're doing it before the launch." I opened my mouth but couldn't say honeymoon without gagging.

His gaze slid away from mine. Did that make him embarrassed or did he know he was planning to honeymoon in outer space? How could I know the answer to that question? He was my dad. I knew daughter things about him, not...guy things.

"Iris was, well, she liked—" his words trailed off, as if he didn't know why they were getting married today.

I nodded. "Do you want me to drop you at work or are you taking today off?" He just looked surprised, so I pushed my chair back. "I'll drop you off then."

"Iris will—I'll see you at the chapel then." A look of anxiety crossed his face. "You won't be late?"

I shook my head. "No, I won't be late."

Chapter 6

I REACHED up to adjust my dad's bow tie, not able to meet his gaze. It was cool in the vestry, but that's not what made me shiver.

Mazan and I had a plan. Not a good one—since most of it hinged on me—but it was a plan. Okay, it was the outline of a plan. Hopefully it would achieve plan-ness before my dad said, "I do."

Peddrenth didn't seem worried. Not that I expected him to be worried, but—the truth was, I didn't know what I expected, other than a horrible death. Mazan was clearly not worried. They'd been over the ship and knew how to stop the launch, but I had to stop the wedding first. Otherwise the ten square miles were going to blow. For now, all they had to do at the wedding was to boost my morale.

Up off the floor.

I took a deep breath to steady my nerves and ran the plan over again inside my head. I had to engage in battle with the Opposer inside my head without tipping off the wedding guests that there were aliens among them. Iris had had eight years to learn how to dig around inside my head and I hadn't even tried to get inside hers for fear of tipping her off. It had seemed easy on Mazan's ship, gazing into Mazan's eyes, and dreaming of a future with the alien who loved me.

Now I faced the reality of playing happy daughter, slash, employee, while mentally gas-lighting the evil Opposer of the Draze. All the while hoping she didn't get annoyed enough to blow up my brain with that implant. Which would actually be better than ending up on a dissection table at Area 51 if the word got out that I was half alien.

I was excited about getting my own little Kobayashi Maru moment. Who didn't want to be an un-sung hero of her own world? Or a dead—

If I fail, Mazan...

She does not wish to involve the galactic monitors either, Mazan reminded me. *She will have to take care in how she responds to you.*

That was the lone bright spot. Mazan had figured out how to tap into my implant, and link it to Peddrenth's, so that he could hear and talk to me, too. It was like getting mental hugs—hugs I badly needed.

I repositioned my dad's buttonhole, moved his tie a millimeter left, then back to where it had been, gave it a pat.

"You look good." I stepped back. In his sober black suit, with the white carnation, he could get married and buried—

He grinned. "For an old dude?"

I managed not to wince at hearing my dad say "dude." He patted my hand.

"You look lovely, Emma."

"Thanks, dad." It all felt so natural, I figured Iris was sending me endorphins as a reward for being obedient.

Our minister, the painfully named Reverend Wolverscampton-wood, who had presided over my mom's funeral, poked his head in. "We're ready for you, Dr. Standish." His gaze flicked to mine, equal parts compassion and worry in there. "You look well, Emma."

I cranked up the edges of my mouth. "Thanks, Reverend Wolverscamptonwood. I am...well." Getting his name out without a stumble gave me the confidence to gesture to my dad. "After you."

Dad hesitated a minute, then followed the Reverend out into the main part of the chapel, with me trotting obediently in their wake. Dad moved into the groom spot, then glanced around like he wasn't sure why he was there. Neither of us liked the limelight, I reminded myself, even though I hoped it was a sign his brain had been messed with. There was a minor rustle from the guests—about fifteen coworkers who looked a bit lost—and then the soft murmur of voices faded away as the organ began pumping out the familiar march. Iris popped into the door at the back, inappropriately eager to get on with the wedding and the killing.

Dad tugged at his tie as she beelined his direction, just a bit ahead of the tempo.

I tensed, even as a heightened sense of calm flooded through me. A false calm for sure.

Be strong, Emma. Peddrenth's voice inside my head was comforting.

We will be victorious, Mazan added. He was in the upper gallery that overlooked the chapel, hidden by his personal cloak. I wished I was with him. I saw a flicker of reptile tail near the last pew, then a snout poked out from behind the wooden base. I looked away as Iris closed on us. What was Peddrenth doing? Wasn't he supposed to be cloaked with Mazan?

Iris reached my dad and gave him a coy smile as she grabbed his arm and almost yanked him around to face the minister.

It was a good thing I hadn't expected to enjoy my dad's wedding.

WITH A LAST, somewhat discordant, wheeze, the music stopped. In the silence between that and the minister clearing his throat, I felt the wrongness of what we planned to do. Though the chapel was small, it was a sacred space, with a majesty that wasn't just about the religious fittings and soaring ceiling. Light shone through the stained glass windows, painting their patterns on stone and wood. I remembered feeling comforted by the sight of them at my mom's funeral—

When do you wish to begin?

The sound of Peddrenth's voice in my head jerked me out of the past. This was not the time to lose the plot. And surely this was a place where it was right to try to save my life, my dad's, some Texas acreage, and, possibly all of Earth.

The slow, solemn words of the wedding ceremony filtered softly into the serious silence. I glanced at my dad. Beads of sweat stood out on his forehead. He glanced at me and his lips moved soundlessly. Was it my imagination that he mouthed the word, "Help?" Or did I just want to believe that?

Let's do this. I think the words were more for me than for them.

As if on cue, I heard the minister say, "Should there be anyone who has just cause why this couple should not be united in marriage, they must speak now or forever hold their peace."

I opened my mouth, felt my throat close, and my thoughts slowed and thickened. She was stopping me—

I have just cause.

I almost let my surprise show at the sound of Peddrenth's voice in my head.

Iris jerked violently. "What did you say?"

The Reverend looked confused. "Um, should anyone have just cause—"

"I heard that." Iris snapped. "You don't have to repeat it."

My dad cleared his throat nervously. "Is there a problem my, er, dear?"

Iris looked around, saw everyone was staring at her in confusion, and gave a fake smile very much at odds with the fire bolts shooting out of her eyes. And possibly some smoke out her nose. "Bridal nerves." Her titter sounded like chalk on a blackboard. With a last, suspicious glance at me, she said, "Please continue, Reverend."

He opened his mouth to continue, but before he could speak, one of the guests gave a small shriek that rapidly grew in volume, swelling into quite the echo, thanks to the vaulted ceiling.

We all spun around. The offending lady encountered a look from Iris and stammered out, "I'm so sorry, I thought I felt...something...cold...brush against my leg..." Her voice trailed off, she looked down, then up again. "I'm so sorry..."

Another woman gave a gasp. "I felt it, too!"

The guests were shifting, stirring, looking down. Pretty sure I knew who was doing the brushing. I hoped the shadowy spaces under the pews would give him enough cover. Did I imagine the faint click of claws against the stone floor?

"I thought I saw—" This time it was a guy, one of the engineers who spoke.

"What do you think you saw?" Iris asked in a deadly tone through gritted teeth. It was weird, because she seemed to swell and her shadow against the wall was kind of dragon-like...

"Eyes..." The word echoed around the room and a flush stained his face. "Nothing. I didn't see anything."

I did. Eyes peered out of the shadow beneath the front pew. His snout hovered between a secretary's nylon-covered legs, so close I wondered why she didn't feel his breath on her ankles.

Iris's gaze swerved toward me. I swallowed. "Maybe you have a mouse, Reverend."

He opened his mouth make some kind of answer to me, but Iris impaled him with her steely gaze. His mouth moved several times, liked a landed fish, but no words came out.

"We came here to get married, not—" Her mouth worked, as if she held back a slew of expletives with an effort. "Could you continue?" Her harsh tone bounced around, building briefly before fading. She managed something sort of smile-like. "Please?"

"Of...of course." He glanced down at his book. "Dearly beloved—"

"We've done that part." The gritting of her teeth sharpened all the lines of her face, erasing her man-bait "it" factor like it had never been.

My dad looked at her in some alarm.

"You are right, of course. We were objecting, I mean, we were asking for objections, I mean—"

"What exactly do you mean, Reverend?"

Her deadly tone drained the ruddy color from his pendulous cheeks.

He is objecting to this marriage. Everyone objects to this marriage. Peddrenth sounded firm, very dragon-like. There was something symbolic about my dragon taking on the dragon lady.

"This is not funny." Iris's eyes kind of bugged out.

It was funny, but I managed to hold back the giggle, because her looks might actually kill.

Iris stared at my dad. "Surely you heard that!"

"Um, what did you hear, um," the Reverend glanced down at the sheet with their names on it, "Miss Smith?"

She stared around the room. "You can't stop this wedding. There is no *impediment.*" She spat the word out.

"Im—uh—pediment?" the Reverend asked, his eyes going side-to-side in that way people do in the presence of crazy.

Her fingers curled into talons. I think she snarled. Or growled. No actual words. Just bared teeth.

I felt a need to look around because her expression was scary. I think I managed to look puzzled despite the bubble of laughter and yes, fear, trying to crawl up and out my throat.

"There's no, um, impediment, is there?" My dad sounded kind of hopeful.

"That's what I said!" Even Iris seemed startled when her words echoed back on her from all corners of the chapel. Her mouth worked for several very long seconds, then twisted up in this half snarl, half smile. "Let's just—"

In almost slow motion, the secretary in the front pew glanced down and saw Peddrenth's snout sticking out between her ankles. Her shriek rose, traveling up and up, increasing in intensity and coming back in waves as echo met echo. She jumped up and then up onto the pew. I couldn't see Peddrenth anymore, but I could track his movement as person after person leapt up on the pews.

One guy, a physicist, added fuel to the panic by yelling, "That's not a mouse! It's too big and scaly!"

I had to give the Reverend chops for not running and jumping up on something. He did cast a longing look at his closest up point —the pulpit. My dad just blinked. Iris looked incredulous. Her gaze swept the room as Peddrenth kept the panic going. And then I think she snapped.

The temper tantrum was impressive and sucked all the angst out of the room, leaving only her frustration and rage. When she finally stopped, and the echoes finally faded, the silence was not a happy one. I think even my heart quit beating.

She pointed her red laser gaze at each guest in turn. One by one, they sank down, though no one put their feet on the floor.

Iris's face was so red, her eyes so bugged out, she looked like she'd escaped from a graphic novel. And I'd swear her nose tried to extend into a snout.

My breathing stopped when her crazed gaze settled on me. Her chest rose and fell. Her lips pulled back in a snarl.

"You," she said. "You did this."

I felt my jaw drop, because yes, I planned to do something, but I hadn't actually done anything yet.

"Iris?" There was a sternness to my dad's tone that I remembered from my younger days.

With a decided twitch, her gaze flicked at my dad. "This is between Emma and I, isn't it, *dear?*"

It took all my self-control to not let even an eyelash flicker on my outside.

Why yes, it is between us, you Kruvox bitch.

I didn't know she'd heard me until her arm lifted back and swung toward me. My dad caught it two inches from my face.

"Iris?" Not just stern, but shocked now.

She shook him off, her gaze never leaving mine.

"Don't play games me with me, little girl."

I'm not a little girl anymore.

"I'll crush you like the little bug you are." Her lips stretched back, revealing sharp canines. There was an echo of Smaug-ness about her and I felt a fellow sympathy with Bilbo, who had also awakened the sleeping dragon. I felt, distantly, the unease that rippled through the benched congregation—did they see or just sense what was happening? I didn't dare look away to find out.

Bug? You're the cockroach inside my head and you call me a bug?

"It's…it's not the done thing, to…to…"

I had to give the Reverend chops for trying. Iris ignored him and another protest from my dad.

Her fingers flexed, then curled into an upturned fist, almost cutting off my oxygen supply. Somehow I managed to keep my arms at my side. I stared at her, then mentally reared back and slugged her. It felt like a real hit, sounded like one, too, though only inside my head.

She reeled back with a shocked look. The hold on my throat eased.

"Excuse…me?" Maybe it was the lack of oxygen making me lightheaded. Or an adrenalin rush. Or maybe I just liked hitting Iris. Inside my head, I took up a mental boxing stance, watching her closely. She swung at me, the physical blow not even close. I mentally ducked and hit back. Then hit her again.

I don't know why she took physical shots at me. I just know it was both comical and scary watching her punching the air and staggering around from my hits.

My dad backed away, though protectively toward me, which gave me a warm fuzzy. The Reverend was less gallant, but I couldn't blame him. This was a lot of crazy to process.

She took a couple more swings. I dodged all but the last one. Managed to not rock back on my heels, though it hurt like a son-of-a-gun. I had a feeling I was going to have a real black eye.

"Do you think you're strong enough to take me on?"

My mom kicked your ass and I will, too.

She kicked off her shoes and took her version of a boxing stance, dancing to one side, then the other.

"Your mother was weak. I killed her and I should have killed you, too," she snapped.

The words echoed and re-echoed around the chapel. She froze. A look of panic twisted her face. It seemed like it took longer for the echo of the damning words to fade away.

She looked left, then right. She had no friends left in this room. Malice replaced panic. "I'll take you down with me you little mongrel spawn of—"

I mentally punched her in the mouth and her head jerked back, a trickle of blood tracking from the side of her mouth. She wiped it away. In the fraught silence, I heard the distant sound of approaching sirens. Someone must have called the cops.

Her head jerked to the side, tilted to listen. I could almost see her trying to figure a way out. Her gaze tracked to my dad. "Did you tell them about her? That she was from another plan—"

I didn't have to think about this hit. My mental fist connected so solidly, the shock of it shuddered through me. Her eyes rolled back in her head and she dropped.

I liked the thump her head made when it hit the stone floor.

Chapter 7

I STOOD next to my dad and watched them wheel his former fiancé out the double doors to the waiting ambulance. My headache was gone and my memories were back, the good and the bad. The EMT's thought she'd had a stroke. I knew better and wondered what would happen when she woke up.

We will deal with that later, Mazan told me. He'd gotten Peddrenth under his cloak and had slipped outside in the confusion. They were going to disable the ship and then—well, I wasn't sure what happened next.

I was glad to feel whole as my dad and I finally escaped the church, both divided and united by our secrets. Overhead, the now full moon—which brought out the crazies, according to one of the cops—both taunted and beckoned with what might have been.

I realized my dad was staring up at it, too.

"What's going to happen to the launch?"

He sighed "It will be cancelled."

I glanced at him, but the night hid his expression from me. "I'm sorry," I said, shifting from one foot to the other.

He looked at me then. "Are you?"

I wasn't. But I was. It had taken eight years to get him to this point. "Are you?" It was a question I could ask in the dark.

He didn't speak for several seconds. "I should be." He sighed again. "There is no fool like an old fool."

His words gave me an out. We could slide past this. Get back to —yeah. Neither one of us could go back to that shadowy status quo. It was weird to realize now that I hadn't known, but I *had*. I'd felt it and just buried my head in the work. I'd let the days slide by, not living my life. So much time lost. Was I really prepared to lose even more? Or not live the days we had left?

I faced him. "No, dad. You aren't, you never were a fool." I glanced around. We were alone, but I lowered my voice anyway. "She…Iris…did something to you." And to me, but I wasn't sure he could handle that right now.

He turned to stare at me, the moon's light now full on his face. His gaze met mine and I saw the person, not just the dad. He'd been young once, had lived, had loved an alien—if we lived through this I really wanted to hear that story—lost her and…gone on. He'd put one foot in front of the other day after day after day. He'd stood between me and Iris, or thought he had. He loved me and I loved him.

Relief broke the shadows in his eyes. We stood there smiling at each other and I realized that even if Iris tried again, we'd won. She'd lost. Dead or alive, she wasn't going home. No one would believe anything she said after her little breakdown in the church. At least my mom hadn't died for nothing.

"Your mom would be proud," he said, almost as if he caught my thought. He went silent again and I could almost feel the wheels turning inside his head. Finally he sighed. "If she did something— then it's not over, is it?"

I shook my head. "No, it's not over yet."

I don't know what he saw in my eyes—or if he could see anything—but he was a genius. He nodded slowly, his shoulders straightening just a bit. Then he looked up at the round, gold moon. "I would have liked to take a ride around the moon."

I looked up, too, started to agree. Stopped. "Maybe we can."

Dad looked at me, his brows arched. I grinned.

"Well, I am my mother's daughter, too."

YOU WOULD THINK that someone who had married one alien, had almost married another alien, and had spent the last eight years building a space ship, would be a little less shocked by Mazan's space ship. Of course, he'd had a more than few shocks in the last twenty-four hours.

"You…wish to fly around your moon?" Mazan had that "seeking to understand" look as his gaze tracked between me and my dazed dad.

Dad looked from the cool tech to Mazan to me. I think he wanted to say something, but instead he indicated the command seat and lifted his brows as if to ask if he could sit down. After a brief hesitation, Mazan nodded.

I stepped up to Mazan, my hand on his arm, our faces close together.

All my memories of him were back, too. I couldn't believe I had forgotten him. No wonder he'd looked so hurt. My heart ached at the thought of our lost eight years. He was my other half. No wonder I'd been a travesty of myself, a lost ghost-like creature drifting through a monochrome life. If I'd fought back sooner—no, now was not the time to look back. But wow, what a difference a day makes. Not just color, but Technicolor had returned, full and vibrant, but also bittersweet because I didn't know how much time we had left. No one was going to call us when Iris woke up. I'd probably know before they did anyway. So I smiled at Mazan and said out loud, "Yes, we really would like to fly around our moon." Inside my head, I told him, *I'm so very sorry. Can you forgive me?*

He blinked, his hands coming up to cover mine, his touch both cool and comforting.

When you look at me like that, I can forgive you anything. But what—

For letting her steal my memories of you. I smiled, totally forgetting my dad was watching. *I love you.* I inhaled his closeness, his familiar alien scent, trying to take it as deep as I could, to live as much as I could in this moment.

His hand tightened on mine. The implant that might kill me linked us together with an intensity that brought tears to my eyes. I felt his love, the loss he'd felt, his joy we were back together, his fear it wouldn't last.

We stared at each because we needed to see each other for as long as we could. The moment was perfect except for lack of kissing, but with my dad a few feet away…

He smiled, taking my breath away. It was the smile I'd missed a few days ago during our second first contact. "I will take you to the moon. To Mars. To the next galaxy. To where ever you wish to go, I will take you there."

And then he kissed me even though my dad was there and I didn't care because wow. As second kisses go, it was a whopper. I felt connected to him in every way two people could be connected, all of it heightened by that crazy implant.

Such a pity that dragon-lady Iris chose that moment to wake up.

I DON'T KNOW if we actually staggered. It felt like we did as fire burned into us, a howling hurricane of rage that rode the implant from me to Mazan and back again. It hurt that she attacked him through me. It helped that she had to fight us both. We drew strength from each other. But…

She had nothing left to lose.

I felt it to my aching toenails. She would rather die than be stuck on Earth in a mental institution or jail. And she planned to take us with her. I couldn't look at my dad, couldn't see him, couldn't tell if she was after him, too. It took all my focus to hold my ground.

And it wasn't enough.

Cell by cell fire burned deeper and deeper into our minds.

It was too bad we really did use all our brains. If I'd only had to protect ten percent—

I think I felt an arm come around my waist. Not Mazan. He still gripped my hands. My dad? Had he joined us in the link—or he been there all along? I didn't have time or focus to be embarrassed by what he might have overheard.

He stopped Iris's progress, but even with dad's help, we weren't regaining lost ground.

Iris was pretty pissed. Her rage gave her power.

Or it helped her maximize the link.

I didn't know. Didn't really care. I wanted to win. I wanted to beat her.

I wanted to believe we could because love should conquer all.

Our love has conquered, Mazan told me. *She has lost.*

He'd come here expecting to die with me, I remembered now. He'd been prepared. I was behind that curve. I felt her find knowledge of his ship in our heads. She could still take out Earth if she exposed it to those monitors…

Did I feel an actual shudder under my feet? Had she somehow managed to take control? No, if she had the ship, she wouldn't be so mad. Her rage built as she felt the ship lifting off.

Who's…flying… I managed the question, barely. It felt like the edges of my mind were starting to disintegrate in the heat of her dragon fire.

We tumbled to the floor as the ship accelerated, the nose pointed toward the stars. I felt air rush out of Mazan and my dad as they tried to cushion my fall.

We were flying.

And dying.

Anger gave me the strength to push back. It surprised her for a few seconds, but she'd had a long time to be mad.

She was both old and evil. I felt her jerk at the word "old" and took pleasure it throwing it at her again and again.

Might have been bad move, since she came back with lots of pissed.

Die….die…die…

We were going to die. All three of us. I tried to protect my dad and felt, I don't know, as if he shifted me aside and stood in front of us…

A hero, like my mom…

I am so sorry, Emma…

Not your fault…

This darkness closing in was not an escape to a merciful release. It was thick and oily and malignant and so hot—it surged and sucked and licked at us, looking for and finding our weak spots. It raced around, digging in here and there and rising to break over us in a fiery wave. We cowered, clinging to each other and bracing for the end…

I love you.

I don't know who said it, me, Mazan, or my dad. Maybe it came from all of us.

In an odd counterpoint to the black slime, I thought I heard Dean Martin singing *Fly Me to the Moon.* That had to be my dad. Huge Dean fan. He always hummed that song when he was really focused…

As one, we faced her. She could kill us, but she couldn't break us—

And then, from behind her, I thought I saw a wave of light. Charged like lightning, but crackling around bright points, rather than the more typical stabbing, jagged lines. It rushed at her, at us.

This is going to be bad.

No one disagreed with me.

Not that anyone could.

I closed my eyes. Didn't matter.

Light met dark.

Even with my eyes closed, I saw it. Light shooting up like a brilliant wall. Dark rising to meet it.

The impact was kind of like touching metal after crossing carpet.

If I'd walked about a thousand miles of carpet, then touched a thousand metal bars.

I flew backwards.

Hit something.

Pretty sure I died.

I DID NOT KNOW it could hurt this much when you're dead.

For some reason, I'd expected better from the afterlife. That didn't mean I wasn't curious to see what it looked like so I opened my eyes. Big mistake. Who knew eyelids could hurt that bad? Made me want to cry, but my tear ducts were, like, no way. That will hurt even more.

I winced involuntarily and it felt like all my cells cried out in protest and then were suddenly not silenced.

A gray expanse, like the bulkhead of a spaceship, met my sore gaze. The unforgiving metal underneath my cringing back cells felt like a space ship, too. I blinked. That hurt bad enough to make me gasp—

Wait a minute. I inhaled. Exhaled. That felt like breathing. The dead didn't breathe, did they?

Maybe I'm not dead. Maybe this is Mazan's spaceship and not the afterlife.

I considered this possibility, while studying as much as I could without moving more than my eyeballs—which didn't like moving any more than the rest of me—and was forced to conclude that I was probably not dead. Was reserving judgment on whether that was the good news or the bad.

My pained gaze found Peddrenth perched in the command chair. Peddrenth…looked like he was flying the ship. My dragon was flying the ship? That was some sassy implant they'd give him. Or Draze dragons were a species smart enough to fly a spaceship.

It seemed kind of right. Dragons should fly, shouldn't they? Well, good dragons. Iris, there at the end, it was almost as if she turned into a very bad dragon—

Out the front screen of the ship, a planet hung in space. The moon? It was. Not the distant moon, seen from Earth. This was the moon up close and personal. A little bit of Earth was visible against one curve. Earthrise on the Moon.

I opened my mouth to ask or say something, but all that came out was, "Ow."

Someone groaned next to me. No, not someone. *My dad.* In

painful inches I turned my head his direction. He looked pretty hammered, and I think I saw little wisps of smoke coming off his head. I couldn't be sure, but his eyebrows looked a bit crispy on the ends.

The sight of the moon appeared to revive him. He struggled into a sitting position, managed to pull himself into the co-pilot's chair. With a hand that visibly shook, he reached out, as if he needed to touch the moon to believe it. That he couldn't was another indication we weren't dead.

"Hello," Mazan said, his mouth close to my aching ear.

I looked his way, not sure I believed what my ear was telling me. It hurt to smile, but I did it anyway. And touched his cheek with my own very unsteady hand. He grinned, then winced.

"I do not believe there is a nerve in my body that does not hurt."

Despite this he managed to scramble up, then reached down to help me. I needed the help. Oh, yeah, everything hurt. Even the ends of my hair, which seemed to be smoking, too. I sank into an auxiliary station seat and blinked.

Was it over or was this just a reprieve? Before I expended energy on rejoicing a possible happy ending or did any kissing, I wanted to know.

Mazan kept hold of my hand as he sank into the seat next to mine. That hand was pretty much my only happy body part. My head felt oddly empty. Had Iris fried my brain?

"Your father is very fond of the moon," Mazan said, looking puzzled by this.

"He's been trying to get here for a long time," I explained.

Peddrenth turned, leaving one claw on the helm. *I hope you do not mind?*

It seemed Peddrenth was of the "seek forgiveness rather than permission" type of dragon. Which was fine with me. I'd wanted to get to the moon, too.

The edges of Mazan's mouth twitched. "No. I do not mind."

My dad turned and looked at Mazan, then at Peddrenth, then at me. He looked like he wanted to ask, but couldn't manage it.

I remembered that feeling from…was it just yesterday? No—I

looked at my watch—it was the day before yesterday. Today was my birthday. The birthday girl had lived. For now.

I made a little gesture, which I quickly wished I hadn't. "This is Peddrenth, dad."

Peddrenth moved his head and waved a paw. Pretty sure it wasn't an act of submission since his beard flared black.

"Didn't you used to have—"

"—a bearded dragon? Yes, I did. He left and then he came back." But I wasn't bitter.

Yes, you are.

Okay, yeah, I was. "Sorry. It's not your fault."

My dad blinked. "Is he...talking?"

"My dragon?" Dad kind of nodded. "He's thinking. Telepathically. He has an implant." I turned to Mazan. "Speaking of, what about the implants in our heads?"

Mazan shifted around to his station and started tapping things. He stopped and spun slowly around to look at us. "According to the latest scans, both of your implants appear to be non-active."

I leaned over and took a look. "The circuitry has been fried." I thought about the wave of light I'd seen. Or thought I'd seen. "What did it?"

I could almost see the wheels turning inside my dad's head.

"The full moon," he said and looked out the view screen. "If we passed through the Earth's magnetotail..." He paused, considering.

The magnetotail extends beyond the orbit of the moon, Peddrenth's tone was musing. *It can cause electrostatic discharges, particularly strong ones when the moon is full.*

I blinked. "Electrostatic discharge?" I asked. I looked at my dad, who shrugged, so I turned to Mazan. "Would that do it?"

"They were constructed out of inferior materials, unlike Peddrenth's," Mazan said. "That is why I was reluctant to attempt removal when the power source was active and unstable."

"Did you think that an electrostatic discharge might destroy our implants?" I asked Peddrenth.

Peddrenth regarded me with much solemnity. *Your parental unit told me to fly you to the moon.*

I opened my mouth to press the issue, then decided not to. Whether he knew what he was doing or not, we'd been saved from the dragon by my dragon. Very cool.

"We should be able to safely remove them from your brains now," Mazan said.

He sounded awfully cheerful for someone talking about digging around in my head. My dad looked as dubious as I felt.

"Can you, um, beam them out?" I asked, tacking on a hopeful smile. I tried to remember if my years of Draze schooling had covered implant removal.

Mazan tried not to smile. "It will only hurt a little."

I opened my mouth to protest and realized he was teasing me. Mazan was teasing me. The edges of my mouth curled up and a small chuckle slipped out. An actual laugh would hurt too much. But there was a nice lightness born of relief bubbling in the air around us.

"It's over." My gaze connected with his. "Isn't it?"

We'd stopped the wedding. Kept Earth from blowing up. Defeated the Kruvox Opposer. Ridden to the moon. We had not died.

Happy birthday to me.

Mazan smiled. Peddrenth's beard flared black, but in a happy way. He turned back to the controls.

I recall a promise to take you to Mars…

His claw wrapped around the helm control and moved it. I stole a look at Mazan. Caught him looking at me. His brows arched and he indicated the hatch. I looked at my dad. He was staring at the view screen, his jaw just a bit dropped, as the moon started to dwindle. I grinned and nodded.

Mazan pulled me upright and yes it hurt, but this looked a lot like a happy ending and a happy beginning. There was still stuff to sort out, but for now…

Mazan's arms closed around me, his head bent, his lips finding mine…

Third time was the charm, I thought a bit hazily, especially when it came to kisses…

😄 ONE LAST **Invitation**

If you enjoyed the **action, adventure, and romance** in these stories, you're exactly the kind of reader I love writing for.

I write adventures where:

things don't always go according to plan

attraction shows up at inconvenient moments

and sometimes laughter is the only sensible response

If you'd like to step into another adventure, I'd love to invite you through one more door.

🖼 **Another Door in Time**

Some stories grow longer.

Some stay short and sharp.

And some appear when you least expect them.

When you join my email list, you'll receive **Another Door in Time** — an exclusive standalone story created just for readers who enjoy action, adventure, romance, and the occasional twist.

It's not connected to this collection.

It's not required reading.

It's simply a thank-you for spending time with my stories.

🔖 **Step through Another Door in Time here:**

Get Another Door in Time (https://BookHip.com/KFKDRCW)

What to expect from me

I write action-packed stories with romance at the heart of them — sometimes serious, sometimes playful, and always driven by characters who refuse to quit when things get complicated.

💜 **A final note**

Thanks again for reading. I hope these stories made you smile — and I hope I'll see you again in another adventure.

Books by Pauline Baird Jones

Science Fiction Romance/Paranormal

Project Enterprise: The Cyborg Chronicles
Cyborg's Revenge: The Cyborg Chronicles Book 1
Cosmic Boom: The Cyborg Chronicles Book 2
CabeX: The Cyborg Chronicles Book 3
AzumC: The Cyborg Chronicles Book 4
MircoP: The Cyborg Chronicles Book 5
ScytheQ: The Cyborg Chronicles 6
OmnitronW: The Cyborg Chronicles 7
TalusH: The Cyborg Chronicles 8
TrackerY: The Cyborg Chronicles 9
Side story: Operation Ark: A Project Enterprise Story
Origin Story: Lost Valyr
Project Universe Series:
The Key (book 1)
Girl Gone Nova (book 2)
Tangled in Time (book 3)
Steamrolled (book 4)
Kicking Ashe (book 5)

The Reboot Books of Project Enterprise
Found Girl (book 6)
Lost Valyr (book 7)
Maestra Rising (book 8)
More Project Enterprise
Project Enterprise: The Short Stories
Time Trap: A Project Enterprise Series Short Story
Operation Ark: A Project Enterprise Story
General's Holiday: A Project Enterprise Story
Claws & Effect: The Otherworldly Pets of Project Enterprise

Other Romantic Science Fiction Stories
The Real Dragon
Nebula Nine (time travel adventure)
Open With Care (Christmas collection that includes, "Riding For Christmas" and "Up on the House Top"
Specters in the Storm: A paranormal/steampunk/science fiction romance novella

Out of Time Series:
Out of Time
Just in Time
Telling Time
Out of Time Series (Three Book Bundle)

An Uneasy Future
(A science fiction romance mystery series set in future New Orleans)
Core Punch (1.0)
Sucker Punch (2.0)
One Two Punch: An Uneasy Future Bundle

Romantic Suspense

The Big Uneasy Series:
Relatively Risky (1)

Family Treed (A Big Uneasy Short Story)
Dead Spaces (2.0)
Louisiana Lagniappe (3.0)
Worry Beads (4.0)
Fais Do Do Die (5.0)
Beaucoup Fracas (6.0)
Pirogue Wipe Out (7.0)
Bourre Brouhaha (8.0)
Soc Au' Lait Stiff (9.0)
Gumbo Ya-Ya Exit (10.0)
The Family Way (A Big Uneasy Short Story)
Guess Who's Coming To Christmas: The Wedding Edition
The Big Uneasy Bundle
An Uneasy Collection: The Big Uneasy Books 3-5

Lonesome Lawmen Series:
    The Last Enemy
    Byte Me
    Missing You
    Lonesome Mama (Bonus short story)
    (The *Lonesome Lawmen* is also available as a digital bundle)

Do Wah Diddy Die
    The Spy Who Kissed Me
    *Perilously Fun Fiction Bundle (*includes *The Spy Who Kissed Me* and
Do Wah Diddy Die. Bonus: *Do Wah Diddy Delete Short Story Collection)*
    Dangerous Dance
    Dangerous Duet

Short Story Collections

Project Enterprise: The Short Stories
    Do Wah Diddy Delete
    Let's Fall in Love
    Take a Chance on Me
    The Real Dragon and other short stories

About the Author

Award-winning author Pauline Baird Jones writes *perilously fun fiction* —from romantic suspense to space opera, time travel and more. With 40+ books, a flair for humor, and a love of adventure, she creates heroines braver than they realize and heroes brave enough to love them. If you crave thrilling plots, smart laughs, and happy endings, you're in the right place!

To find out more about Pauline or her books:
http://paulinebjones.com
pauline@paulinebjones.com